LAW

OF THE

LEMHI

PART TWO

SAVAGE LAW: BOOK 1

Kirby Jonas

OF THE

LEMHI

PART TWO

SAVAGE LAW: BOOK 1

KIRBY JONAS

Cover design by Forrest Design Group

Howling Wolf Publishing
Pocatello, Idaho

Howling Wolf Publishing
1611 City Creek Road
Pocatello ID 83204

For more information about Kirby's books, check out:

www.kirbyjonas.com
Facebook, at KirbyJonasauthor

Or email Kirby at: **kirby@kirbyjonas.com**

Manufactured in the United States of America—*One nation, under God*

Publication date in electronic format for this edition: May 2015
Jonas, Kirby, 1965—

Savage Law 1: Law of the Lemhi, Part Two / by Kirby Jonas.

ISBN: 978-1-891423-27-7
Library of Congress Control Number: 2016918778

To learn more about this book or any other Kirby Jonas book, email Kirby at kirby@kirbyjonas.com

Dedicated to the memory of Gene Ottonello,
a family man and a friend

Also dedicated to his daughter, my friend Barbara, and the rest of his family; we will miss him always

Last of all, to Chris, who also left us too young

CHAPTER ONE

♦ *1972* ♦

Wednesday, November 22

Two men were dead. Barely cold in their graves. And the badge on Coal Savage's chest still felt warm from K.T. Batterton, the last Lemhi County sheriff who had worn it.

This was not the kind of homecoming Coal would have wished for, on himself or anyone else. Two men dead—two of his best friends—and a daughter who hated him.

And then there was the memory of the tragic loss of his Laura, barely cold in her own grave.

Too much death. Too much sorrow. It was going to take Coal a lot of living to blot out the memory of this chapter in his life.

And now, the phone call. One by one, he had talked to them, first his deputy, Todd Mitchell, and then his old friend, retired sheriff Jim Lockwood. And neither of them ever talked to him the way they had that morning. Coal was driving out to something he knew he did not want to see. And there was no way to save him.

The sun was out, but it did not lighten Coal's spirits. Aching, he drove as fast as he dared toward the Erickson ranch. Old man Erickson and his wife, Leo and Sharleen, ran a small Angus ranch twelve miles out of Salmon, Idaho, toward Leadore. They were good folks, kind to everyone, and generous even with people who didn't deserve it. They were one huge reason Coal and his friends had loved to hang out with tomboy Molly Erickson in high school, because at the Erickson place the beverages flowed like water and the food never seemed to have an end. Connie was great for feeding her family, but she was never one to give food to Coal's friends, and back then he just couldn't understand. Connie had seen way too much waste from teenagers, and it was not something she would brook in her household.

As Coal drove, he thought about K.T. If something had happened to the Ericksons, his being sheriff made it his responsibility to go to K.T.'s and notify him, because K.T. was the next thing to a son to the Ericksons, who had never been blessed with a boy of their own. That was going to break K.T.'s heart. And he didn't even want to think of talking to Molly.

It made Coal almost physically sick to think of being the bearer of bad news to them. That was one thing he had seldom had to deal with in the FBI, but something he had run into with a fair amount of frequency as a military policeman. The obvious difference was that in the Army, he generally had not been personally acquainted with the people he had to talk to. It still wasn't easy, but at least it wasn't like family.

Looking out at the beautiful sunshine that spilled across the valley and gilded the already golden and pale green grasses, sparkling on an icy pond here and there, he felt like there should be peace today. He forced himself to take in a huge breath and hold it for a few seconds before letting it out very slowly. That calmed his nerves. Maybe he was overreacting. But on the phone, both Mitchell and Jim had had a very frightening tone to their speech, and the fact that Jim wanted to come and get him—that alone was alarming. He was a big boy; why would Jim have to pick him up?

When Coal neared the Erickson place, his guts tightened up even more as he saw the red lights of an ambulance flickering, mixed in with the blue one on the dash of the brown county pickup Mitchell must be driving. Jim's long, black Thunderbird was also there. And there was a green Impala he did not recognize. So far, he wasn't seeing any people.

He left the asphalt and turned onto a gravel lane, winding through scattered willows along a slough. Soon, a cluster of heads appeared on the other side of the cab of Mitchell's unmarked pickup. He could make out at least seven people, possibly eight. If there was indeed an eighth, it was a head of glistening white hair that was at least twelve inches lower than that of the tallest person there.

Other than the flickering emergency lights, this might have been a scene from some gathering at the end of a house party. Lazy white smoke puffed out of the tall chimney of the tan brick house into the crisp, clear air. Two dogs were running around, tussling near the front porch railing of the house. And the people all seemed to be standing around chatting as if they were enjoying the beautiful, if frigid day.

Coal's heart was beating him to death, and he could hardly catch his breath. He was already tired of being the sheriff of Lemhi County, and ready to go back to D.C. and a land of strange-looking, strange-acting people about whom he cared little. He liked the feeling he had had there of being able to keep up his tough exterior and shed no tears over anything that happened. It let him do his job without his emotions getting in the way.

Coal's Ford was still sixty feet away when everyone began turning their faces toward him. He scanned them all, maybe too fast. There was Sharleen! She was okay. Now... Leo. Where was he? No Leo…

Coal swore. There were many faces, but none was Leo's. Jim and Mitchell started out of the crowd toward Coal's car as he recognized Maura standing with a man he didn't recognize. Another unfamiliar man stood a few feet distant, where he had been in conversation with Jim Lockwood before Jim had walked away.

Mitchell and Jim halted abruptly. Coal had thrown the car into park and was jumping out, and he saw Sharleen Erickson say something to them. This woman was all of seventy-four years old, maybe more. But after she spoke to Jim and Mitchell and stopped them where they stood, she came running toward Coal. Instantly feeling guilty for letting her run, at her age, Coal strode in long steps toward her.

The woman's eyes were red from crying. She held up her arms as she neared him, and Coal had nothing at all to say to her. She fell against him, sobbing. "Coal! Oh, Coal. I'm so sorry, dear. Oh, dear Coal, why did you have to come home to this?"

Coal squeezed his eyes shut, holding onto her tightly. What was he going to say? How did he comfort her? Leo was her whole life. He looked up and saw Jim Lockwood slowly starting to drift in his direction once more. Maura, too, had come closer. The others all stayed a ways off, including one tall, silver-haired man with a walrus mustache and mean-looking dark eyes, and another with a much more affable face, brown hair silvering at the temples, and soft blue eyes.

Suddenly, Coal froze, his gaze focusing in on yet another man, this one with thin gray hair with yet some traces of its former blond. He was walking slowly toward Coal and Sharleen, and there was blood on his hands. The sight of the man jolted Coal clear down to his toes, almost more than any other sight he could have imagined.

It was the owner of the ranch, Leo Erickson!

Coal stood up straighter, pulling away from Sharleen without meaning to, simply because he was so much taller than she was. "Leo?"

The old man, now in his mid-seventies, nodded. "Hello, son."

Confused, Coal stared at him while he kept holding onto the old man's wife, mostly because she wouldn't let him go. His eyes flickered about the group. He noticed how Mitchell wouldn't even look at him, and he caught the absolutely sorrowful look in the gaze with which Jim Lockwood was pinning him in place.

The two strangers looked around the yard. One of them, he surmised, must be Maura's medical partner on this call, and the other had to be the coroner. But... Why the coroner? Leo Erickson was as alive as anyone here!

Jim walked close and clapped a hand on Coal's shoulder. "Sorry, ma'am," he said gently. "Can I borrow the sheriff for a minute?"

As her arms fell limply away, Sharleen Erickson stepped back, staring up at Coal but otherwise hardly even showing that she knew he was there. Coal looked down at Jim and cocked his head, trying to sort through the questions in his mind. Most importantly, why was he here? Jim took his arm and led him away from the others, off beyond the hood of Mitchell's pickup.

"What's the blood all over Leo?" he asked in a quiet voice. "He isn't hurt, right?"

Jim shook his head. He stared at Coal, his face saying he wanted to speak but couldn't. He just stood there with his mouth slightly ajar and licked his lips. Finally, he reached up and wiped at his mustache.

"Son... No, Leo's not hurt." He jerked his thumb toward the brown pickup. "It's K.T. On the other side of Todd's truck."

"*What?*" Coal stared the older man down. "K.T.? What in the hell are you talking about?"

His eyes darted back and forth between Jim's. The former sheriff acted like he wanted to give him a hug, but he didn't. They both stood and stared, and it was plain that Jim was now having a hard time meeting Coal's piercing gaze.

Coal turned robotically and started to walk. He could almost feel his feet—but not quite. He heard footsteps behind him, and Jim grabbed his shoulder roughly. He turned him. "Coal, this is something you don't need to see. Don't go over there."

"What the hell, Jim?" Coal growled. "Nobody could tell me on the phone?"

"Coal, don't." Jim gave a tight little shake of his head. "I tried to fetch you."

"I don't need a babysitter. I'm a damn Marine."

Coal felt Jim try to catch his arm as he turned away again and walked around the truck. He stopped when he saw the body. His heart seemed to stop as well.

Gathering himself, Coal continued on. He would not let the others see him unable to walk all the way to his friend. He stopped over the top of K.T. His friend lay on his face. There was a hole torn through the back of his jacket, just below the collar, and gore and bits of bone sprinkled the fabric, darkening the blue to deep maroon.

Coal didn't have to see K.T.'s eyes. His memory of them was from only the night before. He backed slowly away. Stopped five feet distant, seeing blood splatters on the hard-packed earth.

A hand touched his sleeve. Coal's jaws bunched. Jim. He thought, *Leave me alone. I need to breathe.*

Coal looked down. Although callused and rough, the fingers were long and graceful, but the nails were a little stained and clipped short. Not the tough hand of his old friend. He turned his head and saw the tumbling blond hair, pulled to one side and tied there so it lay across the right side of her chest. He felt, perhaps more than saw, the deep, searching eyes, the pink, parted lips.

Coal needed someone. He needed Connie. Perhaps Jennifer Batterton. Maybe even having Laura there would have been a comfort. There had been a time when all their differences would have gone away in a heartbreaking moment like this. But he was far from certain that he needed the touch of Maura PlentyWounds. By any stretch of imagination, they were not the best of friends.

Maura didn't speak. At least she had that much sense. What did anyone say at a time like this? Maybe she could have said, *I'm sorry for your loss.* Coal wrestled back a strange urge to laugh. The things people came up with to comfort someone.

"He had no idea what was coming."

"No?" Coal turned a little so he wouldn't be talking out the side of his mouth.

"They saw the vehicle."

Coal jerked around and looked at Sharleen and Leo. "They did?"

"Yeah." She pointed quite a ways off along the line of foothills. "I think they said it was parked there, and the killer was up the side of the hill. All they could see was a black speck come down, get in a vehicle, and race away."

"Another long shot. At least nine hundred yards. Maybe more than a thousand." He felt numb speaking the words. It sounded like someone else was saying them.

"That's far, right?" Her blue eyes quested within his.

"For a mere human being."

"What?"

"This man is the kind of a marksman nobody ever sees. Or almost never. Let's put it this way: If a competent marksman carrying a .30/06 saw a bull elk standing six hundred yards away he would be pushing the limits of a responsible hunter to shoot at it. But when the prey is a man, the stakes are a lot higher than a trophy on a wall. And a man is a lot smaller target than an elk."

"I'm sorry for making you talk about this, Coal."

Coal looked down at her. Perhaps it was the cold. Something made her pink lips look more red than usual, and a rose blush splotched her cheeks and the tip of her nose. Her hair poured over the fur collar of her quilted, dark green coat, and a breeze teased one loose hank of it into her face. She reached up to brush it aside.

Coal sighed. Until she had said something, he had forgotten himself in talking about the intricate details of shooting. It was his escape. It often had been. He let his eyes scan back over to K.T. "It's all right, Miss PlentyWounds. You took my mind off K.T. for a little bit. I needed that."

Maura searched his eyes, and she almost smiled but was cool enough to catch it fast. "Miss PlentyWounds? That's kind of out of the blue, isn't it?"

"It's your name, right? Not like I haven't called you that before."

"I thought we got past that."

"Seems to suit you."

"What?"

"PlentyWounds. Fits you."

She frowned. "What does that mean?"

"Seems like someone has hurt you—a lot."

"Do you even want to know where Clarissa is?" the woman asked suddenly.

Coal didn't skip a beat. "Where?"

Her eyes went back and forth between his, speechless for a moment. He knew she had expected a different reaction out of him, expected him to say something about changing the subject or something. He knew the games women played, and he was tired of going along.

"Home."

"Good."

Irritated at his refusal to take her bait, she said, "My boys came home last night. They're with her."

He nodded. He had succeeded in taking her off-guard. Probably about enough. "Maura, thank you for trying."

"Trying? Trying what?"

"To make me feel better."

"You're right about something," she said, purposely veering away from his thank you. "I have been hurt. A lot. I could have kept my husband's name, but I didn't. Because PlentyWounds fit me good and because I didn't need to be reminded of what a bastard he was every time I had to sign my name somewhere. But having this name doesn't mean every man I meet has to add to it."

And she turned and walked away. This time he forced himself not to watch.

Jim and Mitchell walked over, and pretty soon the others came too. Only the Ericksons stayed at a distance, with Maura there to comfort them if she could.

"Another long shot," said Mitchell. "About as far as the first. Did Maura show you?"

Coal nodded and pointed. "There?"

"Yeah."

"What kind of car?"

Jim grunted. "You serious? If it was an airplane they couldn't have told you what kind from that distance."

"At least a color then?"

"Dark. Gray, maybe green. Or a weird shade of brown. Too far. Blended into the brush."

"I took a roll of film with K.T.'s camera," offered Mitchell.

"Good, Todd. Thirty-six shots?"

"Twenty-four."

"Every angle? Did you move the rigs?"

"Every angle, yeah. But no, we probably ought to move all the rigs out of the way and get some more."

Coal looked where the tires were on the brown pickup and on the ambulance. Luckily, it didn't seem that a suspect vehicle had been in the yard. But no one had known that when they pulled up to park.

"We're all shaken up," Coal said, trying to be extra careful how he spoke to Mitchell. They had enough friction already. "But next time you pull in to a crime scene, you should try to park at least fifty or sixty feet away—preferably out on the asphalt."

"Sorry," Jim said.

Mitchell, predictably, looked a little hurt. "Sure."

Nothing Coal could have said would have come across right to Deputy Mitchell.

Jim motioned the two strangers over. "Coal, this is Ronnie Davis." He indicated the big man with the mean-looking eyes. "Volunteer EMT with Maura. He runs the Chevron station."

Coal shook the man's hand, a firm, strong grip. Davis looked capable and determined. He also looked like the kind of man who was drawn to be in charge.

"And this here is Kerry Updyke," Jim went on. "He's our county coroner."

"You're my replacement when I get killed, right?" said Coal, shaking the man's hand.

Updyke's cheeks flushed a little. "Uh, I guess that's how it's supposed to work. I just go along hoping you won't."

"You and me both. What do you do? Other than coroner?"

"I own a real estate office. Gem Realty. If you're looking to buy."

Coal chuckled. "Sorry. Other things on my mind at the moment."

Updyke blushed again. "Oh, yeah, of course. Sorry, I didn't mean to make a sales pitch."

Coal heard him but chose not to reply. "I need everyone to carefully wheel their rigs around and park out by the road. We need to get some photos of the scene the way it looked before anyone got here."

Ronnie Davis instantly turned and yelled Maura's name. When she looked over, he said, "Move the ambulance!"

Coal was put off, and he waved Maura to him as she started toward the ambulance. “You move it,” he told Davis. “I need to talk to Maura.”

Davis looked at him, his eyes narrowing. At last, he simply nodded. He walked to the station wagon, his back stiff, and got in. Coal watched him as he wheeled away, feeling Maura walk up and stop beside him.

“You need me?”

“Not really. I just didn’t like him ordering you around.”

Maura didn’t reply. He felt her watching him for a while, but he didn’t look over. He was looking at K.T., now exposed on the ground, bloody and dead on the hard-packed soil, like a scene from a Clint Eastwood movie.

Still looking at K.T., he said, “I doubt it’s much over fifteen degrees, if that. Can you take the Ericksons in the house? Do you still have time?”

“I do,” she said softly, so softly that he was drawn to look at her. She was waiting for that, and she let her fingers brush his arm. “Thanks.”

“For what?”

“For sticking up for me with Ronnie. Not much chivalry anywhere these days.”

“I just don’t like a bully.” He tried to growl the words. He knew it didn’t sound like a growl, and the trouble was, so did Maura.

* * *

They did all they could in the yard. After all the photographs, they covered K.T. with a white sheet, and Updyke and Davis tried to load him in the ambulance to haul him off to the morgue. Coal stopped them. “Give the Ericksons a chance to say goodbye first.” He turned to call Mitchell over, but Jim was close by.

“I’ll run and talk to them, Coal.” And without awaiting a reply, he hurried away, favoring a hip that hurt him sometimes in the early morning, especially a frigid morning like this.

The Ericksons came out and made their way slowly across the yard. Coal motioned everyone else away with a jerk of his head. He and the others walked over by the vehicles and waited. Mitchell pulled out a pack of Kools, offered one to Davis, and the two of them lit up, polluting the otherwise invigorating November air. But Coal had to admit the cigarette smoke actually didn't smell too bad when mixed with the cold morning.

Maura and Jim walked past the Ericksons and came to join the others. Everyone tried hard to avoid looking at the old man and his wife. But even at that distance they could hear her sobs.

"The p.o. is on his way from Pocatello today," Coal said to Jim.

Jim gave him a slightly amused look. "Fine. Why tell me?"

Coal almost laughed. "Sorry. Habit."

"I'll go with you. Might as well. Bigfoot hates me too. It was both of us put him in the pen, you know."

"Uh-huh. How can I forget? Larry... Trent... K.T. ... You, and me. Damn hard to forget, especially right now."

Everyone looked toward the body, a sober reminder. Three men dead. All of them on a list of which Paul Monahan made no secret. Only two were left.

"I'll go too," offered Mitchell, and Coal looked over and appraised him.

"It would be good to have another hand. But you're going on twelve hours already. You'd best get home and get some sleep. Besides, I don't even know for sure when he'll be here."

"I won't charge the county."

Coal straightened up, meeting Mitchell's gaze. He tried to read beyond his mask. There was nothing to read. What was Mitchell's game? Hard to believe he didn't have an ulterior motive. Was he feeling guilty? He had never showed such bravery before.

"All right, you can come. When he gets here, I'll have dispatch call you both. But I'll pay you."

Mitchell gave Coal a quick and fervent nod. Judging by his lips corners, he almost smiled. The thought left Coal wondering about everything he had ever known of Deputy Todd Mitchell.

CHAPTER TWO

Coal gleaned all he could from the shaken Ericksons after the ambulance and the coroner rolled away. He had left Mitchell and Jim in the yard, searching for the lethal bullet.

Apparently, K.T. had shown up unexpectedly that morning and pounded on the front door, greeting Leo and Sharleen and looking somewhat confused. He told them he had received a phone call from someone down the road who claimed to have driven past the house and seen Leo and Sharleen out struggling to get a handful of their Anguses back into a pen. As K.T. pulled up, the Anguses were gathered in their pen, some thirty steers, waiting to be picked up by a livestock company and hauled off to slaughter. He had assumed the Ericksons had managed to get them in alone, and he told them it didn't surprise him. What *had* surprised him was getting the phone call in the first place, because he had known the Ericksons long enough to know they were more than capable of putting thirty steers back into a corral.

Confused, Leo and Sharleen had assured him that the steers had never left their pen, where they had been put two days ago, with K.T. and a neighbor who had helped drive them in off the flats.

Once everything had been straightened out, they simply shrugged it off and had said nothing more about the strange phone call. They visited a little, and Sharleen cooked her would-be adoptive son some bacon and eggs and finished off the last of a bowl of pancake batter. They sat drinking coffee, then walked out to the corrals to survey the steers, which K.T. helped throw feed out to, since he was already there.

As the three of them were walking back to the house, a bald eagle flew over their heads, and they all turned and followed it with their eyes, enjoying its majestic flight. It had gotten quite a ways out to the west when Leo said K.T. had asked, "What's that?" while watching something far away, below the flight path of the eagle.

Neither the old man nor Sharleen had been able to see what K.T. was looking at, so he had raised a hand to point. Then, without warning, they had heard a whirring noise, then a sound like something close by had been slapped, and Leo Erickson felt warm drops of liquid spatter his face. K.T.'s knees buckled, and he fell forward to his face in the dirt. Leo remembered the sound of Sharleen screaming, right before he realized it was blood that had hit his face—the blood of K.T.

It was at that moment that something drew Leo's eyes back to where K.T. had been pointing, and he saw a faint, dark shape striding down a slope that Leo already knew was pushing one thousand yards away, because it was close to where K.T. used to play around trying to see how far his grandfather's Remington rolling block rifle would throw a 162 grain 7X57 mm Mauser bullet from the ranch house porch on a windless day.

The shape, a man, made it to the flat, where it melded with a vehicle that was obviously what K.T. had been trying to point out but that was well-blended in with its surroundings. The vehicle had sped away in the opposite direction, before turning at right angles some fifteen hundred yards away, merging onto the highway, and vanishing into roadside willows and distance.

That was all the couple knew. There was nothing more to say. The three of them tried their hardest to console each other, but there was no consoling someone within an hour of such a tragic, frightening death. When Coal stepped out on the porch, Leo shook his hand and once more said he was sorry, and Sharleen hugged him and clung to him for a few moments more. Then they let him go to Mitchell and Jim, who were standing with expectant looks on their faces and awaiting him.

Between his thumb and forefinger, Mitchell held up a bullet, right at eye level, for Coal to see. The copper-cased bullet, which was lead-tipped, was mushroomed at the front, but not as greatly as it might have been, and not so much so that he could not identify it. If it truly had been fired from the range it appeared to have been, it wouldn't have been traveling much more than twelve or thirteen hundred feet per second by the time it struck. The damage to its nose had all undoubtedly been done by the bones struck in passing through the body.

Coal held out his hand, and Mitchell dropped the bullet into it. He hefted it in his palm, aware of and trying to ignore the crust of blood and dirt on it. It would have been nearly impossible for a bullet to be more familiar to Coal, for he had loaded easily hundreds of them on his Rock Chucker loading press: the one hundred-sixty-five grain .30/06—this one known as a Nosler partition.

Again, a chill ran all through Coal's body, and he looked from the bullet to that slope some thousand yards away. If Bigfoot Monahan could shoot like this, he was some incredible marksman. Dead shots like that came along only once in many thousands of men who had tried. They had to get this man back in prison immediately, because there was no longer any doubt—Coal, or perhaps Jim, was next.

"Good work, guys." He slipped the bullet in the chest pocket of his jacket.

When he looked over, they were both watching him. Jim met his gaze and held it for a moment, looked far away to the slope where the shooter had been, then looked again at Coal. Coal had been waiting.

"You seriously think somebody made two shots like that, Coal? From *that* range? That don't make any sense. One time can be luck. But two?"

"You remember that racehorse we used to watch, Jim? Kelso? Remember when he took the Racehorse of the Year award as a three-year-old? What year was that? Sixty? Nobody would have dreamed it could happen again, but he did it. I think it was sixty-four. That horse was destined to be great. He just had it in him to be fast, light on his feet, and determined. He was like a human—he had some kind of drive to be the best.

"Well, I saw men like that in marksmanship school too. They came in out of nowhere and out-shot us all. It happens. In this case, he just happens to be a cold-blooded killer. Who would ever have guessed that big brute could shoot like this?"

Jim shook his head. "Not me."

They both looked over at Mitchell, who quickly whipped his eyes away. He made a point of staring out at that far slope.

And almost exactly one hour later, they found it, nearly one thousand yards away: the single casing of a .30/06, thrust an inch and a half into the ground with the head protruding just enough to be obvious.

* * *

Coal had pulled up to the highway, prepared to head back to town, when he saw a big, ugly International Harvester Travelette coming at him from the direction of Salmon. He paused and looked closer, then swore in disbelief.

"Man, that Ken," he said aloud. It was Maura, and Ken Parks already had her truck back on the road.

The woman pulled off the highway and stopped the truck in front of his car, then got out. Coming around to the other side, she flung the door open and reached in, coming out with little Clarissa. He noticed right off that the girl was wearing a dark blue dress and new black shoes, and her hair was glistening, drawn back and tied with a red ribbon. She wore a white coat with fake fur on the collar, snugged up around her ears. She looked like a different girl.

Coal jumped up out of his car and went to meet them. "Well, hi, Sissy. You sure look pretty today. I love that beautiful dress!" He forced a smile for her, and she came close to smiling back.

"Hi, Maura," he said, his eyes shifting to the woman. Her rich blond hair contrasted with the soft, chocolate waves of the young girl's. "Told you Ken was good."

"Yeah. He says I'd better start having him clean it out under there if I'm too lazy." She laughed, trying to lighten the mood in the air. "The carburetor was all clogged up with crap. Simple fix. And cheap."

"The best kind. Well, you're a long ways out from your place."

Maura nodded, joggling her pretty little arm decoration up and down a bit. "My neighbor took the boys out shooting with him, and his wife had Sissy all dolled up when I got back. Can you believe it? Same girl, though. I know it, because she has the same giggle." She wiggled her hand inside the coat and poked Sissy in the ribs, and it was all the girl could do to hold back a laugh. Coal was sure it was because he was there that she fought back the urge. She still wasn't having any of him.

"Well, she *did!* Anyway, I have Sissy now and we're going to go out and see the horses in a while. But... I was wondering... Are you going to see Jennifer Batterton?"

Coal nodded, turning sober. "That's next."

"The Ericksons wouldn't rather do it?"

"I asked them. They aren't up to it. They said they'll go over after I'm done."

"Okay." She hesitated, looking toward his car, then back at him. Then at Sissy.

"Something's on your mind, Maura. That's one thing I can tell about a woman—when they're thinking about something they don't want to bring up."

She laughed. "I'm sorry. So what's on my mind, smartie?"

"Ha! I said I can tell when something's on a woman's mind. I've *never* guessed correctly about what it was! And if I could, I wouldn't dare say it out loud anyway."

Another soft laugh, as her eyes delved into his, trying to read his state of mind. "So hey... Would you mind some company? I don't know Jennifer super well, but we've talked a bit."

"Why would you want any part of this?"

"Don't make me tell you that."

"Ha!" Coal said again and glared at her, aware that Todd Mitchell and Jim were idling their vehicles behind him, waiting for him to get out of the gateway. "After saying that, there's *no* way I'd not make you tell."

She looked into his eyes, and a sad look came over her. She tried to smile. "I feel bad for you, that's all. That's not a job to do alone."

Coal was taken aback. That was her reason? Her sole reason? For *him?* He wasn't quite sure what to say. "Still not sure why you'd get into this. It's going to be ugly."

Maura reached out without warning and gave his shoulder a brisk rub through his coat. "Hey! Stop it. Coal, it's already ugly. I don't want to see you have to go over there by yourself."

With a sudden urge to take this woman in his arms and give her a huge hug, Coal forced his eyes away. "Well, if you're going to go, we'd better get to it and get this little princess out of the cold. Do you want to go for a ride, Sissy?"

The girl's eyes flashed to Maura, then back to his face. She studied him with no hint of a smile. But she seemed to read his eyes, and somehow she must have approved of what she saw there. All of a sudden, she gave a huge nod, which seemed to take all of her effort, from mid-chest up.

"Okay, then. I guess that's a big yes. Want to follow me?"

Maura glanced over at the Travelette and paused. She took a big breath. "Maybe we could leave the truck here for now. Could we ride in with you?"

"Sure, but... We're going right past your house." Coal couldn't help trying to be practical.

She frowned at him. "As if I don't know that. I just thought it would be nice to ride with you for a while. Would it be a huge bother to bring us back after the truck later?"

The words struck Coal in the guts so for a moment he didn't know what to say. He couldn't understand why someone who was nearly a stranger would want to be with him at a time like this. He gathered himself. "Uhh... No, of course not. Okay, then. Why don't you pull off the road farther and park it here? I'll bring you back when this is over."

Maura actually gave Coal a real smile, with real softness in her eyes. He even thought a little mist came into them, a mist for which he had no explanation. She took little Clarissa around and set her in the passenger side of the LTD. Then she walked back to the International and jumped in, pulling past the front of his car and parking in the brittle, frosty grass on the side of the road. When she came back, Coal was waiting by her door, and he opened it.

Maura stopped, a surprised look on her face. She looked down at the open door, then back at him, her gaze direct. "What's that about?"

"What? Opening the door? My mother didn't raise me to be a jerk."

"It happened later, huh?" She giggled when he gave her a surprised look. "Sorry, I couldn't help that. Well, thank you."

"Yeah," he said, his voice dry. "Don't let the door hit you in the butt."

He walked around and got back in, settling into the seat. He looked down at Sissy. "We'll go to town now, Sis. We have to visit somebody." He suddenly felt sick about having the girl see Jennifer's reaction, but it was too late to back out of it now. Maura was a woman. Hopefully she knew what she was doing.

He glanced over at Maura, at her tousled, wind-blown hair, her smoky blue eyes, her firm mouth. Yes, Maura was a woman. And what a woman she was.

Cynthia would be in school. He would have to go after her next, and the thought crushed him. How much could be expected of one man? They pulled up on Hope Street in front of the Battertons', and they both sat and looked at the house for a moment. How ironic that the Battertons should reside on Hope, when all hope now seemed lost. Finally, Maura turned her eyes to Coal and locked on his. His jaws were clenched. He felt dead inside.

Slowly, she reached across Sissy and laid her callused but warm hand over his. "I don't want to go in either. But that gold badge means no one else can do this."

He nodded. His throat was tight, so tight he dared not speak. Jennifer Batterton was forty-one years old, with a lot of years left ahead of her if fate was kind. How did he tell her that her husband, who had left over an hour ago to help push cattle around, was dead? Murdered, no less?

It made him think back some fifteen years. 1957. He was home on leave, and a movie by the name of *Old Yeller* had been released in theaters, with appearances in it by two of his favorite actors, Chuck Connors—who would later win renown as the "Rifleman" himself—and Fess Parker, made famous as Davy Crockett, and seven years later as Daniel Boone. Laura almost never wanted to go to movies, and she especially hated the sad ones, so he went to it alone, down to the Roxy. The main character of the movie was one Travis Coates, who had found a big yellow dog he came to love. When, after a fight with a rabid wolf, the dog contracted rabies and was doomed to die, Travis had insisted on shooting Old Yeller himself. "He's my dog," he had said. Coal could never have guessed that all these years later he, like Travis Coates, would have to apply Travis's logic to an instance such as this. But because he had been close to Jennifer and K.T., besides the fact that he was sheriff, Maura was right: He was the only one who could shoot this particular dog.

* * *

In the Batterton house, four people sat in utter silence. There was no crying. Not even a tear. Maura, who barely knew Jennifer Batterton, sat on her right side, holding her hand. Coal held the left, and Jen was crushing his hand. Little Sissy, on the far side of Maura, leaned back against the sofa and stared at the opposite wall. Even as an almost-four-year-old, instinctively she seemed to know this was not the time for moving around. She seemed hardly even to breathe.

Jennifer didn't look at Coal or Maura. She stared out the window, through lace curtains. The day was but bright. It should have been good. K.T. would have been driving up any time, throwing the door shut to come to his wife and give her a huge hug. She couldn't remember when he had ever missed that opportunity after they had been apart, even if he had only been as far away as the grocery store.

So slowly her movement almost couldn't be detected, the woman began tipping backward, and finally she sank into the back of the sofa. Now her eyes were focused on the ceiling, and her hands still held onto Coal's and Maura's, squeezing too tight. Somewhere outside a dog barked. A car beeped its horn, and someone's motor revved to way too high of an RPM before the vehicle flew south out of town.

Coal heard Jennifer take a breath and let it out slowly. Her eyes shut, and tears began to insist their way out from under her lids. Maura let go of her hand and leaned back beside her, laying an arm over her shoulders, soft as autumn leaves.

And Jennifer cried.

* * *

After the tears, Jennifer washed her face and blew her nose, and they sat at the table. Talk was small. Jennifer wanted to know the facts of K.T.'s death, but they were sparse, and Coal made them more so. No one spoke of life insurance or funeral arrangements. No one said a word about how it would "get easier in time."

Jennifer had looked down and tried to smile at little Clarissa several times throughout the conversation. Finally, she pulled in a little, sobbing breath and looked at her again, holding back the tears that swam in her eyes. "You sure are a pretty little girl."

The girl stared at her for a few seconds, then looked down.

"Sissy's still trying to warm up a little," said Coal.

Jennifer smiled, and looked over at Maura. "Oh, that's all right. She's fine. She's yours?"

"I could only be so lucky," replied Maura with a soft smile. Her eyes went to Coal, who jumped in to help her.

"Her uncle is her guardian, and he's staying with *us* for a while, Jen." He gave her a meaningful look.

Jennifer caught his meaning. "Oh! With *us.* I see." She looked back at Maura. "So you've taken her in until he gets out."

Maura smiled. "Yep. I guess my house was just too lonely during the day."

"I'm being snoopy, but... Who are her folks? Anyone I would know?"

Coal sighed. "I guess they're... Umm, the uncle told us they aren't around anymore, if you catch my drift. He said he's her only family."

"They aren't around anymore? Oh, you mean...? I'm so sorry!" She looked sadly at Sissy. "That breaks my heart. Who is the uncle? Someone from here in town?"

"No. Just some out-of-work fellow from Challis. His name is Roger. Roger Miley."

Jennifer's mouth dropped open. "Roger Mi—" She gasped, and both of her hands came up to cover her mouth. "You did say Roger *Miley*, right?"

Coal and Maura were both staring at Jennifer. "Uh... yeah. Somebody you know?"

Jennifer's hand came down to her chest, and she laid it there as if trying to keep her heart from pounding.

"Coal, Roger Miley is the brother of my brother-in-law—Bud Miley. Linda Miley is my sister. But... she isn't dead."

CHAPTER THREE

Once Coal had spoken for a while with Jennifer about her sister, Linda Miley, and her husband, the woman decided it was altogether believable that she might have been killed in a car wreck and that she not be notified about it. Once she got used to the idea, there seemed to be very little sadness, and absolutely no surprise.

Jennifer went on to tell Coal and Maura how Linda had basically been "lost" to her family shortly before they moved to Salmon from Jackman, Maine, for her father to accept a new job as a manager of the timber company he was working for and which was expanding its operations into the Mountain West. Linda, then a senior in high school, had been seriously dating a young man in his twenties, and she refused to leave him. When that refusal led to Linda physically attacking their mother, she left her crying on the floor with a broken nose and ran away. They stayed as long as they were able to, waiting for her to return, then left a letter and some money with a relative in Jackman, left the police searching for their daughter, and moved west. There had never been any making up. Linda came back, got the letter and the money, sent a hateful letter out to Salmon, and vanished once more.

Linda had since split up with the boyfriend, married or at least attached herself to two or three other men in her nationwide ramblings, become an alcoholic and a drug addict and been huge in the hippie movement of the sixties. All of this Jennifer knew only because of one cousin back in Maine, the cousin with whose family they had left their contact information and the money, with whom, for some reason, Linda kept close contact. And the cousin faithfully sent any news on to Jennifer.

Jennifer's father had many years ago died in a wreck driving down out of the Beaverheads after a freak snowstorm. Coal remembered that horrible day. And Jennifer's mother had died of a stroke maybe five years ago. The rest of her family, three brothers, were scattered all over the West, and she seldom had contact with any of them.

Strangely, it had turned up that, just after the death of their father, Linda had decided to move out to Idaho, to the Challis or Arco area. No one knew for sure why, because she never contacted her family, but they assumed the eventual plan to do so was in her head and that perhaps in time she would come around, a "prodigal daughter," as it were. If that was the case, Jennifer had always assumed it would be because Linda had decided she wanted something from them, and that perhaps with their father out of the way it would be more easy to finagle it out of her mother. In the end, Linda had found herself another husband, this one in the Miley clan, of Challis, and she and Bud Miley had been married now for at least four or five years, according to Jennifer's cousin in Maine.

After all the facts were out, Coal sat there quietly for some time. Finally, he said, "Hey, Jen, is there some place we can talk alone for a minute?"

Glancing back at Sissy, who at that moment was watching Maura smile at her, Jennifer got up and led Coal down a hall to a bedroom. They went in and closed the door, and she leaned up against it with her hands behind her, against her buttocks. Coal put the palm of his hand flat against the door, the other thumb hooked in his pocket. Their faces were inches apart.

"Jen, if it turns out Linda and her husband really died in a wreck, it seems sensible to assume you would be the natural one to have that little girl."

She stared at him, her eyes wide. He could tell she was struggling for breath. Finally, in a voice of breathlessness, she said, "Coal, how could I? How could I take care of a baby like that? I don't even know how I'm going to make a living myself."

"I know. I think it's time you started looking around through K.T.'s records. Most men in law enforcement, especially when they get up in their mid-thirties or so, will start thinking about life insurance. And some men buy it without telling their wives."

"K.T. wouldn't. We did everything as a partnership."

"Well, just don't assume, Jen. Don't leave any stone unturned."

"I won't. But I just don't hold out much hope. And if he had bought one, leave it to K.T. to cancel it right after he lost his sheriff's job. Wouldn't that be ironic?" She tried to laugh, but instead, she cried. Coal held onto her and stroked her hair for a long time.

* * *

Telling Cynthia about her father's death was even harder than telling her mother. They pulled her out of school and took her back to Jennifer to break the news. Then Coal and Maura left them there alone to mourn, taking Sissy with them to the Coffee Shop to get something to eat. It had been a long morning.

Sitting over dinner, which Sissy attacked voraciously, Coal and Maura talked about K.T. He told her about the strange red station wagon that had been parking out in front of the Batterton house.

"I don't know if that car had anything to do with anything. I have no clue who it belongs to, although I'm going to keep looking. It still only stands to reason that Bigfoot killed Larry, Trent and K.T. He swore in front of several people that he was going to, and then right after he gets out they all start dying. Pretty coincidental. And his list included me, which he already tried to get done."

"And he'll try again," she said quietly.

"That's why when that parole officer gets here today I've got to get Bigfoot's place searched. If we can get him on something—anything—he'll go back to the pen, and whoever is on his list now might live. That means me—and I assume Jim Lockwood, too, since he was the sheriff then. It wouldn't surprise me if Judge Sinclair is also on the list, and maybe even the jury members."

Upon their arrival at the cafe, Coal had called his dispatcher to tell her where he could be reached. They were just finishing up when he heard the phone ring, and pretty soon Tammy Hawley, the waitress, came out of the back room. "Hey, Coal! That phone call is for you."

Coal jumped up and strode down the room to grab the phone from her. It was dispatch telling him that a Kevin Wilhelm, Monahan's parole officer, was waiting at the courthouse. "Thanks, Nadene. Can you call him back and tell him I'll be right there? And try to wake up Todd Mitchell at home. Also, see if you can raise Jim Lockwood. Tell them to meet me and Wilhelm at the jail."

He went back to Maura and told her of the new development. "I'd better take you two out to your truck before we do this. Anything could happen at Bigfoot's place."

Maura looked down at Clarissa and gave her a little smile. "I'd like to go with you," she said. "But you're right. Anything could happen—and Sissy's been through enough already."

* * *

They traveled as a parade out of town, Coal leading in his LTD, then Mitchell in his brown pickup, with Jim riding shotgun. Behind them all came Kevin Wilhelm, driving a dark blue '70 Chevrolet Caprice sedan. They had to drive right past the Monahan residence to get to Ericksons' and drop off Maura and Sissy.

At the driveway to the Ericksons', Coal, and then the whole line, pulled over. He was about to ask Maura to wait for him to come around and open the door, but he already knew what her response would be.

She threw open the door and got out, always the independent woman, and held her hand out to Sissy, who climbed out with her. Maura then leaned back down into the passenger side and gave Coal a long, steady look. She wanted to say something, but it didn't seem to be coming to her.

Finally, she just said, "Sheriff, you take care of yourself, okay? You have a lot left to do on this earth." She slammed the door before he could reply, and he watched her walk to her truck and hoist Sissy inside.

Then she came around and opened her own door, pausing to spear Coal with a measuring look. She raised her hand and gave him a little wave, then got in, pulled around, and drove away toward her little homestead.

Taking a deep breath, Coal turned around too, and the others followed.

Finally, around three miles later, just before Monahan's, Coal pulled up alongside the road and waited for the others to do the same. When they were all parked, he got out and went back to Wilhelm's vehicle.

Kevin Wilhelm was a tough-looking man with no nonsense in his florid face. He wore a reddish horseshoe mustache matching hair that had extensively deserted him to leave a shiny dome in the middle. His eyes held a mistrusting look of perpetual anger, and his athletic, muscular frame a promise that it was not smart to tangle with him.

The four of them met at Wilhelm's Caprice. "How do you want to handle this?" asked Coal. "Just drive all three cars on in?"

"No reason not to," said Wilhelm. "Pull in and split off. You drive left, I'll go up the middle, toward the door, and Deputy, you peel off to the right. Shotguns out immediately. This man is huge and dangerous, and there aren't going to be any second chances if he really has that ought-six on him. This sounds bad, but I think you all know what we're going up against, and it's no different than a war. You even *think* you see a weapon, you take him out. Hit him in the chest as many times as you can before he goes down. I never did like this big prick anyway—and I sure don't trust him."

Coal drilled a hard look through Todd Mitchell. "Todd, you take your revolver and stay at the front door to back Wilhelm. I want Jim toting the shotgun, and I want him around at the back door. And if you start shooting and it turns out there isn't a weapon on him, you can't even begin to know the hell that's coming."

Shocked at the flat warning, Mitchell stared at Coal. Finally, he nodded. It was plain he was hurt that he had been singled out, but Coal had no reason to trust him in a tight situation. He would rather hurt his feelings than have Mitchell cause things to go to hell in a handbasket later. They were down to the wire.

Coal popped his trunk and pulled out the Remington pump shotgun. Because the sound of a shell being chambered was such a great tool for quelling someone's desire to fight, he checked the loads in the magazine but left the chamber empty.

And then they loaded up and rolled on in.

Paul Monahan and his family lived in a squat, pale green ranch style home with asbestos siding that was cracked and peeling paint, and a roof that had needed attention for two or three years. There was a board fence off to the right that looked like it had been built to keep livestock in, but it had long since deteriorated and started falling down. At this point, it wouldn't be able to keep in a two legged sheep.

The only other building was what appeared to be a one-time garage out behind the house, with a roof that was slowly giving way to gravity and sagging dangerously downward in the center.

In the yard was parked a hideously rusted dark brown van. Coal's memory was all too clear that the vehicle that raced away from the scene of his near-shooting was dark, and appeared to be a van, or at least a pickup with a camper shell on. It could easily have been this one.

As they had decided, Coal went left, Mitchell right, and Wilhelm up the center. They dismounted with shotguns at the ready, and Mitchell with a .38 special. Coal strode as fast as he could to the left corner of the house, and Jim went around to the back. Then, while Wilhelm took the concrete stairs two at a time, Mitchell stood at the bottom and settled into combat position with his revolver.

Wilhelm stood to one side of the door and pounded loudly with the side of his fist, starting up a flurry of furious barking from some small dog inside. "Probation and Parole! Open the door! Monahan, this is Officer Wilhelm."

There was a yell inside the house, drowning out the yapping dog, but it sounded female. Then for twenty seconds all was still. Coal had brought his shotgun up to his shoulder. Wilhelm, knowing Bigfoot could hear him, racked his shotgun. "Monahan, open up or we're coming in!"

"I'm opening the door," a plea finally came. "Please don't shoot!"

The door clicked, then slowly swung inward.

"Who's there?" barked Wilhelm. His tone of voice left no room for doubt that he was ready and willing to shoot.

"I'm Beverly Monahan. Paul is my husband."

"Is he home?"

"He's at work. Please don't shoot!"

"We don't intend to, ma'am. Now come on out on the porch, real easy."

"Okay, I'm coming. I'm coming." The woman sounded like she was about to cry.

Around the edge of the door appeared a face with splotchy red skin and plump cheeks, a face that might often seem jovial, but now was that of a woman ready to pass out. She wore glasses that made her eyes appear very small, and her hair was curled tightly on her head. Her heavy cheeks pushed her eyes up to make her appear almost squinty. She was holding a Yorkshire terrier that snarled at them ferociously.

"You're Mrs. Monahan?" Wilhelm growled.

"Yes. Beverly."

"Okay, walk down the steps and out into the yard. Mitchell, search her."

Once they had made sure Beverly Monahan wasn't a danger to them, Coal told her he had to handcuff her and put her in his car until their search of the home was finished. Then they scoured the house from top to bottom, going into every single place they could find an opening. The house was clean.

Next, they moved to the garage. In the house, they had searched through the insulation in the attic. In here, they searched the rafters, in spite of a fear that the roof would cave in on them.

Again, nothing. They walked the entire property, and even a little ways beyond it on all sides.

Finally, Coal helped Beverly Monahan out of his car and took off the handcuffs. "Ma'am, let me ask you this question straight. Does your husband have a rifle?"

She instantly shook her head. "No!"

"Any other kind of firearm?"

"No. He was told he can't own a firearm or he will go back to prison."

"That's right. But that hasn't stopped a lot of ex-cons," interrupted Wilhelm, his blue eyes hard and cold.

"Paul doesn't want to do anything wrong," she said, her eyes pleading. "He wants to be with me and our little boy."

"Your little boy?" said Coal. "Oh yeah, you mean the one who flipped me the birdie at the hospital the other night."

Mrs. Monahan's face flushed even redder than normal. "I'm sorry, Sheriff. But you have to understand—the police took Butch's daddy away. That's all he knows about the police."

Coal nodded. "I do understand. Ma'am, we've got to know where Paul is working."

"He works at Lemhi Timber. The one in Leadore."

"Do you have a number where we can reach him?" queried Coal.

"Yes. In the house."

"Okay," cut in Wilhelm. "Let's go get it. And we'll need to use your phone."

"We don't have a phone," she said.

"Oh, okay. Just get the number then."

They all followed Beverly Monahan back into the house just long enough to get the phone number for Lemhi Timber. Mitchell, Jim and Wilhelm went down the concrete stairs, but on the landing Coal paused and turned back to Mrs. Monahan. "I don't know how you reach him in times of trouble, ma'am, but it would be in your best interest, if you're trying to keep on the right side of the law, not to call him at work."

"I won't. I don't ever call him at work."

"All right. I'm counting on that. Also, ma'am, what kind of car is your husband driving to work?"

The woman's reply hit Coal like a kick in the guts: "He drives a red station wagon."

CHAPTER FOUR

Coal had to keep forcing himself to slow his car down. Every time he thought about Bigfoot Monahan and his red station wagon, his blood pressure started going up, and something seemed to press his foot down harder on the throttle. A red station wagon! Could it really be this simple? If it was Bigfoot who had been stalking K.T. and Jennifer in the red station wagon, it was strange that K.T. hadn't recognized him, but it would pretty much clinch Bigfoot's being the killer. All there was left to do now was to find that ought-six, and Coal was convinced that was only a matter of time. Unfortunately, he wasn't sure he would be able to affect an arrest if they didn't find that rifle today. And what did he do then? It wasn't like he and Jim could go into hiding.

It was almost forty miles from the Monahan house to Leadore. They sat across the street from the Lemhi Timber Company, the only logging operation in Leadore, surveying it with binoculars for half an hour before making a move. In that time, there was no sign of Bigfoot Monahan. Finally, they all drove a block or so farther into town, parked on a nameless street, and got into Wilhelm's Caprice so Bigfoot wouldn't recognize the other vehicles.

Wilhelm drove back and parked off to the side of the main office. Again, they scanned the yard through his darkly tinted windows. No sign of Bigfoot. In fact, hardly a sign of *anyone.*

"All right, boys, hold tight a minute. Lockwood and Mitchell, you'd best stay in the car for a minute so we don't make too big of a splash. Savage, why don't you come with me."

The two of them got out, Coal with his service revolver tucked down into the front of his pants and covered with the bottom part of his jacket, his holster left on the floor of the car. Wearing dark glasses, both men scanned the yard again, then nonchalantly stepped to the back doors and unlatched them so the two men in back could make a quick exit if trouble exploded.

"Wait till we come for you or you hear us yelling," Coal told Jim. "We'll be right back."

With Wilhelm in the lead, Coal followed, keeping an eye about the yard. The strong, sweet scent of sawn wood gave Coal a nostalgic feel for his childhood. Woodsmoke curled out of a tin chimney that stuck up out of the roof of the main office, and somewhere out back they heard roosters crowing. This scene of tranquility should never have been in danger of bursting into gunfire.

Hinges squeaked as they eased open the storm door, then pushed through the inner one. A bright-eyed lady in her mid-twenties looked up from a typewriter and a stack of invoices. "Hi! May I help you?"

Wilhelm looked at the name plaque on the woman's desk. "Bobbie? I'm Officer Wilhelm. This is Sheriff Savage. We're looking for one of your employees—by the name of Paul Monahan?"

"I don't think he's in right now," Bobbie said. "Should I call my supervisor?"

"Where is he, Bobbie?" Coal asked.

Bobbie hadn't smiled at Wilhelm after her initial greeting. The tough-looking parole officer didn't lend himself very well to being smiled at. But she smiled at Coal.

"Umm... Probably out back."

"Do you know where Monahan would be?"

"On a truck, I think. I was on the CB with him a while ago, and he said he was driving down off of Rocky Peak with a full load."

"Okay, let us talk to the supervisor then."

"All right. His name is Dennis Pratt." She paged the yard, and within a couple of minutes a burly man in worn-out and greasy brown Carhartt coveralls came stomping in from the back. He sported a blond longhorn mustache that must have been four inches per side.

"Sorry, gents. I was out feeding my chickens. Dennis Pratt. What can I do for you?"

Coal and Wilhelm shook hands with the man. He looked a bit uncomfortably at Wilhelm. "Sheriff Savage and Officer Wilhelm," Coal said before Wilhelm could open his mouth. There might have been a time for ruffling feathers, which Wilhelm's eyes alone made him great at, but this was not that time. "Officer Wilhelm is a parole officer from Pocatello. We're here to check on one of your employees."

"That would have to be Bigfoot," said Pratt with a nod. "Sure, what do you need?"

"How far out is he?" Wilhelm asked.

Pratt turned to the woman. "Bobbie?"

"Never mind," Coal cut in. "Bobbie already told us he's driving down from Rocky Peak. What's that, an hour?"

"Up where they're cuttin'? Sure, maybe. Bigfoot's a steady hand, and he don't take chances with my rigs. Might be a little longer than that. I wish some of the younger boys would take a lesson from him."

Coal nodded. "We need to search his car."

"Yeah? You have a warrant, I take it?"

Coal studied Pratt for a moment. He hadn't seemed like the type to give them trouble. Wilhelm started to speak, and Coal threw up his hand, surprising him and halting his words.

"Bigfoot's on parole, Mr. Pratt, as I'm sure you're already aware. All rules of probable cause are off when it comes to a parolee."

"What are you lookin' for?" Pratt asked. "You know, Bigfoot's turned out to be a damn good worker. I hate to see him not gettin' a fair shake somehow."

"He's a suspect in three murders," growled Wilhelm. "How fair a shake did he give the people he killed?"

Pratt's eyes first widened, then narrowed. "Well, I couldn't say. I don't know the circumstances."

"They were separate killings, Mister Pratt, all ambushed," explained Coal."

Pratt stared at Coal. His face had paled a little. Bobbie had uttered a profanity, and she stood up quickly and tipped her chair back, almost making it fall. "Excuse my language," she said when they all looked at her. Her face had turned red.

"You're fine, Bobbie," said Pratt. "Yeah, we've been hearing about the killings—except there were only two."

"The third one just happened this morning."

Pratt nodded. "All right, boys, come with me. Bigfoot's parked out back."

Coal pushed open the front door and beckoned for Jim and Mitchell to follow them. On the way outside, the supervisor reached up and pulled a set of keys off a hook, glancing over at Coal. "He's a pretty trusting feller. He's hung his keys here since the day he started. I honestly don't even know that he locks it."

The five men wound through a couple of back rooms, one of them a kitchen whose floor was tiled with white squares of Linoleum, and next to it a little break room with a green Formica-covered table the size of a card table, a refrigerator and a TV. *All My Children* was playing, although turned way down low, and Coal was embarrassed to realize he could name that show. It wasn't like he was big on soap operas, but Laura had been.

Out through a creaky back door they went, to a tight parking lot full of mostly pickups and the one glaring red station wagon. The car seemed old, and Coal tried to think back on the age K.T. had said the station wagon that had been parking near his house was. It seemed like he had said it was a Chevrolet, possibly an Impala, and perhaps late sixties. This one was an early sixties Dodge Dart Pioneer. It hardly looked like the one he had in his mind after speaking with K.T. Also, K.T. had said "red and white," hadn't he? The only thing this one had that he might have taken for white in certain lighting was a chrome strip of trim down the side.

No matter. It was still Bigfoot's vehicle. Pratt stopped at the driver's door and started to insert the key, then looked closer and just reached down to pull it open. "See what I mean? Trusting."

Coal nodded. "All right. Let me ask you something before we go through the car. Is there any way any of your drivers could take a hunting rifle up there with them in their truck?"

"Hunting rifle? Hell no! Hunting is strictly prohibited while they're working. We had a guy that used to stop and shoot game all the time. Grouse. Rabbits. Bears. Deer. Whatever. Used to cost us a lot of man-hours, 'specially since he would claim it only took him ten minutes to gut 'em—even the big game, and we couldn't really prove otherwise. No, that's been out of bounds for two or three years."

"All right. Well hang around, would you? It would be nice to have a witness to the search, just in case."

"Don't you worry none about that, boss. I was plannin' on it. I've heard about you boys plantin' guns in houses and cars and stuff, just for a conviction."

Wilhelm's face went even harder, and he took off his glasses, glaring at the big supervisor with a look that could scare flies off a dead snake. "Watch your insinuations, buddy."

"Now you're takin' away my free speech?" countered Pratt.

"Easy, Wilhelm," said Coal before his cohort could reply. "You can't blame him. And it's not like we have anything to hide. Let's just do this and get it over with." He could already see by a precursory glance that the search would likely be futile. There were only a couple of places where something as big as a rifle could be hidden.

Throwing up the back door, Coal unlatched the spare tire compartment and lifted both sides. Nothing but a tire, a jack and a star wrench. That and an empty package of orange-flavored Carefree gum.

Coal crawled out the back of the car again with the empty package. "Bigfoot chew this a lot, does he?"

Pratt chuckled. "That big boy loves his orange gum, he does that."

Coal pondered the package a moment longer, then threw it back in the car and shut the door. Next, they pulled out the back seat. Nothing there, and no room to fit a rifle anyway. Same with the floor under the front seat. As a last check, both men got on the ground and looked up into the undercarriage. Nothing. The vehicle was clean.

Coal got back to his feet and told Wilhelm to turn around, then dusted off his back. Wilhelm thanked him but didn't offer to do the same, which on the instant ticked Coal off.

Pratt, catching the slight to Coal, said, "Here," and when Coal realized what he was offering, he turned and let the big man knock the dust and bits of gravel off his back.

"Thanks, Mr. Pratt." Coal held out his hand and shook the big man's, which rivalled Monahan's for size, although in frame he wasn't as large as the ex-con.

"The car looks clean," said Wilhelm, as if oblivious to what had just taken place. "Is there any place else on your property that a man could hide a rifle?"

"Not that I'm aware of. Well, probably many places that he could, but I think someone would have seen him with one."

All of a sudden, Todd Mitchell, who miraculously had not spoken one word throughout the search, said, "Well, Mr. Pratt, you can tell Bigfoot that if he's the one who was stalking the Batterton house and parking out front, Mrs. Batterton can identify his car pretty easy. He's still got something to answer for."

Coal, on reflex alone, elbowed Mitchell in the ribs. "Why don't you shut your trap, Todd. You don't know what you're talking about." He instantly looked back up at Pratt, who was staring at him in surprise after the exchange. "Never mind him. We already took care of that little problem. That was someone else."

Pratt nodded. "I wasn't worried. None of my affair, I reckon." He spat to one side.

Coal nodded. "All right. Well, thanks again for your cooperation. If you ever get up to Salmon, look me up. I'll buy you a coffee."

"Sure," said Pratt, giving Coal a big grin. "I always like a little road trip. I may just do that someday."

Coal and the others took a route around the building to get back to Wilhelm's car, but while Wilhelm went to the car, Coal opened the front door to the office and leaned back inside to see Bobbie looking up from the desk.

"Bobbie? Thanks for your help—and the nice smile."

"Oh, you are very welcome, Sheriff. Any time. Have a nice day, okay?"

Coal nodded. "I'll try. Thank you."

Out at the car, Jim and Mitchell were standing in a cluster with Wilhelm. They all turned to Coal as he stopped before them.

"Well?" said Jim.

"Well?" Coal echoed. He felt like he was about to explode, and he instantly turned his eyes from Jim to Todd Mitchell. "Up until a minute ago, I thought you had some sense, Deputy. Why the hell would you say what you did to him? Do you *want* to get Jennifer Batterton killed?"

"I was just— I thought we could maybe scare Bigfoot into taking off. Or tipping his hand. Something."

Coal scoffed. "You have to be kidding. How? He's killed three men, Todd. He's not going to scare off."

"Sorry," said Mitchell, unable to meet Coal's eyes for more than a couple of seconds. "I wasn't thinking."

Coal did not reply to that last quiet statement. Anyone could have told him that.

"What do we do about Bigfoot?" Jim asked then, saying with his eyes that he hoped to move away from the contention.

"Nothing. There's not one thing to take him in for."

"So he just keeps killing?" cut in Todd Mitchell, too stupid to know when to stay quiet until Coal calmed down.

You'd probably like that, wouldn't you, Todd? thought Coal. *An almost sure way to get his job as sheriff back, at least until the next election, when maybe they would be lucky enough to find someone with a brain—not to mention some iron in his guts.*

"Unless we find some other way to stop him," said Coal, hardening his jaw. "Wilhelm? Sorry I wasted your time."

Wilhelm smiled, something he hadn't done until this moment. "Not a problem. Got me out of the office, didn't it? Call me back anytime—unless it's snowing."

He reached out his big, hard hand, and after looking at it for just a moment Coal shook it. In spite of the man's hard exterior, Coal had a feeling he and Wilhelm could have a good working relationship, in time. You just had to head off a man like the parole officer sometimes, before he could make the wrong people angry.

Then again, there were other times when making someone angry was exactly the right thing to do. Wilhelm would have been a good man to keep around.

CHAPTER FIVE

While Kevin Wilhelm headed toward home, Coal purposely let Mitchell and Jim go ahead of him, and in a few minutes watched the dot that was Mitchell's pickup disappear in vague distance.

Coal had no more desire to drive fast. He had failed in his quest. He had set out with a sure knowledge that they would find a rifle somewhere on Bigfoot Monahan's property. After their failure to do so there, he again felt certain of success in Monahan's vehicle. Again, no luck. They were no closer to an arrest than they had been an hour earlier, or even several days earlier. What was he going to tell Jennifer Batterton? To say nothing of Kathy MacAtee and the girls. He felt like an utter failure.

Also, it would have been one thing if this disappointment meant only having to wait a little longer to make an arrest. In some cases, it would be nothing more than a temporary annoyance, because surely something was going to turn up eventually. But in this case, no arrest today might mean Coal *never* making an arrest. Both he and Jim Lockwood might be dead before damning evidence was found against Bigfoot now.

Coal wanted to talk to someone. Bounce ideas off a warm set of ears, even if that someone might have no idea what he was talking about. He couldn't bring all this home to his mother. She had been through enough. Besides, the kids would be coming home from school soon. He didn't feel like looking for Jim, because for all he knew the ex-sheriff was still with Todd Mitchell, and after the idiotic comment Mitchell had made about Jennifer's possibly being able to identify the red station wagon, he had no desire even to be in the same room with his deputy for a while. He was afraid of what he might say or do.

There were others he could confide in. Rick Cheatum. Ken Parks or Andy Holmes. Other old friends in town. But none he knew for sure weren't working and whom he would feel okay bothering this time of day. Wrack his brain as he might, there was only one person he might count on, and he was pretty sure he didn't want to.

But he was just about to pass her house.

Coal slowed way down, not seeing the car that was behind him until it flew past him, laying on its horn. "Oops! Sorry," he said out loud. Right at five miles an hour, he came to her drive, and almost automatically, he made the turn. He drove into the yard, then stopped in the grass, a couple of horses leaning over a barbed wire fence to flick their ears and stare at him. Probably wondered if he was bringing them a carrot or something. He looked at the animals, a dun and a deep red sorrel. A look at their strong facial features, and big, honest eyes, their well-muscled forelegs and wide chests suddenly made him long to be riding again, somewhere in the mountains, far from this so-called civilization and impending death. Even from inside his car, he fancied he could smell the scent of their noses, that warm, soft smell that every real horseman loves, that lingers with him for hours after he has turned his mount loose in the pasture.

Coal sighed. Apparently, there would never be any peace in this life. Not for him, at least. He had been making a living for far too many years either on war or on crime and its aftereffects to think he could ever lead an existence of tranquility. At forty-two, there was pretty much nothing he could think of that could earn him an honest living, nothing besides chasing and dealing with criminals.

He checked his rearview mirror. The area of the yard where he had stopped was very tight, but he studied it for just a moment, wondering how many attempts he would have to make to get turned around and head back to town. Finally, he looked ahead again and pulled in a deep breath. Well, maybe Maura would at least have coffee on...

Just then, the dogs started barking. For a few moments, he sat in the car, leaned back against the seat, looking around. He could see the tailgate of the white International just beyond the edge of a dilapidated barn off to the left. So Maura was here, somewhere.

The day was crisp and clear, one of those days you longed never to have end. The sun shone bright on everything, and even though the air was cold, all the furrows made by Maura's tires were dry now, and firm. The grass that grew far enough outside her fences for horses not to reach it had mostly lain down because of its own length and weight, and it was a beautiful auburn color. The few seed heads that were still upright bobbed in the slightest breeze.

Several times as Coal sat there looking for some sign of life besides the dogs and a few magpies and red-winged blackbirds flitting around, he thought about backing out of the yard and heading on to town. He couldn't quite remember why he had stopped here in the first place.

But before he could commit himself either way, he spied movement at the corner of the barn, and his eyes were drawn to it. Maura stood there in a straw cowboy hat and white and green shadow-plaid snap-front shirt covered by a Levi jacket, her boots dirtied by corral mud and manure, her jeans too tight for riding horses, too dirty for dancing, and, for a few seconds, too hard to take his eyes off.

"You just going to sit there and stare?" Maura called.

Coal just sat there—and stared. "You just going to stand there and look like that?" he asked under his breath.

But he immediately got out of the car and eased his hip against the door to press it shut. Little Sissy had appeared now beside Maura, and both of them stood looking at him, the girl with her mouth ajar and her great big eyes wondering, the woman with her gaze full of unspoken questions.

Coal hadn't donned his holster again, and now, after looking about the yard, he chided himself and reached back into the car for it, undoing his pants belt and sliding the brown hunting holster back into place between the first two belt loops on his right side. He might as well live in the wild Old West, he thought. He could not afford to be caught without some kind of protection—old Marshal Dillon would never let him live it down!

Walking toward Maura and the girl, Coal's heart hammered. A part of him was very attracted to this rough-shod woman with the tangled golden hair, direct blue eyes and tender-looking pink mouth. But the other half hated himself for being so easily drawn in, especially to a woman who had treated him so harshly from the time of their first meeting.

He walked up and stopped in front of her, feeling suddenly awkward. Maura surprised him by drawing off her tight, stained cowhide gloves and holding her right hand out to him. *What the hell?* he thought. He didn't remember ever shaking hands with her, but whether they had or not, why now? And while he was still thinking it, his big hand went out to her, and it closed over hers, which in spite of its calluses and roughness seemed simultaneously warm and supple. For several seconds, neither of them even tried to let go. Her lips parted, showing the perfectly aligned edges of her upper teeth, but still she didn't speak.

Finally, the silence stretched so thin it threatened like glass to shatter, and Maura released her grip. "Hey, wanna see the boys?"

"Boys? Aren't they still out shooting with your neighbor?"

"Not those boys!" She smiled, then allowed herself a little laugh. "The hairy boys." She jerked her head toward where the two horses he had seen earlier had turned into four and were standing expectantly at a feeder, staring with perked ears and flaring nostrils at the three people. They knew where to wait.

"Feeding time," mused Coal. "I know how they feel!"

"Hungry belly? Maybe we can fix that. But first, come on. I think it's been a while since you shucked hay to a horse."

A while. Coal tried to recall. *A three year while,* he thought.

They went through a man-gate in the fence, a rail-less opening just wide enough for a human, but not a horse. Sissy stayed right on Maura's heels, and Coal noticed that the woman walked slowly enough for her little shadow to keep up. He had a feeling her normal pace could be much faster. She was not one to dally.

They threw flakes of hay into the feeder, then watched the horses choose their slot and go to eating. None of them fought for a turn, and it was funny to see how each of them lowered its head in turn to start eating. They had their place in the pecking order, and each of them knew it.

Finally, Maura stood back and pulled her gloves off again, pressing them down behind the waistband of her pants. She was smart enough to know they weren't going to fit in a pocket, not as tight as those Levi's were.

She took off her hat and shook her head, letting her tangled tresses fall over a shoulder and breaking free a few stems of hay. At last, she put a hand on Sissy's head, giving the silky hair a little ruffle. "So... You're all alone, Coal." She looked at him, then slowly shook her head as she searched his eyes. “No luck, huh? You couldn’t arrest him?”

Coal mimicked her head shake. “We didn’t find a thing. We scoured that place, too. Even drove clear to Leadore to his work and went through his car.”

“Was he there?”

“No. He works at Lemhi Timber, and they told us he was hauling logs down out of the mountains and wouldn’t be back for a while.”

“So what did the others seem to think of him?”

“Honestly, we only interacted with his boss. But he seemed to think Monahan’s a pretty good hand. If anything, it seemed like he was overly protective of him.”

Maura looked down at Sissy, her hand smoothing down her hair. She didn’t look back up when she spoke again. “So... Now what? You and Jim Lockwood are still in danger, right?” She kept looking at Sissy’s sleek hair.

“Big danger, I reckon. If I got in a rifle fight with this guy, I’m not very sure I could win. Worse yet, it doesn’t look like he gets in gunfights. People don’t see him coming like the old Westerns. I don’t think there’ll be any showdown at noon on Main Street with this guy.”

Coal saw Maura’s chest fill with air. She let it seep out. Then the subject changed abruptly. “So... the black guy is Homer,” she said, pointing at a horse with two rear stockings that were soiled by manure. “He’s the king of the corral and barn, and everyone in there agrees. If you ever come riding, he’s yours.”

Coal looked into her eyes and tried to match her smile. Silently, he thanked her. She knew he did not want to talk about Bigfoot right now. “Okay. Homer. Crappy name.”

She giggled. “Well, I didn’t name him, and that’s what he answers to. I’ve tried a lot of cuss words, and he just ignores them and keeps on doing whatever pigheaded crap he’s doing.”

Coal laughed.

She raised a hand and pointed at the dirty yellow dun. "That's Sarah, and she's my baby. Raised her from day one—with a bottle, mind you."

"You lost her mom?"

Maura nodded sadly. "Yeah. I guess she was just too old. Something tore loose inside her, and she bled out. That was a sad day. Now, the two sorrels are Hilly and Brusher. Hilly has the bald face. Those are steady horses. My boys dote on them."

Coal smiled at her. It was plain to tell when she was talking about something she loved. The sky seemed to reflect even bluer in her eyes, and her cheeks took on a flush of excitement and pride.

"So does a woman like you keep coffee brewing in the day-time? Or are you out with the horses too much?"

"I do. And I sometimes have other things, too. Depending on your mood."

"Like water? Milk? Root beer? Tea? Otherwise, I'm on duty, you know."

Maura sighed. "You're pretty much always on duty, right? That's one of the problems with your life, remember?"

"Yeah. And why I make the big money."

"Come on, soldier boy," she said, taking his elbow in her hand. "I'll buy you a coffee. The alcohol just sits in there anyway, waiting for someone who drinks. I quit that a long time ago."

Coal sat in Maura's little, run-down kitchen later and sipped sour, burned coffee while he stared out the front room window wishing he hadn't asked for any. It wasn't far from one room clear across the other. Beyond their sheltered Lemhi Valley, the Beaverhead Mountains shouldered upward into the expanse of sky, their ridges of smoky blue laced with a frosting of snow, majestic as a painting. A pair of red-tail hawks patrolled the grassland for ground squirrels and mice, now and then landing on the fence or a phone pole to rest.

Coal sat and thought about bad coffee and swore he could never tell Maura hers was some of the worst—at least not until she decided to give him a tongue lashing for something, when of course everything would become fair game.

What did he do next? Something had to break. He was out of cards to play against Bigfoot. But that something that broke could be his own murder, or Jim's...

There were options, of course. Things he had had to do in Korea and Nam and never dreamed he might have to consider again. Things on the back side of the law. He had shot a ten-year-old boy once, and afterward had been glad of it. That boy was strapped with explosives and set to wipe out a squadron of his men. He had killed other people he hadn't felt like killing as well. Other children. Old men. Women with babies. Fortunately, none of them was unwarranted. Every single one turned out to be a sworn enemy, ready to kill as many of his men as possible, and in the worst way possible.

But this... Somehow this was different. There was no war here, not as such. It was one man, Bigfoot Monahan, against whomever he chose to kill. And yet, in its own way, was that not a war? And did not Coal have the skills to do just what Bigfoot was doing? What was to stop him from taking his own rifle, tuning it up with a couple boxes of shells, and then hiding somewhere above Bigfoot's place one morning to wait for him to come outside? Bigfoot's was a remote place. It wasn't likely anyone would even see him. And he had friends with obscure looking vehicles he could borrow, to be on the safe side. Two men could play the game Bigfoot was playing. Why wait for him to roll the ball? Was that something a great warrior ever did—wait for the enemy always to come knocking? Maybe it was time someone carried this game to Bigfoot. Meet him on his own terms. Hell, who was going to miss him? His wife and son, sure. But no more than Larry's and K.T.'s families missed them.

"I guess not then." Maura's voice suddenly broke in on Coal's consciousness.

"Huh?"

"I said I guess not."

Coal felt his face grow warm. "Uh... Sorry, I didn't hear the part before that."

"Yeah, I figured."

She stared at him. Her eyes searched his, while Clarissa leaned up against her leg and fiddled with a toy that Coal suddenly realized was one of the Marx action figures his own children played with—little Josie West, the cute blond-haired daughter of Johnny West, the ultimate cowboy. The little blue figure made him smile, for he thought of Katie at a younger age, a sweet age.

"I really am sorry, Maura. I was pretty lost in thought."

Her face softened. "Well, I had a dumb idea anyway. What were you thinking about?"

"That's not fair," he said, turning more toward her and resting his elbows on his knees. "What was your idea?"

"No, it's okay. I really want to know what you were thinking about. Just drop it, okay?"

"All right. But I can't tell you what I was thinking about either. Too incriminating." After he said that, he instantly wondered if she would think he was having thoughts about her—about them. He started to say something, realized he was just going to dig a deeper hole, and stopped, his face warming up again as he dropped his eyes to Sissy.

At that moment, a big vehicle rumbled up on the highway, and its brakes squeaked as Coal heard it come to a stop. He looked a question at Maura.

"The bus," she said. "The boys are home."

Inwardly, Coal swore. That late already! "I guess I should go." He stood up.

"My boys come home, and you have to go?"

"I have to button things up in the office." His excuse felt lame once he said it, but how did he take it back?

"Okay, that's fine."

She got up too, and Sissy straightened her stance into one of vigilance and watched them both to see what move they would make. They walked to the door, and Coal picked up his hat off a set of mule deer antlers. He fiddled it around in his hands for a few seconds, studying the satin liner inside. Finally, he looked up at her. "Will you tell me what you asked before? When I was day-dreaming?"

"It won't matter now."

"Why?"

"It just won't. Maybe another time."

"Please."

"I was asking if you would like to stay for supper. No big deal."

In her eyes swam hurt, and she immediately looked away from him and focused on the front door as it opened wide. He didn't have a chance to reply. It didn't seem like it would matter now anyway. Either being ignored made Maura really upset really fast, or else she simply had had a moment to realize how stupid the idea was and was hoping to get out of it. Maybe time would tell. Maybe it wouldn't. Besides, if her cooking was anything like her skill at making coffee, perhaps it really was for the best.

Two young boys, one perhaps fourteen, the other a year or two younger, had come into the room and set books down on the end of the sofa. They were good looking, dark-haired boys, somber of skin, with deep-set, dark eyes. Having the same mother and father was undeniable for boys so closely matched.

"Coal, these are my boys, Ty and Sky. Boys, this is our new sheriff, Coal Savage."

"Cool!" said the younger boy, Sky. "Just like our school mascot!"

Coal grinned. "Just like it," he said. "I think they named it after my family. Hi, boys." He held out his hand, and Sky took it in the firm but not over-bearing grip of one well-trained to show his strength without being rude. Sky had a big smile and a row of gleaming white teeth.

When Coal held his hand out to Ty, there was no big smile. He gave his hand only out of respect, and it was a soft, quick shake, dropping away the moment it was able. He looked beyond Coal to his mother. Mistrust and hurt seemed to fill his eyes, if Coal had to guess at any emotions. And he was expert at judging both.

"Uh, I think I'd better get going. You still up for keeping Sissy for a while? I haven't had a chance to see what happened with the judge and Roger Miley yet."

Maura, flustered, pulled her attention away from her oldest boy's scrutiny to look at Coal. In her eyes, there rode confusion. She dropped her glance to Sissy as she realized of a sudden what Coal had asked, and she laid a hand protectively on the girl's head. "You bet. I'm not letting this one go until I absolutely have to. Right, Sis?"

The girl looked up and gave her a huge smile and a nod. Not a word out of her. But the way she encircled Maura's thigh with an arm, tightly hugging it to her, was enough to tell everything she didn't say in words.

The heelers met Coal on the rickety wood landing, and he ignored them and descended the stairs. Putting his hat on as he went, he hurriedly climbed into the Ford and backed out of the driveway onto the road. He puttered down the highway and thought of Maura and the supper she had offered him. He had felt bad about not hearing Maura's request the first time, but now, after Ty's reception, he realized it definitely had gone as well as possible for everyone involved.

His thoughts went back to Bigfoot Monahan. One shot. One kill. It would be so easy. No more issues. No more needless killings of innocent people. One dead man, as justice for the deaths of a few others and to save... how many more? He felt his forehead actually film over with sweat. What kind of a lawman was he, even letting an idea like that come into his head? And yet, what kind of a lawman was he if he let Bigfoot Monahan kill again when he might have stopped him?

It took everything Coal had to force his thoughts away from Bigfoot. He could sense that old feeling coming over him, the feeling he dreaded. The willingness to kill, in order to save lives. But he was not in a declared war here. He was in Lemhi County, Idaho, a place where the law reigned, and things were done by the book. He was a lawman. That had to mean *something!* Could he live with himself if he killed a man here, outside of war, from concealment? And yet here he was, helpless, knowing without a doubt that Bigfoot Monahan would kill again. And that he was supposed to be the protector of the people in this county.

Even if he was caught and sent up for it, perhaps it would be worth it if it saved a few lives, especially if one of them was that of his friend Jim. Perhaps. What was his life really worth anyway? And what was really the worst thing that could happen? Connie ended up raising his children? The answer to that was simple:

She was raising them anyway.

CHAPTER SIX

Thursday, November 23... Thanksgiving Day

In the pre-dawn hours, when no one yet stirred, Coal rolled over in bed and sat up. A chill had finally come to the house, after it had been almost too hot the night before, and he thought about stoking up the fire in the Franklin stove. But he wasn't going to take the time. If he was going, he had to go now, while his world slept.

Stepping to the corner where he had leaned his cased rifle the night before, he laid it on the bed with a box of reloaded cartridges. He stepped into Wrangler blue jeans and tugged on socks and his lace up boots, snugging them tight, then donned a long john top and shrugged into a gray-blue stone-washed canvas shirt. From the night stand, he picked up his gold-plated five-point star badge and turned it over a couple of times in his hand. "Sheriff Lemhi County," it said. And in the center, the Idaho State seal with the words "State of Idaho." Did he really deserve this badge? How was he going to be judged for what he was about to do, here on earth or in heaven?

In all reality, under the circumstances, he was really making of himself nothing more than a vigilante behind a badge. Whatever the future held, it didn't matter. Coal Savage had citizens to protect, and he was going to do it the only way he could see how.

He picked up and hefted his blanket-lined Wrangler coat. He was by nature a hot-blooded man, so he didn't turn to winter coats nearly as early as some, but by the chill in the room he guessed this coat had just about worn out its usefulness until spring. Still, he put it on, then double-wrapped a huge, green silk jacquard scarf around his neck, knotting it in the center of his throat.

The house was still and dark, and it smelled of the apple and pumpkin pies Connie had baked the night before, of cinnamon and cloves, and hominess. He thought about Connie and knew she would be stirring soon, to brew coffee and to feed horses, so he walked extra carefully. He also thought of the children. It seemed so long since they had had any chance to really talk. What kind of a father was he? And what kind of a legacy was he going to leave behind if he was caught and convicted for what he was about to do? His children would be remembered not for their father who had been Lemhi County sheriff, but their father who had taken the law into his own hands and committed homicide. At least, whether free or in prison, their father would be alive.

Coal drove far up Stormy Peak Road, cranking down his window to catch the scent of the spruce and pine trees that were starting to take shape in the gathering light. It had snowed up here not long ago, and that wetness still remained in the deep, black loam of the forest floor, sending out a powerful perfume that sang out like the sirens to a man who loved the wilderness.

He stopped at a wide place in the road, an intimately familiar place. Across this canyon, he and Larry, and sometimes Trent Tuckett, had been known to throw a lot of lead in their younger days. And even on his trips home from Korea and Nam and from whatever post at which he was stationed, he would always come here and go through at least a box of ought-six shells. This was his therapy: the punch of a steel butt plate against the heavy muscle of his shoulder, the long, hollow, deep-voiced *crack* of the exploding powder, the echo that sliced up and down the canyon and made him feel so alive.

Nobody knew the exact distances to the several points along the opposite slope that he and his friends had marked. Certain rocks, certain trees. They had guesses, and they knew from ballistics studies and from later military training that those guesses were fairly accurate. But they could have been fifty, sometimes maybe even a hundred feet off.

All Coal knew was that the farthest point, a spire of upright rock nearly the shape and size of a fat man, was pushing one thousand yards, if not more. And Coal could never hit that rock consistently. In all his years of trying, he had only sent a lucky round into it perhaps three times out of seven—what the military called "confirmed kills."

In fact, there was only one of his friends who could with any degree of certainty hit that rock some nine times out of ten, and that one friend was a phenomenon. Hague Freeman. Old Hague. Crazy as a coot sometimes, often more trouble than any hunting buddy was worth, especially when he started into the booze, but man, that boy could shoot!

Coal sat in the car and stared across the canyon as the memories flooded back. He remembered one day up here, now some twenty years ago, when he had been back on leave for an entire month, and Hague Freeman happened to come home for the last week of that time. All the old high school buddies had decided to get together for a reunion, of sorts. They didn't see each other all that often anymore, now that Coal and Hague had joined the Marines, and the others were living their own lives.

That day, the day of their impromptu get-together, was a day that would live forever in the memories of those who had been there. Out of a box of twenty cartridges fired through his .30/06 from across the canyon, Hague had hit that man-sized rock twenty times. Twenty confirmed kills, seen through K.T.'s spotting scope. Unheard of. Coal had been lucky to hit it eleven—also the most times he had ever scored on that rock.

Hague Freeman. Quite a Marine....

The good times surrounding Hague could never be recalled without the bad ones being somewhere close by as well. There had been some bad blood between Hague and the others for a while. Over a girl, of course—Jennifer Connelly. Coal chuckled. It wasn't funny whatsoever at the time, but he remembered it now with a smile. Hague had wooed Jennifer and asked her to the junior prom, which she accepted. But then he had started following her everywhere, staring at her, and becoming nothing short of possessive of her—even obsessive. Finally, Jennifer blew up and told Hague to leave her alone. In the ensuing argument, she had also told him she was not going to the dance with him.

Hague got pretty rough with Jennifer over the deal, and of course old Mister "Prince of Pushups" himself, K.T. Batterton, had decided to step in and play the hero. He took a bad punch for it, and a kick to the head as he lay on the ground. Unfortunately, that was the kind of thing that always happened when Hague Freeman took to drinking.

When the fight, such as it was, got to be too much, Larry and Trent had stepped in, and finally, to try and calm the situation, Coal had grabbed Hague by the collar and jerked him out of the mix-up. That was the turning point for the two hunting buddies. Hague had turned on Coal with a vehemence none of them had ever seen before. In later days, it would be spoken of often, not only among the friends, but among most of the school. There was always that one fight that everyone seemed to remember, that one epic battle that people would talk about thirty years afterward, and beyond. That battle was the one between Coal Savage and Hague Freeman.

Hague fought like an enraged bull. But Coal, naturally bigger and made more so by the religious use of barbells and dumbbells and by throwing steers to the ground, as well as being far more dedicated in the boxing ring than Hague, who was his boxing teammate, had the upper hand. It wasn't due only to his greater strength and skill, but also to the fact that Coal had the ability to stay calm and calculated. Hague, on the other hand, was a freight train on the loose.

And, in the end, Coal had derailed him.

Coal chuckled again. Damn, that boy had been a wildcat. But joining the Marines right out of high school seemed to have been good for him. Seemed to have actually tamed him down some, so thereafter, when they would come home on leave and happen to meet, they would be able to laugh and joke and even go shooting together—the one place that Hague excelled over Coal, hands down. The fact was, at shooting long-range targets, Hague excelled over everyone in Lemhi County—and possibly half the state of Idaho. Coal sure wished his old hunting buddy was here now. Hague was a Marine sniper, must have killed eighty men, at least ones who were confirmed, and he had a strong sense of justice much like Coal's. Hague would have had no qualms about taking Bigfoot Monahan to the ground. More than any other time, Coal missed Hague Freeman now.

But Hague had gone down in sixty-nine, killed in what was known as Operation Oklahoma Hills. It was a simple clear and search operation mounted in the Quang Nam Province, southwest of Da Nang, by the First, Second and Third Battalions of the Seventh Marines, the Third Battalion of the Twenty-Sixth Marines, and part of the South Vietnamese Army. Hague was the foremost sniper in the Third Battalion of the Seventh, and one of the most decorated snipers in the early history of the war. And, sadly, one of the last to die out of only forty-four Marines who lost their lives during the operation.

He had died, ironically, in a place called Happy Valley.

Coal thought with a sigh of the day they learned of Hague's death. For all the trouble that boy had been back in high school, whenever he stayed sober he had been a fun rodeo and boxing teammate, and one of the greatest shots alive to have along on a hunting trip. Coal always joked about Hague's red trigger finger. He always managed to get his game.

The town of Salmon had mourned the loss of one of their heroes for weeks.

Coal finally got out of the car and pulled a sandbag from the trunk, setting it on the roof. He set his two boxes of shells on the hood, then lay the cased rifle beside them, now and then looking across the canyon at that glowering white rock. He had thought about trying a few shots at some of the closer targets, just to warm up. But something drew him to that white rock. He was going after it first.

Unzipping his rifle case, Coal drew from it a pre-1964 Winchester Model 70, the greatest firearm he had ever wielded, in his opinion. Seated atop it was a Redfield 3 X 9 power telescope, much the same as the one they were starting to use in Nam, and something he had played hell getting his hands on, here in the States. Most of those scopes were going straight to Vietnam as fast as they came out of the factory. He fed five cartridges into the magazine and leaned across the sandbag.

All right, rock. Let's see what you're made of today. Taking a deep breath, he jacked a cartridge into the chamber. Tipping the rifle sideways, he gazed over the side of it at the rock. Took another lung-filling breath. The air was icy cold up this high. It couldn't have been up to zero yet. He found he was shivering. But there seemed to be almost no wind.

Reaching down, he picked up a pinch of dust off the road and threw it into the air. It drifted slightly down-canyon. Coal leaned down into the butt of the rifle and adjusted his sight picture for the wind. One thousand yards. A man. A *big* man. If he could not hit this man, then he could hit no man, not even Bigfoot.

He took a few deep breaths and held them before letting them seep out. He tried to calm his shivering. He adjusted his scope with several clicks. One shot. That's all he had. At least that was what he told himself. One shot, and then he was through. Dead. One shot, and he had to run, win or lose.

Another deep breath. Hold it, slowly let part of it out. Hold again. The trigger was already most of the way down. He had fired this rifle so many times he knew almost exactly, within the half pound, when it would break over.

And then the rifle butt pounded his shoulder, and the barrel lunged upward. That familiar crack and echo reverberated up and down the canyon as with practiced skill he settled the rifle back against his shoulder and stared hard at the rock—his man.

No hit. Get up now. Load the car. Drive fast. Hide.

Coal took a deep breath. It was so cold it almost burned his nostrils. A raven, startled by the shot, had started calling down in the bottom of the canyon.

He removed the empty casing and put it in his pocket, then slid the new one home. Same thing. Rest, breathe, hold, squeeze. *Crack!* Echo. Scared angry birds. He even saw the flash of a deer as it bounded up through the timber in the bottom of the canyon. He smiled, but his smile was grim. He had missed again.

On the third shot, he scored. But it was not going to be good enough. He was going to have to get closer to Bigfoot Monahan's house before he set up his bipod.

There was a white stone, perhaps the size of a man's head, about six hundred yards across the canyon, and consequently much lower down. Coal zeroed in on it and readjusted his scope. Went through all he knew about long range shooting. Squeezed. This time he heard the solid *whack* of the bullet striking home. Coal nodded. Six hundred yards. Still a good shot. Not Olympic medal-winning, but way above average. So he had to get a little closer to Bigfoot. Either way, the murderer was going to die.

Driving down the mountain, Coal's mind turned strangely to Laura. He had kept her memory at bay for quite a while now. It was easy with everything else that was going on. But now here she was, bigger than life. She was looking at him through those soulful eyes, looking *through* him. Accusing him.

"Damn you, Laura," Coal said aloud. Why was she plaguing him? She was the one who made things go wrong. It was her! Not him. He had a job to do in Washington, and he was doing it. What had she expected of him? So he couldn't be home with her all the time, every night. Why had she not been able to understand? And why the drugs? Drugs, of all the things she could have gotten caught up in!

He saw her blue-gray face, her open, glassy eyes. He heard his children screaming for her. Screaming *at* him. He couldn't tell them it wasn't his fault. He couldn't take that last shelter away and unveil to those children what their mother really was. So he let them believe it was him. All him.

Why, Laura? Why? Why did she have to have that job? There were things to do at home too. And... why *him?* What was there in Robert Laine that was so much better than Coal? And why, last of all, did Erin happen? Erin! She was so kind. So understanding. Always there. Always happy. She had a smile for him every time they met. She was lovely, so prim and proper, her black-framed glasses set just right on the bridge of her nose. He had admired her from the first moment he laid eyes on her. He had always seen something in her that was missing in Laura.

But in the end, Erin was only Coal's revenge, plain and simple. Revenge against Laura and Robert Laine, the principal of Warrenton High School. Perhaps not a conscious kind of revenge, but anyone who understood human relations at all would see that she had only been Coal's way to strike out in anger against his wife's unfaithfulness. And even that revenge was not complete—the rumors behind that scandal were overblown, and Coal was too stubborn even to try and prove it to Laura. If he had tried to prove the rumors were far worse than the reality, perhaps Laura would still be alive today.

But after the loss of her job as a substitute teacher, and then what happened with Erin, Laura's downward spiral had gone into high gear. The drugs, the alcohol, the parties. The kids stayed at home. Sometimes, Katie was the babysitter—if she wasn't going to a party of her own. If she did, young Virgil took care of his little brothers alone.

And then one night, when Laura was gone to some party Coal knew not where, and Coal was tucking his little boys in, four-year-old Wyatt had looked up at him through wide, concerned eyes, and said, "Daddy, why does Virgil cry?"

CHAPTER SEVEN

Coal received the radio dispatch on his way down the mountain. Still eight miles left to town. He had just pushed thoughts of Laura out of his head and was thinking about sitting to the table with his whole family, eating Thanksgiving Dinner and hopefully getting a chance to catch up with them. It had been so long since he had really talked to any of them but his mother. But it was not to be...

The radio dispatch came, and his heart seemed to stop beating. His chest constricted to the point that he almost could not breathe. He could barely see the road. He pulled over to the edge, with no worry, considering the freezing weather, that his tires would sink too deep to get back out once he had gotten control of himself.

He couldn't remember all of the dispatch, or his exchange with Nadene. He remembered this alone, with clarity: *Young woman called... Hysterical... hard to understand... Her mother not breathing, cold... possible homicide.* Those were the words his brain picked out. Those were the horrible phrases that stuck in his brain.

His mind was whirling. The mountain spun as well. His hands were shaking on the wheel, and his teeth chattered, although the heater in the LTD was running full blast. With a gasp, he threw open the door and jumped out into the cold. His eyes flashed around him. The trees were blurry. His car too. His hands continued to shake. He closed the right one over the butt of his Smith and Wesson.

He knuckled his left eye. Forced himself to take a calming breath. Then another. He was losing it this time. This was like a dream. A horrible, impossible dream. He would wake up soon, and he would be back in Virginia, and Laura would be still alive. Katie Leigh would not hate him. He would never have gone to that party in Warrenton. He would never have lost his job.

And Larry, Trent, K.T., and *she* would still be alive.

Coal actually wished for tears. They hung in his eyes. They would not come. He was numb. He wiped down his mustache with the webbing of his hand and spat unconsciously on the road. Took another deep breath. A sudden movement caught his eye, and he looked over to see a spruce grouse, an innocent, dumb bird, walk up over the bank from the needle- and leaf-littered forest that sloped away from the road. It looked at him as if he and his car did not exist. The LTD's motor was running, and heavy white steam and smoke rose from its twin tailpipes.

Blinking hard against his blurry eyes, Coal drew the .357 magnum, and with one hand he held it and shattered the life of the fool's hen. It flopped over in the dirt, its chest obliterated. Teeth gritted, he kept firing. Two. Three. Four. Five. Six. His revolver was empty. His ears rang as if someone were blowing a whistle in them. The bird was a flutter of feathers and nearly unrecognizable body parts, strewn for several feet around a rough place in the road where it appeared as if a miniature explosion had just occurred. A few of the lighter feathers fluttered down on the breeze, then curled along the road with the wind, in the direction he had to go.

She was gone. He knew in his heart she was gone. He would never speak to her again. Never hold her in his arms. Never hear her sound advice. Never smell the warm aromas of supper cooking on her stove, or the scent of her wonderful coffee. He could have saved her. Instead, he had killed her. It was happening again. All over again.

Coal turned and almost punched his window. Instead, he hammered his fist down on the roof. Even in his wild rage and sickness, he knew he could not destroy his knuckles. He could not disable his hand. He had failed in saving at least one life. There were two more that would go down, and soon, if he did not make this stop.

Another deep breath. A rub of the eyes. Coal was a Marine. A damn good Marine. *Semper fidelis. "Semper fi!"* Coal heard his own terrible voice ringing down the mountain.

Semper fidelis. Always faithful. Faithful to his country, his men, his calling. His calling now was sheriff of Lemhi County. And he was letting his people here die—left and right. For what? To be law-abiding? To do the "right thing"? Damn the right thing. If ever he had questioned what he was about to do, he did not question it now.

Bigfoot Monahan had sealed his fate.

With a new, all-encompassing chill over his entire body, but this time from something other than the cold of the mountain, Coal reloaded his pistol and climbed into the front seat. He pulled back onto the solid dirt and gravel of the road and drove down the mountain toward the scene of the latest crime.

* * *

There was a blue light flashing in front of the house. Coal pulled up one residence down, in front of the Catholic church, seeing first that his idiotic deputy had chosen to park smack-dab in the middle of any evidence that might be here. He got out and adjusted the .357 on his hip. With grim determination, he started down the street, watching all around him as he walked. He was looking specifically for danger, first. Second, for any strange bystander. Third, for unfamiliar vehicles.

And there was the address, marked in bold numbers: 520. He walked on Hope Street, and yet now, more than ever, there seemed to be no hope.

Coal's mind was made up. This was the doing of none other than Paul Monahan—Bigfoot. But even with that knowledge in his head, he could not cease being an investigator, so he could not cease to scour the scene of the crime.

Farther down the street, beyond Mitchell's truck with the flashing blue light on the dash, Coal picked out Jim Lockwood's idling black Thunderbird. His heart lightened, but only slightly. If Jim was here, maybe Coal could handle what he had to face.

But where was the girl? Where was Cynthia?

A cluster of people stood in the yard, stampeding over any evidence. Coal wanted to explode, but he didn't. Damn the evidence. In the grand scope of things it didn't even matter if they had any.

There stood the baby-faced coroner, Kerry Updyke. And Ronnie Davis, with the ambulance whose driver had at least had the sense to park across the street. Coal's friend, Jay Castillo, was in the yard next to Davis, but there was no Maura PlentyWounds. Farther down on the left, just this side of McPherson Street, were parked two baby blue police cars, Chief Dan George's and Bob Wilson's. The chief's flashing light was on. Bob's was extinguished.

Standing in the yard with everyone else, Bob Wilson looked over and saw Coal coming, and he nudged Chief George, who turned his eyes. George said something to the others standing there, then walked briskly side by side with Bob to where Coal came to a stop at the curb, staring at the house.

"You know the Battertons?" the chief asked without greeting.

Coal's eyes jumped to Bob, who gave him a helpless expression, as if to say he had already confirmed that.

"Yeah." Coal couldn't look at the chief. He didn't want anyone to see what was burning in his eyes.

He realized a shape coming toward them up the short sidewalk to the house was Todd Mitchell. His deputy came and stood in front of him and the others. Coal couldn't look directly at him. He couldn't get it out of his head how Mitchell had told Bigfoot's boss that Jennifer Batterton might be able to identify his station wagon.

"I'm sorry, then," said Chief George. "Really sorry."

Coal bunched his jaws. Speaking was out of the question.

"The body's inside, right where it was found."

"Cynthia found her when she woke up," Bob cut in.

Coal's eyes flashed to Bob. The officer gave him a one-shouldered shrug. His face looked helpless and drawn.

"Where's the girl?" asked Coal.

"With Jim Lockwood," was Bob's reply.

Coal turned and looked down the street. The Thunderbird was a ways away, but he could see movement inside. Dark shapes.

"How is she?"

A moment of silence.

"How's the girl?" repeated Coal, looking at Bob.

"Sorry, Coal, I'm just not sure how to answer you. She woke up thinking about how she was going to face Thanksgiving dinner with her dad gone and found her mom murdered. I mean, how *can* she be?"

Coal held up a hand to stop anything else Bob or either of the others might have had on the tips of their tongues. It had been a stupid question.

"Somebody call Maura PlentyWounds for me. See if she'll come to the scene."

Even as he spoke, headlights turned onto the street from far down the way, possibly off of Daisy Street, and came on slowly, and a big, light-colored truck finally pulled up at the curb down the block, facing oncoming traffic. The truck was opposite Jim Lockwood's car. Coal gritted his teeth harder as he saw Maura descend from the truck. She was two hundred feet away, but it was close enough to see her stop at the front of her truck, look at Jim's car, and then almost run to it.

From the passenger side of Jim's car, a shape flew, obviously Cynthia, and the two shapes collided at the front of the Thunderbird and became one. Tears dimmed Coal's eyes, and he cursed himself for it. He was turning into some old woman, not a Marine.

Semper fi, he thought. *Semper fi. Buck up!* he ordered himself.

Todd Mitchell had on dark brown, soft leather gloves. Coal noticed that as his deputy spoke his name and raised one hand, palm up. Something crumpled and for a moment unidentifiable lay there like a crushed flower.

"I found this on the porch."

His deputy picked the object up with the gloved fingers of his other hand. "It's half a package of orange Carefree gum."

The two city policemen gave Mitchell strange looks, then turned their attention on Coal, awaiting the revelation of this object's importance.

"Just lying on the porch?" Coal managed to say, finding his chest constricted once more.

Mitchell nodded. "I thought you'd want to know."

"Yeah, sure I do. Put it in your shirt pocket and button it up."

"What's that about?" asked Chief George.

"You never know what stuff lying about might mean," said Coal. He was trying to be nonchalant.

"This is Paul Monahan's gum of choice, Chief," said Mitchell.

Coal bit his lip and stared past Mitchell at the front of the house. He hadn't wanted to even look at Mitchell before. Now he wanted nothing more than to knock out his front teeth.

"Monahan?" repeated the chief. "The guy they call Bigfoot?"

Trying to stay calm, Coal looked at Chief George. His plan was sunk. Sunk at least unless he wanted to be the first suspect when Monahan ended up dead in the morning. It was one thing putting *himself* at risk of being looked at. But Todd Mitchell, his jackass of a deputy, had just cinched it that he would be the first one they would suspect if Bigfoot turned up dead. Why? Because he had made it so plain that Coal already suspected Monahan, and the word was probably already making its rounds that they had been unable to find anything for which to take him into custody.

Damn Mitchell. The first chance he had, he had to look for a replacement for this imbecile.

Coal had to go in the house. He didn't want to. He wanted anything but. Yet he had no choice. He had to know.

"Anyone still inside?"

"Uh... Just the woman," replied Chief George. "Not pretty, Sheriff."

"This job never is."

He pushed past Mitchell, trying to keep his cool. He strode up the sidewalk. The yard was well-kept, and mostly grass. Even without all the idiots walking everywhere, there would have been little in the way of tracks to be used as evidence.

Everyone watched Coal as he passed them, having to go around on the grass because they were congregated on the sidewalk. Coal felt the hard eyes of Ronnie Davis piercing the side of his head.

"She's pretty much dead," said Davis. "No need to go in there. The cops already looked around."

Coal paused in his step. But he couldn't turn and face the EMT. Right then, he hated him, and he didn't need that to show. What would make a man say something like that? Maybe Davis didn't know he was a friend of Jennifer's. He hoped that was true.

With another deep breath, Coal went on. He plodded up the steps, taking his gloves from behind his belt and slipping them on as he reached the door. He eased open the screen. The inner door was already standing open. He poked his head inside and immediately saw bare feet, beyond the far end of the sofa. They were tilted to the sides.

Coal walked. He didn't think. He pretended it was someone he didn't know. And it wasn't hard. When he saw her face, he didn't know her, at least not this way. She had been wearing a silk night shirt, but it was torn open, and she was bare. He tried only to look at her face. Her throat was encircled with a piece of wire, and her face gone ghastly purple.

Coal turned away. His knees felt weak, but he couldn't sit, not in here. His eyes scanned the room. He hated Ronnie Davis, but maybe the EMT had been right. He had no reason to be here. Perhaps he had had to see her for himself to be able to admit that she was dead. But now he had seen her. Now he had to go. He prayed that the police chief and Bob would do a thorough investigation, because now it might actually mean something. Coal could go arrest Bigfoot, and he intended to. Even if it was only because of his favorite kind of chewing gum being left at the scene. If only for once, that would have to be enough. He was not going to allow himself to be killed, or Jim, to satisfy some judge's desire for solid evidence.

Coal couldn't sense his feet as he walked from the house and down the steps, then past the cluster of people. He heard Davis say, "I hope he's satisfied," and he kept walking, holding in his urge to knock one of Davis's ears through the one on the opposite side.

He got to the front sidewalk, having managed to hold back the urge to throw up. He turned and walked down the street toward

Jim's car. He didn't want to see anyone, least of all Cynthia Batterton. She was now an orphan, the only owner of everything her parents had had to their names just one morning earlier.

How was that girl going to survive this two days? No normal person could come through this and still be a normal, functioning human being on the other side.

*　　*　　*

When Coal went in to the office that morning, Jim Lockwood came with him. Maura took another day off of ambulance call duty and took Cynthia home with her. And Todd Mitchell simply left the crime scene. Coal didn't watch him go, nor did he care where he went. Probably home to have Thanksgiving dinner with his wife and children.

Coal was sitting at his desk in the office thinking about a ruined Thanksgiving and drinking some of Jordan Peterson's much-improved coffee half an hour later when the phone rang. Jim sat in front of the desk with a cup he had brought from home.

"Jim, would you do me a favor and get that? I really don't feel like talking to any reporters right now."

Jim gave his younger friend a measuring look. Without speaking, he reached across the desk and pulled the black phone off the receiver. "Hello, sheriff's office. Umm... Can I take a message? Who is this?" Jim cocked an eye at Coal, a strange look on his face. "Okay, just a minute. I'll see if he can take your call." Coal looked a question at his old friend. Jim shrugged. "He won't say who he is. His voice is really muffled."

Cautiously, Coal reached across the desk and took the receiver from Jim. "Yes? Sheriff Savage speaking."

You don't know me, Mr. Savage. Sheriff, I guess I should say. But I have some information you need to know. I can't tell you my name. I can't meet you. No one must know we talked. As Jim had said, the voice was muffled, and even beyond that it seemed unreal, like someone was making their voice deeper so it would be unrecognizable.

"All right," replied Coal. "I guess that's working out pretty well for you so far."

The man gave a chuckle. In spite of the strange circumstances, Coal noticed that his voice didn't seem particularly nervous.

I have a friend—I guess I should say a friendly acquaintance. I can't even say how I know him. I can only say that I have hunted with him. His name is Paul Monahan.

Bigfoot...

"I know him," Coal affirmed.

Yeah, I thought you would. Well, you know he is a convicted felon. And convicted felons can't own firearms, right?

"Sure. Right."

Well, I know for a fact that he owns one. We went coyote hunting together just last week. Maybe ten days ago. I had mentioned I was going, and he said he wanted to come along. I thought since he had been in the pen and couldn't own a gun he just wanted to go with me for the fun of being there. I didn't have any idea he intended to hunt.

A chill had come over Coal. He wanted to tell the voice on the other end to take the towel off his mouth so he could understand his words better. But he didn't dare anger him and take the chance that he would hang up. "Go on."

Well, when I went to pick him up, he came out with a rifle in a case. I didn't like the idea of it, but he's a big man, Sheriff. I sure didn't want to make him mad. So I didn't say anything. But when we got out in the hills, he started taking beers out of a cooler and drinking pretty heavy. He was talking kind of scary. Saying something about how he had to 'take care of' a couple of people, although he never said exactly what he meant by that. I was starting to worry that he might shoot me—just for fun. I don't ever want anyone to have to go through that again, like what I felt that day.

I'm no stool pigeon, but if this can save someone's life, I thought I'd let you know about it. It seemed like the thing for a good citizen to do.

"Do you know where he keeps his gun?"

No, not exactly. But when I dropped him off that afternoon I saw him carry it around behind a run-down garage he has back of his house. That's all. It was wrapped in a tarp.

Coal sat there for a moment, thinking back. "Wait, I thought you said it was in a case."

The voice on the other end paused. *Oh. Yeah. Well, that's what I meant.*

"A case? Or a tarp?"

A tarp.

Coal strained to try and catch any hint of familiarity in the voice. "So do I know you?"

The voice paused, this time way too long. Finally: *Listen, do you want me to talk, or don't you?*

Coal sighed with relief to know the informant hadn't hung up. "All right. Let me ask you this: Did you see him shoot anything while you were out?"

Anything? the voice echoed. *Try* everything. *Rabbits, grouse, a coyote. Even a sandhill crane.*

That last one made Coal angry. That was an elegant bird no one had any reason to kill. "How did his accuracy seem to you? Speaking as a hunter."

Another long pause. Then: *Wow. Good question. I have to say I've never seen anything like it. Not in these parts. He dropped that coyote on the run at over two hundred yards with his first shot—through the head. One of the rabbits was more like three hundred, and he was shooting offhand—no rest. He shot that one in the head, too.*

In the head? That struck Coal as odd. Why would someone even *attempt* head shots at that distance? And on anything moving, no less. But that wasn't the most important thing. He took a deep breath. He had that heart-pounding feeling again. "You don't happen to know what caliber of gun he had, do you?"

Why, sure I do. It was a .30-06.

CHAPTER EIGHT

Against the receiver, Coal's pulse mimicked the sound of a strange, steady, distant whip.

Thirty ought-six. It was a common round. In the wide open West, where shooting distances tended to be long, possibly the *most* common. But this anonymous caller's testimony of Paul Monahan's shooting skill, and the proven shooting skill of the sniper who had killed both Larry MacAtee and K.T. Batterton, that was beyond *uncommon.* It simply could not be coincidence.

"I have to ask you an extremely important question," said Coal, trying to keep his voice from shaking because of the adrenaline that flowed in him.

Yeah?

"If we get Bigfoot safely behind bars, then will you come out of hiding and testify? You sound like you're worried about retaliation. But if we can get your testimony in court I think I can put him away for the rest of his life. In fact, it's likely he'll end up with a death sentence."

A long, long pause. *Maybe. We'll have to see when that time comes.*

The voice didn't sound certain at all. In fact, it sounded like the man was just telling him what he wanted to hear.

"How do you know Bigfoot?" he suddenly asked.

Another long pause. *I told you before, I can't tell you that. Too incriminating.*

"Did you know him before prison?"

Uhh... Yeah.

The pause made it seem like the man was trying to decide if the answer would hurt him. Perhaps his usefulness was worn out.

"You know where to find me when you need me again," Coal stated. "When Monahan's in jail, it will be on the news. If you want to keep him there, and save some lives, please think about coming out and talking to me in the open. It's pretty likely when we get that rifle he's going to know who told us where to look anyway. That's something you need to think about."

Another pregnant pause, and then: *Yeah.* And the line went dead.

* * *

Thanksgiving dinner at the Savage residence was somber. There was no happy conversation, no "catching up." Instead, it was the quiet *tink* now and then of silverware against a china plate, or a quiet request for more of some dish or other. The cold from outside, now probably up in the mid-twenties, tried to force its way into the house through every crack. The Franklin stove battled back, kept full by Coal and Virgil.

Katie sat in silence, and now and then her sniffles showed that she was thinking of Cynthia, now an orphan. The girl's tears brought sympathetic ones from Connie, and the males of the house just ate in silence and pretended not to notice. Coal stared out the window at the bright day. The sun shone on the field across the road, finally melting the frost off the barbed wire fence. An occasional vehicle drove past, headed farther up toward the mountains and the junction of Savage Lane with Lemhi Road.

In the background, the television was running, and Coal happened to notice when the new show began to air. One side of his mouth lifted in a wry smile. It was an animated feature by Hanna-Barbera: *The Thanksgiving that Almost Wasn't.* It would have been easy enough to make the title fit this day, Coal thought: *The Thanksgiving that Wasn't.*

* * *

Around four o'clock that afternoon, Coal sat in his office, and the only sound beyond the infrequent vehicle passing by outside or the barking of a dog was the tick of his clock and the occasional sizzling pop as a drop of condensation hit the coffee maker's hot plate.

It had been no surprise to Connie when Coal had told her upon first going home for dinner that he was going to go search Paul Monahan's property again and that he would have to leave to meet the parole officer in town. In fact, she didn't even fight him. With Jen's tragic death on everyone's mind, mostly there was nothing but silence.

There was little for Coal to do now but wait for Kevin Wilhelm, who the moment he had heard the news of Coal's mysterious phone call and the murder of Jennifer Batterton had cancelled all of his Thanksgiving plans and told Coal he would try to be in Salmon around four or five. Wilhelm had spoken quietly into the receiver toward the end of their short exchange, telling Coal he was actually glad for the Thanksgiving interruption, because, as an "outlaw at the in-laws' house", *any* chance to leave was a welcome one.

Coal sat and tried to read the November 20th issue of *Time* magazine, with Richard M. Nixon on the cover sporting a big grin and his fingers making the sign of Vee for victory, the word LAND-SLIDE in huge white letters vomiting up as if out the top of his head. But *Time* was depressing as usual. Stories about Nam, stories about the failure of the British economy, stories wondering what Nixon was going to do for the next four years now that he had been elected and the Republicans had the nuts—and the bolts—of the

White House. Of course, it hadn't printed that last part. That was Coal's special addition inside his head as he thought about the Nation's current state of affairs after the last election.

A fitting sign of the modern times was noticing that a little book called *I'm Okay, You're Okay* had made the *New York Times* best sellers list. Coal had leafed through that book not long after its release a few years back, and it was funny to see it just now hitting the best sellers list. It seemed like a crock to him—some lame-brain psychologist spewing the theory to his readers that no matter their issues, they were still viable human beings. Well, Coal could vouch that this wasn't true. He knew so many people who were worth no more than worm fodder it made him sick to his stomach. The book was just another in the new rush of mollycoddling ideas that were being jammed, and would continue to be jammed, down the throat of America—and the world.

The sad fact was, many people were simply not "okay." Of course, being in law enforcement and in the military all of those years might have colored his opinion on the subject—just a little.

A knock came on the door, and it made him jerk. He wasn't used to anyone visiting, and if they did they normally just walked on in. Before he could bid them enter, the door creaked open, and in a moment the face of a man, then his body, appeared. It took a moment for Coal's brain to switch gears. When they did, and he recognized the face, he leaped up out of his chair and dropped the magazine.

It was Howie Jensen, his furloughed prisoner! And as a huge smile of relief broke over the man's face and he came farther inside, Coal saw that he was dragging some company with him by his right hand—a little girl perhaps nine years old.

"Howie! I'm glad to see you. Say, who is that you have with you?"

"Hi, Sheriff. Sorry to bother you. I went to surprise you at your house, and your mother said you would be here."

"Well, no need to apologize, my friend. I'm glad you came."

"Good. Thank you. Sheriff, this is Trina—my daughter."

"Your... daughter? The one you went to Salt Lake to see?"

"Yes sir, sure is." Jensen's face seemed to glow. "Sheriff, she's all better."

"I hope it didn't cost you too much," said Coal with a hint of worry in his eyes.

"You'll never believe what it was! They found half of a sunflower shell lodged in her windpipe. That's all! Sheriff, I swear to you, it only cost me thirty dollars to pay off the hospital. Can you believe that?"

Coal shook his head, a big, happy grin on his face. "Well, I'll be." He crouched low, to be closer to Trina's level. "You look pretty healthy, young lady. I sure am glad to see you all better."

The girl gave him a shy smile. "Thanks."

"Did you eat Thanksgiving dinner?"

"Yeah. Lots of turkey and potatoes."

Coal laughed. "That's good. The best part!"

"Trina," said Jensen, "this is the man I told you about—the sheriff who loaned your daddy money so I could come to Salt Lake and see you in the hospital. He also got me my job at the mill."

The girl's smile grew, and she looked from her father to Coal's face. It was obvious that she didn't know quite how to word whatever was on her little girl mind, but by looking at the way her mouth was set, it was *something* big. Instead of speaking, she expressed it with her actions. To Coal's surprise, the girl walked to him and put out her arms, and he met her halfway, giving her a tight, quick squeeze which she gave back in kind.

"Well, shoot, I don't know if I deserved all that, Trina!" he said when she stepped back.

"You helped my daddy. My mama was so happy when we saw him that she cried for five minutes."

Coal looked up to see the tears swimming in Jensen's eyes, and a warm feeling came over him. This sheriff's job wasn't that bad after all. In fact, being a human, and helping out folks who were in need, wasn't that bad of a job. He put out his big hand and met the rough one of Jensen, who couldn't hide the wetness in his eyes.

"Thank you, Sheriff. I promise you, someday I'm going to do something for you."

Coal held onto his hand for a moment. "You just keep your word, my friend—keep off the booze, work hard, and some day pay Blake Shear for his tooth, and his horse. And after that you can think about paying me."

"I already got an advance on my wages at the mill," said Jensen with pride. "My boss likes me, I think."

"He sure does. I asked him about you," admitted Coal.

"Well, thank you. He said good things?"

"Nothing but good, Howie. He's very pleased."

The moisture came into Jensen's eyes again. This time he wiped at it and apologized, and Coal just smiled understandingly.

"So I done made a twenty dollar payment to Blake Shear on his tooth."

Coal beamed, and he met Jensen's gaze square-on. "That's how I knew you'd be. Thanks for giving me some faith in human beings again."

Jensen gave a quick shake of his head. "No. No, don't even think of thankin' me. You're the one that did this for me. All of it. I ain't had a drink since I came in here, I'm saving up some money, and I ain't never seen my wife more happy, at least in fifteen years. That's all because of you. I hope I can call you my friend."

"You sure can. You sure as heck can."

He reached and shook Jensen's hand again and then squeezed Trina's shoulder. "All right, honey, you keep your daddy safe now, okay? And keep away from those sunflower seeds." He knuckled her arm.

The girl giggled. "I will. No more sunflower seeds for me—ever!"

* * *

When the Jensens had gone, Coal went and checked on the prisoners, told them he would be out for a while, then put on his jacket and his holstered revolver and went for a drive. A brilliant sun was spilling golden light across the valley, and the sky was bold blue behind the skim of cumulus clouds that billowed around the horizon. But for the bite in the air, it was an ideal day.

Making sure his radio was on full blast, so he could hear Bread crooning out the words to "Everything I Own," he drove out toward Gibbonsville, admiring the big old wooden barns and the grazing horses, cattle and sheep. There was even a deer or two still out, moving along the edges of the trees. "I can do this," he said out loud. "Paul Monahan, this is your last day of freedom. You'd better enjoy it. I'm bringing peace to this county." It felt good to hear the words, for his ears alone. For a moment, his own words even blocked out those of Bread's lead singer, David Gates, on the radio.

Later, he picked up Jim Lockwood and, grudgingly, Todd Mitchell. He still wasn't in the mood to see his deputy, but Kevin Wilhelm had called from the mill in Leadore to say Monahan had just left work and was headed home, and they planned to meet at the Monahan residence.

Coal sure wished old K.T. was going with them.

On a whim, Jim told Coal to pick up big Jordan Peterson, and he directed him to his residence, up on the Bar. They had to pound on the door a few times to rouse him, and he came to the door shirtless and in 501 jeans. His broad shoulders and thick neck reminded Coal of himself at that age.

"How'd you like to go on a weapons search, Jordan?" asked Coal without any greeting.

"A what? Are you serious?"

“I’m dead serious. We’re going out to Bigfoot Monahan’s place, on a lead.”

“Let me grab my shirt,” said Jordan. “Do I need a gun?”

“That’s covered. You’ll take my shotgun.”

Peterson was excited to be included in the search—his first taste of real deputy work. Wearing a beat-up straw hat and a red flannel shirt, he sat in the back seat with Mitchell and fired questions up at Coal. Coal coached him on exactly what would ideally take place at the Monahan residence and how they would conduct themselves, and their search. By the time they arrived in front of the house, seeing Wilhelm’s car parked well down the road, Peterson seemed calm and steady. Maybe more so than Mitchell, who had never seemed all that steady in any tense situation.

They saw Wilhelm’s headlights flash—once, twice, three times, and then he rolled forward. They converged on the driveway at the same time and pulled in fast, descending and taking the same places they had gone to previously, except that Jordan Peterson went around back with Jim, to back him up and also to watch behind them, in case Bigfoot was already outside.

Wilhelm’s barked call at the door brought a flurry of yapping and an immediate, deep-voiced reply from inside. “It’s Thanksgiving! Who the hell is it?”

“The devil!” Wilhelm barked. “Officer Wilhelm. Get out here now, or we’re coming in.”

There was a long pause, then: “Relax. I’m comin’. Don’t break anything.”

The door creaked open, and there stood a massive form, Bigfoot’s six-foot-eight frame more than filling the doorway, with the incongruous body of the little Yorkshire terrier cradled in the crook of his arm. His pale blue eyes slowly scanned those he could see as Mitchell called to Jim and Jordan to come back to the front.

He pushed open the screen door with one gigantic bear paw, and his eyes went past Wilhelm and settled on Coal, whose .357

magnum was centered on the huge chest, and who wanted so badly to pull the trigger. “You came here once before to scare my woman, lawman. And now my boy’s home from school, so’s you can scare him too.” He stepped onto the porch. “I told you one day I’d be back here to kill you for what you done, takin’ me away from my family. I guess it might as well be today as any other. Get your damn gun off my dog.”

With a smirk at the Yorkie, Coal replied, “You call that a dog? Let’s go get your rifle, big talker, and maybe then you can try. But remember, it didn’t work out so well for you last time.”

Bigfoot’s pale blue eyes flattened out. “You came at me from the dark when I had no idea you were there.”

“All right, Monahan, just button it,” cut in Wilhelm. “We came here to search the premises for an illegal firearm. I don’t have time to listen to your petty gripes.”

The hateful eyes turned on the parole officer. “I’ve got a list of men I’d like to snap the spines of, boy. Keep it up and you’ll be on it.”

“Oh, I’m shakin’. Get out here, Monahan. Real slow. Where’s the wife and boy?”

“Inside. Wanna beat ’em up a little?”

“Why? Is that what you do?”

“Listen! I don’t ever lay no hand on my family.”

“Then let’s be done with stupid comments. Get both of ’em out here.”

A word from Bigfoot brought his wife and son outside onto the concrete porch, and with Bigfoot’s back turned Wilhelm searched them both while the others backed him up with weapons at the ready. As he finished with each, he sent them down to the yard. Then he patted down the big logger.

“You sure like puttin’ your hands on me,” said Bigfoot as he finally turned around.

"Actually, I'd just as soon not. Smells like you haven't had a shower in a few days. All right, get down the stairs. Any of you want a coat? We're going out back."

Bigfoot eyed him suspiciously, then let his glance tick across the others, resting a little longer on Peterson. Finally, he looked back at Wilhelm, ignoring the question about coats. "Why you back here? You done looked once. What's out back?"

"Maybe you should tell us," said Wilhelm. "Save some time."

"I got nothin' illegal on this place. You think I wanna leave my family to the wolves again?"

"Let's go see."

So Monahan walked down his steps, and they all trooped around back, including his wife and son. Wilhelm had them sit on the concrete stoop outside the back door, and Coal set Peterson over them with his shotgun. Then he looked at the Monahans for a moment while the others stood there with him.

"Ma'am. You and the boy may want to scoot a little ways away from Paul, all right?" Then, to Peterson: "Jordan, if he makes a threatening move, put two center mass. Understand?"

Peterson nodded. He was trying to act tough, but there was a look of scared anticipation in his eyes.

"Where you all goin'?" asked Monahan as the lawmen started behind the dilapidated garage.

"You tell us," said Wilhelm. "I'm going to get back to Pocatello really late tonight, and my Thanksgiving feast is probably already cold, so the sooner we find your rifle, the easier it will be."

"Ha!" The big man stared at Wilhelm. "If you're lookin' for a rifle on this place, it's gonna be a lot later than you think." He actually had a grin on his face now.

Wilhelm didn't reply. He simply followed Coal, Jim, and Mitchell around the back of the garage. The only obvious thing there, and a place Coal was embarrassed to admit no one had touched on their previous search, was a scattered bunch of faded, gray boards—old siding, it appeared. They looked at each other and then started throwing the wood aside. It was only a moment before they had revealed a pile of musty, blackened straw, about four feet by three.

Wilhelm's cold blue eyes gave Coal a look, and as his lips pursed under his mustache, he stepped closer and kicked the straw aside. The four of them looked at what was revealed beneath, and Todd Mitchell swore. "Hey, what in the world is that?" His voice sounded strange, and Coal looked at him. His deputy was hungrily eying what appeared to be the round top of an old chest freezer.

"Probably not full of food, boy," said Jim with a good-natured smirk.

Mitchell blushed. "Huh?"

"You're lickin' your lips like you're hungry. Oh, never mind," said Jim, looking over at Coal. "Well? The one place I think we didn't look when we were here, huh?"

Coal nodded as he and Wilhelm knelt and started pushing the moldy straw away and cleared off the freezer lid. In a moment, before they opened it, he yelled around the garage.

"Hey, Monahan!"

"Yeah!" came the call in reply.

"What's this here buried in the ground?"

"Huh?"

"Just come back here."

Coal followed that up with a yell to Jordan. "Hey, Deputy, bring all three of them back here, would you?"

Soon, the four of them appeared around the corner of the garage. A smirk was smeared across Bigfoot's face. "Oh, what? You mean you never saw that when you were here before?" He belted out a laugh. "Some great searchers you are."

"What is it?" asked Coal.

"Potatoes and carrots. And a few beets and turnips. Gotta feed the family, you know."

"Nothing else?"

"No."

"Why was it all covered up with boards?"

Bigfoot eyed the gray boards, which were strewn over the ground to the side. "Huh? There was no boards on it. Just straw."

"Uh-huh. Looks like a good way to cover up some place you wanted kept a good secret."

"Sure. Well, those boards was stacked against the garage. They musta fell over in the wind or something."

Mitchell laughed. "Wow! Strong wind down in your part of the valley, Bigfoot."

The big man's eyes narrowed, and he stared Mitchell down until the much smaller man looked away. "Listen, you—"

"Hey!" Wilhelm barked. "That's enough. So there's nothing in the freezer but vegetables, right?"

"Of course not. I told you I ain't stupid enough to have a gun around." The big man's eyes flickered nervously around at the others, then back at the freezer lid. "Just leave it alone. I don't need no bugs fallin' down in there."

"You afraid what I'll find in there?" asked Wilhelm.

Bigfoot glared coffin nails through the parole officer. "Go to hell. Get on with your dirty work and leave my family alone." Bigfoot ran his tongue over his lips, his eyes flitting once more to the lid and away.

Coal shrugged when Wilhelm looked at him. "All right then," Wilhelm said. "Sheriff, go ahead. Just—don't let any *bugs* drop down in there. All right?"

Mitchell laughed nervously. Coal just chuckled, and he reached for the chrome handle.

The lid was tight, and the handle a little corroded, but on the second try it gave way, and he threw it back. Right on top of whatever else was inside, there appeared a big hunk of dirty, greasy tarp.

Coal looked up at Bigfoot in time to see a look of shock wash over his face. The big man growled, "I don't know what that is."

"Uh-huh," said Wilhelm. "Most folks usually don't know what's down in their food storage. Funny how that is."

"I don't!" growled Bigfoot. "I never seen that before."

Coal looked over at Mitchell. "Hey, Deputy. Come here and get this out, would you?"

Mitchell gave him an odd look. Coal felt similar looks from the others. After all, he was right there within reach. They must have thought he didn't want to touch the filthy tarp.

Regardless of his reasons, Coal had given an order, and Mitchell walked closer and crouched down, taking a hold of one end of the folded tarp and hoisting it out. As his hand closed on it, he looked up at Coal, and his jaw clenched.

Coal looked away, his eyes settling on Monahan. "All right, Deputy. Open that up for us."

Mitchell flipped the tarp over to find a loose edge, then slowly unraveled it. With four or five quick movements, he finally set it all flat. There, lying on top of the tarp, was a bolt action rifle.

CHAPTER NINE

Coal's eyes were studying Bigfoot Monahan's face when the rifle came into view. Even if he had had a thesaurus beside him, he wasn't sure he could describe the look that came over the big man's face. He wasn't sure he knew what he had expected, either. He just knew that it was not what he saw.

At first it didn't seem to be anger. It didn't seem to be hatred. It didn't seem to be guilt. It seemed instead to be a whole gamut of emotions, going first from confusion, then to surprise, then shock. And then with the accumulation of all three, at last came the anger that was one of the things Coal would have predicted.

"I ain't never seen that before. You bastards put that in there! Who did that?"

He started toward Coal, somehow singling him out. Jordan racked the shotgun. The weapon went to his shoulder, and its bore was zeroed in on Bigfoot's chest. "STOP."

The big man froze. No sane man, often including one who may otherwise have a death wish, would continue an assault in the face of such an ominous sound. Slowly, Bigfoot's free hand, the one not holding the Yorkie, came out to the side. "I'm stopped. Get that thing off me."

"Keep it there," Coal ordered Jordan. "Shoot him if he moves."

Coal had carefully unsnapped and drawn his magnum, and he pointed it with almost casual ease at Bigfoot's belly. With his other hand, he reached behind him and drew cuffs from his hip pocket.

"Jim?" He tossed his old friend the handcuffs, and Jim caught them deftly.

"We had quite a rodeo last time we took you in," recalled Jim. "And when you got convicted, you swore to kill all five of us. Now three of the five are dead, killed by a .30-06—all since you got out of the pen. With that rifle on your property, it don't look good, Monahan."

The big man glared at Jim. The first sign of real fear washed over his face, right through the acid glow of hate. "I would have killed all of you with my bare hands—or a two by four. Not a rifle. I would have tore out your eyeballs with my thumbs. You bastards put that rifle in there, and you can all go to hell."

"Maybe we'll see you there," said Jim quietly. He walked closer to Monahan. The giant towered ten inches over his head. "You going easy? Or hard?" The older man's eyes flickered over at Coal.

Monahan's gaze followed Jim's to Coal's face. He stared, and the hate pouring out of his eyes was like molten lava. Finally, as he seemed to bring up a memory of something out of the long ago, he smiled, showing broken, browning teeth. Then he laughed. But the look in his eyes was of desperation.

"Easy. You can't keep me anyway. That rifle won't show one fingerprint of mine."

Jim walked behind the big man and put one cuff on, then said, "Give the dog to your wife or son." Bigfoot complied when his wife hurried over. "Now, other hand," commanded Jim, and he closed the cuff on that one too. It was only then that he felt safe to say, "Prints don't matter, big man. People wear gloves all the time, and most any soap or paint thinner or alcohol will take off fingerprints. What's going to matter is a number of people heard you swear you were going to kill some men when you got free, and you haven't been out for more than a month before three of the list are dead—and incriminating evidence left at the house of a fourth one we didn't even know was on your list. I think that'll be plenty, especially for the folks in this county. Let's go."

"What? Who's that?"

"Just move," growled Jim.

They walked to Coal's car, and when he opened the door, Monahan got down into the back seat without a fight. The whole time, he kept trying to see his wife and son. But he never tried to speak to them, and the two of them only stared back. All-encompassing shock filled their eyes. There were no tears.

* * *

Both cars drove to the courthouse together, Jim riding with Coal. They escorted Monahan into the jail without a struggle. The big man wouldn't meet anyone else's eyes.

In the jail, Roger Miley, little Sissy's uncle, sat alone on the back side of his bunk, leaning against the wall. His face was gaunt, his eyes hollow.

They got Bigfoot Monahan strip-searched, and while he was waiting to shower Coal went in and sat for a moment with Miley. "Judge Sinclair's keeping you in here, huh?"

Miley met his eyes. "I'm a flight risk. He says. But I have to laugh at that. Shoot, I got no money to buy gas with. No money for food. And a cold truck to sleep in. In here I got shelter and food, and out there I don't. And somebody's takin' care o' Sissy. I ain't no flight risk. I'm better off in here."

"No flight risk, huh?" Coal repeated.

"Hardly. Look at me. Like death warmed over. How far would I get if I did leave?"

"Good point. So... you want a beer and a good burger?"

"What? You folks change your menu?" asked the scrawny Miley, somewhat sarcastically. "Don't tease me."

"Listen," said Coal. "I've got to deal with this big fellow we brought in. And I'm going to need all my boys in here too, because he can be quite a handful. So... I'm not going to be able to send anyone for food, at least for a while. What if I give you three bucks and you walk downtown and grab a beer and a burger? It'd be doing me a favor, and by the looks of you, you could maybe use some nice, fresh air, too, besides the meal and the beer."

For a long time, Miley just sat and stared at him. "You'd really trust me like that?"

"Shouldn't I? You said you're not a flight risk."

Miley met his eyes, and finally he showed his bad teeth in a smile. "I sure ain't. Yeah, man. I promise I'll come back. I've been achin' for some air."

Coal reached for his wallet.

"Whoa, brother!" Miley held up a hand. "You're not giving me your own money."

Coal stared at him. "Well, where did you expect to have it come from?"

"Man, I don't feel good about that."

"You feel good about fresh air and a burger? And beer?"

After a moment, Miley smiled sheepishly. "Well, when you put it that way."

Coal chuckled, handing Miley three one dollar bills. "You get any change, I want it back. I don't care if it's just a quarter; times are tight, you know. See you in about an hour."

Coal walked Miley to the door and opened it for him. As he stepped out, Miley turned, his eyes measuring Coal. "I never much took to badge toters, sir. But you're a good sort. Salmon's lucky to have you." He held out his hand. Surprised, Coal took it.

"Better get going. That's a bit of a walk."

"That's one thing I can do, Sheriff—walk fast." Miley smiled again and almost ran up the concrete steps, starting along the asphalt driveway. He looked like he had a new lease on life.

* * *

Bigfoot Monahan didn't particularly want to take a shower, but he didn't seem to care, either. Ever since walking down the stairs into the jail, the only thing he really seemed to care about was who would watch out for his family if he went back to prison. And one other thing.

"I'll take a shower. I'll put on your stupid clothes. Just get that ugly little creep outta my sight. I'm tired of him starin' at me."

Coal looked at Bigfoot, who was stripped to the waist and standing outside the shower room door. His eyes scanned over to Todd Mitchell, who was scowling. Jim and Jordan were both still in the room, seated on the far side drinking coffee Jordan had just put through the maker. Kevin Wilhelm was also here. He had decided to get a room in the brand new Stagecoach Inn, on the west bank of the Salmon River, rather than drive all the way along the deer-infested highway to get back to Pocatello.

"You're not going to fight them, are you, Monahan?" Wilhelm's face had taken on a slightly softer look than normal. Maybe all Bigfoot's talk of his wife and son had started to get to him a little. Oddly, it had gotten to Coal.

"No, I won't fight. I just don't want that queer in here."

Jim Lockwood actually let out a laugh, his eyes crinkling up merrily as he looked at Mitchell, who was the obvious target of Monahan's comments. Mitchell, of course, did not laugh.

"Hey, Todd," said Coal with a sigh. "Why don't you go grab yourself a bite to eat. We'll be okay."

Mitchell's glance flickered over at Coal, but then it went right back to Bigfoot. He reached up slowly and from his right chest pocket drew out a package of Doublemint gum, unwrapped a stick, and shoved it in his mouth. All the while, he glared at Bigfoot.

"I wish we had thought of it sooner. I could have sent you with Miley."

Mitchell finally nodded. "All right. You'll be here when I get back to pass off the keys and what-not?"

Coal shrugged. "What keys? Sure, I'll be here. Thanksgiving's pretty much shot anyway."

Mitchell, with one last hard look at Bigfoot, walked over to the door, picked his hat off the rack, crammed it on his head, and left.

Coal looked back at Bigfoot. "Better?"

"Better. Hey, do I get a phone call?"

"Supposed to," replied Coal. "Who do you want to call?"

Bigfoot thought for a long moment. "Well… Nobody, I guess."

Coal suddenly remembered that the Monahans didn't have a home phone. "I'll call your neighbors in a while. Maybe they can get your wife and boy to come to their house and you can call her there. Or she can call you."

Even as he spoke, Coal seemed to hear his own heart beating, drumming sullenly. Why did he even care? This man had killed Larry, Trent, K.T., and then raped and killed Jennifer. It was really a stupid rule. Why should Bigfoot get to talk to his family?

Bigfoot nodded, numbness in his eyes. He started shucking off his shoes and pants, and everyone but Jim, clear across the room with a shotgun not far from his hand, turned away to give him some privacy.

Ten minutes later, Bigfoot came out of the shower room with his jail coveralls on, the legs ridiculously short on him. His dark red hair looked black now, and his beard hung with moisture. He started toward the cell block, then stopped with his left shoulder to the others and turned a sullen gaze on them. The look in his pale blue eyes was that of a man who was dying.

Coal opened up the farthest cell in the back, while the other inmates all stood watching. Monahan traipsed inside and sat down on the hard metal bunk, which sported a mattress not nearly as thick as his upper arm. He put his elbows on his knees, settled his cheeks into his upraised hands, and stared at the floor.

"You want me to arrange a phone call?" asked Coal over the jingling sound of the keys locking the door.

Bigfoot hesitated for five seconds. Finally, he looked partway up, but not far enough to meet Coal's eyes. "Naw. It's okay. Nobody'll want to talk to me anyway."

Watching the man, Coal felt a bizarre pang of sympathy come over him. He knew this man was a murderer, but somehow he just couldn't help but sense his loneliness. The feeling made him angry with himself. He *was* a murderer... wasn't he?

A call suddenly came over the radio. It was the dispatcher, Nadene. *Salmon dispatch to Sheriff Savage. Come in. Salmon dispatch to Sheriff Savage. Do you copy?*

Coal grabbed the mic. "Nadene, this is Sheriff Savage."

Sheriff, get down to the five hundred block of Main ASAP. There's a big fight down there. Deputy Mitchell is in it.

Coal looked at the others as they jumped up. "What are we waitin' for?" barked Wilhelm.

The four of them ran out and got in Wilhelm's and Coal's vehicles and flew down to Main. On the way down, Nadene was on the radio, almost screaming words Coal didn't catch. As they raced over the bridge and down past McPherson's store, Coal saw the cluster of men in front of the area of the Owl Club. Someone must have turned and seen the blue light flashing on his dash, for soon there was a general rout. Men took off running down the street, and some ran into the Owl Club. Two of them sprinted to the other side of the street.

Left was Todd Mitchell kneeling there with his nose bleeding, his hair sticking everywhere, and his hat lying trampled on the sidewalk. His revolver was still in its holster. The knuckles of his right hand were also bloody, and there was a large raspberry on his left cheek. A cut was bleeding into his left eye.

On the sidewalk, a man lay prone, and as Coal jumped out of his car and drew his .357, his eyes fell to that man, and he lunged to a stop. His eyes raised back up to Mitchell.

"Miley?"

Mitchell nodded. He was breathing so hard he almost couldn't speak as he struggled to his feet. "Yeah. I... got down here and... a couple of 'em... was beating him."

"Easy, Todd. Catch your breath."

Coal and then Jim went over to Miley and turned him over. He was breathing, but unconscious. There was clear fluid leaking out of one ear, and blood smeared all over his face. His left eye socket appeared to be caved in.

"Get the ambulance here now!" Coal barked at Jim. He turned his attention back to Mitchell. "Who was it? Did you know them?"

"I think so, or at least some of 'em. It all happened pretty fast."

"Who? You got any names?" asked Coal, feeling his face darken.

"One, for sure. Runnigan. Drew, I think. He's one of them loggers. Big fella. Brownish red hair. Big beard."

Coal drew a deep breath. *Runnigan!* He was one who seemed to be the ring-leader who had caught Miley poaching and had punched him in the head.

"Any obvious reason for the fight?"

Mitchell touched his cheek gingerly. "You serious? There was a riot here, Sheriff. I told them to stop. They jumped me from every direction. Wasn't like we had time to chat."

A police car raced up and screeched to a halt, and Bob Wilson got out. "Sorry, Coal! Got here quick as I could. I was down south of town following up on a burglary. What can I do?"

"We've got to get an ambulance, Bob. Pronto."

Bob looked over at the unconscious Miley, alarm leaping into his face. "He's bad! Can we get him in one of our cars? Hey—lay him in back of Mitchell's truck."

With the emergent nature of the man's injuries, Coal decided it was a good call, especially since the hospital was just down the street. They got Miley loaded, and Coal stayed with him in back until they pulled up to the emergency room. Annie Price was on duty, and Coal gave her a quick rundown of what had happened.

"I've got to get back downtown before the suspects can get out of there," he told her. "I'll be back as soon as I can."

With that, he and Mitchell left, and they drove back to the scene of the fight, where Bob Wilson, Kevin Wilhelm and Jordan Peterson were still standing guard. They had been joined now by police chief Dan George, in civilian clothes with an obvious spot of gravy on the chest of his shirt.

Todd gestured toward the Owl Club. "I know some of them went in there. Not sure if one was Runnigan."

"Let's find out." Coal looked around him at the others, and they all barged through the Owl Club's front door.

It didn't take long to find out that several men had come through the long room, but just as quickly they had gone out the back. The same was true with everywhere else they checked.

Finally, Coal thanked the others and left them orders to pick up Runnigan if they found him. He got back in his car and drove to the hospital. Connie was going to be mad again that he was so late coming home, but she had better get used to it. Unless Salmon changed drastically, it looked like things would always remain about the same. He only hoped by Christmas there would at least be a chance of peace.

Anyway, he could not just leave Roger Miley in the hospital in a state of unconsciousness where he would not be if Coal had not released him illegally to come downtown. This could be big enough to end his job, if he knew politics.

Furthermore, he would not leave Miley in the care of anyone else, not even one of his own friends or his deputy. He was not going to drive away from that hospital until Miley woke up, or at least until he was admitted.

Coal did not dare call his mother. He especially couldn't stand the thought that one of the children might pick up the phone. Like a coward, he went to his car, got on the radio and called Nadene.

Dispatch copy. Go ahead, came the scratchy voice over the air.

"Nadene, I am stuck at the hospital with a victim from the fight, and he can't be left alone. He is also an inmate at the jail. Can you please do me a favor and call my house? Tell them I have no idea when I'm going to be home, and they can eat the pie without me." A feeling of utter aloneness came over him as what he had said sank in. More than anything else, that made it seem final: He had missed this important day with his family.

That's affirmative, Sheriff. I'm sorry you can't be with them for the holiday. Anything else?

Coal had the words in his head. They vied to get out of the back of his throat. He wanted to say, *Tell them I love them.* But anyone with a radio would have heard him say it. He couldn't voice the words. "Uh, no, ma'am. That's all."

He hung up the mic and let his head rest against the seat, taking a big breath. Blue shadows had swept over the city now, magnifying the lonely feeling in his heart. He pushed all thoughts of his family out of his mind.

As he got out of the car and took a walk up the north side of the street, then back down the south, he could think of only one thing: Little Clarissa, temporarily in the care of Maura Plenty-Wounds, had one man who truly cared for her: Roger Miley. If she lost him, she might have had the Battertons, but now, by a horrible twist of fate, both of them were gone as well, before she even got to know them. If Miley did not walk out of that hospital, Clarissa had one relative left that Coal knew how to find, and that one girl, a sixteen-year-old who had become an orphan almost overnight, would be in no shape to take care of a baby. Poor Cynthia. How much could one girl bear?

As Coal stopped outside the Owl Club to gather his thoughts and heard the voice of Cat Stevens break over the radio inside the bar, singing “Morning Has Broken,” he found himself wondering: What did a place like Lemhi County do with orphaned children? And did Cynthia and Clarissa even have a chance?

CHAPTER TEN

Evening, Thanksgiving Day...

When Coal got back to the hospital, Roger Miley was dead.

A massive brain bleed, they told him. From the moment of the hit to the head, there was no hope, or at least that was what they believed. Dr. Bent was guessing that the damage had commenced sometime earlier—probably the first time Miley was struck, at the scene of the poached bighorn.

The body lay in the room where they had tried to work him, now covered in a clean sheet. Miley had no money. The county would have to pay for his burial.

Annie Price could see the news had shaken Coal. After she washed her hands and dried them, she walked close to him and laid a hand on his arm. Sympathy filled her glance. “You okay?”

“Sure.” He was lying. Apparently she could see it.

“Sometimes I pretend too,” she said with a gentle smile. Compassion filled her eyes. He had to clench his jaw and dart his glance away to control his emotions. He just nodded.

"Hey." She gave his arm a vigorous rub. "Coal, by the time you got there it was over. What could you have done?"

He turned his eyes even farther away, and his head too. He could feel her trying to see his face, and he didn't want her to.

"It's time for a break. Do you want to go grab a sandwich or something?"

His chest filled with pain, but with an inkling of hope trying to work its way into him, he turned back to her and took a deep breath. "That sounds good."

She squeezed his forearm. "Okay. Is hospital food good enough? I can't really go far away."

He chuckled. "Sure. With you there, I think anything will taste okay."

She gave him a big smile, tilting her head to one side. "Aww. That was a sweet thing to say. Thank you! I haven't heard anything that nice in a while."

"Well, you should. Let me use the restroom, okay? I'll be right back."

He stood in the restroom, watching his tortured face in the mirror, and thought about Miley. And Drew Runnigan. And Todd Mitchell. And little Sissy...

He washed his hands and splashed water on his face, running his fingers back through his hair, still nearly black when wet but starting to show a strand of silver here and there. He ran the web of his hand down over his mustache to straighten it, staring into his deep-set blue-gray eyes. *You've been sheriff of Lemhi County for a week, Coal Savage,* he thought. *Larry was already dead before you got here, but you've managed to let three other men and a woman get killed while you've been their supposed protector. Maybe they would have been better off with Todd Mitchell after all.*

Coal stepped out of the restroom with a sick feeling inside. He had left his hat in the car, so he went bareheaded down the hall with Annie Price. She was probably five foot five. She seemed diminutive beside him. They went and took a seat in the empty cafeteria, and an older lady came and took their orders. Coal asked for a Coke—his once every other month indulgence—while Annie ordered a sandwich and water.

"How do you stay in shape like you do, drinking that stuff?" Annie asked teasingly.

He laughed. "It's not easy, let me tell you! No, I don't drink much pop—maybe seven or eight in a year. Just sometimes I like that burn in my throat."

"There are better things to burn your throat with."

He laughed. "Yeah, well, I don't drink much hard stuff."

After that, they sat for quite a while without talking. Coal studied the art and photography on the walls around the room, and Annie alternated between studying different parts of Coal and then trying to avoid looking at him altogether.

Finally, he looked over, and she was gazing silently at his hands. He raised his fingers, like the legs of a spider. The movement broke her from a trance, and she looked up at him.

"You've been through a lot since you came home, haven't you?"

He took in and released a quick breath, giving a little shrug, more with his eyebrows than with his shoulders. "I guess."

"You know Mr. Miley wasn't your fault, right?"

He tried to smile and knew it was pathetic. "I let him out of jail. I never should have done that. I gave him three bucks to go get himself dinner."

She studied his eyes, although he had a hard time looking at her right now. "How could you have had any idea those men were there or that they would do anything? Coal, you *gave* him three dollars and a chance for some fresh air. The rest just happened, and it could have happened any time. How can you find fault with yourself for showing a man some human kindness?"

"Because I had a good trainer, I guess."

She searched his face. Finally, she asked him a question with her very expressive eyes and features.

"My wife," he clarified.

"Oh." She laughed. "Sorry. I've not heard about her. Are you still married?" She glanced at his left ring finger, which he knew she had already studied pretty closely earlier. Maybe this time she was looking for a callus or a tan line.

"No."

"What happened?"

"She died."

"Oh, Coal, I'm so sorry! I didn't know."

"No way you would. Not your worry." He looked up, and she was watching his face. Their eyes held. He wanted to get up and put his arms around her. Rather, he wished she would put her arms around him. Big tough Marine! Right now, he just wanted some-one to touch him—preferably Annie. But she kept sitting there, and in a moment tears came into her eyes.

"Hey, now don't *you* start!" he chided. "I'll be okay."

She nodded quickly and looked down. Suddenly, he decided to throw caution to the wind, completely on a whim. He lunged up and walked around the table to her, and as she saw him coming she stood up to meet him. He threw his arms around her and just held her tight. It felt so good to feel a good woman against his heart again.

They were still standing like that when the waitress brought their orders.

Annie was a nibbler. She took a little bite, and he matched it with a tiny sip of Coke. It was too sweet. He usually liked it with water added. He'd have to wait for the ice to melt a little.

As she chewed her morsel, he watched her and put Roger Mi-ley out of his mind. He had no idea what he was going to do with

Clarissa. Or Cynthia. Or if he had any say in any of it at all. But he had bigger fish to fry right now.

"Can I ask you something?" His eyes took in her every beautiful feature.

She shrugged a shoulder, looking nervous. He felt like he was going to fall right into her eyes. "Um... I guess?" She voiced it like a question, like she wasn't completely sure.

"It's a new subject, all right? About Paul Monahan."

"Oh. Okay."

"How did he act in here?"

Her eyes roved around in thought, and then she said, "I thought he was actually pretty polite. Even nice, I would say."

"Really? You'd call him nice?"

She thought again for a moment. "Well, okay, maybe not really nice. But not unfriendly."

"How did he treat his son?"

She threw back her head and laughed. "Wow. Like gold. I loved my father, and he made me think of him—tough as rocks on the outside, but on the inside he was like... I don't know, caramel."

It was Coal's turn to laugh. *"Caramel!* That's pretty sweet."

She shrugged again, her eyes roving off over his shoulder. "Yeah. I don't know, I know that sounds totally weird. But yeah, caramel. He was a little more reserved with others, but he was so doting on that boy."

Coal nodded. That was the image he seemed to be getting of Bigfoot as well—that he really loved his family.

"He killed all those people, right?" Annie asked.

Again, Coal nodded. "Yeah. Well, I think so, at least."

"You don't know for sure?"

"I don't know anything for sure anymore. I just..."

"What?"

"Well, I told you that we found a rifle on his place, and we put him in jail."

"Yeah..."

"So that rifle was hidden in a tarp in a freezer that was buried in the ground for storing potatoes. I was watching him when we opened the freezer and he saw the tarp."

"And?"

"Oh, I don't know, he just seemed really shocked to see it in there. I mean, I've dealt with liars off and on my whole life. I just couldn't see it in his eyes, and believe me, I wanted to. He looked... surprised. Genuinely surprised. And then when we opened the tarp? Same thing again. I've never been more convinced of a man's guilt than I am of his. Ever. I mean, he gets out of the pen, and then the exact men he swore he would kill when he got out start getting shot? Too much for just coincidence, right?"

"It sure seems like it. You know, there are a lot of good liars out there. I've dealt with them too."

There was something hidden behind that comment. Coal could sense it. Something more important than a short lunch break was going to give her time to reveal. He stored the thought away for another time.

"Well, you dealt with Bigfoot. I mean Monahan. Is he a killer?"

She shrugged and shook her head. "How can I answer that? No one can. Anyone can pretend to be the sweetest person in the world when they're in public. I have seen both sides of a person—as sweet as honey and then as mean as a rattlesnake. I'm not going to say one word about Mr. Monahan that could sway you either way. Only evidence can answer that."

Easing back in his chair, Coal gave her a nod. "Yeah, I know. Sure. I couldn't have used your opinion officially anyway. I guess I'm just curious."

"I don't very often make judgments of people, Coal," she went on. "I've tried that, and I've been burned so hard. But I will make a judgment about one person right now, and I hope you can listen to this one. You're a good man. A good father. And you care about people. I trust you to do what's right. You would never be able to rest if you did it any other way."

Even as she spoke the words, all he could think of was how close he had come to lying out on a hill near Bigfoot Monahan's house and shooting him dead...

* * *

It was ten-thirty before the mess at the hospital was cleared up and the undertaker had taken Miley's body away. It would be weeks before all the paperwork from the hospital, as well as Coal's reports, was compiled and ready to be of any use for future legal action.

Even while thinking about home, Coal drove back up to the jail, and Todd Mitchell was there drinking coffee with Jordan Peterson. Coal gave Mitchell a long, level look. His face was wreathed in bruises, and he had a butterfly bandage on his wounded eyebrow. "You going to go ahead and work?"

Mitchell nodded. "There's nobody else."

"Sure," agreed Coal, looking at Mitchell's battered face. "But that looks painful. I could stay." Coal had been about to tell Mitchell to get out on the street and patrol if he was supposed to be working, but after what he had been through earlier, maybe he needed some slack.

"Naw," said Mitchell. "You know what? I at least got to be with my family a little today for the holiday. You haven't."

"No, I did go home and eat with them. You deserve the time home as much as I do." He wanted to say more, but he couldn't get the words out.

Mitchell stood up. "I'm fine. In fact, I'm going to get out there."

He put on his hat and strode to the door, and as he touched the handle, Coal said, "Hey, Todd..."

"Yeah?"

"Be careful out there." It still was not what he wished he could say: that he was proud of Mitchell for jumping into the fight. That he had done a good job. He just couldn't get the words past his throat.

Mitchell nodded, threw a glance and another nod goodbye at Jordan, and went on out. A minute later, they heard his truck start, then watched his headlights flash through the window and across the far wall before he headed out of the lot.

Coal turned his attention to Jordan. "Wilhelm gone?"

"Yeah. After you drove to the hospital, he said he was going to see about getting some supper. Haven't seen him since."

"Jim?"

"Yeah, him too. Said he wanted to spend the last of Thanksgiving with his 'bride'." Jordan thought a moment, then chuckled. "He said he missed his sweetheart, grabbed his hat, and headed out with hardly a goodbye."

"Now that's love," said Coal, feeling a warmth inside. "You know that boy's been married for over forty years?"

"I didn't," replied Jordan, a look of respect coming over his face. "That's neat."

"Yeah." Coal pulled off his hat and looked at it for a moment, spinning it in his hands. *Some men couldn't keep a woman happy for five,* he thought.

"Say, Jordan—what do you think of Monahan, anyway?"

"Damn! That's one mountain of a man!"

With a chuckle, Coal said, "Yeah, he is that. But I don't mean that. More... Well, were you watching him when we opened that freezer?"

"Not really."

"Did you see his face when we opened the tarp then?"

"Yeah, kind of."

"Did it seem strange?"

"Uh... I guess. Sort of like he was sick he got caught, maybe?"

"Really? I swore he looked totally surprised."

"Yeah?"

"Yeah. It's been bothering me a lot. You know, he had to know we'd come back looking some more eventually. Why wouldn't he hide it off his property somewhere?"

"Just stupid, maybe?"

Coal nodded thoughtfully. Well, there was that. There was plenty of stupidity in the world to fill an ocean. But Bigfoot did not come across as stupid.

"Yeah, maybe." So maybe it was only him. Maybe no one else had seen what he thought he had. Possible? Sure. But he had been a Marine for ten years, among many people who weren't the cream of the crop of society. And in the military police for more years than he cared to think about. He had been well-trained to be suspicious of everyone. To trust very few, and almost no one completely. It seemed strange that he, out of them all, would have as much reason as he did to want Bigfoot to be guilty and yet now be having doubts.

Getting up, he went back into the cell block. Either it had just been a quiet time for drunks and everyday thugs in Salmon, or he and Mitchell had simply been too busy to go after petty criminals. Either way, Bigfoot Monahan was the only man back here now.

Coal stopped in front of Bigfoot's cell. "You get anything to eat?"

Monahan just shook his head.

"You hungry?"

Another shake of the head.

"You ever in the military, Monahan?"

The big man raised his head. "No, why?"

"Curious."

"You a hunter?"

"I was."

"Not anymore?"

Bigfoot just gave him a sarcastic smile. "Yeah, right."

"Right what?"

"I can't own a gun now. The government knew it was going to be hard to get a job and feed my family, and that's when they crippled me even more. Can't even own a gun to hunt with. I was just lucky to get that job with Lemhi Timber."

"But you did—own a gun."

"You know damn well that ain't my gun. I been in here long enough in the quiet now to at least realize what's goin' on. You or one of your boys put that there. I ain't no fool. You wanted to send me back to the pen because you don't think my family suffered long enough. So now you found a way."

There it was again. The man didn't mention his own suffering, but his family's.

"What caliber did you used to shoot? When you used to shoot."

"Ought-six, if it's any of your business."

"Well, it kind of is my business."

"Go to hell."

"You don't like to cooperate, do you?"

"You've gotta be kiddin' me!" Bigfoot raged up off his bunk and glared down at Coal. "You've took me away from my family. Again. They're gonna starve for who knows how much longer. Maybe forever, if you pin all them killin's on me. But there ain't no workin' with you. You're railroadin' me, plain and simple. A one-eyed bat could see that. I swore I'd kill you if I could, Savage. I wish to hell you'd let me out of this cell. I should have done it that night at the hospital."

"Why didn't you?"

Bigfoot stared him down. Seconds ticked by while their eyes drilled into each other. At last, Bigfoot stepped back from the bars and a great sadness came over his face. It seemed all he could do to continue staring at Coal.

"'Cause I knowed they'd take me away from my wife and boy again."

Coal met Monahan's eyes dead-on. He couldn't fathom the depths of the heart-rending sadness and loneliness etched all through the hard lines of the big man's face. Finally, he backed away and left.

Immediately as he exited the cell block, the phone rang. Coal looked at Jordan. He wanted him to answer it, but it was well past time to cut into the pies back at home, and he knew who was probably on the other end of the line.

"Hello. Sheriff's office." He felt tired just saying the words.

Hi, sweetheart. Do you plan to come home tonight, or are you sleeping there? Do you want any pie? I made your favorites.

"Hi, Mom. I'm sorry I'm running late. All hell's broke loose in town. I can't explain right now." He sat and waited for the explosion from the other end of the line. Surprisingly, it didn't come.

I know, honey. I know. I heard everything. It's not your fault.

He thought about her words for a moment. Finally, he asked, "Did Jim come by?"

No. Nadine called, and we talked for a while. And also, you had a visitor. Or I should say have *a visitor.*

"What? There's someone there this late? Who is it, Mom?"

Just come home, hon. I have some pie saved for you. Apple and pumpkin. If you're done down there, it would be nice to see you.

"Are... are the kids still up?"

No, they finally went to bed, just a little bit ago.

"Oh." His heart filled up with a sudden feeling of tragedy.

They stayed up as long as they could, honey. It's okay. There's always tomorrow.

"Yeah. Sure."

Saying goodbye to Jordan, Coal drove home, a little too fast, considering the deer out sewing zigzag lines back and forth across the highway. But he made it without incident and pulled into the yard, and there, on the other side of his mother's Cadillac, was a familiar International pickup.

Coal drew a deep breath and stepped out of the car. He settled his hat on his head, his gunbelt on his hip, and listened to the last couple of barks inside the house from Dobe and Shadow before someone hushed them.

At last, he went up the steps. The inner door opened as he was pulling the screen door. Connie looked beautiful tonight, with her silver hair put up and shining in the lamp light. She was dressed in dark gray polyester slacks and a black turtleneck with a shirt over it of blue jean blue, open down the front. "Hi, Son!" She gave him a big, tight hug. "Come on in, baby. You have company."

"Yeah, I saw the truck." He looked past his mother to see Maura sitting in his chair with Clarissa on her lap.

"Hey, Sissy. You look like you should be sleeping!"

Sissy looked at him. He thought she might speak, but she didn't.

Maura leaned forward and said something into her ear, then lifted her up as she rose herself, and turning, put her back on the chair all by herself. The little girl looked like a porcelain doll on that dark, humongous chair.

The woman came over to Coal. She, too, looked pretty—no, beautiful. Even stunning. She wore a navy blue blouse, with her rich, glossy hair tumbling all down the front of it, and snug black slacks with a bit of flare to the leg. Coal hated the modern style of flare-legged pants, but these particular ones looked fine on Maura. In fact, he had never seen anything look bad on her—more because of what was inside than the style itself, if he had to guess.

Maura walked right up to him and said, "Hey, lawman. You doin' okay?"

"Yes, ma'am," Coal replied, instantly thinking he must sound like a sheriff from an old Western. "Is Cynthia okay? She's with you, right?"

"The doctor gave her a sedative. She's in a deep sleep back at my house. There's no way she could have come out and faced anyone—and probably no way she could have stayed there alone, without the drugs. That little girl is scared plumb to death."

"Sure. It's going to take a lot of time for her to begin healing."

Coal was shocked right to the core when Maura came closer still and without any kind of warning slowly, softly encircled him with her arms. He tried to stop the rush of tears into his eyes, but they were too unexpected. He met her embrace fully and held her like she was his last hold on life. Maura didn't let go, at least not right away. Right there in front of Sissy, his mother and God, she held him close and patted his back. It had been a long time since he had felt more loved by a woman other than his mother. She stood on her tiptoes and said in his ear, "I'm sure glad you're okay. There were a lot of people worried about you." Her breath, although startlingly warm, sent chills down his back.

And drawn by a spirit he didn't understand, he whispered back into Maura's ear, "Thank you. That means a lot." Then he said something else, something he had been thinking, but hadn't dared come right out and say to anyone: "Maura, I have to tell you something. I'm not sure anymore that Bigfoot is guilty."

Maura leaned away from him but still kept him in her arms. "What? Why would you think that?"

"Something I saw today. We got Bigfoot in jail now, evidence putting him at the Batterton house, and a .30/06 confiscated from his property. He drives a red station wagon, which is what K.T. told me someone was driving who kept casing his house. But even with all that, I don't know anymore if he did the killings."

"What does it mean if he didn't?"

"It means maybe whoever killed my friends is still out there. Hunting."

CHAPTER ELEVEN

Friday, November 24

Sleep was getting scarce for Coal Savage. He lay awake most of the night, sleeping only in spurts, and even then fitfully, thinking about the look on Bigfoot Monahan's face when the freezer door was opened and the big man laid eyes on the greasy tarp inside. And the even more shocked expression when the rifle was revealed.

Once, he awoke with a film of cold sweat all over him. He had dreamed he was sitting on a ridge, leaned over a rifle and bipod, and he was just about to squeeze the trigger on Bigfoot as he started to get into his car in the morning to go to work. He lay there thinking about how close he had come to going after Bigfoot vigilante-style, how close he had come to throwing aside the honor he had always lived with. What if Bigfoot really did turn out to be innocent? It seemed impossible, but Coal had seen stranger things. What if he had killed him, and then the killings had continued? That was something he could never have lived with. He didn't know how anyone could.

Coal threw off the sheets, which were all that was left covering him by now. They were damp anyway. His thoughts made him sick to his stomach. He had a feeling he was going to get sick for years, every time he thought of taking that shot. Down deep, he hoped he would have changed his mind at the last minute.

Those killings were not his fault! The death of Roger Miley, now, that may indeed have been his fault. But the murders of his friends weren't. He hated feeling helpless, but so far there had been nothing within his power that he could have done to stop them.

Awake before his alarm went off, Coal padded down the hall, looking in momentarily on Virgil, then the twins. His oldest son slept soundly, all rolled into thick blankets and breathing light and easy. Wyatt and Morgan also seemed to be deep in sleep, but unlike their brother they were twisted every which direction, and their blankets covered them haphazardly. Coal sneaked in to cover them better, but he quickly realized if he tried it would just wake them up. Smiling down at their little faces, he decided just to let them sleep on.

Coal went down the stairs, thinking about the time Wyatt had asked him why Virgil cries. What did little Wyatt mean? Why *did* Virgil cry? He couldn't find out for certain from Wyatt if he was talking about actual crying. It seemed so unlike Virgil. But the thought haunted him. He realized way back then that he did not know how to approach Virgil about it. He knew his oldest boy thought of himself as a young man. How did you ask a young man if he had been crying? There seemed to be no answer. And so the thought of it just kept nagging at him, making his heart ache, and his soul seem to die, a little at a time.

Going down into the basement, Coal did a light imitation jump rope—since he hadn't found his jump rope yet from the move, then six sets of fifty pushups as close together as possible, five sets of twenty to twenty-five pull-ups, and last of all one hundred sit-ups, in four hard-squeezing sets of twenty-five. It was going to have to be enough for today. All he could hope to do was maintain.

Back upstairs, he fried six eggs in butter and laid them on medium done toast, smashing all the soft yolk out of them and powdering it all with cayenne and black pepper. He guzzled a glass of raw milk, refilled the glass with ice water and emptied it once more, then set his dishes in the sink and ran hot water on them. A peek out the front window showed him a silvery glow over the Beaverhead Mountains. It reminded him of hunting time, a time he couldn't wait to load all of his gear and his lunch into the pickup with his dad and his brothers and drive off toward the mountains, passing a few mule deer does even as they drove out.

He had to get going before Connie got up. The kids were out of school again, and it would have been nice to be here with them, but he had no choice. And he didn't want to talk about the day ahead of him with his mother, or of his thoughts. He didn't want to talk about Miley being dead or the fact that he had started questioning what he knew in his heart to be true: that Bigfoot Monahan was the killer of his friends.

Dobe and Shadow followed him to the front door, and he knelt down and petted them, putting his face up close to theirs to feel of their warmth and their adoration. He looked into Shadow's old eyes. They seemed to be getting weak, and their bottom lids were drooping, revealing a redness inside that made him sad. Her once-black muzzle was almost all white, and there was a lonesome kind of sadness in her eyes as she looked at him. But there was still that same love as well, and that was what broke his heart. Shadow would not be around much longer. She would be going to hike the mountain trails with his father. The thought made his throat go tight, and he hugged her neck and held her. Patiently, she just sat. Maybe she needed this closeness as much as he did.

On a whim, Coal let both dogs out, and after their morning errands, he let them in the back seat of the car. Probably not the wisest decision, but having them with him made him feel less lonely.

Coal had noticed that, as soon as he stepped out of the house, he did not feel that feeling of security he had been sure he would have after Monahan's arrest. He had still half-expected a bullet to come, out of the dark. How long would it be before that feeling went away? Would it ever?

Today was Friday. He wished he could say goodbye to his children. He needed to. He needed to look into their eyes. And yet he didn't know what to say. So the brave Marine chose the coward's way out and left long before they would rise.

He drove out to the main highway, then turned toward Leadore. The dogs were in their glory, standing up and looking out the windows, smearing the glass with slimy noses. Coal just laughed. It was like the old days.

As he drove south, he thought of Maura and felt an even deeper loneliness sweep over him. Thoughts of that woman confused him, so he pushed them aside. She was a conundrum, and one he did not think he would ever completely figure out. He wanted to go get her, to ask her to come for a drive, but he knew he couldn't. Her holding him last night was done out of sympathy. Because she was a woman, and women did that kind of thing—comforted others. There was nothing else to it. Besides, he couldn't ask her to leave her boys, Cynthia, and little Sissy alone.

He kept on driving, as the sunlight emboldened the sky behind the mountains. Two miles later, he sat in his car on the roadside grass in front of the Monahan property. *Why was he here?* he wondered. What would he really accomplish at this place? This woman wasn't going to tell him the truth, even if she knew it. Nor was the boy, Butch—or Danny, or whatever his name was. All either of them wanted was to have their provider back in the house with them. Their loved one.

Coal got a little jolt at those two words when they came into his mind: Loved one? Bigfoot Monahan? Could someone really love a man like that? A big, angry, taciturn wild man? He never smiled. He always seemed ready to take on the world, even if he had no reason. He couldn't possibly be much different at home... could he?

Steeling himself, Coal pulled into the driveway and parked in front of the house. The little Yorkshire terrier came yapping at the other side of the door when Coal knocked. It was free now, with no Monahan to snuggle it in the crook of his arm—a vicious guard dog on the loose.

Beverly Monahan opened the inner door wearing a house coat and slippers, and for a moment she stared through the glass at her early morning visitor. It was as if her mind was trying to register the fact that the sheriff was actually back.

Finally, she spoke through the door, reaching down to pick up the dog and cradle it the way her husband liked to do. "What do you want?"

"I'd like to talk to you."

"Sure you would. You came back to get more evidence against Paul."

Coal was taken aback. The woman had seemed so meek before. But then again, she had had a whole night to think about being alone again, with her man gone back to prison. That thought seemed to have brought out a defiant streak in her.

"No, ma'am," Coal said. "I really do just want to talk."

"You got a warrant?" She seemed to be saying all the things she had rehearsed in her mind, perhaps things she wished she had said earlier.

"No warrant, Mrs. Monahan. This is completely informal. If you really want to help your husband, you need to open this door and let me in."

After a long pause, while her suspicious thoughts swam in her eyes, Beverly Monahan opened the door. "Come in then. But I guess you already done the damage. I don't see how talkin' can help now."

"I don't either," Coal admitted. "But we can try."

She brought him to the dining room table and bade him sit down. She was about to sit on the opposite side but stopped. "You drink coffee?"

Coal glanced quickly around the kitchen. As he had thought on their first search, it seemed well-kept, not what he had originally expected from Monahan's residence. "Yeah, sure."

"Let me start some." She went over to the kitchen and set a coffee pot full of water on the stove to boil, then started grinding coffee beans with a hand grinder as Coal watched. She was squat and heavy, her hands pudgy, her face ruddy, not unlike her husband's, but much rounder. She seemed well-practiced and efficient in her work.

Feeling slightly nervous, Coal glanced around. "Is your boy awake?"

"He gets up kind of slow," she said. "Plus, I think I'm gonna let him sleep in today. He's not up to doin' chores."

"I don't blame him," Coal said. "I wouldn't want to either. His name's Butch, right?"

The woman looked over at him, her eyebrows coming up. "Uh, yeah. Right. Well, it's really Danny. Paul calls him Butch, and he likes that."

"He's had a tough time, huh? Growing up without any other kids around, and without a dad."

The woman nodded. Then she hurriedly looked away from him, checking the coffee pot. Seeming satisfied, she poured the grounds into the pot slowly, watched it boil for half a minute or so, then pulled it off the heat. She brought it over and set it on a hot pad on the table in front of Coal. She went back and got two cups and carried them back over, then set one in front of each of them.

Abruptly, she plopped into the chair across from Coal. "I'll let that brew for a little bit."

He nodded. "Sure thing."

Her eyes, made puffy-looking by the over-abundance of flesh beneath them, met his, watery through her thick glasses. "I'm surprised you remember my boy's name."

Coal smiled. "Yes, ma'am. And you're Beverly, as I recall."

She gave him a shy smile back. “Yes.”

“Talk to me about your husband, Beverly. Can I call you Beverly?”

She hesitated, glancing down the hall as if to see if her boy was up yet. “Um... Sure, I guess so.” She seemed pleased by the familiarity.

“What has it been like since Paul’s been home?”

“Real good,” she said, smiling. “We’ve been happy.”

“Happy how?”

“I don’t know how to answer that.”

“Do you do things together? How do you spend your time?”

Tears came into her eyes, and she looked down, studying her hands. Suddenly, she looked back up, but not at Coal. Instead, she looked at the coffee pot. “I’ll bet that’s ready.” She stood and poured both of their cups full, then set the pot down again.

Looking in his cup, Coal guessed the coffee should have sat longer. Of course he didn’t mention it. Instead, he just waited. Sitting back down, the woman finally took a deep breath, not looking at him.

“We go for walks sometimes. Sometimes we drive and watch the deer. One morning he got me up early, and we left Butch in bed and went to watch the sunrise together and saw a big bull moose. And then we like to read.”

“You read? Really? Does Paul read to you and the boy?”

She smiled, a shy smile. “No. He never really learned to read. I read.” Coal waited, silent. “I read *Huckleberry Finn. Tom Sawyer. Little Women.* Don’t you ever dare tell Paul I said this, but he loves those Louisa May Alcott books.”

Coal sat quietly absorbing this. “Those Louisa May Alcott books” sure didn’t seem like the kind of thing Bigfoot Monahan would care about.

"Oh, and of course he likes his cowboy books, too. Luke Short. Ernest Haycox. Zane Grey. He's crazy about those cowboy heroes."

"Oh yeah?" Coal chuckled. "Do you go to the movies?"

"Not usually. But we do if it's John Wayne. They were still playing *The Cowboys* as a Saturday matinee when Paul got out. We saw that, of course. He's still mad that John Wayne got killed."

Coal laughed. "Yeah, even back east a lot of folks were mad about that. You know, that came out in the theaters last January, and I took all my boys. My little guy Morgan cried his eyes out."

Beverly echoed his laugh. "Well, don't you ever tell a soul this either," she said, leaning forward with a conspiratorial whisper, "but our Butch did too. I'm not positive, but I think Paul had tears in his eyes himself, but he tried to hide it."

Tears came into her own eyes then, and one or two rolled down her cheeks. "Will you excuse me for a minute?" She got up and left the room, going down the hall. After a minute, she came back and sat down again.

"You have to forgive me, Sheriff. That was a special afternoon for us. My big old Paul, he saw Butch cryin', and he never even told him to stop like he used to. Instead, he put his arm around our boy and pulled him close to him. I never saw him do anything like that before." She took off her glasses and wiped them, putting them back on. "Sorry about all this emotion. I don't know where that comes from."

"You don't need to apologize for being human. Some of the rest of us could take a lesson from it, in fact." And he was talking about himself. "So... It sounds like you and Butch and Paul were really living a happy life."

"We were, Sheriff. Oh, we truly were. We thought little Butch would be all growed up when his daddy got out of jail. We never dreamed he would come back to us so soon."

"I'll bet he never planned to leave you again," said Coal.

"Not ever." She hurriedly sipped her coffee, trying to take her mind off her thoughts.

"Did Paul ever talk about me, Beverly? Or the old sheriff, Lockwood? Or K.T. Batterton?"

Beverly's face got serious then, and she looked down at the cup, cradled in her hands. "He used to wake up nights, sometimes swearing. Always sweating. He would lie there and breathe hard, and I would ask him what was wrong. He would finally say he was just thinking about... those men who put him away." Then her eyes jumped up to Coal's face. "But he woulda never took a chance on going back to jail, Sheriff! I promise you."

"No, it sounds like he wanted anything but that. I have one more question. Ma'am, a lot of people have died lately in this valley. It's got to be stopped. Everybody, including me, has thought it was your husband. If it was, then you've got to help us. You can't really want any more people to die, right? If it is Paul."

She shook her head. "No, sir. I reckon if it was Paul, I would feel real bad."

"And you know he would need to be out of society, right?"

"Out of what?"

"Society. Back in jail."

Her eyes filled with tears again. "Yes sir. I suppose so, yes."

"Then tell me this: Was there ever a time in the last week or two when Paul got up early and left, and you didn't know where he went off to?"

"No sir. That I can swear to. Every morning, Paul would make us all get up together. Then he would wait for me and Butch to say prayers—because Paul, he never agreed with talking to a man he couldn't see—and we would eat breakfast together, and he would drive off to work. He always left here at seven a.m."

"Always? Never was late one day for work?"

"No sir. That's the honest truth. And I will swear to it forever."

"You may be called to. In court. Are you prepared for that?"

"I am. My man never killed no one. Ever. He got turned down for the Army, and he once told me he was actually glad because he didn't want to ever be forced to kill nobody for no man. My man isn't the mean person people think he is. He just likes to pretend. I'll go to my grave knowin' he's innocent."

* * *

After leaving the Monahan place, Coal decided to head straight for Leadore. It was still early enough that maybe he could catch some of the other workers at the lumber mill before they all headed out for the day.

He got there around 8:45 and parked in front of the office, getting out of his car to the sounds of men's voices yelling back and forth across the yard. The pungently sweet scent of pine and fir logs saturated the air, a smell that must fill the halls of heaven. Coal breathed deeply and remembered again how glad he was to be out of Washington, D.C.

He pushed open the office door, in time to catch the secretary, Bobbie, pouring cream into a cup of coffee. At the jingling of the doorbells, she turned halfway around, and a big smile leaped to her face. "Well, hi, Sheriff! Welcome back. You sure are out and about early."

"No banker's hours for me," he replied with a grin. "How are you, Bobbie?"

"Oh wow! You remembered my name. I am just fine, Sheriff. Just fine. Can I help you, or did you just come to visit me?"

"Well, sure I just came to visit you," Coal teased. "But first, since I'm here anyway, I don't suppose Mr. Pratt is around, is he?"

"Both Mr. Pratts are around," she said with a smile. "Dennis, or Robert?"

"Well, it was Dennis who showed us around the other day. How about him?"

"Okay. I'm sure he'd love to talk to you, too. Paul Monahan didn't come to work today."

Coal's face went serious. "Yeah. Well, I might know something about that."

She winced. "Ooh. That doesn't sound good. Okay, let me get Dennis." She stepped to the door leading to the break room and called for Dennis, and pretty soon he came lumbering in, dressed in the same brown coveralls he had been wearing the first day.

He looked for a second at Coal, and then recognition came over him. "Mornin', Sheriff! What the hell you doin' up this early?"

"I might ask the same of you."

Dennis gave out a laugh. "Say, you didn't steal my boy from me, did you? Paul?"

"Well, that's what I'm here about, Mr. Pratt."

"Call me Dennis," said the big man, waving a hand across the front of him. "Damn, do I look like a 'mister' to you?"

"I can't say you look like a missus," countered Coal with a laugh. "Okay. Dennis. Before we talk much more, I'd like to question your drivers before they take off. Would that be possible?"

"Uh... Sure. They don't get no work done this early anyway. But first, what about my best driver? What'd you do with Monahan?"

"I'm afraid he slept on the county's dime last night." Coal shrugged in reply to the grimace Dennis gave him.

"What happened?"

"I got an anonymous tip about him from a guy who said he knew him and that they went hunting together. Even told me where he last saw him lugging his rifle off to."

Dennis Pratt's face had gone very serious. He nodded as he listened to Coal speak. "I sure have a hard time believin' it."

"Did he ever say what logging company he worked for before you?" Coal asked.

"Well, he didn't have to. It was us!"

Coal was taken aback. "So he worked here? Before he got sent up to prison?"

"Sure. He started here back in sixty-two or so—whenever he first come to town."

"All right. That's good to know. But maybe I'd better talk to your crews before they head out. You and I can talk later."

"Sure thing, boss. Page the boys in here, would you, Bobbie?"

When the workers had answered Bobbie's general call and come to the office, Dennis Pratt gave them the order to stick around the yard until the sheriff had talked to them each personally. At that point, Coal dismissed them all but one.

As Coal conducted a preliminary questioning of all the employees, a few things began to be clear. The first was that Bigfoot had no one here who called himself a friend. And no one worker could think of any other worker who might be friends with Bigfoot and just not want to admit it to Coal. Second, Bigfoot had confided in none of these employees about wanting to actually kill any of the recent murder victims. He had on different occasions mentioned wishing he could take some of them apart with his bare hands, but he had never said anything specifically about killing them. Further, two of them recalled a conversation in which, when the news about Larry MacAtee's murder first came across the news, Monahan seemed furious, claiming they had stolen his right to justice from him. And one of those men, who seemed to Coal to be the only one Bigfoot confided in with any regularity, said he had had the same reaction with Trent Tuckett, and that by the time he heard about K.T. Batterton's death, he had started to act what that employee could only describe as "scared."

The third big question Coal got an answer to, an answer that was the same across the board, was that none of these men had ever heard Bigfoot brag about taking any game animal or even talk about hunting at all. Back before his prison sentence, the few men who were still here and remembered him said that when it had come to the subject of hunting, Bigfoot had seemed to have a big lack of knowledge of firearms and shooting, and, as he had come from someplace in Alabama, very little knowledge of the kind of hunting one did in the state of Idaho.

When all the drivers and lumberjacks had finally headed out to their job sites in the forest, Coal settled in to interviewing first Dennis Pratt's brother, Robert, and then Dennis himself. Robert, a little shy at their first meeting, much like Dennis had been, quickly warmed up to Coal and became more than friendly and helpful. He and Dennis both admitted that if they knew Bigfoot Monahan had killed anyone they would never allow him on their property, much less in their employ. And both of them averred that Bigfoot Monahan had never been late for work, not one single day, either before his imprisonment, or after.

"What time would Monahan have to report to work?" asked Coal at last. "Say back on the seventeenth?"

"I don't know what time he *had* to report here," said Robert. "Eight, I guess. But he was never here at eight."

"Wait. Never here by then? So he might have had some free daylight before he got here?"

"Oh, hell no!" said Robert, and Coal saw Dennis nodding, affirming what he knew Robert was about to say. "I said he was never here *at* eight, not *by* eight. He was *supposed* to come in at eight, like everyone else. But old Paul, he always showed up at least half an hour earlier—if not forty-five minutes. No, I would say Paul Monahan *never* had free daylight before he got to work. And if you were to ask specific about these past two weeks, I'll swear to that on a stack of Bibles."

* * *

Once he got back to town, Coal thought about stopping at home to say hi to Connie and the kids. But it was easier not to, so he just drove up in front of the drive, got out and let the dogs out to find their own way back to the front door, which they did gladly, looking for food. Then he drove up a little farther, got onto the old Lemhi Road, and took it all the way back into town so he wouldn't have to turn around and go past the house again and risk being seen. He had never felt like much more of a coward.

He pulled up to the curb in front of the Coffee Shop and went in, greeting Jay Castillo over the counter with a nod. Tammy waved from the doorway to the kitchen. "Hi, Sheriff!"

"Morning, Tammy. Got hot coffee?"

She gave him a look of mock reproval. "Well, of course we do! Fresh, no. Hot, yes." She laughed. "What do you want, black? Sugar? Cream?"

"Wow, you don't know Coal Savage," said Jay as he wiped the counter in front of a couple of customers waiting to be served. "That should be easy to remember, Tam—black as coal!" The cafe owner laughed. "Have a seat, buddy. You want some food too? It's on me."

"I should then," said Coal, grinning. "But no, just the coffee this time."

"So what's new?" asked Jay later as he leaned up against the counter across from Coal. Down the long line of tables in the deep, narrow room, the other customers were chattering noisily and eating, so Jay had a free moment. "Any break in the murders?"

"I shouldn't talk about it. But let's say... no. I don't think so. If you'd asked me that yesterday, I'd have given you a resounding yes. There's one more thing I have to do to be sure, but until then, I'm going to have to keep this one under my hat. Sorry."

Jay shrugged and swiped his rag haphazardly across the counter top. "Well, that's probably for the best. I'd probably rather not know anyway. More coffee?"

Coal looked down into his cup, swirling it around. "Naw, I guess not. I'd better get."

He had started to dig into his pocket for some change when he happened to look out the front window and saw a vehicle drive past, going a little fast. The look of the car, once it registered on him, gave him a jolt. It was a red station wagon. Possibly a Chevy

Parkwood. But there was an even bigger difference between this one and the one driven by Paul Monahan. The top of this one was *white!* Suddenly, K.T.'s description of the vehicle driven by the man he thought had been stalking him came back to Coal with sharp clarity. It wasn't simply a red station wagon. It was red and *white!* And possibly an Impala, K.T. had said!

Coal whirled back on Jay. "Hey, Jay, did you see that car?"

"Sure."

"Have you seen it before?"

"I think so. Up on the Bar."

Coal dug in his pocket for his keys. "Tammy, I'll catch you with a tip later today, okay? Promise!"

With that, he darted out the door and headed for his car. A glance up the street showed him the Impala station wagon had already disappeared. That seemed odd, as it was quite a climb up the bar, but perhaps the car had really picked up speed after it went past the Coffee Shop. He jumped in his LTD and fired it up, then gunned it and headed for the Bar.

Coal drove all the way to the top of the Bar on Courthouse Drive, then cruised the neighborhood for a while. There were no red station wagons at all, and definitely not the red and white Chevrolet. He stopped at the stop sign on Cobalt Street at Courthouse Drive and swore.

Finally, he sighed and drove down to the courthouse, going into the jail. He looked in on Monahan, but the big man was in no mood for company, so he left him. He needed to see to Roger Miley's affairs anyway and start getting things cleared up with him. He was going to have to figure out how the whole burial thing went, when the one being buried was a pauper. With that thought in mind, he gave Jim Lockwood a ring. He hated to keep bothering him, but now that K.T. was gone, Jim was his only good source of information about how to do his job.

While he waited for Jim, he went down and got some food to bring back to Monahan, who took it sullenly, but when Coal looked in a minute later was eating with an obviously hearty appetite.

Jim Lockwood arrived, and he and Coal sipped coffee for a few minutes as they went over the specifics of a pauper's burial. While they were still talking, Coal pulled out the envelope he had put all of Miley's worldly possessions in, besides his rifle, revolver, and his pickup, of course. He tipped the manila envelope upside down, and everything slid out onto the desktop.

There sat the half stick of gum, the used movie ticket, two folded slips of paper, a worn-out business card for a bail bondsman, ten pennies, a dime and two nickels. Last and most valuable, the plastic Casio watch and wallet.

Coal went through every pocket of the wallet, finding nothing but a worn-out piece of paper with a nearly illegible phone number on it. He saw another number, this one a little clearer, on the back of the bondsman's business card.

He dialed the first number, talked to some man from Challis who had no idea who Roger Miley might be, but he had put a classified ad in the paper a few weeks ago trying to sell camping equipment, and anyone could have written his number down.

The second number picked up with a simple *Hello,* and Coal asked who he was speaking to. The voice replied with *Who's this?* When Coal introduced himself, the line went dead, and when he tried the number again he got a busy signal. That was going to bear some further investigation. It was a Salmon phone number.

He started sliding the things that meant nothing into one pile, and the others, like the wallet and the business card, he wrote the details of on the receipt Miley had signed upon his incarceration. Finally, he unfolded the first slip of paper. It was two first names: Bud and Linda, and a phone number. That had to be Jennifer's sister and brother-in-law! The last item was the final slip of paper. He unfolded it and laid it out on the desk.

Something hit him in the guts, and for a moment he only stared. This was a list. He sat and started to read it, then stopped. He looked at it closer, shot a glance up at Jim, who sat fiddling with his watch across from him.

Coal dropped his eyes to the paper once again. There on the paper was a list of names, written in a strange, semi-fancy but semi-sloppy script. The first of the names had a pencil line drawn through it, although the names themselves were written in blue ink.

The names stood out to Coal as clear as morning, as harsh as the voice of a fire and brimstone preacher:

Larry MacAtee—with the line drawn through it.
Trent Tuckett
K.T. Batterton
Jennifer Batterton

And the last name...

Coal Savage.

CHAPTER TWELVE

Coal's fingers were trembling as he stared at the list of names. The wheels of his mind tried to turn, but they were stuck in a muddy bog. He could hardly breathe. He was trying to fathom what this list of names being in Miley's possession could mean.

The first thing his fevered mind grabbed hold of was the idea that Miley was the killer he had been searching for. But that notion quickly flew. He was in jail when both of the Battertons were murdered. Also, his light-colored pickup was definitely not the vehicle that had fled the scene the day someone shot at him. But this list... Five names, one of them his, and four of them belonging to people who were now dead—assassinated, as it seemed. And there had been a failed attempt on his life.

By now, Jim had caught the change of atmosphere in the room and was staring at Coal, his mouth ajar. He waited as long as he could for Coal to tell him what he had found, then finally set down his coffee cup. "What is it, son? Don't just sit there like a squirrel with a mouth full of nuts."

Without even cracking a smile, Coal told him about the list. It was hard to get his words out, so tight was his throat. He thought suddenly of Miley's signature at the bottom of the inventory list of his belongings and looked at it closer, then at the list of names. He was no handwriting expert, but there was no way the same person had written both. Jim was now standing beside him, and he turned his head to look at Coal. Their eyes met, and Jim shook his head.

"You got a piece of paper and a pencil?" asked his old friend.

Coal simply nodded, pulling paper and a pen from a desk drawer and handing them to him without asking what it was for. Jim walked back into the cell block. He was back there for a while before he came out. "I told the list of names to Monahan and tried to get him to write them for me, but he couldn't do it off the top of his head. So I wrote them myself, and he looked at mine and copied them." The retired lawman plopped the pad of paper down in front of Coal. It was as if some preschooler had written the letters. There was no way Bigfoot could even fake being that bad.

Coal dropped back into his chair, and Jim sat on the corner of the desk. After half a minute listening to the clock tick, Jim looked over at Coal. "When's the last time you took a day off, son?"

"You mean as sheriff, or do you want me to count the fun days traveling here from Virginia with a fifteen-year-old daughter who despises me?"

"You choose."

"Seven days since I got here, I think," Coal said after counting back. "Thirteen if you count the trip."

"You gotta be worn out, boy. Maybe it's time for a vacation."

"And who do I leave in charge? Mitchell?"

"Son, it's not so long since I wore that badge myself. I bet between the two of us we could convince the county clerk to hold your spot for you. Hell, they know as well as you and I how bad it's been for you since you got here. You got five dead people in eight days. Outside of car wrecks on the highway, that's gotta be some kind of record for this valley. And they tried to kill you too. It's a little quick to take a vacation, but who wouldn't understand?"

"Thanks, Jim," said Coal, coming to his senses. "I appreciate the thought, but I can't do it. Not till something's resolved. I can't keep waking up to dead folks in my county, even if I'm sitting in Acapulco listening to someone tell me about it on the phone."

"Coal, what are you talkin' about? I was thinkin' more along the lines of Australia or someplace."

Coal laughed. The sound surprised even him, for he wouldn't have thought laughing was possible right now.

Suddenly, a call came over the radio: *Salmon police to sheriff's car. Come in? Salmon police calling Sheriff Savage.*

Coal cringed. He was starting to hate the sound of anything coming over this radio. He strode over and snatched the mic off its base. "This is Sheriff Savage. That you, Bob?"

Bob Wilson's voice crackled back over the air. *Yes sir. Meet me down at the 7-O Saddle Shop. Bring a stick. And put a hustle on it.*

"Copy. Sheriff out," said Coal, re-fixing the mic on the base. "Jim, you want to come? Sounds like Bob's got something."

"Then let's go."

They got in the LTD and flew down Courthouse Drive, turning onto the side-street where the 7-O Saddle Shop sat on a corner. Bob Wilson's baby blue Chevy Caprice was parked half a block down the street, and as he saw them, he got out and stood beside the car. He motioned them on, so Coal drove down to where he was, then spun the car around and parked behind him.

When they got out, Bob met them at their car. "I think your Runnigan fellow is in the saddle shop. Drew Runnigan, right? Big, brawny guy, a little taller than me, with a bushy beard?"

Coal felt his chest go tight. "That sounds like him, all right."

Bob turned and pointed at a metallic bronze sixty-seven Dodge Charger that was parked directly in front of the business. "That's Runnigan's. Pretty recognizable."

"Did you actually see him, or just the car?"

"Well, just the car."

"Okay. Hey, Jim," said Coal, "can you go around back and make sure he doesn't slide out that way? Bob, you come with me."

They gave Jim a minute to get around back with his shotgun, and then Coal and Bob stepped through the front door of the saddle shop. A good-looking, clean-shaven young man in a cowboy hat looked up at them from a saddle stand, a mallet and leather stamp in his hands and magnifying glass clipped in front of his eyes. Other than the young man and the delicious smell of new and old leather and leather dye, the room was empty.

"Can I help you?"

"Looking for Drew Runnigan," said Coal tersely.

"He dropped off a saddle," said the young man. "I don't know that he'll be back today."

"His car's out front."

The saddler shrugged. "Then I guess he will."

"I'm Sheriff Savage," said Coal, stepping forward. "Coal Savage."

The man set down his mallet and smiled. "Joshua Olschewski. Most of my friends call me Josh."

"Good to meet you, Josh. So let me tell you, Runnigan and his brother and some of his friends are wanted in a killing."

"You mean that fight last night?"

"Yeah, that fight. The man they beat up died at the hospital."

"I heard that. But I didn't know anybody knew who did it."

"Well, apparently Runnigan doesn't realize it either."

"I'll call you if he comes back," said Olschewski.

"I'd appreciate it. In the meantime, he's going to have a little flat tire problem out front here. At least that's what I foresee."

"You a fortune teller, Sheriff?" asked Josh Olschewski with a twinkle in his eye.

"Call me a dream maker. Good meeting you, Josh."

"Likewise."

Coal and Bob walked back out front and scanned the street both ways, looking into shop windows across the street. An old man and woman were walking arm in arm across the street. Other than them, and a black and white dog that lay on the sidewalk in front of a bakery, the street was without life.

Coal and Bob went around behind the leather shop to collect Jim, then returned to the street. "What do we do now?" asked Bob. "Go door to door?"

"Pain in the butt," said Jim.

"Well, first we make sure Drew Runnigan doesn't go away," said Coal, and he walked toward the front of the Charger.

"You gonna seep some air out of a tire?" asked Jim, with a grin.

"Yeah. That's it. 'Seep' some out." With a straight face, he pulled a pocket knife from his pants pocket, popped open a blade, and with all the nonchalance in the world poked a hole in the side-wall of the right rear tire. Within seconds, the tire was flat against the ground.

Coal turned to see Bob Wilson with eyebrows raised. "I didn't see one thing," said the officer. "Well, I guess that's one sure way to keep him from leaving town in a hurry."

Coal stepped back into the saddle shop, making the door bells jingle. Again, the wave of leather and dyes hit him, and he felt a sudden longing to have a life like Josh Olschewski's, a life of quietly working on leather, a life without worrying about who killed whom.

Coal walked to where Olschewski was working, pulled a pad of paper and a pen from his pocket and scratched a number on it, handing it to the saddler. "I'll be at the Coffee Shop. That's the number. Keep an eye on that Charger out front, would you, Josh? You see Runnigan come back, please call the second you can. I have a feeling it won't be going anywhere fast."

"I will," Josh replied with a grin. "In fact, I'll move my work table right over in front of the door so nobody can stir around out there without me seein' 'em. Sheriff?" The word stopped Coal turning to go back outside. "I like your style." The young man nodded and winked.

Coal smiled back at him.

It was half an hour later when the phone rang, and Coal, taking a chance, picked it up. "Coffee Shop. This is Coal Savage."

Coal, this is Josh, at the saddle shop. Runnigan came back. He's madder than hell.

"All right, Josh. Thanks."

With that, Coal dropped the receiver on the base and thanked Jay for his hospitality and the use of his phone.

"Let's move, boys."

They left their cars parked in front of the Coffee Shop, out of sight of Olschewski's business, and walked down the street. When they rounded the corner, Runnigan was pulling a spare tire out of his trunk. They were half a block away.

The three of them started toward him, as quietly as they could walk. But as Runnigan hoisted the tire and started around the car, he saw them out the corner of his eye. A look of alarm leaped into his eyes. Coal barked, "Hold it right there, Runnigan! Don't move."

And of course holding it was the last intention Runnigan had. Dropping the tire, he took off sprinting down the street.

With his gun still in its holster, Coal hit a long run behind Runnigan, leaving the other two quickly behind. The wind flew into his face, and his heart started pounding. Fresh, cold air pierced his lungs. It felt good to be alive.

Coal's sport in high school was rodeo—his main event, bulldogging. If he had to choose, it would always have been rodeo and bulldogging. But he also excelled at two others—boxing... and track. The second of the two they had come recruiting him for, because Coal was famous in Salmon for his ability to sprint, and his ability to pass any challenger at any distance up to half a mile. And there was no mile for Drew Runnigan to flee.

Down the block, Runnigan spotted an alley and tried to take it. But his bulky body didn't agree with the right angle turn he hoped for, and which his legs attempted. By the time he could slow his momentum enough to make the turn, Coal was vaulting through the air. Coal's two hundred fifty pounds struck Runnigan hard in the right shoulder, and Runnigan careened to the side, finally going down, with Coal on top of him. They were half a block away from Bob and Jim, but Bob was coming on fast as Runnigan and Coal rolled over and leaped to their feet.

Like a cornered animal fighting for its life, Runnigan's fists came up. He knew now it was impossible to flee. Without thinking, Runnigan went into pugilism mode. But Coal went into karate. The first swing by Runnigan Coal knocked aside with a middle block. It was not only the first, but the last swing Runnigan made.

Coal whirled and delivered a side kick to Runnigan's jaw. Even without Coal's heavy boots on, even had he been barefoot, it would not have mattered. There was no defense for Runnigan. The blow hit him before he even had time to think about reacting, and it knocked him sideways to the ground.

When Bob came huffing up, trying to catch his breath, Runnigan lay in a heap, and Coal stood there with his revolver drawn, looking down at him. The revolver would not be needed.

"Call an ambulance, Bob," said Coal, as he knelt down and clapped handcuffs on Runnigan, and silently, for his own satisfaction, said, "You have the right to remain silent."

When the ambulance arrived, it was Ronnie Davis by himself behind the wheel. His partner today, Jay Castillo, had walked straight over from the Coffee Shop. Jay looked up at Davis as he stopped beside him. "What do you need, Jay?"

"Get somebody to help you bring the cot. We got a broken jaw."

"What happened to him?" queried Davis, giving Coal an irritated look as he noticed him standing there.

"What happened to him?" repeated Jay Castillo, jerking a thumb at Coal as he stood up. "Coal Savage happened to him."

CHAPTER THIRTEEN

Coal left Drew Runnigan at the hospital under the guard of his friend Bob Wilson and went back to the office. He thought back on the face of the unconscious Runnigan, lying there with his jaw askew and an oral airway sticking out of his mouth. IV tubing ran out of his arm and up to a bag of lactated ringers. And Coal didn't feel one bit sorry for putting him in that condition.

At the same time, he couldn't stop thinking that Roger Miley, the only caregiver to little Sissy, had had something to do with the murders of his friends. He also couldn't help believing that, in spite of how badly he had wanted it, Paul Monahan didn't.

He went and pulled the .30/06 found on Monahan's property out of the evidence locker and gave it a careful inspection while wearing cloth gloves. They had dusted it for fingerprints and found none, but just to be on the safe side, he didn't feel like making his be the first. The rifle seemed sound. He loaded cartridges in it from his own supply, then worked the bolt five times and let them drop out on the desk. Nothing seemed to be mechanically wrong. The odd thing was it had a pretty plain four power Bushnell scope on it. Hardly an optic to be taking one thousand yard shots with. And besides, Coal hadn't been able to find a single person to tell him Bigfoot was even much into hunting, to say nothing of being an expert sharpshooter. There were very few men in the world who could make successful thousand yard shots on any kind of regular basis, and the murderer had made two. It just didn't stand to reason that this could be Monahan. Wouldn't *someone* have known if he was that kind of dead shot?

On a whim, Coal got out the phone book and looked up a number, then dialed up one of his father's old hunting buddies, who also happened to be the most famous gunman in Salmon, a fellow by the name of Elmer Keith. In fact, Keith was one of the most famous gunmen *anywhere.* He had helped develop not only the .357 magnum round, but also the .44 and .41 magnums. And he had written at least three books that Coal knew of on rifles and big game hunting. Keith was one man Coal could rely on to make a thousand yard shot if anyone around Salmon could.

Keith came right down to the jail as soon as he got Coal's call. He heard him thumping down the concrete stairs, and then Keith pounded on the door, it sounded like with the side of his fist. Coal bade him enter.

Into the room came a tough-looking man in his early seventies wearing a huge silver-belly cowboy hat, a "ten-gallon hat" if any piece of headgear ever fit the name, and a cigar about the size of a monkey's forearm sticking out of his mouth, giving his lips a comical sneer. On his right hip, he wore a Model 29 Smith and Wesson revolver, the bigger brother to Coal's Model 27.

"Coal Savage," greeted Keith. "It's been a few years, son. How the hell you been?"

Coal smiled and shook Keith's outstretched hand. "I've been good, Elmer. At least until I got back to Salmon."

"Yeah. Rough stuff. I've been meaning to come grab a cup of coffee with you, but it seems like every day there's something new. So how can I help you, anyhoo?"

"Well, I've got a rifle here that we found in a search of a suspect's property. Maybe you know him—Bigfoot Monahan?"

"Sure I know him," said Keith, tugging the cigar out of his mouth. "Big surly s.o.b. Hard to forget a mountain like that."

Coal chuckled. "Yeah, tell me about it. Anyway, Bigfoot swore back when we put him in the pen to kill me and several other people if he ever got out. He mentioned several names, and now three of them are dead—leaving just me and Jim Lockwood."

"Another surly bastard," said Keith with a chuckle. Coal knew he was joking. Jim and Elmer Keith were great friends and loved to rib each other over coffee—and sometimes something stronger.

"What folks don't know is that two of the killing shots were made from somewhere between nine hundred fifty to one thousand fifty yards out."

Elmer gave out with a long whistle. "Damn, son. That's some impressive shootin'. Not many folks hereabouts could do that."

"Including me," agreed Coal. "Not many folks *anywhere* could do that. I'd like you to take a look at the rifle."

He went and picked up the rifle and handed it to Keith. It appeared to have some kind of Czechoslovakian writing on the barrel, which had a big nick in the end of it. Keith inspected the weapon briefly. "A four power scope? And he made two killing shots at a thousand yards? Seems pretty preposterous."

"Could *you* make those shots?" Coal asked.

"Well, I can if anybody can," said Elmer with his typical humility. "But with a four power scope? Even I have my limits."

"Do you think we could take it out and you could try?"

"Huh? You serious?"

"Well, yeah. Sort of."

Elmer chuckled, stuffing the unlit monkey's forearm back in his mouth. He raised the rifle up and set the stock on his knee, looking it up and down. "Sure, why not. Let's go give her a try."

They took ear muffs and a case of cartridges loaded with 165 grain bullets to the car, along with the rifle, then drove out to the MacAtees'. "This is where the first shot was made."

"Yeah," said Keith. "Right before you got home, eh?"

"Yeah."

"How disturbin' will this be for the missus, son? She home?"

Coal looked over and saw Kathy MacAtee's car parked on the side of the house. "Yeah. Afraid so."

"Well, let's go talk to her. See what she says. I'm sure it won't be any less disturbing if we went to the Ericksons."

Kathy greeted Coal with a warm embrace when she opened the door to see him standing there. She also greeted Elmer and shook his hand, asking after the health of his wife, Lorraine. "Oh, that old gal will be shootin' prairie dogs fifty years after I'm pushin' daisies!" Elmer replied. Then he chuckled: "Or shootin' daisies fifty years after I'm pushin' up prairie dogs, as the case may be!"

Kathy laughed. "What can I do for you two? I assume you're not here for a friendly visit."

"Kathy, we found a rifle on the Monahans' place, hidden out in a freezer that was buried in the ground. A thirty ought-six."

Kathy's hand came to her mouth.

"Yeah."

"So it was him for sure. Did you get him, Coal?"

"He's in jail right now. But... Kathy, there's something wrong. A lot of somethings that just aren't adding up. So I brought Elmer out here to see if that old rifle we found can even make a shot like that. At first glance, it looks decent, well taken care of. But the more I've looked at it, the more I wonder."

"How can it be anyone else, though?" Kathy asked.

"I don't know. I wish I could tell you. I just have a bad gut feeling about all this. I can't talk about all the specifics of the case, but I know you'd understand if I told you everything. Is it okay if we try to take that shot?"

"Um... Sure, I guess." She looked over at the straw stack, then seemed to mentally line up where the shot had come from with the straw, then with her house. "Do I need to get the girls out of the house?"

Elmer chuckled, chewing on his long, fat cigar. "Ma'am, that rifle may not be able to hit what I'm shooting at, but don't you worry your pretty little head—it won't hit your house. I'll give you my hat if it does."

Everyone knew how proud Elmer was of his big hat. Kathy smiled. "Okay, Mister Keith. I trust you."

"Darn straight," he said with a big nod. "Thank you, good lady."

He and Coal went to the stack of straw, where Coal set up a big cardboard box from the barn. Then they drove out to the place from where the shot had been taken. Elmer got all set up and crouched on the ground. Even at seventy-three years of age, he seemed rock-steady. Coal waited in suspense. His ear muffs were high quality, so he would barely hear the shot. He simply waited to see the punch of the rifle against Elmer's shoulder.

Suddenly, Elmer rose from his shooting position, giving the rifle an odd look, and pulled off his ear muffs. Coal did likewise.

"What's wrong?"

"Not sure," replied Elmer. "But it didn't fire. Seems to be a slight problem—for a murder weapon."

"Huh?"

"It didn't fire, I'm tellin' you. I squeezed it off. Had a pretty decent sight picture, actually, even with that piss-poor scope. But nothing."

He jacked the cartridge out on the ground, and Coal reached down and picked it up, studying the firing pin. It actually didn't take much studying. There wasn't even a dent in the primer. He turned the butt end of the cartridge to Elmer, who glanced at it, then looked back at Coal.

Elmer popped the bolt out of the rifle and peered at it for a moment. "Coal, if this rifle made that shot—or *any* shot—then I'm a Christmas duck. The firing pin has been sheared clean off."

"What? Well... Could it have happened since the shots were made?"

"My first thought too, when I saw that primer. But nothing corrodes that fast, son. Take a look for yourself."

Coal hefted the bolt and glanced down inside the recess at the firing pin. It was broken off at least a sixteenth of an inch back. And what he could see of the end of it was covered in rust. An old break.

A cold feeling ran down Coal's spine, and slowly, he raised his eyes to Elmer. "It wasn't Monahan, was it?"

"Somebody went through a lot of work getting a rifle on his property, looks like to me. I guess they didn't stop to see if the rifle would fire. It would be pretty coincidental if he had another rifle somewhere that he used in the killings, I reckon. But not impossible, I reckon. I don't think I'd go running to let him loose on that evidence. Not yet."

Coal sighed. "Yeah, but that's not all. There's more."

On the way back to town, Coal decided to tell Elmer about the investigation. It wasn't the most professional thing he had ever done, but when it came to something like this he was pretty sure he could trust his father's old friend to keep things quiet. Even as much as Elmer Keith liked to talk, most of his talk was about his own prowess with firearms, especially now that he was in the twilight of his years. And Elmer was not the type to hang a friend out to dry by sharing what he had been told in confidentiality about a murder investigation.

By the time they reached the jail, Elmer had the entire story. And his active and agile mind also had some good suggestions. When Elmer had gotten back into his old car and driven off, Coal went to work acting on one of them immediately.

He had not seen the red and white Impala station wagon since the first time, so he could pursue nothing in that regard. But there was one thing he could do. He went down to the Battertons' house and across the street to the place K.T. had said the station wagon would park when its occupant watched the house. The gutter there was full of leaves and litter, and he dug through it piece by piece, working all the way from just in front of the house down to the corner, where the gutter ended. Every single piece of litter, which amounted to a couple of pop tops, an almost illegible receipt, and a few cigarette butts, he looked over carefully before leaving them in place. There was nothing else there. Nothing which could serve as a clue.

Back at the jail, he made a phone call, his heart pounding. Todd Mitchell responded to the call and came right down to the jail, hungry for the few hours' overtime Coal had offered him if he came in early.

Mitchell was furious when Coal lied to him to inform him that Judge Sinclair was doubtful they had enough evidence to hold Monahan. Coal calmed him down, then took him into his confidence. There was one more thing they might be able to do, he said. One thing that might give them a stronger edge in the case, which appeared to be all but slipping away from them now, since not one fingerprint could be found on the rifle. Coal asked Mitchell to go down by the Batterton house and to search the gutter across the street for any evidence he could find. There was but a slim chance this test would actually work, Coal knew, but it was a question that had to be answered.

Todd Mitchell left, and he was gone for what he must have felt was an appropriate amount of time for such a search. When he returned, he gave Coal a grim smile. "Well, it appears that the guy with the red station wagon must have been there watching K.T.'s house for a long time, Sheriff. I don't know what kind of power this will hold in court, but it may sway a jury." With that, he tipped his hand over on the desk, depositing in front of Coal an empty package of gum and four wrappers. The package was Carefree—

orange flavored. And all of the white paper wrappers smelled of orange.

CHAPTER FOURTEEN

Coal took a deep breath. For some reason, his heart was not hammering away inside him like he thought it would be. Sometimes, in moments like these, he found that his body reacted exactly the opposite of what the experts would predict. This was one of those moments.

Coal got up and walked around the desk until he was face to face with Mitchell. He looked long and hard at his deputy, and Mitchell did his best to meet his gaze. But his eyes kept flickering away. He knew something was wrong.

Finally, in a demanding voice, Mitchell asked, "What?"

Coal kept looking at him for a couple more seconds. Strangely, he felt a little sad. After his experiences with Mitchell, that surprised him. His feelings now must stem from how Mitchell had jumped, seemingly without fear, into the melee with Drew Runnigan, trying to save Roger Miley. It was not something Coal would have expected, considering Mitchell's sketchy past.

"It seems we've got a problem, Todd."

"A problem?"

"A problem," Coal repeated. "I need to see your gun."

Even as he spoke, Coal reached up and unsnapped the thong over his own Smith and Wesson's hammer. He rested his hand on the gun, ready to draw. The left hand he raised toward Mitchell, motioning with his fingers.

Mitchell was only two feet away. And he knew Coal Savage. He had seen him move—on the day when Mitchell ran the other way. The fact was, Mitchell had to know it was impossible for him to beat Coal—in any kind of fight.

Mitchell was starting to shake a little now, and a pale glow had come to his skin. He carefully reached down and unbuckled his revolver, lifting it out of the holster and placing it butt-first in Coal's hand. Coal felt his body relax as he flipped open the cylinder, let the cartridges spill out, then lay the gun among them on his desk.

"Was it you who put the rifle in Monahan's freezer, too, Todd?"

"Wait. What?" Mitchell's eyes took on a look of confusion, then grew big.

"Come on." Coal's voice was calm, even quiet. He would have thought at a moment like this he would be crowing triumphantly, glad to be rid of this thorn in his side. But he wasn't. "I know about the gum wrappers. You can stop the charade. I hardly know what to say to you right now, Todd. Do you suppose I should read you your rights?"

"Hey, I don't know what's going on," complained Mitchell.

"Shut the hell up," Coal growled, finally feeling some of the anger he had expected. "It's a felony to falsify evidence." Coal reached over and picked up the gum wrappers, holding them in his cupped right hand. One part of him almost hoped Mitchell would take advantage of the situation and try something. Take a swing at him. Anything. Anything to make this easier.

"Gum wrappers, Todd? You'd risk your whole career, your freedom, for *gum wrappers?"*

A sick look washed over Mitchell's face. He stared at Coal as if his eyes were glued there.

"So what about the rifle, Todd? I want the truth. Yours?"

"No."

"The truth, Todd. It can't get much worse."

"I didn't put that rifle there! I've never seen it before."

"How do I believe that? Give me something."

Mitchell abruptly sat down on the desk, now closer to his gun.

"You're not going to try something stupid, are you?" Coal motioned toward the gun with his eyes. "Although it would make this whole thing much easier on me if you did."

Mitchell looked down, saw the gun, and jumped away from it as if it were a rattlesnake, holding his hands out to the sides. "Hell, no! I won't try anything. I swear."

Coal picked up the Smith and Wesson and slid it behind his back, down inside his waistband. "Go ahead and sit back down."

Mitchell did so.

"Talk to me." Inside, Coal felt sick. When he saw how Mitchell had jumped into the middle of the fight with Roger Miley, he thought perhaps he was a changed man. Perhaps things were going to be all right between them, after all these years. Now there was no chance. There was something inside of Coal that kept suggesting maybe it was even Mitchell who had killed Larry, Trent, K.T. and Jennifer. That now he was trying to frame Bigfoot just to take all the attention away from himself. But he couldn't believe that. In the first place, he didn't think Todd could shoot all that well. "Go on, Todd. Tell me all of it. It's going to come out anyway."

When he began to speak at last, Mitchell's voice was soft, beaten. "We both know Bigfoot killed K.T. And Larry and Trent. And neither one of us is stupid enough to think he didn't kill Jen Batterton too." Tears suddenly rose into his eyes, and he took the Lord's name in vain, staring blankly at the floor.

"Go on, Todd."

Mitchell's chin started to quiver. "You know he did it, Sheriff. You have to know!"

"Do I?"

"He swore he would kill them, all except Jennifer. And he swore he'd kill you too, and he already took a couple shots at you. All right after he got out of the pen. You know he did it."

"And?"

"And you're gettin' soft. It's like you're trying to find ways to let him go. He *hates* you. Don't you know that? We've finally got him back behind bars. Sunk. He'll get convicted if we let it all ride. Why would you try to stop that?"

"What about the rifle?" Coal repeated. "Is that yours?"

"Damnit!" Mitchell growled. "I told you I've never seen that! It's *his!*"

With a deep breath, Coal said, "I went down and scoured that gutter for evidence before I sent you down there, Todd. You come back with gum wrappers that weren't there an hour ago. You try to convict a man on planted gum wrappers, how can I trust anything else you say? Let that sink in for a bit."

"I couldn't stand to see him get away. I just had to hope it would be enough."

"So you went and paid a nickel and bought some gum, threw down a couple sticks of it at the Battertons', then a couple of wrappers across the street. You're going to go to prison, Todd. It's a ten thousand dollar fine and five years in prison for falsifying evidence. Man, for ten cents? What were you thinking?"

Some of the color had been coming back into Mitchell's face, but once again it went white. Tears dimmed his eyes. "I guess... I wasn't."

Coal waited. He waited for Mitchell to beg and plead like the old Todd Mitchell would have. He waited for him to whine and get on his knees, asking Coal to let him go, "just this once." But he didn't. Finally, he just started taking things out of his pockets and putting them on the desk. His hands were shaking. He set his hat down, took off his gunbelt and holster, put up his feet, one at a time, and took off his boots, pulling a knife out of a sheath that was sewn to the inside of one of them. Last of all, he set his wallet down next to the other stuff, resting his fingers on top of it for a moment.

"Can I call my wife?"

Coal wanted Mitchell to fight him. He wanted him to curse him. To scream. To throw a tantrum. Anything but this calmness. But there was no help for either of them. He only nodded, then walked to the window and stared out at the parking lot. He tried not to listen to the low sound of Todd's voice as he spoke with his wife, a very short conversation, and then hung up with a quiet click.

Turning, he indicated the direction of the cell block with a tilt of his chin.

Mitchell marched there slowly, and he opened the door himself. Coal picked up the ring of keys as he went by the cell block door. Once inside, with Bigfoot Monahan staring them both down, Coal said, "Pick your poison."

Mitchell glanced down the line of five cells, finally choosing the one farthest down, as far away from Monahan as he could get. He went in and shut the door after himself, and Coal locked it tight.

Coal couldn't even speak now. He turned to go, and Mitchell's shaky voice stopped him. "Sheriff?" He walked closer. "I'm sorry about all this. I let you down."

Again, Coal could only nod. His eyes flew to Bigfoot Monahan, and their gazes held for a couple of seconds. Then Coal turned and marched out, praying to catch his breath.

He sat down at the desk and stared at Mitchell's belongings. He had no deputy now. He was all alone to run the entire county of Lemhi.

Coal sat there for a long time, then at last got his senses about him. He got up and prepared everything he could, gathering Bigfoot Monahan's belongings, getting out the inventory of anything they had taken from him upon his incarceration. He wanted this to be fast.

Then he walked back into the cell block, trying hard not to look at Mitchell, even out the corner of his eye. He strode to Bigfoot's cell and unlocked it, thinking about how they had ruined Monahan's Thanksgiving celebration. When the big man just sat there on his bunk, staring, Coal said, "Come on, let's go."

"What? What're you doin'?"

"Let's go, Monahan. I don't have all day."

Monahan loomed up off the bunk, looking like a huge black troll in the dim light of his cell. He stared suspiciously at Coal. After a moment, he looked down the way at his new cellblock mate. Mitchell lay on the bunk with an arm covering his eyes.

Monahan edged to the door. Coal stood there holding it. Monahan sidled past him, watching him with wary eyes. Finally, he was free of the doorway, and he walked to the door that led into the main office. Coal came behind him, and he followed him into the other room.

"Take the coveralls off, Monahan. Get your clothes on and get your stuff. You're going home."

Monahan had a strange look in his eyes. A look of suspicion mixed with wonder. He fumbled with the zipper on the coveralls, then stripped them down to the floor, leaving him standing there in boxer shorts, his wide chest covered in a mat of long, blackish-red hair. Hurriedly, as if to get dressed before Coal could change his mind, he pulled on his pants, then his shirt, and last, he sat down on a nearby chair to tug his boots on his feet.

Coal finally forced himself to look at the big man. There was a look of hope in Monahan's eyes, but it vanished the second he knew Coal was watching him.

"Just so you know, all the charges against you are gone," said Coal. "Dropped. You're free, as long as you keep yourself clean."

"I don't get it." Bigfoot's pale blue eyes came up to meet Coal's. "Why you doin' this?"

"That rifle we found doesn't shoot," Coal explained. "The firing pin is broken. And it has been for a long time. Somebody was trying to frame you. Apparently, they bought a rifle and forgot to check if it even worked. My guess, anyway."

Bigfoot stood up. Dead shock filled his eyes. "But... why?"

"Why anything?" asked Coal. "Somebody covering their tracks, I suppose."

"Why me?"

"Because you were the obvious choice. If you had gotten out of the pen two months from now, none of this would have ever happened to you."

Coal drove Paul Monahan home, not as a criminal, in the back, but as a passenger. He had an eerie feeling with the big man sitting on the seat beside him. But he couldn't very well justify putting him in the back now.

Nine miles out of town, he pulled the car right up to Monahan's front porch, and soon the door opened, and the little Yorkie came running out, yapping. It ran straight to Bigfoot as he got out of the car, and he reached down and picked it up, holding its squirming little body as it struggled to lick his face.

On the front porch, Beverly Monahan stood crying, her hand over her mouth. Butch was beside her, staring at his dad, trying to comprehend what was happening. Monahan didn't even give Coal a backward glance. He simply climbed the concrete steps and pushed his wife and son inside, then ducked under the doorframe, disappearing after them. Coal had climbed out of his side of the car, but after that, he didn't move. He just stood watching Monahan go.

He was still standing there after the door closed, just about to climb back in the car, when the front door opened again, and there stood Monahan, half his huge body revealed past the door. The big man's eyes met his, and one tough man stared at the other. A look in Monahan's face said that he was trying to find words to speak, but he couldn't. Finally, he just stepped back inside, and the door shut with flat finality.

Coal drove back to town thinking about Bigfoot, about all his friends who had died, and about Todd Mitchell. The more he thought about the situation, the more he wondered if Mitchell was telling him the truth. Coal's life experiences had not given him any trust in people. It was sad, in a way, but at least it protected him against being hurt. Right now, his inner thoughts were screaming one thing at him: DON'T TRUST TODD MITCHELL.

Coal thought about what he would have told someone if they had caught him for doing something stupid like planting gum wrappers at a crime scene when in reality he had planted something far more incriminating: a .30-06 rifle. Coal's head rang. His mind called out a warning. Was Mitchell really the killer? Could he truly make those shots? Coal had no idea. He realized suddenly that he had never seen Mitchell shoot a rifle.

The only thing he knew about Mitchell for sure was that the night he took down Bigfoot Monahan on a warrant for manslaughter, he saw Mitchell sneaking off the other way. Leaving to what he must have thought was sure death a man who was not even a fellow officer. A man who had simply come back to town on leave and was doing the sheriff and his deputy a favor by going after Bigfoot when he could as easily have gone home to be with his family. At the time, Mitchell was only a part-time deputy, because Jim Lockwood was still sheriff and he had K.T. Batterton to back him. But part-time or not, the fact was he had left another man to face the wrath of Bigfoot Monahan alone, when it was he who carried a badge and a gun, he who had sworn to uphold the law.

Coal tried to think of a motive. He couldn't. What motive *could* Mitchell have? What motive could anyone have? Could it be that he had only wanted K.T. and Coal dead, so he could take over the sheriff's job again, and the others had had to die just so he could blame the entire thing on Bigfoot Monahan? That seemed extremely far-fetched. But he had heard of stranger things.

He was driving back into town when he saw a vehicle pull up to the stop sign at South Church and turn onto Main, heading in the direction of the Salmon River. The car was a block away, but the distance was minimal. Not nearly enough to hide the fact that it was a red station wagon with a white top!

Coal gunned the LTD, fumbling for his blue light and putting it up on the dash, turning it on. The car sped up ahead of him as he yanked the mic loose and called dispatch and told them he was in a pursuit. He dropped the mic in his lap as he flew over the bridge. He expected the station wagon to head up Courthouse Drive, but to his surprise it turned right after the bridge and screamed up Highway 93 toward Carmen, with Coal in hot pursuit.

Coal slammed his booted foot down on the throttle, coming closer and closer to the station wagon, and now sure it was a Parkwood. What he had under this hood, a Boss 429 engine, was making a joke of whatever the Chevy came equipped with.

Even before they reached Carmen, Coal's LTD was screaming up beside the Parkwood, and he veered toward it, causing it to run off the road into the grass. As he slammed on his brakes and looked back, he saw the Parkwood come to a stop, and he threw his car into park and leaped out, drawing his revolver.

In his excitement, he forgot to even tell dispatch he had run down the car.

Coal walked slowly back toward the Chevrolet. His revolver was up and ready, and he moved with his right side toward the station wagon, trying to keep his silhouette as slender as possible.

The door of the Parkwood flew open suddenly, and the form of a man came out and fell to his knees. He got up and stumbled sideways, throwing his arms in the air as Coal yelled out, in his best MP voice, "FREEZE!"

The man's arms stayed bolt upright as Coal closed the last twenty feet to him. "Turn around, slow," growled Coal. "I guess I should tell you I forgot to call for backup. So nobody's going to be here to see me put a bullet in the back of your head."

"*What?* Hey, man!" the Chevy man screamed. "I'm beggin' you, don't shoot! Buddy, I ain't done nothin'! For hell's sake, come on."

Coal got close and kicked the man in the back with the bottom of his boot, shoving him onto his face in the tall grass. "Get your hands behind your back!"

The man whipped his hands behind him, and Coal thrust his handcuffs over his wrists with no attempt to be gentle. Having done so, he growled again, "Now get up!" and with his left hand grabbed hold of the man's upper left arm and helped him lurch to his feet. With the momentum of his rise, he ran him forward, throwing him hard over the hood of the Parkwood.

"Any weapons on you?" Coal asked.

"No, man!" wailed Chevy man, his face shoved up tight against the hood so he had a hard time making himself sound human.

"What's your name?"

"They call me Pinky," said the man. "Pinky Cruze."

"I don't care what they call you!" Coal spat off to one side. "What's your *name?*"

"Trevor. Trevor Cruze."

"All right... *Pinky.* Start talking, and talk fast. What do you know about Larry MacAtee?"

"Huh?"

"Larry MacAtee!"

"Never heard of him."

Coal slammed the back of the man's head so hard his face seemed to sink into the heavy metal of the hood.

"Ahh! Hey, man, take it easy."

"Larry MacAtee!" Coal yelled again.

"Okay, yeah. MacAtee. I know the name."

"Tell me about it."

"Uhh..." He hesitated too long, and Coal shoved his face harder against the hood.

"Talk!"

"He's the guy that got killed, right?"

"Yeah. You know. How about Trent Tuckett?"

"Officer, I ain't never heard that name eith—"

Coal grabbed the man's hair and lifted his head, slamming his face into the hood. "I'm going to beat every tooth out of your head if I hear another lie out of you, Pinky. Trent Tuckett!"

"Yeah. He got killed too."

"Let's talk about the Battertons now."

"Hey, why you doin' this, man?" Pinky Cruze whined. "Why you hurtin' me?"

Coal grabbed his arm and rolled him over so he was now on top of his bound wrists, a very painful position. He stared up at his tormentor. His lips were crushed, and blood started oozing both ways down the sides of his face. "You tell me, you slime ball. Why were you casing the Batterton house? Huh? Spit it out fast!"

Resignation ran over the man's face. "Hey, man, don't hit me again. I'll tell you. Please just stop."

Coal lowered the bore of the magnum to the man's throat. He was doing everything he knew he shouldn't be. Everything all his training told him not to. But no one who has never been in a high-speed chase can understand the adrenalin that fills a man's blood stream when he has. No one who has never had friends killed—murdered—should ever be able to blame a man who has when he loses control. At least that was what he told himself.

"Start talking, mister. I've got a worthless old Saturday night special in my car, and it's going to be found on your dead body by the time anyone else gets here if you even think about lying to me."

The man was shaking all over. "Okay, man. Relax! I said okay. A friend of mine came into town a month or so ago. I don't know, maybe it's been a month and a half. Came to see if I'd help him with somethin'. Brother, I had no idea what it was. All I know is I got laid off work, I didn't have hardly a dime to buy bread and peanut butter, and all of a sudden here's this friend tellin' me I can make some dough if I just do a couple little things. Nothin' illegal, though. I swear I ain't never broke no laws."

"What little things?" Coal was a little calmer, but he didn't let on to Pinky.

"I was supposed to follow some people, see what kind of things they did. Where they went. Who they visited. I had to keep a log of every move they made. Sometimes this friend of mine would call me, and if I had enough, I'd go meet him down by Pahsimeroi Road, and he'd get the stuff from me."

"So what was he doing with it?"

"He had some other guy payin' him to provide all that. He never said who it was, or even why. Said he was real dangerous, and he couldn't talk about it. That's all I know. He was payin' me five dollars a day, man, and that's all I cared about."

"But you knew what he was doing with all the information."

The man let out a sob. "Well, I didn't at first. I had no idea, I swear. They didn't start gettin' killed until my friend quit callin' me."

"Bull! You were still casing the Batterton place after the first two murders."

Pinky took a deep breath, and it made a chattering sound as it came back out of him. He shook his head resignedly, and his eyes fell away from Coal's. "Okay. Yeah."

"What does the name Todd Mitchell mean to you?" Coal asked suddenly.

"Todd Mitchell? That's your deputy—right?"

"Sure is. He's the man who was paying you and your friend."

Pinky stared at Coal for a few seconds, then let out a laugh. He looked at Coal again. "Wait. You're serious!"

"I am."

"He wasn't the guy! You're crazy!"

"How do you know it wasn't him?"

"Because Mitchell was always harassing me, pestering me. He would have loved to have me out of town, if he could have, or even in jail, ever since I lost my job. Besides, the man payin' my friend lived over around Challis somewhere."

Coal nodded. That was the first decent lead he had gotten from this man yet. He filed the information away.

"Where in Challis?"

"I wish I could tell you. You'd have to ask my friend."

"Okay. Tell me his name," ordered Coal. He already knew who it was, but he wanted to hear Pinky say it.

"Ah, come on, man! I can't! He trusts me. And what kind of friend would I be then?"

"Okay. What if I tell you it doesn't matter? He's dead."

"Huh?"

"You ever pay any attention to the news? Read the paper? Watch TV?"

"Yeah, right! I barely have enough money to eat. I hawked my TV three months ago, and I sure don't spend good money on newspapers."

"Well, if you did you would know your friend Roger is dead."

"What?" The man tried to rise, his eyes leaping open in surprise. He sank slowly back down on the hood when he felt the pressure of the .357 barrel against his throat. "Rog is dead?"

"He is."

"Wha— How?"

"How do you think?" asked Coal, suddenly feeling devious. "The guy who was paying the two of you for all that information must have got scared. Decided Roger was a liability."

"No!" Pinky practically screamed. "No way, brother! Roger never would have said a thing! He was— He had a little girl he was tryin' to watch after—his brother's daughter. He would never have told. Ah, man. Please tell me this ain't true."

"How'd you know Roger Miley?" asked Coal.

"Man, we worked together at the Blackbird Mine. Got laid off the same day. They said they was lettin' a dozen of us go for the winter. Like we could just eat snow 'til they needed us again."

"Things are tough," agreed Coal, his voice softening. "Well, just so you know, that last part wasn't true."

"Huh? Rog is still alive?"

"No, I'm sorry. He's dead. But he was killed by a local man who was mad that he poached a bighorn sheep last week."

"No way! Some guy killed him for a damn sheep?"

"It was a little more complicated than that, but yeah, I'm afraid that was the catalyst."

"My hell, Sheriff. This world ain't a fair place."

"You've got that right."

The man sank back again, closing his eyes. "Am I under arrest?" he asked, looking up.

"For what?"

"I don't know. Runnin' from you?"

Coal chuckled. "How can you claim anything that pathetic wagon did was running? You just gave my Ford a workout, that's all. Where are you living now, Pinky?"

"Up on the Bar, on Fairmont. But not much longer. I paid two months ahead for rent, but that's gonna run out soon."

"So if I need you, you're not going to be around, are you?"

"I don't know how I can stay, man. I gotta head to the Falls and look for a job before my gas money runs out too."

Coal couldn't explain why he thought it was funny to say, but somehow he did: "Well, maybe if you get to the Falls they can give you a job at the temple." He was referring to the Idaho Falls LDS temple, where the Latter Day Saints went to perform their special ceremonies and no unworthy member—which most certainly included Pinky, if he was a member at all—would be allowed.

"Real funny," said Pinky. Then he managed to actually let out a chuckle, more a sound of relief than of humor. "So what if I ain't there when you need me? The judge issues a warrant?"

"I doubt I'll need you. But let's take down your social security number and date of birth, just in case. Then when you get settled, get hold of me with your contact information. Otherwise, yes, there may be a warrant issued." Coal took out a pen and wrote Pinky's information down on the palm of his left hand. Then he looked at the far side of the Parkwood, which was tangled up in a stretch of barbed wire it had taken out when he careened off the road. "You'd better get rolling. Before this farmer sees what you did to his fence."

With that, he backed away and made Pinky turn around, so he could remove his handcuffs. Then he watched him dab at his battered lips as he limped to the driver's door, climbed into the Chevy and started it up. It took some backing and going forward in the tall grass and dirt, but finally he got his back tires onto the pavement. Then, without much effort, he backed it around and headed toward town. The car, like its owner, seemed to be limping.

CHAPTER FIFTEEN

After contacting the farmer about his damaged fence and leaving a card and his promise that the county would pay for repairs, Coal drove slowly back to town. It was somewhere around three-thirty. His thoughts whirled around everything Pinky Cruze had told him. Five minutes into the drive, he mechanically reached out and turned on the radio. The first song coming out of the speakers was announced as being by Johnny Nash, a colored singer who had been around a while but about whom Coal knew next to nothing. For the first little bit, the song barely registered on him.

Then he heard the words, "I can see clearly now—the rain is gone. I can see all obstacles in my way." One side of Coal's mouth ticked up in a wry smile. For him, things couldn't be much muddier.

When he got back to the office and called Flo Hawkins, the woman who usually acted as dispatcher and answered the phones and radio traffic during the day from her house but who had been off for the past week, she told him he had a message. It was from Paul Matthews, sheriff of Custer County, where Challis was the county seat.

He didn't say much, Flo told him. *Just said to call him, and it was urgent.*

Coal hung up and immediately dialed Matthews.

Coal Savage! came the voice on the other end of the line. *Welcome home and congratulations on the job.*

"Thanks, Paul," said Coal. "It's great to be back." Paul Matthews and Coal's father, Prince, had been good friends and had hunted chukars along Morgan Creek, near Challis, for years before his father's best hunting dog, a white setter speckled with black, bred in France and known as a Braque D'Auvergne, died unexpectedly of what appeared to be a heart attack. The hunting of chukar partridge had died with the dog, for there was too much sadness in the pursuit.

"So my dispatcher tells me you left a message."

Yeah, Coal. Some strange stuff. I've been keeping notes, and I thought you ought to be made aware of this. There's some fellow hanging around town here asking a lot of questions, according to friends of mine down at Bux's Place. The establishment Matthews referred to was one of Challis's most famous landmarks, a local bar and grill. *Some of his questions are about you.*

"What kind of questions?"

Well, we can round up a few of these old boys and you can talk to them about that if you want. The thing is, though, that folks started really clamming up around this guy after a while. At first, it was pretty obvious he was a local, so nobody much minded him. But he was just asking weird stuff about people in Salmon, mostly. Who was left there from way back when, where they worked—you know, stuff like that. Stuff you'd think he'd just drive on into Salmon and ask about if he really wanted to know. Then he hooked up with this weird little guy we had living around here for a while, and he just kind of disappeared, so I didn't think anything more about it.

"Is he still gone?"

No, Coal, that's the thing. That's why I thought I should call you. That weird little guy I was telling you about just showed up in the paper—dead. And then this stranger shows back up in town.

A chill passed over Coal. "Do you know this other guy's name? The dead one?"

Sure. Roger Miley.

Coal was not surprised. He would have been surprised, in fact, had it been any other name. "Can you pick this man up for anything, Paul?"

A long pause, then a scratchy chuckle across bad phone line. *This is Challis, Idaho, Coal. But it's not the Wild West. I'll do whatever I can.*

Before hanging up, Coal got Paul Matthews to give him a description of the stranger, in detail. He was six feet tall, muscular but lean, his cheeks sunken in, jaw bulging with muscle. He wore sandy blond hair hanging shaggy partway over his ears and a beard so patchy it seemed a sin to call it a beard, and generally he wore a camouflage jacket, Levi's 501 jeans, and hiking boots, with an olive drab baseball cap. He drove a root beer brown 1968 Mercury Cougar X-R7. It bore what appeared to be Washington state plates, but no one had been able to get the number because it was usually smeared with mud.

Coal stared out the window and drummed a pencil on the desk, watching people in the parking lot as they came and went from their vehicles, preparing to go home for the weekend. He tried to envision the face of the man Sheriff Matthews had described to him. It could match dozens of Challis and Salmon residents. Or it could match none. Ex-military? That much seemed likely. Other clues? None, not beyond the fact that he had the speech patterns of a local, and he knew local landmarks, people, and establishments.

The biggest clue was obvious. Challis was home to just over seven hundred people, pushing eight. Paul Matthews had been the sheriff for years, a deputy for years prior to that, and he had lived there his entire life. After some sixty years of residency in Custer County, Matthews did not know the man who drove the brown Cougar, and that meant one thing to Coal.

The man in the Cougar was from Salmon.

* * *

Coal needed to think. And he needed help. He had no K.T. Batterton anymore. He had only old Jim Lockwood, who was supposed to be retired, and big Jordan Peterson, who had never even been through the police academy yet and was about as green as they come. Completely untested, other than the tame arrest of Bigfoot Monahan.

Coal gritted his teeth and swore. As much as he hated to admit it, the man Coal needed was Todd Mitchell. And now the man was a criminal.

There was no one yet who knew about Mitchell, about what he had done. He had not filed any paperwork, surely against policy—even whatever weak policies Lemhi County would have in place, which he had yet to read through because from the beginning there were just too many things more important to take care of. He had had the papers in hand, ready to take before the judge. But for some reason he had hung onto them. Maybe it would get him fired. At the very least, it would cause him to have to do an awful lot of explaining. And still he held onto them. Why? Only he could know, yet even he did not.

The phone rang, and Coal picked it up reluctantly.

"Sheriff."

You may as well sound official with me, Son, as often as I see you anymore.

Coal winced. "Hi, Mom."

Hi. Say, do you remember having some little people you left here at the house with me? I think they remember you—at least barely.

"Mom, I've had me a day. Boy howdy!" He tried to lighten the mood by quoting one of his favorite television characters, Heath Barkley, from a now-off the air Western called *The Big Valley.*

Connie was not amused. *Nice, Heath. So have we. A real day. Funny, we thought the dogs were lost, but they showed up mysteriously later.*

"Yeah. Sorry I didn't have time to stop."

Have you even eaten yet? she asked.

"Uhh... No, I guess I haven't, not since before I left."

And you're supposed to be some kind of bodybuilder? I thought you had to eat every few hours.

"Ha. Yeah, well, it's not like I've had time to throw any iron around a gym lately, is it? Mom, I'll come home soon. But I really need to take a drive first."

A pregnant pause. Disappointment wove among the static on the line. *You usually do. I'm sad, Coal.*

"Don't be sad," Coal said with as much pleading in his voice as he could muster. "This will all be over soon. Then we can have some family time. I promise."

For Christmas, you mean?

"Stop it. It won't be that long."

I don't think you can make that promise anymore.

A thought struck Coal, and he took a deep breath. His mother had always been there for him if ever he got the nerve to ask her to talk. Maybe he needed her now.

"Hey, if I come right now and pick you up, can you go for a drive with me?"

The same pause, now mingled with a feeling of hope. *Sure, Son, if that's what you'd like.*

"It is. I've got to get your opinion on something."

Coal locked up the jail after checking on Todd Mitchell, then drove straight home, hardly seeing the familiar, close-packed businesses as he rolled past on the quiet gray street. He was going to pick up his mother, and he was about to commit a serious breach of legal etiquette. But right now he didn't care. Sometimes there was no one in the world but a man's mother who could understand what he needed to say.

Leaving the kids with a promise to be back within an hour, Coal got Connie in the car, and they drove south toward Leadore.

On the way, they passed Bigfoot Monahan's house. It was not until there that Coal was able to push himself to speak.

"Mom, I've got a big dilemma."

"You mean one I don't know about?"

"Well, at least one." He tried to smile.

"I'm good with dilemmas," she said, reaching out to squeeze his arm.

Taking a deep breath, Coal sighed most of it back out, then clenched his jaw. With a strange feeling in the pit of his stomach, he began to tell her about Todd Mitchell, Bigfoot Monahan, and pretty much every bit of the case that had led him to where he was today.

"You're not supposed to talk about an investigation with anyone who isn't involved, are you, Coal?" Although this was worded as a question, it was more of a statement. And a little late, too, since he had already spilled the entire case in her lap.

"No, I'm not. Some places would probably fire me for what I just did."

"That's how I know how important it was for you to tell me."

Coal gave a close-mouthed smile and a little nod.

Connie watched the highway for a moment. Evening's gray had fallen over all the world around them, and only the majestic Beaverheads were swathed in the sunlight's golden beauty. The crystal-clear sky seemed to crackle with icy cold.

"I'm still digesting this new idea that Paul Monahan isn't the murderer."

Coal nodded. "You and me both."

"Perhaps your deputy couldn't come to grips with this idea either, Son."

"Well, maybe."

After a pause, "Are you thinking he might be the killer?"

Coal raised a hand and rubbed his lower lip. He brushed at his mustache. "It sure crossed my mind. What man would want to blame an innocent man of a crime more than the one who's really guilty?"

"That's true, I suppose." A long moment of silence. "Do you want to know my gut feeling?"

"I don't know, do I?"

A patient smile. "Yes, you do. Coal, I think your deputy has seen a lot of guilty men walk free. Our court system is often very imperfect. I think you have seen that too. My inner self is telling me that everything you have seen and been told is the truth. Your deputy was trying to help out the case the only way he knew how."

Coal frowned. "By committing a felony," he said flatly.

"By any means he knew how. After all, every one of you was convinced that Mr. Monahan was guilty. Are you saying you would have let him go free on a technicality if you could find some way to stop it?"

The radio was playing in the background, playing almost soundlessly. But suddenly the distant sound of the music seemed to jump out of the radio speakers into Coal's ears, and a chill washed over him like a January ocean wave. For the second time in as many hours, they were playing Johnny Nash, and the words, although muffled, came clear to Coal's ears: *I can see clearly now; the rain is gone....*

Coal's thoughts raced back, back to the moment up on Stormy Peak Road when he had held his rifle in his hands, and upon every cartridge he slid into its magazine he had mentally scratched the name of Bigfoot Monahan. Here Coal was, ready to take away Todd Mitchell's entire way of making a living and send him to prison for falsifying evidence, when not so long ago he himself had been set to murder Bigfoot Monahan in cold blood! He had never felt like a bigger hypocrite than at this moment. But sadly, this was something only he could ever know. He could never admit even to his mother how willing he had become to take another man's life.

"Mom, you're right. You're totally right."

She reached over and squeezed his hand. "It's good to be right for a change. You ready to go home?"

"I have to go talk to Todd."

"But, Son, you promised..." She paused. Then she sighed and said flatly, "No. No, this time you're right. You need to go talk to him."

And so they returned to the house, where Coal dropped Connie off, then drove back down to the highway and headed into town. On the way, he pondered on who the real killer might be. Who had reason to kill those who had recently died? Obviously, the answer lay with the mysterious man Paul Matthews had told him about. But even with that thought in mind, Coal had to make one more stop before going to the jail.

He drove up on the Bar, made four turns, and stopped just shy of a shabby looking pale green house on Lincoln Street. At the curb in front was parked a beat-up white Ford station wagon, and various disabled or disowned toys littered a lawn that consisted of more dirt than grass. A streetlight not far away was kind to the residence, for it shone on it only dimly, through the skeletal branches of a dying box elder tree.

Coal gave a sigh and stepped out. The sidewalk here was as broken and neglected as the sun-faded toys. An elm tree hung over it, many times chopped at the base, giving it more the form of a big, obnoxious bush than a tree. He walked past and went to knock on the door.

A racket of arguing kids stopped suddenly, and in a few moments a voice came from inside. "Who's there?"

"Mrs. Mitchell? It's Sheriff Savage, ma'am."

Long silence. The smell of rancid grease and cigarette smoke, used kitty litter and frying bacon came sliding out of every crack under and around the door. Nauseating.

Finally, foot falls. Then the opening door made a cracking sound, and the unkempt face of a woman with stringy blond hair poked through the slot that appeared. "Yeah?" The voice was leery. Not unfriendly, yet not welcoming.

"Can I talk to you for a minute?" Coal almost hoped she would say no, so he wouldn't face any closer assault of the smells seeping out of the run-down house.

"I don't see why, really," she said.

"I'm not sure I do either," Coal said after a moment. "But maybe you can help your husband if you do."

She tried to search his eyes, but whatever past that had beaten this woman down made her drop her gaze to his black boots. She paused, and a cat yowled back deep in the cave of the house. A stiff breeze nudged at an untrimmed elm branch and made it scratch against the window pane to Coal's right.

"It's sure cold out here, ma'am."

"Yeah. I reckon so. Come in. But I haven't had time to clean up yet."

Coal pursed his lips and nodded, sweeping off his hat. "Not a problem." But it *was* a problem. The problem was she hadn't had time to clean up in months, at least—neither the house nor herself. And soon he saw in the faces staring from the shadows of another room that the same thing applied to at least three smudgy children aged from three to six.

"You want to sit?" asked Todd Mitchell's wife.

Coal cringed. "Uh, no thanks, ma'am. I won't take too long." In truth, he had no idea how long he would be, but sitting in any chair this house had to offer made him think he was likely going to have to throw away his brand-new Wranglers.

The children kept staring. Coal could see bacon sitting in a bath of grease in a bumpy black cast iron pan. "Didn't mean to interrupt your dinner."

The woman laughed, not a pleasant sound. "Not much dinner," she confessed. "Bacon. Bread's almost gone."

Coal swept the kitchen with his eyes. An empty Jiff peanut butter container stood sentinel on the counter near the fridge, two or three flies crawling in and out of its mouth. A potato chip bag lay on the floor under a table covered in faded red Formica. The floor was stained by a thousand untended spills. One cupboard door stood open. There was nothing inside.

"What do you need, Sheriff?" The woman had seen his eyes glancing about the room. Her pride, what little she might have, overcame her.

"I need to know more about Todd, ma'am."

"Like what? Like he don't have a job?"

"That part I know," he said softly.

She scoffed. "Of course you do."

"Of course," he repeated. "Say, why don't you let the kids in? Cold bacon's no good."

"Kids, come and eat this," she said over her shoulder without looking toward the three dirty children Connie would have referred to as "urchins." There was no scrambling, as Coal half-expected. The three children walked in slowly, single-file, and the first one, a boy, tentatively took two strips of bacon right out of the cooling grease. He put the end of one in his mouth, started to walk away with the other, then looked down at his dirty little brother. Finally, he handed the second slice to the little guy, then took two more, keeping one for himself and giving the little boy the other. The third child, also a boy, took two of his own, and that left nothing swimming in the thick warm grease.

"Why you here, Sheriff?" the woman asked again. "You ain't done enough damage? I'm not going to tell you anything about Todd to get him in worse trouble than he already is."

"Did he tell you what kind of trouble he's in?" Coal asked bluntly.

"Sure. He's fired and sitting in jail. What could be much worse?"

"Ma'am, I don't think you understand. Todd is looking at prison time if he's convicted for what he did. Maybe a big fine, too."

After a moment of shocked silence, the woman laughed again and looked around the house. "They won't get a lot, will they? Maybe they can have his old underwear."

Coal ignored that. "Did your husband kill anyone?"

"What? Are you crazy?"

"Somebody has killed four people in this town."

"Yeah, by the name of Bigfoot Monahan."

"It wasn't Bigfoot."

"That's not what Todd told me!"

"No, I'm sure not. He thought it was Bigfoot. Everyone thought it was."

The woman stared. Coal stifled a sneeze. The dust in the house was tickling his nose. He hated thinking he was breathing any of this into his lungs.

"Todd's in bigger trouble than he's ever been in, ma'am. If you know anything about all this, you'd better talk. He could be implicated for murder." Coal didn't really think this was true. But he simply had to get this woman to talk, if she would.

The oldest boy came over and leaned against his mother. She had been staring at the floor, chewing on the knuckle of her thumb. Tears came into her eyes, and she looked down at her son, who put one arm around her waist. "It'll be okay, Bub," she said softly. "I don't know what to do, Sheriff." She looked back up at Coal, tried to force herself to meet his gaze. Dropped her eyes.

"Just tell me the truth. Anything might help."

The woman turned abruptly away, leaving her son standing in the middle of the room. With fast steps, she went to the kitchen sink and raised her hands to support herself. Her shoulders shook briefly, then she raised her hands and wiped at her eyes. She spoke as if she were talking to her darkened reflection in the window.

"Todd didn't want you to come to Salmon," the woman said.

"I know."

She lowered her chin, making her next words come out in a mumble. "Then... When he got working for you for a while, he kind of started to change. Finally, one night he told me you were a good man, and he was glad you were the sheriff. Todd don't say things like that very much."

Coal just stood there. Knowing what to say to those words was well beyond his capability. He was stunned.

Finally, the woman turned back around, realizing Coal wasn't going to reply. She wrung her hands fiercely in front of her, contending with her own conscience. "Todd found out that Bigfoot fella liked orange Carefree gum. He told me he had to find some way you all could prove he did the killings. Said you all knew it, but you couldn't find the proof. Said you was too law-abiding to ever do anything wrong, and you would never go along with it, but he wanted to help you. He said if he didn't do something to keep Bigfoot in jail, you might be next to get killed."

"What if it really wasn't Bigfoot?" he asked.

"Todd never said nothing about that. He said you were all sure. That there was no way in the world it wasn't him. He told me what he was doing was risky, that he could lose his job and the respect of everyone at the sheriff's office. But that he couldn't live with himself if he didn't do something and Bigfoot got out and killed you."

"Why would he care?"

The woman brought up a hand and swept it back over her unkempt hair. "He told me he didn't want to be sheriff anymore. He said nobody would elect him anyway. He wanted you to be his sheriff. He said he thought everything between you could be fixed now."

Coal just stared. It was so hard for him to wrap his mind around all of this, considering how things had been before with Todd. At last, the woman raised her eyes to him. They were blood-shot. This time she held his gaze. "What was between you, Sheriff?

"It was a long time ago," Coal replied, then lied: "I don't even remember now."

Coal left the quiet house and went to the IGA, down at the bottom of Courthouse Drive. He returned to the Mitchell house with three loaves of bread, a jar of peanut butter and a case of Chef Boyardee spaghetti and meatballs. Todd Mitchell's wife wept.

CHAPTER SIXTEEN

Before going home, Coal returned to his office. He sat at his desk, alone and chilly, because he didn't bother turning up the old radiator. It whined and groaned and clicked too much, and he knew he wouldn't be able to gather his thoughts with all the racket.

Pulling open the desk drawer where Todd Mitchell's paperwork skulked, he tapped it on the desk, as if to straighten it. He stared at Mitchell's name. Not very long ago, he would have loved to see that name there, listed as "suspect." Anything to get rid of worthless baggage. Now... It didn't make him happy like he thought it would. Why? More reasons than one. For one, Mitchell had jumped into the middle of a fight he couldn't hope to win to save Roger Miley. That wasn't like the old Mitchell that Coal had once known. For another reason, they had suffered this string of murders together, side by side, and now that Coal had time to think about it he had to admit that Mitchell really did seem to care.

Could Mitchell be the murderer, and Bigfoot a likely scapegoat? Coal took in a deep breath and let it seep out. No. That was not the case. His guts alone told him that truth, but any evidence would also bear it out. The man had committed a felony, in the line of duty. He had stupidly planted evidence intended to send Bigfoot Monahan away for a very long time, because he believed a guilty man might otherwise go free. But he was not a killer. And who was Coal to put Todd Mitchell in jail for planting evidence anyway? He himself had intended on murdering the same man Mitchell was trying to get thrown back in prison! If Coal had any conscience, he would step down from this position as unfit. Maybe *he* was the man who should be in prison.

Coal could smell old coffee and cigarette smoke. For a moment, he even thought about brewing a new pot. Just something to comfort him against the cold. He stood up, but his eyes were drawn toward the cell block door. He thought for a moment about going back to talk to Mitchell. But in the end, he hid the paperwork in the drawer again and drove home. Mitchell would have to wait. His big mistake deserved at least that.

* * *

When Coal got to the house, it was bright inside, or at least bright against the jet black of the night. He heard Shadow bark a couple of times then go silent. He stepped out of the car, and the bite of cold pinched his cheeks. Pulling off his hat, he ran a hand back through his hair, trying to see movement in the house. What new challenges was he going to face with his children? For that matter, with his mother.

He pulled his collar up around his neck and waited, feeling the flow of the night air around him, the bite of it through his jeans. The door opened a couple of feet, and the dogs came running down the stairs to see him. Dobe got there first, as was his place as the younger dog, and his solid, short-haired body wiggled up against Coal's leg. He knelt down to feel the animal's face against his, knowing that the dog only loved him *more* because he had stayed away so long, not less. The same was true for the shaggier Shadow.

Nothing in the world can make a man feel loved like a dog. Nothing was more true than the joke about learning who loved you more by locking your wife and your dog in the trunk of a car for two hours and then opening it up to find out which one of them was happy to see you.

In the black sky, the stars flickered as bright as distant light bulbs. It put Coal in mind of the Christmases of his childhood. Christmastime was coming, and he hadn't given one thought to what this one was going to be like—the first Christmas without Laura.

Coal waded to the house through a sea of dog parts and eased inside the front door. The assault of warm air pushed him back, stifling after the biting cold on the other side of the door. Connie smiled at him from the kitchen, a rolling pin in her hands and a flattened pie shell on the counter top. She gave him a wink and a soft smile.

Neither Virgil nor Katie was in sight, and the twins kept watching TV in the living room, to his left. It was an episode of *Sanford and Son.*

Coal walked into the kitchen, and Connie dabbed flour on the end of his nose. "Mom, what do you let those boys watch that junk for?"

Connie leaned around him to peer at the television. "Oh, Coal! What's wrong with it? It's just a little harmless entertainment."

"They could be reading or playing. That stuff's going to pollute their minds."

Connie laughed. "Lighten up, lawman. They could be galloping horses down the asphalt on Main Street instead—taking their lives in their hands! I've heard of worse things than watching *Sanford and Son.*"

Coal flushed. It was a direct hit. "We were teenagers."

"Sure. Is there an age when you're safe from a horse's shoes slipping on the pavement and making you fall and get rolled over?"

"All right, Mom. I get it. So... Why the pie? Wasn't Thanksgiving yesterday?"

"I'm making turkey pie for my long-lost son."

"You're too much, Mom. Thanks. Say, where is Virgil?"

"Doing what you want the twins to do—reading in his room." A long pause. "You going to ask about Katie?"

"Right. I was hoping to avoid the name. It brings an evil spell over the house."

Connie frowned. His attempt at humor did not set well with her. "Well, just so you know, she's gone to Maura's. Maura thought Cynthia needed someone more her own age right now."

Coal took a deep breath. He had been trying to put Cynthia Batterton out of his mind, for his own peace. Face serious, Coal put his hand on Connie's arm. "How is she doing?"

"Cynthia? Or Maura?"

Coal felt his face flush. "I'm talking about Cynthia."

A direct gaze, searing in intensity. "How *can* she be, Son? I don't know how someone even lives through what she has. She needs professional help."

"I'm sure Chief George must be working on something."

"Well, it's not fast enough. This is going to drive Maura crazy too, you know."

"Did she say that?"

"How could she? That house isn't big enough for her to get far away from Cynthia and really talk. But any fool can see this is too big for her. She's never had any training for that."

"Yeah, Mom, have you ever talked to a shrink? I have—in Nam. And they're crazier than any of the people they pretend to help. If you ask me, they go into their field just because they're trying to figure out why they're so cracked themselves."

"That's not nice," Connie chided.

"I know. I'm sure it's only ninety-nine percent of them that give all the rest a bad name."

Before Connie could even respond with a laugh, the phone rang. A wary look came over Connie's face. Coal could tell she wanted to ignore it, but with Katie out of the house, they couldn't. Her own hands were covered in flour. When it rang again, Coal picked it up off the receiver.

"Savages."

Hey, Sheriff! Red Levine here. At the Owl Club. Would you be interested to know Bigfoot Monahan's in here tonight?

Coal was stunned into momentary silence. "You're joking, right?"

I wish. I don't like it, Coal.

"Has he been drinking?" Coal didn't want to hear the answer. If Monahan was drinking, it broke the conditions of his parole—but his parole officer was five or more hours away.

Long pause. Too long. *Yeah, dang it. Yeah, he has.*

"Hard? Or soft?"

Huh?

"Whiskies or beer?" asked Coal impatiently.

Beer.

"He at the bar?"

No, playing pool, at the moment.

Coal swore, then looked apologetically at his mother. "All right, Red. I guess you can't throw him out, huh?"

Funny! Can you?

"I guess we're about to find out."

Coal hung up the phone. Even though he wanted to slam it on the base, he held back, but even so, the bell jingled with the harshness of the motion. Coal stared at it. Finally, he looked up.

Connie was watching him quietly. "No pie tonight, huh?"

"I saw you about as much when I lived in Washington, didn't I, Mom?"

Connie pursed her lips. "The kids are busy anyway, I guess. I somehow thought... I just thought we'd have a nice evening together."

"I'm wondering if we ever will while I have this job."

"Who is it, Son? Who did they call about?"

"I don't want to tell you." He wiggled his hat back down on his head and shrugged into his Wrangler jacket.

"I don't really care if you want to or not."

"Mom." He pleaded with his eyes. "You already know."

Her face fell, and she nodded. "Yeah. I was hoping I was wrong."

* * *

Driving down the dark, snow-packed road, Coal thought about Dobe. He wished he could have brought him along. But sometimes dogs led to even more trouble than a man was trying to avoid. And besides, pool cues and steel-toed boots could do fearsome damage to his beloved friend. He had to do this alone.

Why did he have this sudden desire to keep Bigfoot out of trouble? Was it his own guilt over his recent plan to ambush and kill him? An innocent man? That thought came to him out of the blue, where many of Coal's thoughts came from that had merit. The truth was, he should be calling for backup. Lots of backup. But if he did, Paul Monahan was going back to prison. What could be hidden when the only man involved was wracked by a guilty conscience could not be kept secret if other law enforcement officers were involved. Coal knew he had to do this alone, win or lose.

As he pulled quietly into downtown, he looked up at the top of the furniture store to see if the light was lit that informed the police to get on the phone in the nearby phone booth and call dispatch for a pending call. The light was dark.

He glanced up at the marquee over the Roxy Theater. They were playing *The Valachi Papers,* starring Charles Bronson. Now there was one tough man he would not have minded having on his side tonight. Charlie would sure know what to do.

He parked across the street. As usual, the curb in front of the Owl Club, and down the entire block, was jammed with pickups, and a car or two. He gritted his teeth. When he stepped out of the car, he could feel the weight of the gun on his hip. He paused and took a couple of deep breaths. Then, wondering if he was committing suicide, he took off the holster, refastened his belt, and stuck the holstered pistol under his seat.

He looked up and down the street. It was too cold for any boisterous outdoor crowd tonight. But he could hear voices inside the Owl Club and some of the other bars. He closed his eyes and tried to calm himself. Tonight was going to tell Coal Savage an awful lot about certain people—mostly about himself.

Inside the Owl Club, it was like a scene from a Jack the Ripper movie, a foggy night in the Whitechapel area of London, only here the fog was not cold, it was hot, and it was all made out of noxious cigarette smoke. Coal felt his face instantly begin to sweat as he searched the smoky shadows for big Paul Monahan. The place was packed to overflowing, but when Monahan stood up, clear at the back of the room, Coal recognized him instantly. He was nearly a head taller than anyone near him.

Bigfoot seemed to sense Coal, too, and his eyes flashed up and toward the door. Their gazes met, and froze.

CHAPTER SEVENTEEN

"Hey, there. Sheriff!"

The voice to Coal's right side startled him. He turned and came face to face with a raw-boned man wearing a gray turtle-neck sweater, the cliché kind old-time dock workers were famous for. The man's mustache hid whatever expression might have been on his mouth.

"Hello."

"Say, you come in to drink? No badge, no gun?"

"I came to meet a man."

The man laughed, a forced sound. Other men of his ilk were gathering around him. "Well, you're meetin' one."

"I'm busy."

"You're right, you're busy." This time it was a voice from behind Coal, and without completely taking his attention off the first man, Coal tried to see the new speaker. He couldn't look at both.

"What can I do for you boys? Make it quick."

"Oh, it'll be quick, all right. We've been hopin' for this night for a long time," said the man in the gray sweater.

Suddenly, Coal felt strong hands clutching both of his arms from behind. On instinct, he threw himself backward as hard as he could, but instead of bringing his assailants down as he had hoped, he ran square into another one who had closed up tight against him.

A leering grin stretched the face of Gray Sweater as he raised his hands, licked his right thumb. "Ever hear of the Runnigan family, boy? Well, we stick up for our own, and we got a lot of friends. Say your prayers, sucker." And he came in for the kill.

Using a move he had seen Robert Conrad perform many times on the science fiction Western, *The Wild Wild West,* Coal, relying on the strength of the hands that held him, threw himself upward and struck out with both feet. His heels took Gray Sweater square in the abdomen. With his eyes bulging out, he flew backward and slammed against the bar. But it didn't matter. Already, others were swarming in.

The sheer mass of their numbers made many of their blows ineffective, for one man's fist might strike into another's as he strove to hit Coal in the face or body. But those same numbers made the odds of a good, solid blow landing now and then much greater too, and several did.

Suddenly, one of the men's fists caught Coal directly under the rib cage, in the solar plexus. He felt his own eyes bulge this time. He couldn't breathe. He fought to turn to one side and managed partially to make it before another man struck him a blow of shattering force over the right eye.

As his eyes came open, and before the blood began to flow in and block his vision, he saw a sight he had always prayed he would never see: Bigfoot Monahan was lumbering toward him toting a pool cue, and there was blood in his eye.

It wasn't going to matter much, Coal thought way back in his consciousness. He realized that with seven or eight rough men pounding on him he was doomed anyway. But these men might simply have intended to rough him up. Bigfoot Monahan was big and strong enough, and seemed just mentally unstable enough, to put him in his grave without a thought. There was a time he had believed his karate skills might carry him through, but that was out of the question now. He had not the slightest bit of strength left even to fight a normal-sized man, to say nothing of monstrous Paul Monahan.

Something in Coal simply gave out. He had used all of his strength fighting the arms that held him, and the multitude of fists that had driven into his abdomen and groin and battered his face to what felt like one giant boil took away his will even to remain conscious. But something forced him to watch as Bigfoot finally reached him, arriving in slow motion. Was this the end?

Bigfoot Monahan, with a savage look in his widened eyes, reared back with the pool cue, and with all his might he swung.

For a moment, as the cue came crashing down and shattered in half, Coal was stunned. But he was not stunned in the way he thought he was going to be—stunned, or dead. Instead, he saw the man who had been before him flop down to his knees, then pitch over sideways. With the half pool cue remaining in his hand, Monahan, still with that wild look in his eyes, and now, with a backward stroke every bit as fierce as the first, hammered an attacker slightly to Coal's left with a facial blow that must have broken his jaw. Roaring, the mountain of man grabbed a third attacker who was still foolishly holding onto Coal's left arm by the neck and flung him like a sack of dog food at the bar. Coal heard him hit but could not see what became of him after that. Everything now was blurred by blood and the tears adrenaline can sometimes bring.

The man behind Coal, who had been holding him around the chest, let go, and Coal heard his scrambling footsteps making toward the front door. Bigfoot reached out a huge hand and grabbed the man at Coal's right arm by the front of his shirt. By now, all of the others had scattered.

As Monahan jerked the man loose of Coal, and around toward the front, Coal felt his knees give way, and he went limply to the floor, pitching onto his side. He heard the big man who had become his protector roar in a voice that must be much like that of his namesake, and it took just a second for the words to register on his foggy brain.

"That's the law! You don't fight the law." And then the sound of his fist striking the other man in the face, the sound of stumbling footsteps, and the body hit the ground several feet behind Coal.

The room was swirling around him now. One moment, his eyes would come to focus on Bigfoot, and the next he was just a blur. No one seemed to be moving. It might have been a tomb, but for the pall of smoke that wove like spirits through the dim-lit room.

Sirens registered on Coal's brain, and he struggled to get back up. Soon, he heard the sharp crack that any hunter, cop, or thug recognizes—the working of the pump lever of a shotgun. The faint voice of Red, the bartender, came through the murmuring of the crowd. "Stand right where you are!"

Then the front door burst open, just as Coal struggled to his knees, feeling blood run down his face. He sensed, more than saw, a clot of men who had tried to run for the back door, stopped now between him and the place where he had heard the shotgun. He realized that Monahan's big hand was stuck out in front of him, extended with open palm. Barely able to grasp what it meant, instinctively Coal reached out and took it, and Monahan helped him to his feet. When he started to go down again, the big man caught him around the waist with one powerful arm. "Easy now. I got ya."

Coal could hear other voices, but those last three words alone registered on him. *I got ya.* The voice of Bigfoot Monahan. *I got ya.* Nothing seemed real. The room was a kaleidoscope of nauseating smoke and light. Monahan's face was broken into shattered pieces, but his arm around Coal was as powerful as a Clydesdale. Coal didn't think he could fall if he tried.

Someone was talking now, talking to Coal. He heard the voice, only broken, meaningless syllables. Did not recognize it, just knew he should. Then another voice registered, and it was Red's. "No! He saved the sheriff, boys. He's one of the good guys."

Silence. Long and filled with a sense of disbelief. Then someone spoke again, and the words seemed to come more clearly. "...rest of them to the hospital, or up to the jail. And somebody better get Coal to the hospital, too."

Coal shook his head. He sensed that this made blood splatter off his lips. He talked. He knew what he was saying, but it sounded almost unhuman. Another voice said, "What? Coal, I can't understand a word"

"I'm fine!"

"The hell you are!" It was Bob Wilson's voice that registered now. "You're anything but fine, buddy."

"Fine as anything," Coal mumbled. It wasn't what he intended to say. Not really. But it was what came out. "Need some water," he mumbled, and he heard Bob's voice again.

"I think he said he wants a drink."

The sound of scraping came to Coal, and soon a tall stool bumped into the backs of his legs, and Bigfoot Monahan eased him onto it. It was the strangest sensation to feel the big man's arm remain there then, steadying him.

"Here ya go, Sheriff." Bigfoot's voice. Coal's eyes half focused on a sparkling glass of water, reflecting the yellow light of the room. It came to his lips and tipped, and he sipped. It tasted like blood and smoke. "Get a rag," a gruff voice ordered. Again, Bigfoot Monahan.

A minute later, the feel of a cool rag dabbing his chin, then his lip, registered on Coal. He managed to open one eye and tried to focus on Bob Wilson. After swishing his mouth out and spitting it back into the glass that was being held in front of him, he managed to say, "Bob, man, get these men out of here. I'll be along. Gotta take care of something."

"Uhh... I think I understood you that time, buddy. You want me to take these men out of here. What about you?"

"I told you. Gotta take care of something."

His head was pounding. His whole body was beginning to throb. He was sick to his stomach from the blows to his groin.

"How you going to get home?" Bob asked.

"If I'm still here when you come back, we'll think about that. But don't worry. I'll get there." He tried to sound confident. Capable. Inside, he felt like dying. He knew if it weren't for Monahan's arm around him he could not have even stayed sitting on this stool.

"All right, Coal, but you'd better be okay or I don't know what I'm going to tell Connie."

Coal tried to force a smile. His face felt like he had just come from the dentist and his lip was the size of his nose. He waved a hand weakly toward the door.

There was a commotion around the front doors, an army of footsteps, and then the door closed, and for a moment all was still.

Paul Monahan's voice broke the stillness. "You got a big bowl or a pan you could put warm water in?"

"Sure," said Red, and his footsteps faded away.

Somebody else walked over, and the voice came out very meek. "You going to be okay, Sheriff?"

Coal had no idea who this was, although he had seen the face. At least he thought he recognized it, though things were still blurry. "Fine. I'll be fine. Thanks." The man faded away into the shadows, but Coal could feel him and everyone else, watching from every dark corner of the room, beneath the pathetic glow of the ceiling lights that trickled through the weaving snakes of smoke.

Red brought a pan of water and a rag, and Coal tried to wash his face. After a minute, he heard Monahan's gruff voice. "Here, give me that." The rag slipped out of his numb fingers, and in a moment it was gently dabbing all around his face. "Lean over," Monahan commanded, and when Bigfoot Monahan gave a command, you didn't hesitate. Coal leaned over, and the big hand cupped water and gently bathed his face, especially his nose and mouth, and around his one eye that was swollen shut.

Coal's thoughts were coming much clearer now, at least as clear as the smoke-filled room. Here he stood with Bigfoot Paul Monahan, in a bar where the big man had just been drinking, breaking his parole. He had also been in one rip-roaring fight. It had all the earmarks of a man going back to the penitentiary. A man who might have just saved Coal's life.

"We've got to get out of here." Coal suddenly stood up. He couldn't see out of one eye at all, but through the other he was beginning to make out the room with all clarity. However, he must have started to sway, and Monahan's big hand came out and rested on his shoulder, steadying him.

"Who's getting out of where?"

"Let's go," Coal insisted. He turned, moving slowly, and walked to the door. As he opened it, he held on to the handle, because that was how he stayed upright, and turned back to the bar. "Hey, Red, thanks." He meant not only for stepping in with the shotgun, but for the initial phone call. But he wouldn't give the bartender up like that with Bigfoot right there. The bartender nodded his understanding.

"You take care, Sheriff. You sure you'll be all right?"

"My own sons have roughed me up worse than this," Coal joked.

"Hell, I'd be lookin' for a new family."

Coal gave a painful chuckle and walked outside, letting Bigfoot shut the door behind. "Where we goin'?"

"You been drinking?"

Bigfoot nodded.

"How many?"

"Maybe four."

"Why?"

"The taste of freedom."

"You don't have the luxury."

"I know. It was my last."

"In your place, I'd say that too. Can you walk a line?"

The bigger man paused for several seconds. All of a sudden, he chuckled. Coal was sure he had never heard him make that noise before. "I don't know. Can you?"

Coal held back a laugh of his own. He knew it would have hurt, and he didn't want Monahan to know he thought it was funny anyway.

"Walk a line."

Bigfoot was unsteady.

"Stand on one foot."

Bigfoot was unsteady. He didn't last two seconds.

"Can you do anything sober people can do?"

"Can you?"

This time Coal really had a hard time not laughing. He felt so at ease with this big brute of a man who could have helped kill him just minutes ago but instead had saved him from a far worse beating than he was sure to have received—if not from death.

Coal motioned across the street to his Ford. "Go get in the car."

"I have my station wagon here."

"I said go get in."

Monahan drew a deep breath. He glanced up and down the sidewalk both ways. The only people in sight were going into the Lantern Bar, trying to act casual but unable to hide the shock in their eyes at Coal's appearance.

"What if I don't?"

Coal just stood there. *What if he didn't?* he thought. *What if he didn't?* It wasn't like Coal could do anything.

"You will." His words were flat and final.

Monahan sighed. "You going to at least cuff me, so I don't look so foolish?"

"Do I need to?"

Monahan stared at him, his eyes starting to turn sullen, then angry, then finally defeated. "No. I reckon not. I know what I've done."

"Just get in."

Side by side, they walked across the street. The whole time, rather than feel threatened, Coal had the strange sensation that the big man was waiting for him to start to fall so he could catch him. In a way, it was a very unsettling thought. Not long before, they had wanted to kill each other.

Monahan began to open the back door of the Ford, and Coal said, "It's against my policy to have someone in the back seat out of handcuffs."

Confused, Bigfoot stared at him for a moment. "I sure don't get you. Now you're saying you *are* gonna cuff me?"

"No. I'm saying you're going to have to sit up front."

"Huh. Can you even drive? Seems like even with four beers in me I'm a safer driver than you."

"Driving drunk is illegal. There's no law against driving beat-to-hell. Besides, how would it look for the sheriff to let a drunk man drive him somewhere?"

Coal imagined hearing the perfect reply: *Good point.* Instead, Bigfoot just stared his one good eye down. After a moment longer, he went around to the driver's side, steadying himself by gliding his fingers along the ice-cold metal.

When his fingers finally touched his door handle, he saw Bigfoot reach down and open the passenger door. "What about my car?"

"It'll be all right here."

"I've heard that before."

They got in, and the doors slammed shut as one. Coal fumbled with the keys at the ignition. When finally, inevitably, they fell, Bigfoot reached over before Coal could get up the gumption to brave the pain and picked them up for him. Then he slid the key in the ignition and fired it up. Coal watched him without a word. Monahan turned back to the front. "We're gonna get killed before we get to the jail."

"Could be," replied Coal. With that, he threw it into drive and wheeled around in the middle of the street, now facing back to the south. Bigfoot started fidgeting, but he said nothing. He kept turning to glance back up the street as the businesses quickly faded away behind them in twilight blue, one by dark and lonely one.

Finally, at the far edge of town and driving past the last establishment, he looked over at Coal. "Ain't the way to the jail. Where you takin' me?"

Coal looked at him blandly. "Did you move, Paul?"

"Huh?"

"This is the way to your house, isn't it?"

A long moment of silence. Deep breathing by both. "Yeah, it's the way to my house." Monahan sat still for a moment longer. "But I was drinkin', and it's against the rules of my parole. And I was in a fight."

"What fight?"

With a sudden realization of what was happening, Bigfoot finally sank back in his seat. No more sound came from him for quite a while as Coal drove very slowly down the highway, trying to see the road in spite of the mist that kept fogging over his good eye, which was hurt, just not as bad as the one that was swollen shut. Once, about six miles out, Monahan cleared his throat, but still he held his tongue, as if he had wanted to speak and changed his mind. He just stared straight ahead.

Coal pulled off the highway and up in front of Monahan's house, and they both stepped out. By now, Coal's left eye was a throbbing boiled egg of pain. His shirtfront was soaked in blood from his lip and nose, both of which had started to bleed again once they were driving and the vehicle got warm.

Monahan peered closer at Coal in the glow from his porch light. "Man, you're worse than I thought. You ain't even gonna be able to drive back home."

"Just get in your house. And remember, next time it could be someone else coming in that bar—like Wilhelm. Is that hooch worth your family having to stay here alone?"

"No."

"All right. Go get some sleep. I'll be here at eight to go get your car with you."

Bigfoot just stared at him. "I don't get you."

"Yeah, me neither. Just be glad you're home. Now let's keep it that way."

A wave of dizziness swept over Coal, and what would have been a certain fall found him up against the hood of the Ford. He felt the urge to throw up.

Soon, he heard Bigfoot's feet crunching in the icy gravel as he hustled around the front of the car and grabbed his arm. For a second, an unreasonable fear bolted up inside Coal, and he straightened up, trying to tug his arm away. Luckily for him, Bigfoot didn't let go, because at that moment Coal felt his knees buckle, and then the big man's powerful arms closed around his torso.

"All right, you ain't goin' nowhere. Come on."

Coal tried to move his feet. It felt like he was standing in a foot of mud. His head spun, his eye turned upward, and the world swirled around him. And then he felt himself fall backward.

But Coal did not touch the ground. Like a baby, he felt his two hundred fifty pounds of dead weight being lifted up, cradled in incredibly powerful arms. He could see the stars overhead making little whirling circles in the sharp black sky. And then all was dark, and Coal knew nothing.

* * *

Coal awoke to a feeling of warmth—maybe too much of it. He felt his face and clothes soaked in sweat. He tried to open his eyes.

Someone was standing on them. He tried again. Whatever tiny person was standing on his eyelids must have moved, and the good eye opened. A shaft of light stabbed in. He sneezed violently, and a woman's voice said, "Bless you." He tried to reply. His tongue was glued to the roof of his mouth, and his throat was swollen. He opened his eye a sliver again and could see red light flashing dimly in the room.

He lay on what must be a sofa, and it felt like he was being pushed deep down into its soft cushions. A blanket, or some other five hundred pound weight was crushing him. He couldn't breathe. The weight. The heat. He needed outside!

"Easy, man. Easy." For a moment, he stopped breathing, waiting, mind a-whirl. Finally, the voice registered on him. Bigfoot. Maybe he didn't like the name Bigfoot. Maybe he should think of him as Paul. Maybe the giant had saved his life that night.

Coal sucked in a deep breath, clear down into his toes, the way he used to draw on a Marlboro. He forced his eye open, blinked it hard, opened it again. Monahan was crouched there by the couch, watching him. He held a glass of water and some aspirin.

"I had to have my woman run over to the neighbor's and call the ambulance on you. You ain't quite the man you think you are, I guess."

In spite of the sick feeling gurgling through his guts, Coal gave a lopsided grin when he saw the humor about Bigfoot's face. There were times he had wondered if the big man had that kind of capacity in him, to understand the concept of humor.

He closed his eye again, wanting the nausea to go away. Wanting just to sleep. A hand rested on his forehead. Too soft to belong to Monahan.

Coal heard another voice, a man's voice. Soft, kind. A voice he ought to know. "Hey, amigo. You on duty? Or you just like to run your face through a stamp mill on your time off?"

It was Jay Castillo.

"Hey!" He tried to smile and opened his eye. The hand on his forehead dropped away suddenly, but to his surprise it had not been Castillo's. It belonged to Maura PlentyWounds.

"Well, hello." The woman's voice was soft, and Coal thought they had tears in them. She reached down and squeezed his hand. "Jay thought—" She stopped suddenly, her words catching in her throat.

"What?" He looked over at Castillo, who crouched farther up toward the head of the couch. His old friend shrugged and looked over at Maura.

"Sorry." The woman cleared her throat. "I was just saying that Jay thinks you look like you went through a stamp mill, and I was thinking this looks more like a meat grinder." She sniffed and wiped brusquely at her nose. He was watching her eyes, and this time he was sure they filled with tears again as they roamed over what must be a horrible looking face. Now he felt bad for making her feel this way. And he also felt surprise.

"I was in the hospital when they brought all those men in," she went on. "They didn't look so good either."

Coal closed his eye for a moment, feeling dizziness twirl him around the room. Then, "Well, that wasn't any of my doing." He looked up at Monahan, who had now stood up in the center of the room behind the two paramedics. The big man nodded, his face embarrassed.

"You're lucky he was there," Maura said. "Well, we have the cot inside, so let's get you loaded up."

"What?" Coal tried to sit up, lay gingerly back down.

"The cot, Coal. I don't think you can walk yourself out to the ambulance."

"I can walk, but I'm not walking to the ambulance. I'm going home." This time, with all his willpower, he came to a sitting position, while all the while Castillo and Maura tried to dissuade him.

"You're going to the hospital if I have to carry you myself!" Maura said when he was facing her.

"Maura. I am *not* going to go to the hospital. There's no way you can change that. This is nothing but a few flesh wounds. I'll be over it by morning."

"Good hell." Maura exploded to her feet, slapping her leg. "Are you serious? Should I get you a mirror?"

He couldn't help a laugh escaping him at the look on her face. He looked over at Jay Castillo. "Come on, buddy, you know me. I don't need a doctor."

Jay shrugged. "Don't look at me! I've never seen you lookin' like *this* before."

Coal grunted and looked up at Monahan, still standing beyond the woman and holding the water glass and aspirin. "Can I have those?"

"Sure." The big man lurched forward, holding both in monstrous hands. Coal took the three aspirin and swallowed them gingerly with a swig of water. When his throat felt lubricated, he drank a little more.

Coal turned so his one open eye could look directly into the woman's, who had calmed back down enough to crouch again in front of him. "Maura, I appreciate you coming, but I'll be all right. Seriously. I just need some rest."

"You need stitches in your eye and your lip, Coal. You are never going to look the same if you don't listen to me. You haven't seen yourself."

Coal looked a question over at Jay "She's not kidding, buddy. It's pretty bad, all right. I'm pretty sure you're going to wish you got it sewn up if you don't."

"Maybe in the morning," Coal finally said with a sigh.

"Morning will be too late," said Jay, as Maura was lunging to her feet again. She whirled on Jay now.

"You can take the ambulance back. I'm at least going to drive this stubborn jackass home so he doesn't run off the highway."

"We're not taking him in?"

"Right. You know him better than I do. He's made up his mind."

Jay stood up and looked down at Coal, who now was watching him, waiting. "Yeah, you're right. Okay, old buddy. You're going to look pretty bad if your wounds all heal up looking this way. I hope you know what you're doing."

Coal struggled to his feet while the others all watched. No one raised a finger to help him. He recognized the fact that they were testing his strength. His resolve.

Jay turned to Maura. "You sure about this? What are you going to do, walk home?"

"Connie will give me a ride. Or I'll just take his car home. I guarantee he won't be needing it for a while."

Coal's eye was throbbing horribly. His head ached worse than he had ever felt. His guts felt poisoned. He was at least smart enough to know Maura was right about him driving home.

At last, Jay shrugged and looked at Coal. "Wow, you sure can cause a lot of trouble when you decide to."

CHAPTER EIGHTEEN

A thermometer in the Ford would have said it was warm. But driving back north from the Monahans' house, Coal felt as cold as it looked outside. It was a feeling emanating directly from Maura.

For a mile, he rested his head against the seat back, his eye closed, trying to ignore his aching guts, his dizzy head. Finally, to lighten the mood, he glanced over at his chauffeur. "You're taking kind of a big chance assuming Mom will take you home, you know."

"I don't care. Like I said, I'll take your car. It's a sure thing you couldn't stop me."

In this game, a player was only allowed one strike. Coal had struck out. He sat there willing away the chill. He thought about Cynthia, Sissy, and Katie and wondered what Maura had done with those three. Did she just leave them home alone? He wasn't fool enough to ask at the moment.

"Coal, why are you doing this?" The sentence sounded something like a lighted stick of dynamite exploding suddenly into a desert cave. "Why are you so proud?"

Coal looked down at his lap. He raised a hand and prodded his bruised and swollen lips with his fingers. "Proud? That's the last thing I am."

"Yeah. Right. Why can't you let anyone help you?"

"You're helping me."

"Funny. I'm not talking just about a ride home—a ride I forced on you, I might add. You should be going to the hospital to get some real care—and some x-rays."

"X-rays for what? Nothing's broken."

"Right. What is wrong, Coal?" A rock dropped into a metal drum. "Why are you so hard?"

He didn't have an answer for that. There were a lot of things he had no answer for.

"So you know you can't go back to work for a while. Are you going to let Katie take care of you when you're laid up?"

"That's real funny. Take care of me with an ice pick?"

"Why do you say things like that?"

"Why? Have you seen how that girl feels about me? You shouldn't have to ask."

"I *am* asking. Why does she act like that? What happened between the two of you?"

"I killed her mother."

Now Coal had dropped his own rock into the metal drum, only his was a boulder. Maura looked over at him a couple of times. Said nothing. Finally, she took a deep breath. She was getting ready to say something she didn't want any answer to. "I know that's not true, Coal. Why would you say a thing like that?"

"You don't know me. Nobody knows me. Nobody really knows anybody."

Again, a pregnant silence, and now they were nearing the turnoff to Savage Lane. "Coal, I really want to. You can tell me what happened. You've never talked about this, have you? Never. To anyone." She slowed the car and pulled off the highway onto Savage Lane. Only fifty yards onto his road, she pulled to the shoulder—which basically served to make it into a one-lane road, and shut off the engine. She left the parking lights a-glow.

She folded her hands in her lap and looked slowly over at Coal. "You know when we go inside your mom's going to make you go get stitches, don't you?"

Coal chuckled. "She'll try. You're two sides of the same broken record."

He was lumping her in with his mother, and Maura knew Coal loved his mother. So she held back a reaction that had flashed in her eyes. "Well, you'll look tough when you scar up, I guess. I guess tough-looking is good. At least for other men."

"Why not me?"

"Give me a break. You already looked tougher than anyone in town. Oh well. I'm sure you'll get lots of storytelling over it."

Coal grunted. Maura, with her gaze, reached deep into his soul through his eye. Slowly, very slowly, she reached out and laid her hand on his. "Hey. Can you talk to me? Please? You've gotta break that hard shell sometime. What happened to your wife?"

Maura had the right look in her eyes, the perfect tender tone in her tough-girl voice, the ideal warmth in her hand. Before he could prepare for it, tears welled up in Coal's eye. He whipped his head away to gaze out the passenger window, into the dark. He sought something to say, some cute reply, some comment, perhaps, about the moose he had run into. *Anything.* But there was nothing. Nowhere to escape.

"I don't think you really want to know about that." His voice was gruff. He was holding back his emotion. He still couldn't look back and meet her gaze.

"Look at me, Coal Savage. Damnit. *Look at me!* I *do* want to know. And I really think you need to talk. I won't leave tonight until you tell me." She squeezed his hand, almost too hard, and shook it insistently.

Maura was right. Coal had never talked. Never told a soul. Not a shrink, a cop, his boss—nobody. At least not everything. Only Connie knew most of it, but even she did not know all the details before *that day*. A lump rose in his throat. He thought of Laura's body, hanging there, the life drained out of her face. The barn was cold. The smell of the hay and molasses feed still haunted him.

Coal had been gone. A lot. His job was becoming his life. He was good at it. He was respected. He was revered. He was the toughest federal agent in town, both in body and mind. Coal had a partner, Tony Nwanzé. But he did not need him. Coal needed no one.

No one.

It was a long drive into the capital from Broad Run, Virginia. Over forty miles. And Coal insisted on being to work before the rush, and before anyone else. He had to get a jump on the day. Coal was a hard charger, they said. He always had been.

So Coal got up early every morning and was gone down the road. At first, he would wake Laura, give her a kiss, tell her he loved her, say goodbye. That became less and less frequent. Then, in time, he would just go. No goodbye. No kiss. No *I love you.*

No nothing.

Laura was alone on Roland Farm. She walked with the twins in the woods. She strolled with them along the pond and threw bread crumbs to the ducks, to the bass and blue gills that swarmed beneath the surface. In season, they picked the little red strawberries festooning the banks, and they watched the heads of turtles that floated out in the water, just black dots. They caught little tadpoles along the edge of the shore and chased bullfrogs that would leap so far away that none could ever be caught. They watched the dogs chase cottontails, and sometimes there were whitetail deer, or long black snakes. Coal knew all this only because the twins would tell him. After a time, Laura didn't say much at all.

In time, they didn't kiss. Didn't even hug. And they surely never made love. He would forget when it was their anniversary. Sometimes forgot her birthday, and sometimes on his own big day an important case would keep him in the city, so that even if she planned some wonderful surprise for him with the kids, he missed it. Laura would get upset and cry and tell the children not to say anything about it. But sooner or later they always did.

After two and a half years in Virginia, Laura finally started talking one winter about getting a job, and she did. With her beauty, charm, and natural abilities with books, and with children, it wasn't hard. She began substitute teaching, at the grade school in Warrenton. Some other teacher had had trouble with her pregnancy and was on leave. So Laura would teach, and she would leave the twins with the neighbors. This was the first thing they had actually felt strongly enough about in a year or more to fight about out loud. Coal wanted her home, raising the children right. She didn't care. She needed a life. She needed to feel needed.

The worst fight was toward the end. Laura broke down and cried. She told him what she needed. He told her he would change. The old scenario, played out ten million different times in a million different households across the world.

Coal didn't change, Laura didn't quit her job, and they grew ever farther apart that fall, and fast. Then she found a man. *The* man, the one who was really sympathetic to her, who understood everything she was going through. He was the principal at her school.

The affair was short-lived. Only three or four weeks, perhaps. But only because they were found out. The superintendent got word of the affair. He summarily fired Laura and informed her that she was going to have to tell Coal why, or he would do it for her. And the man didn't even know Coal. Of course, the principal was too good of a man to lose, and friends with the right people. The superintendent gave him a reprimand. It was rumored that he got a day off, but whispered that it was with pay. It was two men who were friends, in a man's world. And Laura came home to tell Coal her sin before the superintendent could make the call.

It was a quiet scene in the kitchen when Laura opened her soul to her husband. The children were all in bed. Laura thought he would yell. Maybe throw something. Stomp out of the house and slam the door. He did none of that.

He left quietly, not in a fury like she seemed to expect. He drove into D.C. and stayed the night by himself, in a hotel. Three nights he stayed there, working every day in the same suit of clothes, missing his gym time because all his workout clothes were home. He lived those three days sickened in his heart.

Before Coal could decide to go back home, he was called to help in the arrest of a criminal wanted for murder in Venice, Italy. The man was deadly, and he had friends. The arrest went bad. Guns were pulled, and Coal killed his first man since the war—Ilario Luccetti. The name would ring forever in his head.

The investigation lasted three weeks, and in that time Coal bought two new suits of clothing and stayed in the city. He made his partner, Tony, call Laura and tell her what was going on, so the children wouldn't worry.

Coal started going for walks, most often to the Lincoln Memorial, then across the Arlington Memorial Bridge to walk among the rows and rows of sparkling crosses from soldiers who had died throughout the decades. One day, he found the marker for one of his friends who had died in the war, Pete Shank. He was sitting at his grave when a young woman came up, a beautiful young thing with black hair swept out of eyes of a deep chocolate brown. Her name was Erin. The miracle of the meeting was that she was Pete's widow.

Soon, they found themselves meeting at Pete's grave around the same time every evening. Erin was soft and gentle, ready with tears, for Pete and all the other boys taken too soon in Nam. He started to think he was falling in love with her. She seemed to know him, inside and out. She didn't have the reserve that he felt with Laura. That he had felt since coming home from the war.

The police in Warrenton managed somehow to reach Coal at work one day and told him that his wife had spent the night in jail, on drug charges. He was devastated. He raced back to Warrenton and baled her out, but all the way home there was nothing but silence. That night, he slept on the couch downstairs, his heart aching with thoughts of Erin. She would have been at the cemetery that evening. She would wonder where he went. He had no way to reach her and tell her everything was all right.

In the bedroom, while Coal tried to sleep, Laura was drinking from a bottle of Jack Daniels whisky. Coal didn't know until it was too late. She stumbled into the kitchen to get a drink, and he could tell she was inebriated. He had never been a hard drinker, but he knew plenty who were, and there was no question what state his wife was in now.

He challenged her, foolishly, about drinking while the kids were just upstairs. She told him to go to hell. Then she opened up about a lot more. She admitted she had not only been smoking marijuana, but she had even tried heroine. The revelation made Coal almost physically sick. She began verbally to attack him then, telling him he probably killed the Italian in D.C. because he would have liked to kill her instead and was taking it out on an innocent man. Her abuse, her accusations, became volatile. He tried to keep her quiet so the kids wouldn't hear, and fortunately for her he succeeded. It was fortunate because Laura usually only fought with him if the children were nowhere around. That was how she had kept the notion in their heads that she was some kind of saint. And Coal was not about to destroy their dreams by admitting what their mother really was. His children didn't even know him. They wouldn't have believed him anyway.

In the morning, Laura was passed out, and Coal tried to shake her awake. Finally, he dumped a glass of cold water on her. She came up sputtering, ready to fight. He told her if he found out about any more drug use he would take the kids from her and leave her alone. Then he left, headed back to the city. The children were asleep, and he didn't tell them goodbye.

The first afternoon back in D.C. the department cleared Coal of all charges in the shooting and allowed him to come back to work. To celebrate, he went right at five-thirty to Pete's grave, at Arlington, and there was Erin. She ran to him and threw her arms around him as if they were old lovers.

They went for a long walk, first along George Washington Parkway, then crossed over the rippling Potomac on Francis Scott Key Bridge, and ended up at a well-known restaurant, Clyde's of Georgetown, where they feasted on crab cakes. Here, after dinner, Coal told his new friend about what had happened with Laura.

It was dark by the time they walked once more along the Potomac. In Coal's mind, he could hear an old Civil War song his father used to sing: "All Quiet Along the Potomac Tonight." When Erin asked him for his thoughts, that was what he chose to tell her. They stood in the dark, looking at the river, lit beautifully by the city lights across the water. It was peaceful here, and calm, and the night was warm and a little humid. Down along the edge of the water, in the grass, and soon flickering into the night sky, the twinkling of fireflies appeared. Erin laughed with delight and called them "little Tinkerbells." He tried for a while to catch one for her, and finally he did, and it sat still on his thumb. When he touched a finger to it, it lit up. Erin touched it, and it glowed again, just a brief flame, then went dark again. He threw it up into the air, and it sailed away, and as it went out across the water it blinked one last time in goodbye.

Somehow, Erin's hand had rested on Coal's, and he looked down at her. With her lips parted, she was watching him. And their lips met. They shouldn't have, but they were two terribly lonely people, drawn together like lost souls, and they did. They kissed passionately until going down on their knees in the grass, and they kissed some more. And finally, happy and sad all at the same time, they just knelt there and held onto each other.

Coal forced himself to go home the next day. He had to go to Laura and the children. He had to see if there was anything left.

As it turned out, sometimes even in big cities things happen much like they do in small towns. Someone from the Bureau had seen Coal with Erin. Someone with a big nose. Coal pulled up in front of the house only to be confronted by his wife in the driveway. She knew he was having an affair. She knew because she had received a phone call that morning from someone who begged not to be identified.

She screamed at Coal that it was over. She didn't love him, and he didn't love her. It wasn't until that particular moment when he realized that she was on some kind of drug again, or at least drunk. If the latter, it had to be on vodka, because he hadn't smelled a thing.

In anger, he went in the house and collected the twins, then took them over to the neighbors' house and asked if they could keep them until he returned home that evening. Then he went back home and told Laura one more time that she had better get some help or he was going to take the kids and move to D.C. without her. It was an empty threat. He knew he couldn't take them away from their mother. They would hate him forever.

He remembered Laura's last words as he grabbed the handle of his car door. In a screaming voice, she had said she would be better off dead than being married to him. And his own words in reply rang clearly in his head. As long as he lived, they always would. *Yeah, maybe you would be!* They were the last words he had ever spoken to his wife in her presence.

Coal did not want to tell the rest, but he had started, and it was like a flash flood. It was going to have to run its course, and Maura was going to hear it all. Maybe she would never speak to him again when it was over. Win or lose, it was too late to go back now.

Laura had called him at the office at noon, happening by sheer chance to catch him there when on any normal day he would have been out on the streets. This day, however, he had been called in to be part of a deposition being taken by one of the federal prosecutors on a case he had been working for some time, involving the murder of one high-ranking government official by a local mob member who felt he had not lived up to his part of a deal to feed him information from inside his office.

The secretary was adamant, and Coal left Tony Nwanzé in the deposition and went to take the call. His salutation when he picked up the phone was very curt. By the sound of Laura's speech, she was under the influence of something, either drugs or alcohol. One moment she would say something loving, something maybe a normal wife would say, or at least a wife like Beaver Cleaver's mother. The next, she would be crying, then laughing almost hysterically, then screaming at him.

He had warned her that he was going to hang up on her, but she stopped him cold and told him he had better make it home before the children did if he loved any of them anymore. Coal hadn't even said goodbye. He just slammed down the phone.

Here, his voice broke. Maura reached up and rubbed his upper back, one of the few places where he didn't seem to be hurt. "Coal, you can stop if you want to."

"No, I can't. If I don't keep going I'll never get this out. And you're the one who asked."

And so he finished the story, while Maura sat there with tears rolling down her cheeks and didn't even try to stop them.

Coal had not gone home like Laura asked him to. He stayed to finish the deposition, and he planned to see Erin, at Arlington Cemetery, and tell her what had happened, about how small the world was and how nosy people were. Back in Broad Run, the children had walked from where the bus always dropped them off, at the main road, all the way a couple of hundred yards to the house. They had gone right past the big barn on the last leg up the lane. In the house, Katie had found the note on the kitchen table. The note intended for Coal to find.

The words on the note were still etched in Coal's mind, indelibly. Sometimes in his nightmares someone held the note in front of him, an ownerless hand, and he was forced to read them, over and over: *Coal, you did this to me. I hope it makes you happy. You said maybe I would be better off dead. Well, if that's what you want, then I am going to help you out. Have a great life. I'll be in the barn. I doubt you ever loved me or the kids anyway.*

Katie had finished reading the note and walked down the lane to see if she could find her mom in the barn and ask her why she wrote the note. She found her mother hanging by a rope from the rafters. She had been dead for hours.

Coal got the secretive call from the county sheriff, and he rushed home as fast as he could drive. He had no details, only the knowledge that something was seriously wrong. He didn't know his life was about to change forever.

Coal had tried to hold his emotions in. He was a Marine! No one needed to see the tears of a Marine. No one *wanted* to. But as he finished his story, he made the mistake of hearing Maura's soft voice as she leaned toward him, and it was his undoing. "I'm so sorry, Coal."

Then she was crying, and he was crying. At last, after all the months of torment, the sorrow was breaking free of his soul, and his sobs seemed to shake the car.

CHAPTER NINETEEN

Maura and Coal sat there in the car for twenty minutes and held each other. At last, Coal drew in a long, deep breath, then let it out slowly. "Why don't you go ahead and take me to the hospital? I don't want my mom and the kids to see me this way."

The woman pulled away from him and looked into his eye, then finally smiled. "Thank you, Coal."

He just nodded and leaned back in his seat.

Maura had to pull up past the house to turn around. She could have turned around in the driveway, but he didn't want to take the chance that Connie would come out to see what was going on. At the hospital, Annie Price was the first person they saw walking toward them.

Coal's heart felt like it skipped a beat. Every time he saw this woman she looked prettier. Her heart must have skipped a beat too, for she came to a stumbling halt, and both hands flew up to her mouth, gasping. Dropping her hands away from her face, but still holding them together, in praying fashion, she exclaimed, "Coal!"

"That's right. Just me."

She walked to him and put a hand on his arm, looking over at Maura. "Why didn't you come in sooner, when the others came?"

"Business to tend to," he said, trying to smile. He knew he had failed, and the woman's eyes moistened. "So, they tell me I might need stitches."

"Come with me," Annie ordered, seeming completely oblivious to his lame attempt at humor.

She brought him into one of the rooms and had him sit down, then ran for Doctor Bent while Maura waited beside the bed he was sitting on. There was a long silence after Annie Price left. It was broken by Maura, who Coal had seen had something on her mind for quite a while.

"You and Annie seem to have gotten to know each other pretty well."

"We have?"

"It sure sounded like it."

"Huh. I didn't notice."

He kept watching her after she dropped her face to start watching the all-important operation of cleaning under one fingernail with another. He knew she could sense him watching, and she didn't look up again for a time. Finally, she grunted and wiped her hand on her pants. "Stupid horses. I'll never have clean hands again."

"Like a mechanic," he joked. It was not difficult to intuit that she was thinking about anything but her dirty hands, or her horses.

She looked up at him and *humphed.* "Yeah, I guess."

Footsteps clicked in the hallway, and soon Annie reappeared with Doctor Bent. "Wow! Annie wasn't kidding."

Coal shrugged. "I haven't seen myself. But everyone else sure seems impressed."

"Pretty impressive, Sheriff. Sure is that. I'm surprised you're conscious."

"He wasn't," cut in Maura.

"Oh? Tell me about it, Sheriff."

Coal told him everything he remembered happening, during the fight and after. He told him about his sick stomach, his nausea, and passing out at Monahan's.

"All right. Let's get you lying down here and figure out what to do with some stitches first. Then we'll see how you feel later and find you something to deal with the rest of it. I'll tell you one thing: You're going to be sick for a day or two. Maybe more."

Coal nodded. "Yeah, I know. Been there before."

"If you're experienced, maybe your body's accustomed. Maybe it won't be as bad."

"Huh." Coal could offer nothing more.

The doctor made him lie down, and he and Annie worked together cleaning off the caked blood while Maura stood back and watched, her eyes worried. "How much do you weigh, Sheriff?"

"Two fifty, maybe two fifty-five."

"That's a lot of muscle. Annie, why don't you work me up a dose of lidocaine, would you? Make it... let's start out with three and a half. He's a pretty big boy."

"Yes, Doctor."

Coal could hear the nurse getting into a cupboard and drawer. The doctor, peering over a pair of spectacles, prodded at Coal's eyebrow with a swab. "That's pretty deep. Sheriff, we're just going to give you a local anesthetic, all right? Now, this won't put you out. It'll just make it so you don't feel the pain—just the same as if you're at the dentist. You'll be able to tell I'm sewing, but nothing more. You aren't squeamish, are you?"

"I was in Nam."

The doctor frowned. "Then no. All right. This could make your heart speed up a little and a few other side effects, but it's not likely. It could give you more of an upset stomach, maybe a little more nausea. But I'm guessing you'll do fine."

Annie came back over, and the doctor softly fingered the area of Coal's worst wound just before Coal felt a prick, then the cold feeling of the fluid going in. In a few minutes, he felt a little lightheaded, but probably from the fight itself, not the drug. Within another three minutes, the feeling around his eye was gone altogether, with no worse nausea than what he had felt before. He just felt very sleepy.

Groggy, and feeling as if he were somewhere else, he only vaguely felt the pressure of the needle and thread pulling away, trying to drag his eyebrow with it. He shifted his gaze to Annie. She had a mask over her mouth and nose, but her eyes were open wide, shielded now behind glasses—prescriptive glasses, not safety. Even in his state of lethargy, she looked so pretty. The room was warm. Slowly, his eye faded shut.

"No, we're just friends."

Coal jolted awake. The words were ringing in his head. He turned his head and looked around, finally spotting Annie and Maura, seated together. He lay there and tried to decide whose voice had spoken.

But now they were both looking at him. He was awake, they knew it, and there would be no more of the conversation he had stumbled into.

"How are you feeling?" asked Annie. "Are you awake?"

"No, I'm asleep," he replied. His mind felt groggy, but not *that* groggy. "Keep talking."

Both women laughed and looked at each other. They looked like the children caught with their hands in the cookie jar. "How long have you been listening?" Annie asked.

"Listening to what?"

This time Annie looked at him askance. "Be still." She walked around behind his bed. "I'm going to raise you up a little, all right? We'll go slow, so I can monitor your vital signs. Tell me if you start feeling sick, okay?"

He just nodded. He felt her raising the head of his bed. Soon, his torso was at a forty-five degree angle, and he was looking straight at Maura PlentyWounds. In spite of his injuries, which in real life were not glamorous at all, it struck Coal that this was the stuff spy novels were made of. The tough agent is wounded, waking up in some hospital with two beautiful women hovering over him. *Bond,* he would say. *James Bond.* He smiled with one side of his mouth. The two women would not get his humor.

"What's funny?" asked Maura.

He shook his head. Did he look stupid to her? That was a joke he refused to let her in on. "Oh, you just look concerned."

She scoffed. "Concerned? Coal, you have twenty stitches in your face. Your eye is swollen shut and looks like a green golf ball. You have bruises everywhere. Why would I be concerned?"

He smiled and closed his eye, taking a deep breath. "Well, I'm not dead."

Annie walked around in front, and she stood side by side with Maura, the top of her head about even with the top of Maura's nose. Two of the most beautiful women that must live in this little town, and here they were, staring at him.

"James Bond," he said quietly.

In unison, the women said, "What?"

"Oh, nothing. No idea where that came from."

They both frowned, feigning momentary displeasure. "I'll go get the doctor." Annie turned and left.

"She asked me if we're dating."

Coal knitted his brow. "She... What?"

"Oh, you heard."

"Huh."

"Yeah, huh."

Suddenly, Coal heard his name exclaimed out loud. He turned to see Connie rushing toward him. "Mom!"

"Oh, Coal! Look at you. They really did work you over. Who are those men?"

"I can't tell you," he replied. "I know you'd try to kill them."

"You're damn right I would!" she said angrily. Then she blushed. "I'm sorry. Excuse my language," she said, turning to Maura. "How are you, sweetheart?"

"I'm okay."

"Sure?"

"I'm sure. He doesn't mean anything to me." Coal looked at her in time to see her wink. He sniffed in disdain.

"The girls?" Maura was looking at Connie.

"They came. I left them in the car, for now."

"The girls are here?" said Coal. "Mom, come on. They shouldn't see something like this."

Connie looked at Coal and shook her head quickly, piercing his eye with hers—her look that told him to shut up because he was in over his head. He had seen it many times since he was a child.

Maura reached over and edged the door almost shut, all the while searching Connie's face. "How is Cynthia, Connie? How does she seem to you?"

"Broken." Connie shrugged. "I don't know how she'll make it through this. I honestly don't. How can anyone go on after what she's been through?"

"And... Katie?"

"She's... Katie. What else is there to say?"

Maura smiled apologetically, glancing over at Coal. When she saw him watching her, she quickly looked away. The uncomfortable pause was broken by the entry of Annie and Doctor Bent.

"How are you feeling now, Sheriff?"

"Like a million bucks. In a house fire."

The doctor laughed. "Worse than before?"

"No. About the same. The pain's back. And I'm still nauseous."

"If it's not worse, I think we'll let you go home. No sense putting even more junk in your body that we don't know how you'll react to. Can you sit up?"

"I thought you'd never ask."

Coal struggled to get his feet over the edge of the bed when the doctor pulled back the sheets and the single blanket. He got his feet on the floor and took a deep breath. In truth, his stomach actually felt better than it had when he came in.

"What do we do with the girls?" he asked Connie.

Connie looked over at Maura.

"If Katie wants to stay the night with us, she can."

"Would Cynthia like that?"

"I know she would. She needs a lot of love right now."

"Well, then maybe you can take Coal's car and take the girls with you. I'll drive Coal home."

Maura looked quickly over at Coal. A brief look of what might have been disappointment passed over her eyes. "Okay. That would be fine."

Coal frowned and looked down at his clothes. He was happy to see they had not undressed him for the simple operation. He looked over at the doctor, questioning him with his eyes.

"Questions?"

"No, just am I free to go?"

"Sure. No pain anywhere else?"

"Pain *everywhere* else."

The doctor chuckled. "Okay, but does it feel like anything's broken?"

"No, just my pride."

"Take it home and nurse it with a lot of tea and chicken soup. Maybe you'll get lucky and not get sick. I want to know about that if you don't. I'll use you for some kind of study. Your body isn't used to having to deal with something like this. It has to react somehow."

"Well, if I don't get sick, I'll call you. How's that? We'll go grab a bite to eat at the Coffee Shop."

"My pleasure."

"Thanks, Doc," said Coal, and standing up he shook the doctor's overly-soft, feminine hand. It had taken a while, but he was finally getting used to it.

Saturday, November 25

The next morning, Coal was wracked with fever. He had hoped the doctor would be wrong, but now he was too sick to care about it either way.

He woke to a wet washcloth on his forehead and Connie hovering over him. "Good morning, tough guy."

"Not so tough right now," he mumbled.

"Some of us think you are." She glanced to her left, and Coal looked that way. All three of his boys were standing there waiting for him to see them.

"Hey! How are my big men?"

"Good!"

"Boys!" Connie's warning bark stopped Morgan as he was about to launch into flight and land on his father. "Come on, boys, what did I tell you? Your father is very sick right now."

Morgan's face fell. "Oh, yeah."

"That doesn't mean I couldn't stand some hugs, though," Coal said. In reality, he didn't know if he even had the strength to hug. But the look in his little boy's face was even more painful than the pains in his face and body.

Morgan smiled and came over to lie partway across his body. Coal patted his back. Next came Wyatt, and he held onto his daddy extra long. Virgil was last. He stood there, awkward in his teenness. Coal did not want to push him. At last, he held up his hand. Virgil seemed shocked to see it there before him. He stared at it, then finally looked up at his father's face. At last, he took the hand and shook. Something was wrong. Even Coal could see that.

"Wow, that's fatherly love," remarked Connie.

Coal looked at her. "What?"

"Oh, never mind."

Wyatt was staring at his father's eye. "Will you ever be able to see again?"

"Yeah, Daddy! Are you going to have a patch?" asked Morgan.

"No, boys, no patch. In a few days I'll be as good as new."

He looked over to see Connie watching Virgil. Once again, his gaze fell on his oldest boy. What did a father do if his son did not want to give him a hug? It was not something that could be forced.

* * *

Later, the door opened, and Coal rolled over to see Connie. He could hear the theme of *Bewitched* playing on the television in the living room. "Can I sit?"

"Sure, Mom."

He felt dizzy. Groggy. Worn down to the ground. But how do you tell your mother to just go away?

Connie sat down on the bedside. "You should have asked him for a hug, Coal."

"What?"

"Do you ever listen to anyone?"

He laughed quietly. "Sorry. I heard you. I just don't know what you're talking about."

"Oh, hell. Virgil! He wants to be a grown-up man, Coal. But he's not. He's a little boy. He wants it to be okay to hug you like the other boys."

"Huh."

"Why do you say that so much? Do you not care what I'm telling you?"

"No, Mom, I do. But how do you even know that? Did he actually say that?"

"Well, of course not, you dope. He's a teenage boy. He's not going to tell his grandmother something like that."

"So...?"

"So what? You think I don't know my own boys? Even a blind man could read it in his face."

"But not me."

She was still. "You're trying so hard to be grown up too, Coal. But you're never going to be so grown up that you don't need the love of your children. The fact is, as you get older you might need it more and more. You're so busy being tough that you can't see your big boy is just like you: busy trying to be tough. Like his dad. Break out of it, buddy. You will regret it for the rest of your life if you don't."

She patted his leg a couple of times, and with that, she was gone.

Coal stared at the ceiling. It was daylight outside, although an ugly gray daylight, and dim rays glanced through the blinds and speckled the bedspread on top of him. It was hypnotic. He fell asleep thinking of Virgil—and Katie.

Sunday, November 26

It was black when Coal awoke again, and when he clicked on his flashlight and aimed it at the wall the clock said 5:00. He lay there staring at it, still groggy, but his dizziness gone. He reached up and gingerly touched his swollen-shut eye. The swelling had gone down appreciably.

He heard scuffling by the bed and was soon accosted by two wet noses. Dobe and Shadow were vying for his attention. He petted them and scratched their ears until his arm got tired, then rolled back over. In a moment, he heard them plop back down on the floor.

Five o'clock, he thought. Night was only beginning, and he felt like he had been asleep for many hours.

He was lying there on the verge of going back to sleep when the bedroom door cracked open, and a shaft of yellow light streamed in out of the hall. He held still.

"He's fast asleep. I think he went back to sleep around noon yesterday, and last night we couldn't even wake him up to drink some broth. He really got beat up bad, honey. Do you want to just go look at him? I promise we won't wake him."

A whisper... "No, I can't. Please." It was the voice of his little Katie Leigh.

CHAPTER TWENTY

Coal could not sleep after hearing his daughter's voice, although he never let on to them that he was awake. He had been surprised to learn that the time was five in the morning, not at night, and he had slept all night without waking.

He felt much better, physically, and his appetite was starting to come back. But he couldn't stop thinking about Katie. Connie had come in just after sunup and told him how his daughter came to be at his doorway so early in the morning. She had had a nightmare while sleeping at Maura's. She dreamed that someone was trying to kill her, and Coal came to save her but was shot by the killer. She woke up screaming, and Maura insisted on bringing her back home so she could make sure everyone was all right.

Coal pondered this news, sleepless. Did his daughter really have a part hidden deep inside that still cared for him? It was something he had not seen, or even dreamed of, in months. Something he had longed for, but lost all hope of ever seeing again.

He also learned something about Virgil. When Connie had gotten up in the middle of the night to use the bathroom, she had checked on the boys, and Virgil was not in bed. She found him lying on the floor with Dobe and Shadow, beside his father's bed.

In spite of his bad beating, and the stitches he would carry for a while now, this morning had brought Coal Savage so much hope he had not known two days before. Maybe with time, and a little prayer by his mother, someday he and his children could be a real family again.

* * *

The last meeting of church was held at three o'clock in the afternoon. Connie and the boys were getting ready to go, and Coal sat on the sofa, drinking coffee, watching the Pittsburgh Steelers humiliate the Minnesota Vikings, and listening to the banter among his family as they prepared. Only Katie Leigh remained silent in her room.

Coal's swollen eye no longer really hurt, and in fact he could even see a slice of light through it. But he had looked in the mirror, and the skin around his eye was a deep purplish-blue, almost black. There were several other places on his face that weren't much lighter—places he didn't even remember being hit.

His ribs still hurt, but he had his midriff still wrapped tightly with linen, and he could move around all right without too much discomfort. Much less discomfort, he was sure, than what the Minnesota Vikings were going to experience after this game was finished. Fran Tarkenton was in fine form, throwing the ball for the Vikings, but Terry Bradshaw was burning up the field with his arm of gold, and running back Franco Harris was flat-out unstoppable.

Cole heard the sudden sound of Katie's voice from down the hall, calling to her grandmother. Connie, glancing over at Coal with surprise, turned from messing with her hair and went down the hall. When she came back out later, she walked over and sat down beside Coal, drawing him away from the football game that was starting to bore him back to sleep.

"Katie just asked me if I thought she could come to church with us."

Coal turned from the television, staring dumbly at his mother as he tried to digest the words. Finally, he said, "You're kidding."

"I'm not. She wants to know if I think makeup would cover her bruises."

"I don't know what to say, Mom. You know, she hasn't been to church in months. Maybe half a year."

Connie raised an eyebrow. "Have you?"

With a sigh, Coal said, "We haven't been in a churchy mood in our house for a while."

"Well, I'm going to help her get ready. Even if we have to go in late, I won't be the one responsible for a troubled teenager missing church if she is interested in going."

After that, Coal sat trying to watch the game and drive the guilt out of his mind. It didn't work. It was on a whim that he pushed his way off the couch twenty minutes later and went to his room. He pulled a light blue shirt out of his closet that seemed to be growing a little loose across his chest in the absence of regular workouts. A black tie snugged up to the unbuttonable collar of the shirt. He had been using ties to make it look like his shirt collars could actually button for twenty years, since his neck got too big to buy regular shirts that didn't have to look like a tent on the rest of his body. A pair of black slacks and his cowboy boots, then a slightly too tight suit jacket turned Coal into a different man than he had seen in his mirror since leaving the Bureau. But he didn't shave. His face hurt in too many places, and not shaving was the one way remaining that he had to remind himself that he was going to go to church as the sheriff of a small Idaho county, not some highly respected agent for the FBI.

Coal puttered in his room until he could no longer find any excuse. In fact, he waited until he heard the muffled sound of Katie's voice going down the hall. Then, taking a deep breath, he stepped out after her. His daughter and his mom were walking together, probably expecting still to see him sitting on the couch.

That guess was proved when they both came to a confused stop at the entry to the living room, staring at the deserted room.

"You ladies sure look beautiful today," he said, stopping mid-way down the hall.

Connie turned about in surprise, and Katie started to, then stopped. "Why, Coal! What are you doing?"

"I'm taking my family to church. What does it look like?"

He didn't know what he expected out of his mother. But he sure hadn't expected her to cry.

* * *

In spite of his horrible appearance, those in attendance at church seemed genuinely pleased to greet their new sheriff and to see that he was a man of God. They had no idea how many times recently he had wanted to walk away from all of that. They took Katie in and treated her like gold as well, and for the first time in months Coal got to see his daughter's smile up close. She didn't sit by him in the pew, but she was just on the other side of Wyatt, with Morgan against his left leg, and Virgil on the far side of him. Connie sandwiched Katie between herself and Wyatt, giving her that last skin of protection against this world of friendly strangers.

One man spoke of obedience. Obedience to God's laws, no matter how hard they could seem. An older lady in a blue, flowered dress, with silver hair that was straight on top, curled on the sides, got up and spoke with full, smiling cheeks about forgiveness. He would never remember her exact words, but Coal remembered thinking about Paul Monahan, about Todd Mitchell, Katie Leigh, and Laura. Once, goose bumps came and covered his skin, and his eyes filled briefly with tears before he could blink them away. He wished everyone could hear words like this, and heed them, before they ever got into places like he had been.

After singing together, "God Be With Us Till We Meet Again," and then saying a closing prayer, many came to greet Coal's family before they headed home. He couldn't help but smile when one young girl Katie obviously knew from school came up and gave her a hug right before they left.

All were quiet on the ride home. As they drove down the highway, the quickly melting snow splattered up behind the car, and the world, absolutely windless today but for what the car itself was creating, seemed almost warm and inviting. Sunshine glared off the snow-laden Beaverheads, in the distance, and joyful deer romped in the meadows between them and the river. Several miles outside town, a bull moose stood alone, black as tar, defiant, staring them down. Coal wondered what Katie thought of him, since it was his kind who inadvertently had caused her broken nose. Her face, when he dared to look at her in the mirror, seemed serene.

Somehow, Katie had ended up getting into the car next to Coal, and she didn't even try to keep her leg from touching his on the trip home. Coal ached to reach down and put his hand on her leg and give it a squeeze, but he didn't dare. The moment was too idyllic to take that kind of chance. Instead, he just relished in the feel of some part of her against him. And in his head, he said a prayer. He tried to be hopeful, but he knew this kind of peace could not last.

* * *

After watching Mutual of Omaha's *Wild Kingdom,* starring good old Marlin Perkins and his tough-as-nails cohort, Jim, *The Wonderful World of Disney* came on, playing one of the boys' favorites, *Charlie, the Lonesome Cougar.* When it was over, Virgil suddenly got up and started getting his boots and his coat on. Both dogs leaped to their feet in anticipation.

"What are you doing, Virgil?" asked Connie.

"Taking the dogs for a walk."

"Oh! Well, okay. They'll love that. Make sure you dress warm. It's starting to get cold again."

Coal looked at his boy. His big, mature boy who so often seemed alone within himself. His heart was full, after today's church service, and the spirit inside him made him recognize an opportunity he may not soon find again. "Hey, Virg. Would you mind some company?"

Virgil met his eyes for only a moment, then pretended to busy himself pulling on his gloves. "That'd be okay, I guess."

Coal jumped up and got his coat. He was still wearing his boots. The twins jumped up too, but Connie quickly stepped in. "Wyatt and Morgan, why don't you boys help me get some cookies ready?"

Wyatt's eyes went from his father, to the dogs, then last of all back to Connie. His mind was torn, although Morgan had already caved. "Daddy, can we go again tomorrow?"

"Sure, Son," said Coal with a smile, tousling the boy's hair. "You just make sure and remind me, okay?"

Wyatt smiled broadly. "Okay!" And then he was off into the kitchen to the Pied Piper-like lure of the chocolate chip cookie, where Connie was already bringing down a bowl, and Morgan was searching the jungle of cupboards for the flour.

Coal and Virgil walked up Savage Lane to Lemhi Road, the dogs running out ahead of them. On days like this, Shadow seemed almost as spry as Dobe, although she had never had his incredible speed and agility, even as a two-year-old.

Other than the crunch of gravel, and Coal laughing now and then at the dogs' antics, they walked in silence for a while. Then Virgil, with both hands firmly down in his coat pockets and staring at the mountains ahead, said, "Dad, do you think Shadow's going to get too old to run soon?"

Taken by surprise, Coal looked at his old dog, running, playing, full of the spirit of life. But he was no kid anymore. He had lost many dogs, and he knew the signs. "It's pretty hard to tell how much time a dog has left, Son. They can be like a pup one day, and then all of a sudden the next day they can't get up off the floor, and the next day they're gone."

They walked for another quarter mile in silence, while Virgil's eyes kept roaming to Shadow, and then his head would turn and he would look out over the fields and the thickets of willows toward the highway. Finally, a sniffle he couldn't suppress revealed his deep emotional moment to Coal.

"I bet she'll be with us for a while, buddy. Let's just think about enjoying her while she's here."

Virgil didn't look over. He kept his eyes trained on something off toward the highway—or possibly toward nothing at all.

"What are you thinking about?"

Not looking at him, Virgil simply shrugged.

"You doin' okay?" Coal pressed on. Virgil just nodded, but still he didn't look. Suddenly, one of his few lucid moments as a father came over him, and he thought back to the time Wyatt had asked him "why Virgil cries". He took a deep breath.

"When I was about your age, Grandma used to have kind of a hard time knowing how to talk to me, Virgil. It seemed like sometimes she could tell something was wrong, so she might ask me if I was okay. But if I lied and said yes, she would just brush it off and go on talking about something else—something that was important to her, in her busy life. She didn't know I really wasn't okay, because she didn't know how to make me open up. And I never really learned that I had to hurry and tell her the first time she asked. I never learned that she didn't know how to coax me. So I just quit talking to her much. In fact, after a while I could only tell our old shepherd, Juno, what was hurting inside me." He smiled at the old memory, but it was not a smile of humor. Deep inside, those memories still hurt. His dad's old German shepherd was the only living being he would confide in, and Juno, although a great listener, never once had a morsel of sage advice for him.

"I'm not going to let that happen with you, Son. I can see you're hurting about something. You've got to talk to me. I won't just stop asking like Grandma did to me."

That was the breaker of the camel's back, it seemed. Coal had stumbled onto just the right words—the dynamite that blew the dam. The key that opened the lock. The password into Virgil's soul.

Without warning, Virgil stopped and whirled, throwing his arms around Coal. It was only the strength of a thirteen-year-old boy, but with it Virgil fiercely tried to crush the breath out of his father. Coal hugged him back, and when Virgil began to sob, it couldn't help but bring tears to his father's eyes too. It had been so long, so very long, since he and his son had really talked, really touched.

They stood that way in the road for what seemed like an hour, but in reality was probably more like five minutes, before Virgil's tears subsided.

Coal finally began to stroke his son's hair. "You know, buddy, men can cry too. My daddy used to tell me they don't. He would tell me to toughen up. But sometimes a man has to cry, just like anyone else."

"You never cry, Dad." Virgil's voice sounded muffled against Coal's coat.

"You're wrong there. I've cried a lot since your mom died."

A few seconds passed, and then Virgil pulled away and looked up at him. The boy's eyes were red-rimmed, and his cheeks puffy. "Really? You cry about Mom?"

"I have. I loved her more than anything, for a long time. And she gave me all of you kids. You guys became my whole life."

"Then why'd you go away?"

Coal didn't expect his boy's words to be so blunt. For a moment, he had no response. Finally, he said, "I didn't mean to go away from you kids, buddy. But sometimes when two people grow apart, they just can't get along in the same house anymore. I'm really sorry I wasn't strong. But I knew you kids needed your mom more than you needed me. And she needed you, too."

Another frank question: "And you didn't need us?"

Virgil would probably never know it, at least not for many years, but it was taking Coal a lot to open up too. So long he had been trained in the school of life to keep his deepest emotions to himself. "No, Virg, I needed you kids bad. I just couldn't let you know. I didn't want to make you feel torn between me and your mom."

Virgil hugged him tighter again, and Coal, in the light from the waning gibbous moon, basked in this feeling of warmth. The dogs had disappeared now into the gloom. But it was okay. They were safe here, for traffic at this time of year was sparse as Christmas rain.

Coal understood something this night, or at least he thought he did. He almost asked his boy why he had finally opened up, but it seemed plain, and whatever it was, it was enough. It must have been a shock for the kids to see Coal so beaten, so helpless and lying asleep so long in bed, unable even to wake and drink broth. It was the shock of Coal's traumatic beating that finally brought Virgil around, and for that, Coal could not help but be thankful.

Coal and Virgil walked for a long time after that, and the dogs came to check back in with them from time to time. Coal and his boy talked like friends. Like men. It was not only that Virgil was opening up as he had not done in a long time which made Coal so happy. Virgil had never opened up like this in his entire life.

At one point, on their way home, Coal brought up a subject that changed the tone of their entire evening. It was Katie Leigh.

It seemed that, in spite of their short time in school, and in spite of the bruises and black eyes that Katie had been so worried about, she had already started making friends. She was hanging out with one boy in particular, mostly around lunchtime, and if the boy was even going to Salmon High it wasn't quite clear to Virgil. This made Coal's ears perk up, and he listened closely to every detail Virgil could share with him. In this new climate of openness, that was pretty much everything.

It stopped Coal cold in his tracks when Virgil told him what the boy drove—a dark van. And he wasn't sure, but he thought he had heard someone call him Lance.

Lance.

It didn't take a statistician to guess who this Lance was. Possibly out of school. Driving a dark van. And Lance had already been seen talking to Katie Leigh at the Battertons' the night Coal went to find her there.

It was the Lance who had just walked out of Cynthia Batterton's life. The Lance Coal had hoped never to hear of again.

And now he was with Katie Leigh.

CHAPTER TWENTY-ONE

Monday, November 27

The temperature dropped overnight, and the ground the next morning was covered with heavy frost when Coal went out with the dogs. Snugging the wool collar of his coat up around his ears, Coal walked, and the dogs ran, all with big gouts of steam boiling out of their mouths. The sun burst bright over the mountains, scattering brilliant diamonds on the bed of frost.

Coal could not stop thinking about Katie, especially after being told about the attentions of the randy Lance. He had hoped the boy had the fear of Coal's wrath in him from their last two meetings. He guessed he was going to have to step his pressure up a notch.

But whatever he did, he had to at least say something to Katie first. Now, before she went to school. She must at least be warned, even if it caused a fight—which it inevitably would.

Returning to the house, Coal hung up his coat, beating his hands together to warm them. He walked to the stove and held them out to the heat, glancing over his shoulder at Katie, who was eating a pancake. He was glad to see that her bruises had turned light green and yellow now. Her young body was healing them fast. As for his own, they looked awful. Something out of a horror movie. He was going to live with them for a long time.

Coal turned to look at Katie again. The bus would soon be here. It was now or never. He took a deep breath... And the phone rang.

The ringing phone had begun to be a bad thing in the Savage home. Connie's eyes jumped up to Coal's, and both froze. Slowly, she reached out and picked the phone off the receiver. "Hello, Savages." A pause. "Yes, he's right here, Sheriff. Hold on please."

She held the phone at arm's length as Coal strode across the room. "Sheriff Matthews from Challis."

Coal looked at his mother for a moment, took another deep breath, and answered the phone.

He's back, Coal!

Coal didn't need to ask who "he" was. "Can you pick him up?"

He hasn't done anything.

"Come on, Paul!" Coal barked. "Help me out here."

Coal, damn it, don't put me in that position. Listen. I got in a lot of hot water a few months ago, and my name got smeared all over the papers for doing just that. I arrested this local guy to hold him for a while when I didn't have any solid grounds for the arrest. I'm still in trouble over that, buddy. Don't ask me to risk my job.

Coal sighed. "All right, Paul. You're right. Is he still driving the same rig?"

No, as far as I can tell the only rig out there that could be his is a late forties Power Wagon. Green. Kind of a weird green, all splotchy.

"All right, Paul. I'm on my way. If there's any way you can stall him from leaving, please do. I'll get there as fast as I can."

Wait! Coal!

Coal heard the words as the phone was clicking down on the receiver. He scrambled to find the number to Challis's sheriff's office, but then the phone rang again. He snatched it up. "Yeah?"

He just came out, Coal. I think... Yeah, he's taking off. A pause. *He turned it around and he's heading your direction.*

"Okay, I'm on it, Paul. Thanks!" He slammed down the phone. "Mom, I've got to go. It looks like our man may be headed this way. Kids, be good today, okay?" He meant to say he loved them. Somehow, the words got stuck in his throat. Exasperated, he grabbed his heavy wool coat, his hat and his holstered revolver, and then his keys as he headed out the door.

It seemed to take forever to get the Ford warm. Coal whipped it into Ken's automotive repair shop when he got into town and parked behind the building. Going inside, he found Ken working on an older Belair. "Ken!"

Ken peeked out from under the hood. "Hey, bud. What's up?"

"I've got a situation. I have a feeling I'm going to end up someplace I can't take my LTD. You got anything around here I could borrow for at least a few hours?"

"There's that green GMC out there. It's only a year old."

"Does it have four-wheel drive?"

"Yep."

"What's wrong with it?"

"Not a thing. Just another guy from the mines. Lost his job and has to sell."

"You're kidding!" Coal had seen the pickup in the back parking lot. It was a beautiful teal shade of green and didn't appear to have a scratch on it. He almost hated to take it, but he was desperate. If he found the Power Wagon, and the driver caught on that he was being tailed, he was likely to take to the hills, and there was no way to follow him in the sedan.

"I'll leave you the keys to the LTD. Where are the keys to the truck?"

"Under the seat, like always."

"All right, thanks!" Coal tossed the car keys to Ken and then was out the door. He drove out on S. Challis Street, which became Highway 93, and punched the gas. Some three hundred horses roared to life—a beautiful sound to a General Motors man—and Coal was soon driving seventy miles an hour out of town, and before long paralleling the mighty Salmon River.

He got out to Twelve Mile Creek Road before he decided there was no reason to go any farther. If the man he was looking for was coming to Salmon, he had no other recourse but to come this way. Coal pulled off the highway and down a little ways into a dip, to wait.

He shut down the GMC for thirty minutes, then turned it back on again. It was about an hour's drive from Challis to Salmon. If the Power Wagon was coming, it would be soon.

Coal's hand came up and touched the butt of his Smith and Wesson. It felt coldly reassuring to his touch. It was all he had thought to bring, but it was going to have to be enough. The minutes ticked by. Now and then, a vehicle passed, but never the one he was waiting for. It was an hour and twenty-five minutes before Coal realized the Power Wagon was not coming. Even if anything had changed and Sheriff Matthews had tried to reach him, he didn't have a radio in this truck, so he would not have known.

Coal puttered back toward town. He could feel the adrenalin seeping back into its sleeping place in his body. His pounding heart went back to normal. Both would have to wait for another day.

The day was uneventful. Coal visited Annie Price at the hospital. Her attitude toward him today was inexplicably reserved. She didn't even have time for lunch. So he drove back out to the ranch.

Connie was making tomato soup enough for ten people. The twins, who had morning kindergarten, were playing with the dogs in the living room when Coal came in. Both boys ran to hug their father, surprising him. He had gotten out of the habit of expecting this kind of reception.

Later, as they sat eating their soup and sandwiches, Wyatt studied Coal's bruised eye. "Will your eye get better, Daddy?"

Coal laughed. "Sure it will. It's getting better already. At least I can open it partway now, right?"

Wyatt nodded. He seemed relieved. From across the kitchen, Connie spoke. "Do you boys want to see a photo of your daddy another time he had an eye like that?"

In unison, the boys shouted yes. Connie went to her room and came back with Coal's senior high school annual. She flipped through the pages for a moment before coming to a stop on a section of photos from the Salmon boxing team. One of them was Coal. It pictured him with a crew cut and a seriously bruised eye—the same eye that sported the bruises now.

Both boys stared at the picture in amazement, and Coal laughed. "It's not that spell-binding, boys!"

"How did you do that, Daddy?" asked Morgan.

"Well, *I* didn't do it. A friend of mine did it."

The boys both continued to stare, and Coal laughed again at the obvious question in their eyes. "Well, he wasn't exactly my friend the day he did that!"

"Who was he?" Wyatt asked.

"His name was Hague Freeman. He was a real scrapper. He beat up K.T. Batterton the same day—but K.T.'s mom made him get another photo taken."

"Why didn't you, Grandma?" Wyatt queried.

"Ha! I tried," said Connie, leaning over them with a hand on Coal's shoulder. "Your dad wouldn't hear of it. He wanted the tough look in his picture."

Coal laughed. It was the first good laugh he had had in a while. Connie was right. He had been pretty proud of that eye. Especially because it was the only good hit Hague had gotten on him before he got a much worse beating himself.

"Where's the other man?" asked Wyatt. It was funny for Coal to hear the word "man" applied to them. They had all been nothing but kids when that fight happened.

He showed them Hague Freeman's photo. Even more than Coal's, Hague looked like he had been through the mill. The boys thought that was pretty neat. Too many movies with fist fights in them had colored their perceptions of life.

After lunch, Coal and the boys migrated to the sofa, one settling in on either side of their daddy, happy to have his attention for so long. Coal's mind was wandering. Seeing Hague's photo had made him start to think of how much things had changed since his return to the valley. Of the group who had hung around in high school, a loyal gang of "Musketeers," he was officially now the only one left, unless he counted Molly Erickson.

Laura Hutchinson. Larry MacAtee. Trent Tuckett. K.T. Batterton. Jennifer Connelly. Susan Lane, the first girl Coal had kissed by his own choice and who later had died in a highway crash. Hague Freeman. All of them were gone now. Only Coal remained. It was a lonely feeling, especially for a man of only forty-two years.

After the kids lost interest in the photos in the book, Coal went nostalgically to the pages at the back, which were packed with sappy and stupid sayings and wishful thoughts and signatures. He smiled at Laura's heartfelt emotions, sprawled out there so Coal could never forget them. Larry had to use one of the stupid poems that had been worn out as far back as junior high: *If all the girls were across the sea, what a wonderful swimmer you would be.* Larry had been Coal's best friend, but neither of them had ever been very good at expressing their true emotions with each other.

And then Coal's eyes fell on the writing of Hague Freeman. He stopped and stared. Recognition hit him in the guts like a sledge hammer. They were typical words Hague would write: *Bye, Coal. See you in the war. Your buddy, Hague.* He wrote them because they were both going into the Marines. But it wasn't the words that hit Coal so hard. It was the strange, flowery writing, so atypical of a boy, and especially a tough boy like Hague Freeman, that made Coal do a double take.

And it was the same strange writing style Coal had seen on the list of names in Roger Miley's pocket. The list of names partially crossed out. The list of people who were destined to die by a sniper's gun.

CHAPTER TWENTY-TWO

For many seconds, Coal stared at Hague Freeman's writing on the page. His heart pounded, and it seemed suddenly very hard to focus on anything but those words. Where was Miley's note? He had to get that note.

Coal stood up numbly. The boys were both snoozing, and the room was quiet. His eyes turned to Connie, who had been sweeping the tile kitchen floor but seemed to sense the change in the room's atmosphere. She stared at him with a mix of concern and curiosity.

"What's wrong, Son?"

"Mom, I don't know."

"What do you think is wrong?" she pressed.

Coal walked to her, not even feeling his feet hit the floor. It felt like someone had picked him up and was moving him toward her. He stopped beside her and pointed to Hague's inscription. She stared at it blankly, then finally shook her head and look up at him. "So?"

"So... it really looks like the same writing on the note Roger Miley was carrying when he was arrested. The list of names. Mom, most of those people are dead now."

Connie's face paled. "Okay, Coal, calm down. Hague Freeman was killed in Vietnam."

"I know, Mom. I know. But that isn't just any writing. How do you explain that?"

Connie shrugged. She searched his eyes. "There has to be some explanation, Son. Don't go scaring yourself."

"I have to go back to the office." He turned abruptly and went to his coat and hat, putting them on. Dobe got up and ran to him, and Shadow followed, but much more slowly. He patted them on the head, but in truth, he hardly noticed they were there. His mind was spinning.

In his office, the smell of burned coffee was strong. He went over and shut off the hot plate. It was ice-cold in here, so he turned up the radiator, then went and peeked through the window into the cell block. It was empty except for Todd Mitchell, clear down on the end.

Coal went and picked up the phone. He dialed a number that he had been calling for four years, a number that would take years to leave his memory banks—if it ever did. It was the number to his partner, Tony Nwanzé, at the FBI.

Tony was overjoyed to hear from him. In spite of the urgency he felt, Coal was happy to hear the man's voice. Tony was from Nigeria, and his skin was as black as that of anyone Coal had ever met. The whites of his eyes had a brownish yellow cast to them. Tony was tall and slender, and his heart was far too full of love for his fellow man for him to be an agent for the FBI. Perhaps that was what made him one of the best Coal had ever met.

"Hey, buddy. Man, it sure is good to hear your voice."

I know, man! I've been wondering every day how you were doing out there in cowboy land.

Coal laughed. "Well, Tony, I almost hate to tell you. In fact, I really don't even have *time* to tell you. But not good."

Hey, my brother—what's up?

"Tony, we've had a string of murders out here that started the day before I got back. And I'm on the list."

Say what? What the hell! Man, I am so sorry! You got a line on the killer? Brother, I'll be out there in a day if you ask me to. Ain't nobody gonna mess with my man like that.

"Thanks, pard. Not much you can do. But I need you to run a check on someone for me. A Marine."

Sure, buddy! Fire.

Coal gave Tony all the information for Hague Freeman. "The thing is, Tony, he's supposed to have been killed back in sixty-nine, in an operation called Oklahoma Hills. Happy Valley, to be exact—of all the ironic names."

So what's this all about, Coal?

"It's too weird to explain right now. Can you just check him out and call me back? I want to know where he was buried, and when."

Half an hour later, the phone rang, and Coal stared at it. He had anxiously waited for that sound, but now he was half fearful to actually hear what Tony had to say. On the third ring, he answered.

Coal, buddy, if this guy was a friend of yours, I sure hope you're sitting down.

Coal glanced over at his chair. It was too far away—all of seven feet from where he stood—and he couldn't wait. "Shoot, Tony."

All right. Well, your Sergeant Hague Freeman was fighting in Operation Oklahoma Hills, all right. Nineteen sixty-nine, just like you said. Quang Nam Province. First, Second and Third Battalions of the Seventh Marines and the Third Battalion of the Twenty-sixth. This Freeman guy, he was the head sniper in the Third Battalion of the Seventh. Pretty decorated, too. Killed him a lot of Vietcong.

There was forty-four Marines killed in that operation, Coal. But your Sergeant Freeman wasn't one of them.

Coal sat listening intently. He had forgotten to let out his last breath. Now he remembered, and with a gush it escaped his lips.

"What are you talking about? Then what happened to him?"

That part's a little hazy. The only thing I know for sure is this: That boy lost his mind. I hate to say it, bro, but this is some pretty deep stuff here—confidential as hell. I'm sure they wouldn't like me bein' in here. You know the government, though. There's some real cryptic things wrote in here. But from what I make of it, he went berserk on some civilians. Killed four or five of them, unarmed, up close. Just cracked. Shot 'em point blank. They shipped him home with a less-than-honorable, and that's all he got. Too much bad smoke by sixty-nine—I'm guessing they didn't want this all gettin' out to the news media.

Coal brushed his hand down his face. He wished he could do the same to the goose bumps all over his flesh. "What happened to him after that?"

Not real sure. His statement was that he was heading home. To 'the West'. After his discharge, there are a couple of notations, because apparently they wanted him kept track of for a while, to make sure he settled in all right. Kinross, Michigan, for a couple of months. Republic, Texas—five months. Some place called

Guffey, Colorado, maybe half a year. I'm guessing they're all pretty out-of-the-way, quiet places. Then he vanishes. Or they just stop keeping track of him. Maybe he was quiet for long enough they decided he wasn't a threat to society. Whatever the case may be, the last page says, 'Location unknown. Case closed.' Is that what you needed, buddy? Coal's pause was long. Far too long. *Hey, bro—you still on here? What's up, man?*

Coal sucked in a deep breath. "Sorry, Tony. Sorry, didn't mean to go to sleep on you. Hey, this is exactly what I needed, my friend. Thank you."

No problem. Anything for a brother. You gonna be all right?

"I wish I could answer that. Keep watching the papers. You might get to see me back in the national news."

* * *

It was four in the afternoon when Coal drove out on Highway 93 to the home of Don and Nonie Freeman, twenty-three miles outside of town, just shy of Elk Bend. It was still coat-weather cold, with mist lifting off the dark blue riffles of the Salmon. Cold, but starkly beautiful, with autumn's auburn grasses sparkling in the afternoon light and the ragged mountains hemming the highway in on both sides.

Coal was still driving the 1972 GMC pickup he had borrowed from Ken Parks. The more he drove this thing, the more he liked it. Gravel crunched as he pulled up at the corner of the house and stopped. He got out immediately, Smith and Wesson palmed, and stationed himself on the far side of the pickup, watching the house. Finally, with a deep breath, he approached.

He stood back from the door knob as he reached over and rapped three times with his left hand. He still had the pistol out, but it was down and hidden by his leg.

The door cracked open. It was Nonie Freeman. Her eyes looked tiny behind the lenses of her glasses, and her nose button-round. Her face was round as well, and florid, matching the red and white plaid shirt she was wearing. Nonie's body had been let go to apple pie and lack of exercise. She had always had a kind look to her, but now it was more nervous.

"Oh, hello, Sheriff."

"Hi, Mrs. Freeman. Is your husband around?"

"Yes, sir, he sure is. What's the matter, Coal? I mean 'Sheriff'?"

"It's okay, you can call me Coal."

Nonie smiled shyly. "Do you want me to fetch Don?"

"I do, ma'am. I'd like to talk to you both if I could." As she turned to call him, Coal hurriedly holstered his revolver.

Don Freeman was a mousy man, fat in the belly and saggy in the shoulders, his white hair sparse, his glasses crooked on his nose because one ear was slightly farther down than the other. One short leg gave him a gimpy walk, and he had a high-pitched voice that grated on Coal's nerves, along with a sense of humor that had never been fully developed and always seemed to be used at the wrong times. He had no sense of personal space.

"Sorry you came all the way out here, Coal," said Don upon seeing him. "We already ate all the food."

Coal chuckled. The Freemans had always made fun of him for eating so much as a teenager. But Don always went way overboard, until Coal finally quit coming over. A person could only take so much funning.

"Well, come on in, since you're here," Don squeaked.

Coal stepped in and pulled off his hat, shutting the door.

"How can we help you, son?" Nonie was now standing to one side, purposely making herself a shadow. She wouldn't meet Coal's eyes head-on.

"I'd better get right to it, folks," said Coal. He didn't like this at all, but it had to be done. "I guess they made quite a big stir in town in sixty-nine, when Hague was killed, huh?"

"Oh, yeah!" confirmed Don. "It was quite the shindig. I guess old Hague was pretty well-liked."

Coal couldn't tell if the old man was being facetious, or if he was simply deluded. Most folks, in truth, hadn't thought all that highly of Hague Freeman. But then dying always upped a man's popularity by several hundred points—not to mention his life-long saintliness.

"You folks might want to sit down," said Coal. When they told him they were fine standing, he cleared his throat. "All right. I don't think Hague is dead."

On cue, both of the Freemans' faces went white. "What?" shot out Don. "What's that supposed to mean?" He had indignation in his face, but Coal immediately knew. This was the kind of indignation that had to be planted in place.

"I just got off the phone with my partner in the FBI, Don. I'm sorry. I don't mean to dredge up whatever it was the two of you wanted not to get out, but I know what happened in Nam."

"That's not true!" wailed Nonie, coming to life. "That's just not true at all. Coal, you know! You of all people know how our Hague was. He was tough and strong and good. He went over there to save those people. You know!"

Coal nodded. He wondered how long Nonie had been waiting for this moment. Definitely so long that he hadn't even had time to make a challenge before she had started trying to counter it.

"Tell him, Don!" Nonie's voice went up another notch. "Come on, you tell him!" Her eyes turned back on Coal, and any timidity from before was suddenly gone. But her eyes were filled with tears. "Hague was a hero. He died in Vietnam. Happy Valley, it was. He was leading his squadron, and..."

Don had been peering closely this whole time at Coal's face. He read the kindliness there. But he also read the truth. Coal knew everything. The charade was over.

"Okay, honey. Okay. Stop it. Stop it now." He tried to put an arm around his wife, but she pushed away from him, almost falling. Coal leaped forward to try and catch her, but she managed to remain upright.

"I don't care what any of you say! Hague was a hero in that war. They done him wrong!"

Coal raised his hands in front of him. "Please don't go any further, Mrs. Freeman. I know this is hard. It's hard for both of us." Reaching into his pocket, he pulled out the list of names from Roger Miley's belongings, holding it out to Nonie, then to Don.

"Do you recognize this handwriting?"

"I've never seen it," Nonie shot out.

"Then why does it match exactly to what Hague wrote in my senior annual?"

"Mama, stop it now," said Don Freeman when Nonie started angrily shaking her head. "Hush now. He already knows anyhow." Don looked solemnly at Coal, his jaw set. "Can I see that?"

Coal handed him the list of names, and Don took it and looked at it quietly, then flipped it over. When he saw the back was blank, he handed it back to Coal. "What is that for?"

Coal stood there quietly meeting the man's gaze. Now he wasn't sure how to go on.

"That's the list of people who have been getting killed in town," said Don, reading the truth. "And it's in Hague's handwriting. But Hague isn't anywhere near here. He's... Actually, we're not sure where he is. We asked him not to come around here anymore."

"When did you last see him?"

"Sixty-nine," admitted Don. "He came home right after he left the Marines. He thought he could stay here and I told him I didn't want him bringing shame to our name. I sent him away, and we've never heard anything from him since."

Nonie started crying, and that embarrassed her, so she began to strike Don in the shoulder. "You had no right to do that, Don. No right at all."

"I'm sorry, Mama. I told you I wished I could take it back."

With tears flooding over her cheeks, Nonie Freeman hurried out of the room. Coal didn't see her again.

After she left, Don turned back to Coal. "We didn't want anybody to know our boy was still alive, Sheriff. You understand that, don't you?"

"I guess."

"He wasn't the same boy we knew. Not the same at all."

"It's okay, Mr. Freeman. You're sure he hasn't been back here though, right?"

"Oh, hell no! We would have known."

Coal was thinking back to high school, back when Hague had saved up his money and bought himself a shiny new rig—a black Dodge Power Wagon, one of the first four wheel drives in that area. With Sheriff Matthews telling him the stranger was now driving a Power Wagon, he couldn't help but wonder...

"Whatever happened to that old Power Wagon of Hague's?"

"It's out in the garage. When our boy left here, he was pretty upset. I kind of figured he'd come back for it sometime, but he never did. It's just sitting out there, all covered up."

"When's the last time you've been out there?"

"Oh, hell fire—a week, maybe two, I guess. I'll go out every couple of weeks and start it up, to make sure things stay lubed up, but I don't ever drive it anywhere, at least not more than a few miles at a time."

"Say, what color was that thing, anyway?"

"You don't remember? Black. Black as night."

"Yeah, that's what I was thinking." Coal knew it was black. But Sheriff Matthews had sworn the one in Challis was green.

"Would you mind if I take a look at it?"

"No, I guess not," said the little man. He went and got his coat, and they traipsed out together to the garage. Freeman threw up the rickety old overhead door, and no dust or any other kind of debris fell off of it in the opening, as Coal had been watching for. His heart began once again to pound.

They walked clear to the back of the over-sized garage, and there on the floor lay a tarp, covered in filthy gray dust. Don Freeman stared at it. "But, Sheriff, it was right here. Right here! I swear it was just yesterday."

"I thought you said you hadn't been out here in a week or two."

"Well, I don't mean *literally* yesterday! Sheriff! Somebody stole Hague's pickup."

The old man was staring at Coal. Suddenly, he caught the significance of the level gaze Coal was giving him back. "Oh my Lord! No. My boy is back."

CHAPTER TWENTY-THREE

Coal phoned the Challis sheriff's office, and he had to wait half an hour to get a call back, at Freeman's home. Nonie had never come back out of her bedroom, but Don was waiting patiently in the dining room with him.

Sheriff Matthews, when asked again about the color of the Power Wagon, swore that it was green. Even different lighting could not have made a black truck look the shade of green that one had been.

"It looked like it was sort of meant to be camouflage, Coal. Like a bunch of different colors of green. But black? No way. I'll give up my job if I find out my eyes are *that* bad. Any number of guys over here will tell you the same thing. It wasn't any normal rig. Everybody noticed it."

Coal asked Matthews to do some checking around and see if anyone knew of a black Power Wagon getting painted a splotchy green like Matthews had described in the past couple of days. It seemed far-fetched, if the paint job was as shoddy as Matthews described. But he had to know he was no longer looking for a black rig.

On a whim, Coal turned back to Don, still holding the phone. "What's your most recent photo of Hague?"

"One from the service," said Don. "Sixty-five, maybe."

"Can I borrow it?"

"You can have it," Don growled. But when he went to take the photo out of a drawer, his hand was shaking, and there were tears in his eyes he couldn't hide when he handed the snap shot over to Coal. "Get that out of here." And then he turned away without seeing Coal to the door.

Coal got Paul Matthews's private address from him, then hung up the phone and let himself quietly out. A minute later, he was speeding off toward Challis.

* * *

Paul Matthews lived out on Challis Creek Road. Coal could have reached his house by cutting off on Stephens or Jobe Lanes, but he wanted to drive around town for a few minutes, on the off-chance he might stumble into the green Power Wagon. After cruising around downtown for a while, then hitting some of the outlying roads, he gave up and drove on over to the sheriff's place. The sheriff's car was in his drive, and Coal pulled up behind him.

Leaping out of the truck, he went to knock on the door, but Matthews met him, pushing open a squeaky screen door. Matthew's most recent breath had been drawn inside the warm house, so it seemed like when he exhaled it made an extra-large cloud of silvery steam burst forth.

"Hey, buddy, what you got?" asked Matthews as he was shaking Coal's hand warmly. "You wanna come in?"

"I don't have a lot of time, Paul. Just wanted you to see a photograph." Once again, Coal could feel his heart starting to pound abnormally hard. He held out the snapshot of Hague Freeman.

Matthews studied it in the fading light, then reached back into the house and flicked on the porch light. He looked at the photo again for a moment. "A sight more clean-cut, Coal, but I'm pretty sure that's the man. I could pick him out of a line-up."

The words hit Coal like a physical blow to the chest. His ears began to ring. Even though he already knew what he was up against, Paul Matthews's word was like the last nail in the coffin of any chance that he might have been wrong. He had no clue why Hague Freeman had returned to Salmon, why he was killing all of the people he used to call friends. But one thing he did know, beyond any doubt: Hague was indeed the assassin.

Another thing he knew was that he was like a naked quadriplegic with a six-foot rattlesnake in his lap. Hague Freeman was as likely to kill him as he was to be taken into custody.

"You all right?"

Coal nodded. "Not really."

"Who is this guy?"

"Hague Freeman. I went to school with him. Around Salmon, he was about as famous as Davy Crockett, once you put a rifle in his hands."

"Say! Is that the fella... ? Wait—I thought he got killed in Nam."

"Yeah, so did everyone else. What he really did in Nam was go nuts, Paul. And his parents made up the rest of it to save face."

Matthews's face paled. "So... you think he's the guy who's been doing the killings over there?"

"I don't think, I know."

"Damn, buddy. That's rough."

"Rough isn't the half of it. Thanks for your help, Paul. I'd better get back to town. I'm going to have to start spreading the word."

"Cup of coffee for the road?" asked Matthews, motioning toward the inside of his house. The dimly lit opening was spewing forth warm air that called to Coal like a beacon.

"No, I'm plenty awake with adrenalin. Thanks anyway."

Coal drove way faster than he should have as the last of the daylight faded. But coming back this way there were a lot fewer deer out on the road than on Highway 28, so he drove seventy miles an hour in the borrowed GMC and ached with knowing what he was up against now. He was going to need every bit of grace God could spare him. For some reason, Hague Freeman wanted all of his friends dead. And so far, there was nothing stopping him.

Back in town, Coal drove by Ken Parks's house and knocked on his door. Ken answered with his typical dry grin. "Jeez. It's gettin' pretty bad when the local sheriff starts stealing vehicles!"

"Sorry," said Coal sheepishly. "I got in a spot where I needed to move fast and didn't have any time to come back by the shop. How do I get the car?"

"Do you need it tonight?"

"Not really."

"Keep the truck."

"I'd like to!"

"Really? He's only asking a thousand."

"Wow. It's a nice, clean piece. Who's the seller?"

"Sam Redd? No one you'd know. Just some drifter. When he sells the truck, he's drifting on over to the Falls to look for work there."

"Wouldn't make sense for the sheriff of a mountainous county like this not to have a four-wheel-drive truck, would it?"

"You'd be a fool, I think."

"You must be making a commission."

Ken laughed. "No, I just think it'd be cool for somebody responsible to get a nice truck. I've got too many already or I'd buy it myself."

"I'll get back with you in the morning," said Coal. He said goodbye and started to turn away, then turned back. "Buddy, I need to do some figuring before I blow the lid off this, so please keep it quiet, but since you went to school with him, too, you might as well know—Hague Freeman never really got killed in Nam."

"*What?* Where'd he get killed?"

"He didn't. And he's back."

Confused, Ken stared at Coal for a few moments, then suddenly swore, and his eyes widened. He swore again. "You're not telling me—"

"Yeah, that's what I'm telling you. Keep your eyes peeled, would you? It sounds like he might be driving his Power Wagon again, but now it's green. A pretty shoddy paint job of green, too. Shouldn't be hard to spot."

"I'll call the second I see it, Coal. Man! Good luck."

* * *

Coal got in the pickup to drive home, but a sudden thought hit him. He took a deep breath and exhaled it, blowing steam out into the truck cab. He looked toward home, then up toward the Bar. Finally, he started up the pickup and drove up to the courthouse.

He walked slowly down the concrete steps to greet Jordan Peterson. "Howdy, Sheriff!"

"Hi. Say, Jordan, there's been a break in the case you need to know about—for your own safety." He made the big deputy wait while he got on the phone and dialed up Jim Lockwood and asked him to come up.

It took Jim only five minutes to get there. He had felt the urgency in Coal's voice.

Jim took the news about Hague Freeman like an old soldier would. He stared at Coal and bunched his jaws, and in his eyes plans already began to form. Jordan was not quite sure how to take it, as he had never known Freeman and knew nothing about him other than the big fuss they had made all over town when news came back that he had been killed in the Oklahoma Hills operation. So Coal made sure he *did* know how to take the news, and exactly what kind of man they were dealing with—or at least the kind he *had* been. In reality, no one could know what kind of a man he was now, not even his own parents. And that was the most frightening thing of all.

Coal let Jordan go home early, then said goodbye to his old friend Jim. Now he was alone in the office. And he had never felt more alone. He was the only one left, as far as the list of names from Miley's pocket. He had never *felt* more alone, and he had never *been* more alone.

He suddenly got up and picked up the keys to the cells. He went into the cell block, satisfied and happy to see all the cells full of the men he had fought at the Owl Club. All were silent now, either feigning sleep or trying not to look at him as he walked by. He went straight to Todd Mitchell's cell and opened it.

"Come outside, Todd."

His words were flat. He turned and walked out of the room, and half a minute later Mitchell came out and shut the door.

"Sit down." Mitchell looked at him for a moment, then dropped into the chair that always sat in front of Coal's desk. It had probably been put there long ago as a hot seat for deputies to sit in when the sheriff was chewing on them. But traditionally it had become a place where people sat to visit.

Coal sat down in his own chair and reached down into the lower left drawer of his desk. Mitchell's folder was still on top, and he plucked it out and dropped it on the desk between them.

"Todd, I've been doing a lot of thinking."

Mitchell looked at him, noncommittal. That made Coal happy, because what he needed to say he had to say without inane interruptions.

"Nobody had any way of knowing Bigfoot Monahan didn't kill those people. Everyone involved in the case thought the same thing—me, most of all." He still wasn't going to tell Mitchell how he had actually planned on ambushing Monahan and killing him. He would never tell that to a soul as long as he lived. "Old Jim's a wise bird, and he's been in this business probably longer than you or I will be alive. And he was still fooled. Somebody went through great pains to make sure we were fooled. They had the perfect scapegoat."

Mitchell finally lost his cool. "Okay?"

"You went to bat pretty hard for Roger Miley that night."

Mitchell blinked, then nodded.

"You didn't have to do that."

"I was on duty."

"I have a feeling you would have done it anyway."

Mitchell stared. He was sitting up straighter in his chair. The proverbial wheels were turning a hundred miles an hour in his brain. He wanted to speak, but it took him some time. "I don't know. It just kind of happened."

"That's what good officers are made of, Todd." He let those words sink in, and when he was about to speak again, Mitchell said, "Thank you, Coal." Mist had come into his eyes, and he forcefully blinked it away.

"Todd, I'm going to be needing you."

"What?"

"I'm going to need you backing me up."

"I... I'm not sure I understand."

"That folder there?" Coal indicated the manila folder between them. "It's going into my Franklin stove when I get home tonight.

As far as I'm concerned, nothing that's in there was ever written, and if it wasn't written, it never happened. You understand?"

"I, uh... Sure. But... not really."

"We started out on a bad foot, Todd—a long time ago. But since I got home I've started to see a different person. Someone I need to back me. Of course, when I tell you what I'm about to, you may not *want* to stay here and back me."

He pulled his keys from his pocket and opened a taller desk drawer, down low on the right. Reaching into it, he drew out Mitchell's belt and holster, with his service revolver still in it. He also drew out his badge. He laid them all out on the desk on top of the manila folder.

And then he told Todd Mitchell who they were up against, and every detail he now knew of the case. When he finished, Mitchell was staring at him, working his jaws.

"If you want me on your side, Sheriff, there's no place I'd rather be. You won't regret this. Not as long as I live."

Coal smiled. "I know I won't, Todd. I know I won't."

As Todd stood up, Coal went to a footlocker behind him and dug out his clothes. "Go get dressed, would you? That suit doesn't fit you."

* * *

On the way home, on a whim, Coal stopped to see Maura, Sissy, and Cynthia Batterton. The teenager was quiet, as Coal expected she would be. As he also thought she might, she walked to him with emotion bursting out of her at the sight of him and threw her arms around him. He was one of her last links to her parents now, and Cynthia squeezed him with all her might and sobbed uncontrollably. He wished he had come sooner.

Maura walked over. Those beautiful blue eyes of hers, that could be so expressive of any emotion, from anger to happiness, now held a vast sense of sadness. She started rubbing Cynthia's back, all the while watching Coal's face with her lips pursed. After a while, her gaze started to make him feel uncomfortable, so he closed his eyes. He couldn't help thinking about the Battertons, and about Katie. Someday, his little girl could be in the same place Cynthia was. He wondered if she would struggle with any of these same feelings of grief, or if for her it would be only a sense of relief—a burden off her shoulders. To her, the killer of her mother would be gone. Perhaps that was all she would see. And that made Coal almost want to cry too.

Coal actually thought to call Connie after Cynthia let go of him and tell her where he was. He then sat on the couch, Maura and Sissy on his left side, with a foot of space between them, and Cynthia on the right, as tight against him as could be, with her head on his shoulder and a hand on his chest. He squeezed her close to him with his right arm. He ached for her loss and her sadness, and he longed to have a closeness like this with his own daughter.

Coal looked over at Maura. He wanted to tell her about Hague Freeman. But it wasn't really her place to know, plus she didn't really know anything about the man, so maybe it would make no difference to her anyway. More than anything, he just wanted to talk. But that's what Connie was for, he thought.

After Cynthia had cried off and on, enough to make her sleepy, Coal and Maura got her and little Sissy to bed. Cynthia, clutching her Teddy bear, Buddy, seemed more like a child than a young woman right now. Coal leaned down and kissed her forehead, and all at the same time she tried to smile and started softly crying again.

As they were walking out of the room, Coal started to turn off the light, and he felt Maura's hand close over his. He looked at her, and she shook her head adamantly. Nodding understanding, he dropped his hand, and they left the room lit, the door ajar.

"It's hard to be a tough guy with this one, isn't it?"

Coal looked up at the woman sharply. Before he could make a retort, he realized that she wasn't trying to abuse him. He rebuked himself inwardly for always being so ready for a fight. But Maura always brought that out in him, because most of the time she too was ready for a fight.

"It's hard. I don't know what to say to her."

"Who could? Only time can ever say the things she needs to hear, Coal. Tonight, you came here to see us, and that by itself speaks volumes—to her *and* me."

"Oh, well, I just—"

"Coal, can you shut up? Just for a second? I'm trying to say something nice to you."

He laughed. "Sorry."

"What I was trying to say is you came here when Cynthia needed you the most. She needed a man—a man to remind her of her father. And suddenly here you are. And then you let her hug you as long as she needed and cry all over you, and you didn't try to be the tough guy and push her away, or tell her not to cry. Coal, that little girl did more healing tonight with you than she has the entire time she's been with me."

He sighed. "I'm glad."

"And you needed it too," she added.

"What?"

"Put the tough guy away, buddy. I already know you, remember?" She reached up and lightly brushed at his eye. "We have an understanding. What I'm trying to say is I think you needed that hug too, and you needed every last one of those tears of hers on your coat. Because I think that little girl in there is every bit as much your little Katie right now as you are a father to her."

CHAPTER TWENTY-FOUR

Tuesday, November 28

Bacon-scent filled the hallway in the morning when Coal stumbled out of his room. As usual, only one person was up before him, and that was Connie. She had already been out and fed the horses, taken the dogs on a short walk, and now was cooking bacon, French toast and hashed browns.

Connie liked to serve Postum with fresh cream in it that she scooped off the top of her wide-mouth milk jars after it rose to the top. Although Coal was a coffee drinker, he had grown up with the smell and taste of his mother's Postum, and to him it was every bit as tasty and just as welcome of a frigid morning like this. She poured him a cup full as he told her what he had learned talking to Virgil, about Katie and Lance.

"He's trouble, Mom. But I don't know what to do, short of leaving him for dead in an alley."

Connie frowned at him. "Coal, you stop that, now. Have you thought of taking the time to get to know this boy?"

"I *got* to know him!" He told her of the incident the day he was shot at, the day he made Cynthia Batterton's acquaintance.

The farther Coal got into the story, the darker his mother's face became. She began stirring the potatoes faster and faster in the pan, long before they had a chance to turn brown on the bottom.

"Well, I can't say it's unnatural, but okay—you're right. I don't like Katie being around a boy like that. You'd better talk to her."

"You think so? Maybe *you* should."

Connie stopped stirring the potatoes and put a fist on her hip. "Coal, it's time for a confrontation. She needs to know you still care about her. Avoiding each other sure isn't going to do that."

His mother had never steered him wrong. Coal knew that. But this didn't feel right. It felt like a sure way to start a fight.

"Who's going to pick up the pieces if it goes south? You?"

"I won't be able to, because I agree with you."

"Then we're taking the chance that she gets mad enough to take off."

"Coal, what is the alternative?" She suddenly remembered the potatoes, and began turning them over. "If he is the kind of boy you're talking about, Katie has enough trouble already."

"And telling her not to have anything to do with him will solve the whole thing, right? It worked so well when I told her not to use drugs."

Again, Connie frowned. "I know. I know, honey, it doesn't always work. But at least she would know you care."

"Yeah, that'll come to her when she's twenty-five or so. Until then, I'm just a meddling piece of crap who won't let her live her own life."

"Tell me about it. I raised you three boys, remember?"

"Sure. Now try to tell me that boys are even close to as hard as girls."

"Okay, probably not. I never had to find out. And you were pretty much heaven to raise, most of the time."

"Wow, thanks, Mom."

"Don't let it go to your head. But your brothers were a different story."

"Yeah, they still are."

Connie found it in her to laugh as she finally dumped the potatoes out onto a warm plate, added some oil, and started cracking eggs into the pan.

"I'd talk to her, Coal. It's not going to get any easier. At least she'll know how you feel."

"Then be prepared for the dynamite. That's all I can say."

Coal went outside with the dogs to breathe in some icy cold air. The temperature had dropped close to ten degrees from the morning before, and in the night a skiff of snow had fallen. The dogs frolicked across the property while Coal went out and climbed up on the top corral rail to watch the horses eating a deep green pile of alfalfa hay.

Katie Leigh. He watched the horses, the steam coming off their flanks, their long hair matted with ice, hot breath coming out of their nostrils in clouds, and thought of his little girl. What had he done to make her how she was? Where was the fork in the trail that made her turn against him? Was it his work? If he had been home more, would it have made any difference? He was out saving the rest of the world while his own family was falling to pieces.

He sucked air in through his nostrils and felt that old familiar feeling of them briefly sticking together. He remembered that sensation from standing waiting for the school bus to come when he was a kid, long after the ice on the puddles had become solid and he was no longer able to stomp on it and collapse it like ultra-thin sheets of dirty glass. When he was a kid, he had been fascinated by the feeling of his nostrils sticking together for that piece of a second. Now it was just annoying, a sign that it was too cold.

It was time for the kids to get up, so he would wait for them to get some breakfast, and then he would go approach Katie. He couldn't let his mother think her advice unheeded. And he couldn't let her think he was too cowardly to talk to his own daughter.

When the cold on his backside became unbearable, Coal jumped down off the icy pine rail and brushed the frost and snow off his pants. He took another deep breath, gave the contented horses one last look, then called to the dogs and went inside.

The children were finishing up with their food. Katie was at the bar, looking so darn beautiful, even with the remnants of bruising around her eyes. It was no wonder he was having to deal with boy troubles. Who wouldn't want to be with this lovely girl of his, so much like a mix of her mother and dad?

He went and sat down on the stool next to hers. "Hi."

Katie looked down. "Hi." The sullenness was gone from her voice. For that reason, he almost retreated. Although it wasn't a sound of joy in her voice, at least it wasn't a sound of war.

"Your bruises are just about gone away, sweetie. You sure look pretty today."

Katie wouldn't look at him, but at least she didn't turn her back on him. She kept herself in profile. "Thanks."

"How are things in school? Are you making any friends?"

Coal noticed Connie had moved to the far side of the kitchen and was pretending to busy herself wiping down the handle of the fridge door. The boys had gotten up and gone to their rooms or to the bathroom, except for Wyatt, who had found a *Lone Ranger* rerun on TV.

"Yeah, I guess. Sort of."

"Good." He sat and mined his thoughts for a way to bring up Lance. There wasn't any good inroad there.

"Say, can I ask you about something?"

"I guess." She scraped with her fork at some egg yolk on her plate. He didn't know if her body tensed up or if it was his imagination—just something he was expecting her to do.

"So I heard that Lance boy was starting to come see you at school."

"What?" This time she finally turned her head, and their eyes met.

"You know—Lance? The kid that was over at the Battertons'?"

"Yeah, I know who he is. Lance Cooper."

"Oh. So it's true?"

"What is this?" The tone of her voice was growing sharper. Now he knew the tension that seemed to have come over her was not his mind playing tricks.

"What's what?"

"I should have known you weren't just asking me about school because you cared."

"Wait, Katie. That's *why* I'm asking—because I—"

"Go away," she burst out, jumping up. "I'm not even allowed to have my own life with you around."

With that, she stomped off to her room down the hall, and a minute later she came out with her books, slapped herself angrily into her coat, and slammed the front door going out. He turned and watched her stiff back as she went out to the road where the bus would be coming—although not for another twenty minutes.

Coal took a deep breath, and he felt his throat flutter. He took another, trying to hold down his anger. "That went well."

"I'm sorry, Coal." Connie had walked over, and she rubbed his shoulder. "It wasn't like we didn't both expect it."

"So you think that was okay?"

"Like I said, at least she knows how you feel. She knows you're aware of his interest and that you'll be watching her. Even if she doesn't take it as you caring right now, maybe it will at least make her cautious in what she does."

"Yeah, cautious. Sneaky is more like it. It wasn't that long ago when I was a kid, Mom."

Connie couldn't even reply to that. She just gave his shoulder a last couple of firm pats, turned and walked off.

* * *

After taking the pickup back to Ken Parks and collecting his LTD, Coal took a call at the office that morning that didn't surprise him. It was Don Freeman.

"I thought you'd want to know this, Coal. I went digging in my garage last night and found something. There's a rusted old garbage can at the back that I hardly ever use except in summer. Too cold out there to do wood work this time of year. I got curious and looked in it, and there's six or seven cans of spray paint in there. Fresh cans."

"Let me guess. Green paint."

"Yes sir. Three or four different colors of it. He had the nerve to paint that truck right here under my nose. Must have come in late at night."

"Where'd the car go that he drove there?"

"Search me. All I know is there's no reason to be looking for a black Power Wagon anymore.

"Nope. Thanks, Mr. Freeman."

"Sure. Hey, Sheriff?"

"Yeah."

"I know what-all I said when you were here. But I'd sure take it as a favor if you don't hurt him. And I wouldn't mind having that photo back sometime."

"I wish I could make a promise about not hurting him, Don. That will have to be his call, though. But I'll get the photograph back to you. That much I will promise. Thanks for your help."

"Just wanted to make things right with you. This is all I can do anymore to help."

Coal had lunch at the Coffee Shop, and while there Tammy Hawley came and sat down across the table from him.

"How come you're not at the counter, Coal? Where you usually sit."

"Not in the mood for chit chat, I guess. Sorry."

"Want me to go?"

"No! Of course not. It's the inane banter I can't take right now."

"Well, the lunch crowd's gone. You want to talk?"

Before he could open his mouth, the front door bells chimed, and Tammy looked up and sighed. "Rats."

He turned his head and was surprised to see Annie Price standing there just inside the door, letting her vision adjust to the dim light, after being out in the bright sun.

When she spotted him, she came to the table, slowing down as Tammy stood up to greet her partway. "Hi, Annie. Just you today?"

"Um..." Annie looked down at Coal, who was trapped in his booth seat by the table. "Are you by yourself Coal? Are you just getting here?"

"Yes, ma'am—to both."

Annie turned back to Tammy. "Well, I came in to see if I could find the sheriff, so... If it's okay with him, I'll just sit here and make it two of us."

Coal smiled an apology at Tammy but nodded at Annie. "It's great with me. Take a seat. Sorry for not getting up."

Annie laughed. "No! It's all right, I know I'm interrupting you."

Tammy, now back in her waitress role, smiled at the two of them. Coal sensed some disappointment in her eyes, but her smile belied it. "What will you have to drink?"

Coal turned his attention to Annie, his heart jumping a little as he caught the look in her beautiful eyes. She always did that to him. "I guess I'll have a Coke?"

"I'll take coffee," Coal added.

"A Coke and a coffee. Be right back." Tammy walked away.

"What brings you over here, Annie?" Coal asked.

"You."

"How's that?"

"Well, I just got off work and was driving home when I saw your car. I thought I'd try to catch you and say hi."

"Well. I'm glad you did. How are things?"

"Good," she replied lightly. The lights overhead sparkled in her eyes. "You?"

"Rough."

She pursed her lips. "Anything you can talk about?"

"Probably shouldn't. But what the heck. I might not be around to tell you tomorrow."

She frowned. "Sounds serious."

He nodded and went on to tell her, with one lull in the conversation when Tammy came to take their orders, about all that had transpired in the past few days. That was a dark enough subject, but perhaps worse was the one of Katie. He told all about his most recent run-in with her, giving her as little detail as he could about why she had gone off the deep end without leaving the entire thing a puzzle. He also brought up Cynthia and little Sissy, both now living with Maura, who was not equipped in any sense to handle the burden.

"There's a counselor who comes to town now and then, Coal. In fact, she will come when we call her for things like this—traumatic deaths in the family, sexual abuse. All that kind of thing. Sorry—I know, none of it's comfortable to talk about. But that's why we have people like Nancy. Her full name is Nancy Pearson. I think you should call her and set up an appointment. All three of those girls should talk to her."

"I will. Glad you brought it up. I've been at a total loss what to do with those two girls, to be honest with you. If it weren't for Maura PlentyWounds, I don't know where they'd be now. I have a feeling they'd be living at my house, though. My mom was always good at taking in strays."

"Can your mom talk to Katie at all? They seemed to be close."

"Nobody can talk to her when it comes to me, Annie. And now there's this new boy—'young man' is more like it—who's interested in her, and he's too old for her. Besides, I already saw what he's all about a week or so ago, and I don't even want them hanging around each other. Mom agrees with me about him, so for her to talk to Katie would just make them into enemies too. I'm totally at a loss."

"Wow, Coal. I'm sorry. I can't imagine being where you are."

"You have kids?"

Annie's eyes flickered, and she suddenly dropped one hand over the other, rubbing it. "Umm... Yes. Three."

He searched her eyes. "Not with you?"

"No, they're with me sometimes."

"Oh. Sorry, wrong guess."

"No, don't be sorry. Yeah, it's a complicated mess with them. Someday I'll tell you. Right now you have your own worries."

The food came, and conversation died. Coal had his back to the window, which until now he hadn't even realized, so while Annie kept watching what was going on outside, in the way of passersby and traffic, Coal had only her to look at—not that this was a bad thing. They ate and pondered the problems of life, and Coal for a moment had a break from his own cares when he began to ponder Annie Price. She was a beautiful woman, so kind and caring and seemingly full of life. Yet she didn't wear a ring, and he was pretty sure she was not married. What was her story? Was it anywhere near as dark as his, or what Maura's seemed to be?

Coal had one bite of his hamburger left when his thoughts turned to Maura, then to the two girls in her care. "I should get going. I'm sure glad you stopped by. I'll get that counselor's number from you soon, okay? I think it's the right thing to do."

"Okay. Come see me tomorrow at work. I'll be coming in at eight P.M."

"Okay."

She caught his preoccupied look. "Promise?"

"Yes, I promise. Eight o'clock."

"Okay." She reached out and squeezed his hand. In spite of hers being cold, a warm shock ran up his wrist.

* * *

Coal pulled into Maura's drive and sat. The horses were moving around in the corral, but no dogs were in sight. Steam rose from the heated water trough. Horses, steam—no other movement.

He stepped out and went to knock on the door. The curtains moved, and within three seconds the door edged open, just enough for Maura to squeeze out. "Hi, Coal!" She seemed excited to see him. For a tiny moment her tough exterior was gone, and the old school girl excitement of childhood took over her expression. "I feel privileged to see you again so soon."

He smiled, when another time he might have grinned. He felt lucky to have recently left a woman as gorgeous as Annie Price only to walk right up onto the porch of another who rivaled Annie's beauty as closely as Maura PlentyWounds did. Two more beautiful women could not have existed in this town—perhaps anywhere, when it came right down to it. Of course, his vision was a little clouded by loneliness.

"I wanted to tell you about something."

She stopped and searched his eyes. Her hands came up, as if to grasp his forearms, or at least his coat sleeves, but then her eyes flickered—a moment of uncertainty—and the hands fell back to her sides.

"All right. Inside?"

"No, out here is better. I just came from talking to Annie Price." Coal was only a man, thus blind to many things about women, but even he saw the change in Maura's face at the sound of Annie's name. He couldn't worry about that, so he bulled on. "She told me there's a woman named Nancy Pearson who's a counselor, and if we set up an appointment with her she will come to Salmon and talk to the girls. I'm going to call her for Katie, but I think Cynthia and Sissy could both benefit from talking to her."

Maura brightened a little. "That would be so good, Coal. I think Sissy's going to be okay. She's young. But Cynthia... I don't know what to say to her. Her whole life as she has known it has been completely destroyed."

"You can't be expected to know what to say. I think you've done way more than anyone else could have already."

Maura's eyes darted back and forth between his again. "Coal..." She paused.

"What?"

"I feel stupid saying anything."

Her tough woman act seemed to have vanished. In her face was the vulnerable look of a teenage girl who had lost her self-esteem, and thus her composure. This was not the Maura PlentyWounds Coal knew.

Instinctively, Coal reached up and curled a finger under her chin, raising her face so their eyes met. In hers, there was a lost, almost frightened look. "Don't feel stupid, Maura."

"I ... Coal, would you think I was an idiot if I asked you to hold me for a minute?"

Stunned, Coal stood there for a moment, looking like a man—which was quite understandable, he thought, but not acceptable. He caught himself before he could make any serious blunders of speech or movement. "Hey, Maura! Hey. Why would I think you were an idiot for that? Hey, come here." He reached out and drew her to him. It wasn't until right then that he realized how strong she really was. He thought he was going to have to ask her to let him breathe, so powerfully did her arms enclose him.

For a long time, they stood holding each other on the rickety porch of her trailer house, and the frigid air that had been around them before was gone. Even through his thick coat he fancied he could feel the warmth of this woman.

After a few minutes, Maura said something into his coat that he couldn't hear, so he asked her to repeat it. She lessened her constricting grip around him and looked up. "I have a place I want to take you. Maybe when some of this stuff is settled."

He smiled down at her. He was close enough to suddenly better understand the Beattles' words about the girl with "kaleidoscope eyes" in "Lucy in the Sky with Diamonds," because Maura sure had them. Her eyes seemed in this lighting to be a mix of blues and greens, even a little silver and gold. There was a sparkle in them like the diamonds that had been sifting down out of the sky that morning on his way to work, glittering in the sun.

"I'd be glad to. We'll talk about it soon." He thought about the girls inside, especially Cynthia. He knew he should go in and see her, but he was already in emotional overload with Maura. "I'd better get back to town, okay?"

She nodded. A thin veneer of toughness slid back over her face, and she gave him two slaps on the back like a couple of beer drinking buddies might do, then pulled away. "Yeah, sure. Yeah, you should go. Um..." The little girl peeked through again. "Maybe you could call me sometime—to check on the girls."

"I will. And I'll try to make that appointment today for them."

With that, he went back to his car and drove away. He drove straight to the hospital, rather than wait for Annie to be there, and got Dr. Nancy Pearson's number from the receptionist. Then, while he was still at the hospital, he called her at her office in Idaho Falls and set up a time for them all to meet.

The day had flown by the time Coal took a drive out toward North Fork, stopped in to visit a few folks he had known years ago, drove up to Gibbonsville for a while, and then headed back to town. He was purposely trying to get back at two forty-five so he could be over by the front of the school when classes got out. But he came across a truck that was broken down near the little post office town of Carmen, and by the time he got some help there for them it was three-thirty. Disappointed, he drove back into town. When he passed the high school, on Daisy Street, there was no activity around it. The buses had long since come and gone.

He didn't have anything to do back at the office. Todd Mitchell was on duty now, watching out for things, so Coal decided he would head home early. Maybe he could suggest the whole family go out to a movie. The Roxy was playing *The Valachi Papers* at nine, with Charles Bronson, but at six-thirty it was John Wayne in *The Cowboys.* The boys would love it, even if Katie didn't. Connie would enjoy it as well.

Before that, maybe he could ask Katie to go for a walk with him. He longed to find the right words to say to her, something to make her see how much he loved her, and how badly he wanted them to be close again.

That was it—a walk. In fact, he could take her riding. They could go into town and have a root beer float at Wally's. Coal took a deep breath. He badly wanted this to work. Bad enough even to be willing to pray about it—and for Coal that said a lot. He had been out of the habit of prayer for a long time.

He pulled up in the gravel of the yard, and the dogs came running out to greet him when Wyatt opened the front door. Both of the twins followed in hot pursuit of the dogs and threw their arms around him. If only a five-year-old boy had any clue how that made a tired father feel at the end of the day. Sadly, until they had children of their own they never would understand. Coal held them close until they started to squirm.

"Can we go for a walk, Daddy? Can we?" Morgan shouted.

Coal was taken aback. This wasn't exactly in his plans for the evening. "Umm... I guess we could—a short one."

"Yay!" Wyatt jumped in the air. "Hey, Daddy, did you know Katie didn't come home on the bus?"

Coal stopped short. "What?"

"Yeah, Katie didn't come home."

He clenched his teeth. A feeling of heat ran all through him. Why did this kind of thing always have to happen? Here he was feeling so optimistic about the evening, and now... It was going to get a lot hotter around there before it got cool again.

"I'm sorry, boys, but we're going to have to wait on that walk. Maybe tomorrow, okay? I need to go find your sister."

In spite of the chorus of groans, and what for a moment sounded like it was going to turn to real tears, Coal jumped up on the porch and threw open the front door to find Connie staring at him from the other side of the room. Her face was a mix of disappointment and the inevitable worry of a good grandmother. "I guess you heard."

"Yeah, Wyatt just told me. No phone call or anything?"

"No."

"Do you think she could have somehow gone to Maura's? It wouldn't surprise me, after our little deal this morning."

"I guess. I can call her if you want."

"Uhh... No thanks, Mom. Let me call." He picked up the green phone and began to spin the dial. One ring. Two. Three. Cynthia picked up, and he talked with her for a brief few sentences.

Finally: "Is Maura home?"

Yes. Hang on.

Soon, Maura's voice, sounding hopeful. *Hello?*

"Hi, Maura. Hey, I don't suppose Katie came over there, did she?" He wondered if he sounded as hopeful as she had.

No, Coal. I haven't seen her in a while. The excited tone had gone out of her voice. *She didn't come home from school?*

"No. I just got home and the boys informed me she wasn't on the bus. I think I know where she might be, though—or at least with who. Remember that Lance kid I caught with Cynthia the day your truck broke down?"

Oh, yeah. I remember you talking about him, anyway.

"Well, I think she might be at his house. I'd better go hunt them up."

Be patient with her, Coal, I—

Coal hung up the phone. He didn't have time for people telling him how to raise his daughter.

"I guess I'm going to Lance Cooper's house," he told Connie. He had taken great care to learn exactly where that young man lived, a couple of miles farther out on Twenty-Eight.

"Should I come with you?"

"No, Mom. I need you to stay here in case she calls. Besides, I doubt you're going to like anything I do or say to her when I find her—or him, either, for that matter."

"Coal." She had that half-worried, half-warning mom look. "Remember, you're the sheriff here. You've got to uphold the law. If you don't hold yourself back, you might be looking for another job. Remember what happened in Virginia."

He took a deep breath, hoping it would calm him. It didn't. "I remember. I'll try, but I can't promise anything."

Coal drove too fast down the icy lane out to Twenty-Eight, then turned left and punched the gas. For two miles, he tried deep breathing, he tried meditation, he tried every concept he could think of to calm him down. His mother was right—if he ended up hitting Lance or something like he had done with Charles Bryne back in Warrenton, there was a good chance his popularity in town would gain him nothing. He had to keep his cool—if he could. But each time he tried to relax, his anger came back, and each time it was at a higher level. Then he saw the black van he recognized as Lance Cooper's, ahead on his right. Within fifty yards he would be at the drive.

Suddenly, the radio started crackling, and he heard the dispatcher say, *Salmon dispatch, calling any county unit on the air. Anybody out there?*

Coal swore and grabbed the mic almost viciously. "It's me, the sheriff."

Thank heavens! came the sound through the crackles. *Sheriff, what is your ten-twenty?*

He told her, and she came back sounding like she had just won a big poker game.

Ten-four. Sheriff, I just got a phone call from someone reporting a car wreck right out that way, this way from the Monson place. It sounds like someone ran into the river. They may be stuck inside!

Again, Coal cursed. But this time the tone of his voice was different. Katie had to take a back seat now. There might be lives on the line.

Although he was already speeding, and he had passed several foolish deer playing along the road edge already, he took his speed up another notch, oblivious to the danger. Then, around the next corner, he spied a cluster of vehicles stopped in the road, and people rushing around like ants in a kicked anthill.

He screeched to a halt. Getting out, he popped the trunk, lit a couple of flares and set them on the road well back from his car. Then he hurried to the scene.

A sedan was on its side, partway into the river and hanging precariously to the bank.

"The sheriff's here!" he heard someone scream.

And then another voice, and words that make a law enforcement officer's blood go cold:

"There's a baby still in the car!"

CHAPTER TWENTY-FIVE

By the time Coal got into the car, by climbing through the upper back window while seven or eight brave people braced it on either side, some of them standing in the river, the baby was cold. He could detect no breath or heartbeat. He handed it out the window, and someone took it from his reaching hands. For a moment, he was forgotten inside the car, until someone started yelling for the others to stay where they were.

At last, soaked with frigid water and feeling frozen clear through, Coal clambered out the window, but only with the help of some man's strong hands, which were pulling on him. When he was mostly free, the man let go, and he tried to jump over the side of the car to the ground, but he couldn't even feel his feet. The man grabbed him, and both of them nearly went into the river. A second person got hold of his coat, then another came up behind, and they got him over onto the bank. The car teetered where it was for a moment longer, then finally crashed over onto its roof, its wheels all spinning crazily now that they were free.

Coal had lost all contact with the baby, but he was being ushered into someone's warm car when he heard a roar go up among the rescuers. A woman passerby was sent to find Coal and bring him word. Somehow, someone had gotten the baby breathing again!

He lay there in a stupor for he knew not how long when a voice began to register on him. "Sheriff? Sheriff, you all right?" A gentle hand was clapping him on the shoulder. He opened his eyes and finally brought them to focus on the face of a man who was bent over a little too close to him to see clearly in the fading light. It was Howie Jensen, the man who not very long before had been a tenant at his jail.

"Hi, Howie," he said weakly.

A huge grin overcame Jensen's face. "I'm sure glad to see you're all right. That was sure a brave thing you done down there, savin' that little baby. I'm proud to call you my sheriff."

Still a little disconcerted, Coal forced a smile and then, blinking, he looked around him, hearing the hum of excited voices outside. "Say, what are you doing here, Howie?"

"I was the one down in the water with you," said Jensen. "It was me that pulled you outta the car."

A slow smile came over Coal's face. "Well, I'll be, buddy. Looks like we're even."

Jensen smiled, somewhat shyly. "Not the way I look at it. I'll owe you for the rest of my life."

After Jensen was gone, Coal lay there on the back seat of the car, feeling the warmth seeping through his clothes into his body. He ached all over from the cold, and now the parts of him that had been in the river were beginning to tingle.

That tingling was what kept him from passing out when the car became so warm that fatigue tried to overcome him. But after half an hour or so, when the ambulance had come to take the hapless young couple and their baby away to the hospital, Coal, even though his pants and the lower parts of his coat and shirt were still wet, had started to get his wits about him again.

The first thing he thought of was Katie.

A middle-aged woman with a huge hair-do obviously dyed black leaned over the front seat, gazing down at him with big eyes. "You okay, Sheriff?"

"I am. But I've got to get to my daughter." He sat up, looking around. There were four or five cars still there, all pulled to the roadsides but leaving only a narrow alleyway down the middle of the road for other cars to pass through. He looked out the back window, and his LTD was still sitting where he had left it.

"Thanks for the use of your car." He started to open the door.

"Hey, the medics told us we should bring you to the hospital with us."

Coal tried to laugh. "No, thanks. I'm just cold. I don't live far from here. I'll go get some new clothes. Thanks all the same."

Without listening to any further protest, he struggled out of the car. The outside air hit him like a deep freeze. He got over to his car as fast as he could, threw open the door, and fell inside. For a moment, he leaned against the seat, his eyes closed. Then, gathering himself, he cranked the heat all the way up.

He wasn't going home—not until after he went to pay a visit at the Cooper residence and take his daughter with him. And she and Lance Cooper had both better pray that's where they were.

He drove back the way he had come, to the place he had been approaching when the overturned vehicle call came in. Taking a deep breath, he turned into the drive. The black van was still sitting right where he had last seen it. At least that was a good sign. Maybe Lance had learned one thing from their last two encounters—that Katie's father was not to be trifled with.

Steeling himself against the cold, he threw open his door. He got out, and practically leaping up the concrete steps, he pounded ungently on the storm door glass. He could already feel his trousers starting to stiffen up again. He heard someone grumbling as they approached the door.

The inner door swung open to reveal a tough-looking mustached man in his mid-forties, perhaps a few years older than Coal. He was starting to growl something—probably about Coal pounding on his door—when he recognized the badge on Coal's chest.

"Whoa! Hello, Sheriff, what can I help you with?"

"Is this the Coopers?"

"Yes sir. I'm Todd."

"I'm looking for my daughter—Katie."

Todd Cooper cocked his head and gave Coal a strange look. "I think the cold's gettin' to your head, Sheriff."

"Where's my daughter?" Coal ignored the man's comment, and his voice rose.

"Don't get testy with me. There's nobody here but me and my family."

For a moment, Coal was taken aback. "Whose van is that?" He jerked a thumb at it. He was beginning to shiver uncontrollably, both from the cold and from his own inner wrath.

"Mine, and my son's."

"His name Lance?"

All of a sudden, Lance appeared over Todd Cooper's right shoulder. He had a scared look painted on his face. "Howdy, Sheriff. What's up?"

Coal stared at him. "Katie didn't come home from school today, and I was told she's been hanging around with you."

Lance gave him a shocked look, then hurried closer. "Hey, Sheriff! I saw her today, but she didn't go with me. Her uncle came to get her."

His jaw clamping shut, Coal bore his eyes into Lance's head. His fevered mind tried to digest the boy's words. "What the hell are you talking about, uncle?"

"Yeah, some guy came to the school. He got there before the buses came and before the bell rang. I was the only one out there. I was sittin' in the van. He came over to me and asked me if I happened to know Katie Savage, and I told him yeah. I was pretty surprised because I thought he must know me, but I guess he just got lucky. So he tells me he's her uncle and you sent him to pick her up and take her home. He said he hadn't seen her in a few years, so he wanted me to point her out when she came out. Said he was going to surprise her.

"Pretty soon, she came out, and I told him it was her. He just thanked me and said I could maybe come see her at the house tomorrow, and then he headed over to her. I wanted to see her. We were kinda plannin' on it. But I didn't want to ruin the surprise, so I just drove off."

Coal's heart was pounding so hard he could barely breathe. He no longer felt the cold of his soaked clothing. "Lance, I do have a couple brothers, but I... What did this guy look like?"

"I don't know. Tough. Had a beard. He was a few inches shorter than you."

Coal mulled this over. The description could fit both of his brothers. Why would they come to pick Katie up and not tell Connie or anyone?

"Did you say you saw what he was driving?" The question left Coal's lips along with a prayer that Lance was going to tell him a rust-colored Lincoln, a blue station wagon, a damn white Torino. *Anything* but what he suddenly feared.

"Yeah, real strange looking green pickup. It looked like a cheap job of camouflaging."

Coal felt the old familiar kick in the guts. He knew his face must have gone white. Todd Cooper took a step back. "Hey, man, you okay?"

"No. No."

He didn't even thank Lance Cooper or his father. He couldn't. He couldn't say anything but the word "no". Almost stumbling, he backed away and rushed out the door.

His eyes were filled with tears of terror. The tears seemed almost instantly to turn to ice. He rubbed at them, trying to focus. He flung open the car door and jumped down into it. For a few seconds, it felt like he was somewhere else. He realized he was in his car, and he tried to start it. The horrible grind reminded him it was already running.

Throwing the car into reverse, he slammed on the gas and flew backwards right out into the highway. A car was passing, and it swerved and laid on its horn. He didn't even have time to feel embarrassed. Looking wildly around, not knowing which way to go, he finally took off racing toward Savage Lane.

He slammed on the brakes when a deer came flying out in front of him. Luckily, it made it all the way across half a second before he would have killed it. He was doing ninety miles an hour.

At Savage Lane, he screeched his brakes and careened off the highway, hitting the iced-over gravel road already going twenty-five and almost sliding off into the barbed wire fence. By the time he skidded off the lane into his mother's driveway, he had gotten up to forty-five, on a road that didn't justify thirty.

He jumped out of the car, but stood for a moment with the engine still running. What was he going to do now? Where was he going to go? Where was his little Katie Leigh, in the grasp of a mad man?

A feeling of sickness and despair like Coal Savage had never known swept over him, and suddenly he fell to his knees on the frozen grass. "God! God, help me. My girl is gone. I'm begging you!" He fell forward, his forearms on the ground. He didn't realize it, but tears were already streaming down his face.

He didn't hear the front door fly open. He didn't hear the footsteps coming.

Without warning, a hand touched him. It wasn't until then that he heard his name being yelled. He came to his feet ready to swing, both fists cocked. Only his tear-blurred vision kept him from throwing a punch.

"Coal!" The voice of his mother finally registered on him. "Coal, what's wrong? You're pants are soaking wet!"

"Mama, he got her!" He tried to see Connie through his tears. He was shaking all over again, but not so much from the cold.

"Mom!" He punched himself in the leg as hard as he could. "Mom, he took her. Hague Freeman took Katie!"

The look on Connie's face was full of terror. He heard her saying, over and over, "No, Coal. No. No. No, Coal. You're wrong."

"I'm *not* wrong!" he screamed. "Mama." Crying, he fell onto his knees again. With his fists, he struck the hard lawn, over and over and over. In horror, Connie stood back from him. She wasn't openly weeping, but tears stained her cheeks. She seemed frozen in place.

Finally, Coal felt hands grabbing him. Looking up, he saw the face of his boy, Virgil, and Connie on the other side of him. With the strength of people in terror, they hauled him to his feet almost without any help from him, and they started guiding him toward the steps.

He caught sight of the younger boys staring out the window and now could hear Shadow and Dobe barking, and he saw them clawing at the front window glass. If Dobe wasn't his own dog, he would have been terrified by the look in his face. He seemed to want to come right through the glass and tear out someone's heart.

Coal stumbled through the front door, and he heard it slam. "Get those wet clothes and boots off, Coal. Come on, Virgil, help me." He felt his coat buttons being undone, and then his sleeves were being wrenched off either arm at the same time. The process was repeated with his shirt. Coal's teeth felt like they were going to crack once he realized how hard he had them clenched. He looked wildly around the room, now bare-torsoed.

"You boys come here," he said, wanting to cry. He dropped once more to his knees and swept both of the twins into his arms, squeezing them hard enough that they were never going to get away. "I love you boys," he cried. "I love you so much."

Both of the boys were scared now by Coal's demeanor. Shadow was dancing around the room barking in a piercing, shrill voice, and Dobe was back up on the couch, searching outside the window and hitting the glass with his feet, barking with a sound that would have stopped the devil himself in his tracks. He knew there was something out there in the dark that had hurt his master, and he was going to have a piece of it or die trying.

"Virg, get Dobe, buddy. You've got to calm him down." Coal heard his own voice. It sounded like someone else. Then Shadow, hearing his voice sound calmer, came over to him, whining, and he hugged her around the neck and buried his face in her fur.

He could feel Connie caressing his bare shoulders. "It's okay, buddy. It's okay. It'll all be okay." She told Virgil to grab some clothes, and Coal heard him run down the hall.

Twenty minutes later, they had the fire in the Franklin heater stoked up, and Coal stood in front of it, dressed in a dark green plaid shirt and tan Dickies, with his badge pinned to his shirt pocket. Still shaking, he stared into the flames in the stove, while all his family gathered around him. The twins clung to their father, afraid they would lose him forever if they let him go.

No one spoke. There had not been the sound of a human voice in ten minutes.

"I don't know where to even begin, Mom," Coal said, his voice, after so many minutes of breathless silence, sounding like the crack of an old tree in the forest. "She's out there in the dark somewhere, alone, scared to death. She could be anywhere." He didn't even voice the first, most obvious thought in his mind, that perhaps she wasn't even alive at all.

"You go to the office and talk to Todd and whoever you can find," Connie said, forcing her voice to sound calm. "I'll start calling people. Jim... Maybe Elmer Keith?"

"No, not Elmer. He's too old to help with this. It would only make him feel bad that he couldn't be of any use."

He left his family there and started driving. On his hip, he was carrying the .357 magnum that Jim had given him years ago. On the seat beside him were the Winchester Model 12 shotgun and Model 70 .30-06 Winchester he had hunted with for years.

At the courthouse, Todd Mitchell came rushing up the steps to meet him. Connie had already been on the phone.

"Hey, Coal! Man, I'm sorry about your daughter. What can we do? I'll do anything it takes to help."

Coal stood staring at his deputy for several seconds. He had never dreamed he would be happy to see this man, but he was. Coal reached out and grabbed his arm. "Thanks, Todd. I know you will. Let's go inside."

When they got in, Todd told Coal that Jim was on his way as well, as were the police chief and Bob Wilson. Coal had to chuckle, in spite of the terror raging in his chest. Connie was trying to call in the cavalry from everywhere.

Big Jordan Peterson came in from the cell block and gave Coal a look of sympathy. "Anything you need, Sheriff, you just ask."

Coal could feel for these men. They needed to say something to fill the silence. They had to speak to make it sound like *something* was being done. But in reality, he wasn't even sure why he was here. He knew, and he knew they all knew—it was Hague Freeman's move, not theirs. There was not one thing they could do until they heard from him. He held not only the best hand—he held every single card in the deck.

CHAPTER TWENTY-SIX

They were all sitting in the sheriff's office, seven men with one common purpose: to bring Hague Freeman to the ground and save the life of Katie Leigh Savage.

Rick Cheatum was among those gathered in the office that night. Coal had thought of Rick last of all, but with his old friend's skill with a rifle he should have been one of the first to get the call.

Besides Rick, the list read thus: Coal. Todd Mitchell. Jordan Peterson. Jim Lockwood. Dan George. Bob Wilson.

Lucky seven. Seven men. One girl. One killer. And millions of acres of snowy, rugged, mountainous terrain to search. It would have been much easier searching for a single flea on a Kodiak bear—while it was attacking.

This was one of those times when a military commander would have taken control away from Coal. He was too emotionally involved. But even as good of friends as these men were, not one of them could possibly care as much about this hunt as he did. He was glad he was no longer in the military.

Jim Lockwood came and stood by Coal as he talked, a solid force of support and wisdom backing him up. Instinctively, Jim always knew just what to do in a crisis. That was what had made him the best sheriff Lemhi County ever saw, and a legend in those parts.

Coal stood there and told them all exactly what they were dealing with, and with whom. They already knew his daughter was gone, but none would have guessed that Hague Freeman was still alive, and that he could possibly be the Lemhi County murderer. Each and every one of them had been at Hague's memorial, in sixty-nine. They had all removed their hats, bowed their heads, and had a long moment of silence for him. They had all stood at the solitary cross in the corner of the cemetery and wished the fallen Marine a safe flight home.

And now here he was, back again.

"I wish I could hand you each a pistol and a rifle and give you a concrete assignment," Coal said. "We could get in our rigs and go out hunting and know within a tiny area where to go. But I can't. It's pitch-black out there. It's thirteen degrees and falling, by my thermometer. And we've got hundreds of thousands of acres we could cover—or more. There's no proof they didn't hit the road and head for Montana. Or Idaho Falls or Pocatello. Or anywhere else." Coal's own words almost choked him up, but he bulled on.

"I've already got APB's out on who we're looking for. They're going out all over the West right now. But judging by Hague's M.O., he isn't going anywhere—at least not far. As far as we know, he has been hanging right around here—between here and Challis—killing only people he used to be associated with. He's got my name on a list of people, and every other one of them is dead now. Now he's got my daughter—" he bunched his jaws hard to keep from choking up "—and if anyone thinks she is anything but bait to bring me to the trap, they are a fool."

Coal looked around the room at these men, his friends. Every one of them was tough. Capable. Intelligent. But none of them was psychic. None of them was a miracle worker. None of them could find Katie Leigh any more than he could.

"I guess you're all wondering why you're here tonight, in the dark." Coal's eyes met those of Rick Cheatum as he said that. His sight blurred over, and he blinked hurriedly, trying to clear his vision. He ground his teeth and took a deep breath. "I'll try to tell you without sounding like an idiot. In all the years I've been away from this valley, some things have remained constant. And true. You boys are among those things. Nobody wants to admit they need other people, but I'm here in front of you admitting it now. If you ever tell this to anyone, I'll tell them you lied."

He tried to laugh, but instead he got tears in his eyes again. This was tearing him apart. He felt like he had already lost his girl, but he refused to give up hope.

"So I guess what I'm saying is I needed to get among a bunch of friends I trust, because honestly, if I had to go through this night alone, I don't know how I'd stay sane."

There were no jokes cracked, as there would have been almost any other time. A tough man, a Marine, had bared his soul in front of a bunch of other macho males, something Marines didn't do lightly. His daughter had been kidnapped by a murderer, and no one had any clue where to begin to search for her. Even among a room full of tough guys who could find humor in almost any bad situation, there was nothing funny about tonight, or about Coal opening up to them. Someday down the road, perhaps. Depending on how this ordeal turned out. But never on this dark, frigid night when a man's family was in danger.

Coal had just finished his speech, and he was sweating because of the intensity of it, when the phone rang.

Jordan Peterson was closest to it, and he picked it up and answered. A moment of silence as he listened to the other end. Then: "Yeah. Hang on."

Jordan held the phone out toward Coal. To the question in Coal's eyes, he shrugged, face baffled.

Coal walked over and took the phone, and the room waited in silence.

"Sheriff Savage."

Sheriff Savage. Sheriff Savage—the last four syllables very enunciated and drawn out. The voice on the other end began to laugh, slowly at first, then building almost to hysteria. *Who would ever have thought I'd hear those two words together from a guy who was always in trouble like we were?*

Coal had grown cold all over. He wasn't actor enough for every man in the room not to be able to tell by his face who was on the other side of the conversation. Every man had come erect and was staring at him intently.

"Where's my daughter?"

She's safe. What do you take me for? You think I'd hurt an innocent girl?

Coal choked on a reply. So many things he wanted to say, but none he dared to. What could set Hague Freeman off? This man was likely psychotic. He would kill without remorse and by any method. Shooting men from ambush was one thing; it was the killing of Jennifer Batterton, brutal and up close, that set him apart.

"I didn't say that. I just asked where she was." He couldn't even bring himself to say this man's name to him. "Where are you calling from?"

Crazy laughter. *Oh, yeah! Wouldn't you like for me to tell you that? Hey, Sheriff, I've got a question for you. You got any idea how easy it is to make nitroglycerin?*

Coal froze, trying to think ahead of Hague Freeman, but unable. "Not really. Why?"

Do you also know how unstable that stuff is? Man! You ought to see it when you hit it with an ought-six bullet from a couple hundred yards away. Holy BAM!

Coal's heart was racing. To anyone else, it would sound like Hague was just talking crazy. But Coal knew enough about him to know he was not *just* talking. Hague had always been a little crazy. Now he had gone totally over the edge. But he never talked only to talk. Somewhere in this equation, Coal knew there was nitroglycerin involved. The stakes had just gone way up for Coal and all his friends.

"I don't know anything about it." Coal knew his voice sounded dead. He didn't know how to make himself sound to keep Hague calm—if that was even possible. He knew nothing about this new Hague that had finally gone all the way over into the deep end.

Well, I know enough for both of us. I know what a quart of it would do to a trapper's cabin. So, Coal? You want to have a hunting competition?

Head spinning, Coal said, "I'm not sure what you're talking about."

Ah, jeez, Sheriff Coal! Really? A hunting competition! Think about it. But here's a little something else for you to think about before you get thinking too hard: I can shoot a tick off a bull's ear at a thousand yards. And I know somebody else that can't. The crazy laugh came again, not building up slowly, but zero to sixty in one second. *We used to compare our hunting skills, one on one. No brush poppers. No radios. Winner took all. And I bet you can remember who the winner always was. ALWAYS.* Crazy laughter dug deep into Coal's guts. *No guests allowed on this hunt, Coal. No guests! Got it? I see a sign of any 'guests', a bullet goes into a jar of nitro, and anyone who might happen to be sitting tied to a chair on a trapper's porch, right above that nitro... well, it might not be too pretty for them.*

By the way, my mom and dad's house.

Coal was taken by surprise. "What's that?"

I'm calling from Mom and Dad's.

And then the line went dead.

Coal was frozen in place. He stared at the receiver. The deafening quiet of the room pressed in on him from every direction. Faces waited expectantly, eyes glued to him. The faces of his friends. His friends who now could not do one thing for him, because Coal was all of a sudden completely alone. Katie's life depended upon his alone-ness.

Finally, Bob Wilson couldn't hold back. "Hague?"

Coal nodded. Everyone already knew.

"What? What did he say?" Bob went on.

"He said he'll call again tomorrow around noon and I'd better be here by the phone if I wanted to see Katie again."

Coal couldn't meet the eyes of his friends. He was not a good liar. But he had to become one, fast.

"We'd better all get some rest," he said at last. "Any of you who can, I would appreciate you being here tomorrow. I guess there's nothing else we can do tonight."

With condolences, the would-be rescuers slowly cleared the room, all but Coal, Jim, Todd and Jordan. Jim came over and laid a hand on his younger friend's shoulder. He spoke quietly, trying to hide his words from Todd and Jordan.

"The rest of them don't know you like I do, son. Listen. I don't care what that nut told you. You can't try to do this all alone. He's had a lot of time to make a plan. He has it planned so there's no way you can get out alive. Even without hearing his side of that conversation, I can tell you that. You know, sacrificing your own life won't save Katie. For once, you've got to rely on your friends."

Coal almost snapped back, but he was able to take a breath and calm himself. He nodded. "Thanks, Jim. You've been a good friend. I'll call you tomorrow."

Jim nodded and laid a hand on Coal's shoulder. Then, without warning, he gave him a bear hug and a slap on the back. Neither of them could speak after that.

After Jim and Jordan Peterson left, it was only Todd Mitchell and Coal in the office. Todd kept watching Coal, but whenever Coal looked up at him he would hurriedly glance away. It was obvious that he wanted to say something comforting, but there was nothing to say.

Coal dialed the hospital on a whim and asked if anyone from the earlier wreck was still there. When they told him the young parents and their baby were still being cared for, he asked the receptionist to make sure they didn't leave, and then he said goodbye to Todd and drove down the hill.

At the hospital, a scene that likely was chaos earlier had settled down. Coal found the young couple sitting with their now sleeping baby. The little guy was pink and perfect, his chubby cheeks relaxed, his body bundled up and resting under a heat lamp.

When the young woman saw Coal, tears rushed into her eyes, and she jumped up and hurried over to him. "Thank you so much for what you did, risking your life." Without warning, she threw her arms around him and hugged him fiercely. He hugged her back. It filled him with joy to see that baby lying there in peaceful slumber when not very much earlier it had seemed to be gone from this world forever.

"You're welcome. You can thank me by raising that little guy right."

The father came over and shook Coal's hand. "We will. I promise you. If I could name him again I would name him after you. He would have died without you."

Coal smiled. "I think God had more to do with that than I did. Hey, I wanted to ask you something. In all that excitement, I didn't get to talk to you. But I heard something about somebody running you off the road. Can you tell me more about that?"

Anger came into the young man's eyes. "Yeah! We were coming up to this white car that was approaching from town, and they had a pickup behind them, coming fast. Then all of a sudden the pickup shot around them, right into my lane! The only way not to hit him head-on was to swerve, and that's why I ran off the road."

Coal was covered in goose bumps. He knew the man's next answer before he asked his question. "Did you notice much about the pickup?"

"Just that it was a pretty old one, a Dodge Power Wagon, I think. And it was kind of a weird splotchy green."

"Okay." Coal had gone still inside. "That's what I thought. Thank you."

"Do you know who owns it? I'd sure like to give them a piece of my mind."

"I do. I sure do. I'll be talking to them... soon."

* * *

Coal left the hospital and sat in his car, letting it idle at the curb. Every piece of this puzzle had now come together. Even if someone else had been listening to his phone conversation with Hague Freeman, they could not have deciphered the killer's cryptic words. But Coal could. Coal alone would know what his old schoolmate was talking about when he mentioned a trapper's cabin and a hunting competition, with such seeming casualness.

During the last two hunting seasons when they were together, their last two years of school, Hague had challenged Coal to a competition. A friendly bet. They would meet up above McDevitt Creek, at an old trapper's cabin, a relic from the twenties. Back then, the Freemans lived the other way out of Salmon, out off Highway Twenty-Eight, about half a mile up McDevitt Creek Road. And the old cabin was on the Forest Service land several miles behind them. Someone, perhaps Hague himself, because he loved the place so much, had taken it upon himself to keep the cabin up. They had varnished the outer log walls and kept new shingles on the roof—although "shingles" was a word that Coal thought of a little loosely, as it seemed that to whoever the self-appointed caretaker was, just about anything that would last a year or two on a roof might be considered shingles.

The teenagers would start out from the cabin when first light was only a gathering consideration on the eastern horizon, and with rifles in hand they would pick a route and start up the canyon. Whoever got their elk or deer first was the winner. And both years of this competition, both for elk and deer, and one year even with a bear, Hague came out on top. Where some people have a green thumb for gardening and can grow anything, anywhere, when it came to hunting, Coal always said Hague had a red trigger finger. If there was game—and sometimes it seemed like even if there wasn't—Hague would fill his tag.

This was where Hague would be when Coal went after him, not at his parents' house.

Coal could not sleep that night. He sat on the sofa keeping the fire alive and watching it flicker and wave its orange flags through the endless hours of waiting. Connie went back and forth between the living room and the kitchen, stir crazy. Finally, she fell asleep on the sofa beside Coal, her head on his shoulder.

Wednesday, November 29

And then the hour came. The time to go. Coal got up and dressed in layered clothing: long johns; tee shirt; light cotton shirt; wool shirt; black and blue buffalo plaid wool coat. The last, he wore because if he brushed against a branch, it would make very little noise, as opposed to his heavier coat.

He laced up his boots, then threaded on the holstered Smith and Wesson and loaded the Model 70 .30-06. Last, he got out the .44-40 Winchester. It didn't have the same power as his ought-six, but it carried sixteen rounds if he had one chambered, and it had always been his good luck rifle. He had killed more game with it than any other. Besides, when he was carrying the lever action, it seemed like his father, old Prince, was walking along with him. And today, more than ever, he needed his old man. On a whim, he also took out the old Colt Peacemaker.

Before leaving his house, Coal suddenly had a thought, and he dialed up Todd Mitchell's home phone. Mitchell answered the phone trying to wake up. *Yeah?*

"Hey, Todd, sorry to call so early. Can you do me a favor? Something I didn't tell anyone last night is Hague Freeman was calling from his folks' house. He won't be there, but... Do you think you could go check on them for me? And you might want to alert whoever the ambulance crew is today before you head out there."

Sure thing, Coal. And I'll be ready for later, all right? Make sure you call.

"I will."

Promise?

Coal chuckled, although he felt anything but light-hearted. "I'll see you later, Todd. And Todd?"

Yeah?

"I'm sure glad things have worked out like they have. You're a good man. Lemhi County is lucky to have you. Take care."

Before Todd could reply, he hung up.

Connie was awake now, and Coal went to her and hugged her, long and tenderly. He patted her back and then kissed her on the forehead. "Our family never said it much, Mom, so I don't know how it sounds. But I just want to tell you I love you."

"Oh, I love you too, Son." She pulled him back against her. "I love you too."

The dogs tramped at the doorway as Coal picked up the keys and stared out into the night. He patted them each and then he knelt down and hugged them to him. He petted his good old girl and his strong young boy on the head, wished like crazy that his sons could be awake, and then walked out into the piercing cold. The thermometer on the front of the house said four degrees, but Coal's blood was pounding fast. It felt like thirty to him.

He fired up the LTD and drove into the dark of morning. Over the eastern horizon hung the morning star. But there was no point in wishing on it, except maybe for Katie Leigh.

Today, Coal Savage was going to die.

CHAPTER TWENTY-SEVEN

Coal drove first into town, where as he expected he found the keys to the green GMC under the seat behind Ken's shop. He left the LTD parked nearby with a note on the seat, thanking his friend for everything and telling him where he could find the pickup later, if Coal didn't make it back.

From there, he turned southeast on Highway Twenty-Eight. Finally, as the sky was blooming silver in the northern sky, over the snow-covered Beaverheads, Coal eased off the throttle and turned south onto McDevitt Creek Road.

Here, he paused, looking up at the sky-lined mountains ahead. His little Katie was back there. He knew it. He felt it. But saving both of their lives was going to take something more than a miracle. He knew that more than he knew anything else. He was about to embark upon the deadliest mission of his life.

McDevitt Creek Road wound along through farm fields and pastures, with loose shocks of willows standing sentinel here and there along the roadside. Once, he startled a cow moose with a big, gangly calf. They ran off out of the range of his headlights, and he kept driving. Wildlife watching was the farthest thing from his mind.

He came to the old Freeman place, which bordered a nice ranch where Coal used to help roundup and brand cattle in the spring and fall. Here, the road bent sharply right, and he followed along. Shortly, it elbowed once again to the left, running in the same direction it had started, up into the mountains.

As he drove the road, it began to descend into a canyon, and now it was flanked by steep slopes on either side, tree-covered and sprouting with huge lava outcrops. Most of this he only knew from memory, for this world he was driving in now was black and foreboding. Death and destruction seemed to cry out with every rattle of rocks, every bounce of the pickup bed.

Mormon Canyon Road soon branched off to the left, but he continued to follow along winding McDevitt Creek, now driving in a crunchy frosting of snow. After a while, he lost track of the names of creeks and roads and canyons. Perhaps he had never even known most of them to begin with. Somewhere ahead in the dark loomed Watson Peak, the only big landmark he would see in that direction once the sun came up.

He found his heart pounding harder, partly because it had been years since he spent any time on these roads, and he was growing uncertain that he was still on the right road. The thing that made him almost sure was that he was still following the freshest set of tire tracks in the frozen snow. He had branched off McDevitt Creek and made several turns onto different forest service roads, and old growth timber surrounded him on every side.

Suddenly, the road made a bend, and a wide, brushy meadow opened up before him. His heart leaped. This was it! He brought the pickup crunching to a halt in the snow, which was now half a foot deep in many places, and by January would be much deeper. It was actually not as deep as it might have been, and for that he was thankful. The GMC might not be able to go all the places Hague's specially rigged-up Power Wagon could.

A wave of unexpected trepidation came washing over Coal, leaving goose bumps in its wake. In spite of the heat inside the cab, it suddenly felt very cold. He found himself wracking his brain, calling up old memories, trying to place all the landmarks in this canyon from the hunts of his youth.

The trapper's cabin would lie almost directly across from him now, in the shadows of towering Douglas firs and aspen. Beyond it, the slopes rose sharply upward, and there elk and deer trails meandered through the deep wood. If these woods were the same as twenty years ago, they would be crawling with bears, too, and an occasional cougar. Although he had seen very few, he had often crossed their sign.

He took a deep breath. What did he do now? He was where Hague Freeman had wanted him. Would he give him some kind of sign?

As if Freeman was reading his mind, a light flashed on the far side of the meadow, probably a flashlight, for it was very dim at this distance. Coal drew in another deep breath. If Hague was choosing to play their old game, the contest would start from the cabin—only this time they would not be hunting any game animal.

This time, their prey was each other.

Coal's gut told him that Hague would not just shoot him now, as he had done the others. There was something different about the relationship he and Hague had shared. They were more equals in this realm of the mountains. Worthy rivals. Coal sensed that Hague would not want to spoil his moment of triumph. He would at least want to talk first, before pulling the trigger. And more likely, after missing in his one attempt to kill Coal from ambush back at the house, he had concocted some spectacular plan to show off the prowess he had honed in Vietnam. If he had wanted once more to try assassinating Coal from hiding, he was certain he could have done it.

Coal reached over blindly and felt the Winchester .44-40 rifle. He ran his fingers along the pump action of the Model 12. He fondled the grip of the magnum on his hip. And last, he reached far over and hefted the rifle case off the seat, the case in which his old ought-six rested. But it was probably useless, for he had had no time to sight it in. He wasn't even sure why he had brought it along.

Same with the .44-40 Peacemaker, kept by his father so he could use the same cartridges in both it and the lever action Winchester. On a whim, he put that one, still in its case, under the seat. In case Hague ended up killing him, and later ransacked the pickup, maybe he would miss that one. It would be nice for the boys to have to remember him by, and as a memento of their grandfather.

One big breath. Two. Three. Four. And then he reached down for the shifter knob, threw the truck into first, and started to crawl across the meadow through the snow and brush. Shift to second. Now he was going five to seven miles an hour, and in this deep snow, and uncertain of the terrain, he would go no faster.

He drove until he saw the cabin appear dimly in his headlights. He slowed even more. He clenched his jaws until they hurt. How he hated Hague Freeman right now, more than he had ever hated any other man.

Forty feet out from the cabin's front porch, Coal pulled the truck to a stop, throwing it into neutral. He clicked the brights once with his left foot, flashing glaring light over the cabin and the timber behind. The other man's flashlight flashed once in reply, from the side of the cabin.

He rolled down the window and leaned his head out.

"What now, Hague?" His voice sounded unnaturally loud in the meadow, echoing up through the trees and vanishing against the ebony sky.

"Turn it off!" the call came back.

Coal reached and flipped the key back, and the world went completely still. His headlights had dimmed a little, but still they continued to illuminate the house. A paler light was beginning to creep over the sky to the south and east. And the snow in the meadow backlit everything there in its own eerie way, making it so the canyon was anything but coal black.

Coal leaned out the window again. "You going to shoot me when I step out?"

A barking laugh echoed back from the trees. "Nah, I tried that back at your house, remember? What the hell? You think I went through all this work just to do that?"

Coal knew this was one time when he could actually trust this opponent, even as crazy as he had obviously gone. Hague had something to prove, and for whatever reason, he had decided that shooting a sitting duck was not going to make things right for him.

Rolling up the window, Coal raised the door handle and pushed open the door, stepping out into the snow. It crunched loudly under his lug soles.

The flashlight beam reached Coal, shining dim. "Is that a gun on your hip, Coal?"

"Yes."

"Take it off. Any other weapons too. If you come over here with a weapon on, I shoot you in the guts. I didn't come here to fight a damn cheat. And then I kill your girl."

Unreasonable anger surged up into Coal's throat. "Katie?" he yelled.

"Daddy!"

That word coming from a girl with whom he had been at odds for so long almost made Coal want to cry. "It's okay, honey. Let's just do what he says."

"That's right," Hague responded. "Now take off the gun, and put it in the cab."

Coal complied and then rebuckled his pants belt. He was now completely unarmed. He slammed the door, which sounded like an explosion in the snow-locked, frozen world. Slowly, he began to make his way across the snowy field.

He could feel his face aching with the cold. Up here in these high woods, it had to be well below zero now, perhaps fifteen below. His hands, even inside his wool gloves, were already feeling the ruthless bite of the cold.

Twenty feet from the cabin, Coal saw the flare of a match. It moved to one side, and as a lamp's wick was lit, the yellowy-orange light flared up around a lean, bearded face, the shadow of a man from Coal's ancient past, wearing a ball cap and camouflage coat and pants.

Reaching up, Freeman hung the lamp from a nail protruding from one of the cabin's roof supports, which also served as the front corner post of a porch that ran the length of the cabin. About five feet to Freeman's left sat a chair, and in that chair was what seemed like a tiny form, all wrapped in bulky blankets—Katie.

Freeman reached up and pulled a sidearm from a leather holster on his right hip. Coal heard the sucking sound of the leather relinquishing its hold on steel from twenty feet away. He flinched when the gun came level, aimed at his chest.

"You don't get a gun, buddy, but I do. I won't use it, though. We don't want to do away with all the fun."

He flicked the switch on his flashlight and shined it to the left. Beside Katie's chair was an object, some kind of jug.

"You see that, Coal? That bottle's full of nitroglycerin. One quart, I think. Hell, maybe two. I was bored one day. Just kept making it and lost track. Anyway, it's enough to blow this place to slivers, along with half the trees in the neighborhood. I don't need to say what it will do to that little slut sitting by it."

Coal ground his teeth together, and Hague laughed. "Aw, come on, butthead. You're not going to let a little thing like that bother you, are you? She's a woman, like all the rest of them. If you think she's something besides a slut, that doesn't say much for your intelligence. But you just keep on believing she isn't, Coal. Yeah, go right on ahead. You aren't gonna live long enough to know for sure one way or the other."

"Get on with it, Hague." Coal had a lot of things in his head that he wanted to call this man, but he wasn't sure what might set him off. For once, he was able to keep his temper in check. Katie's life depended on it.

"How far did you come with that nitro?" Coal asked.

"Five hundred miles, I guess."

"And you weren't afraid it was going to go off?"

A long pause, followed by a raucous burst of laughter. "Oh, yeah. Real afraid. What the hell's there to be afraid of, Coal? It's not like I have any kind of life left. Between this damn valley and the Marines, they took everything I had."

"What happened, Hague? Why'd they kick you out?"

"Bastards!" Hague suddenly spat forcefully against the snow. "Why? They sent me out on a mission. In the middle of this thing called Oklahoma Hills. I don't know—maybe you were there too? Put me in the middle of this godforsaken spot called Happy Valley." He laughed again, a forced sound. "Happy Valley!" He shouted the words, and they echoed through the trees. "Real happy place. Me and some boys found these people there. A family. Six of 'em. Could have been there to blow us up. It was a war. How was I supposed to know? It happened all the time. I lost a bunch of friends to those little creeps. They'd send some kid to bring us bread, and he'd have a bomb in the basket. Blew the head right off this friend of mine once. Splattered me with blood and brains. Killed the little kid too—pecker. He deserved it. If he hadn't blown himself up, I would have carved him into little pieces."

"That's a long answer, Hague. Still doesn't tell me anything."

"Oh, go to hell. You know good and well what happened. I shot all them people down. Shot 'em down right then and there and didn't give 'em a chance to blow me up, or any of the boys I was with. We did it all the time. It was them or us."

"So?"

"So then this piss ant so-called buddy of mine called Bucky Knight gets all religious on me. Never said a word till the whole thing was over, and then he turns me in to the El-Tee as soon as we all get back together. He took it all the way up the line, and this Colonel Braeger gives me a court-martial. What the hell? I did what we were all doing over there: saving lives."

"Did that family have bombs?"

"Well, not as it turned out, no. Not right then, anyway. But that doesn't mean they never would have."

Coal felt bile rise up in his throat. Some men could not be soldiers. Hague Freeman made that clear. His motto: *If they have brownish-yellow skin, kill them. Just in case.* It could not long be justified, war or no war.

"Why didn't you just kill me, Hague?" Coal asked suddenly.

Hague started to laugh. "Like I said, I tried. Your damn dog saved your life when you reached down to pet it!"

"Yeah, but you could have tried again."

"You know what? I thought about it. I didn't do it for the same reason that I killed all them others."

This was the moment Coal had hoped for. He at least had the right to know why his friends had been murdered. "Well, I still don't know that, either."

"Oh, come on! You remember the fight. That whore Jennifer turned on me and told me where to go. Then Batterton, Larry, and Trent had to jump in to save her. Then when it got ugly, you came in. You know what? I didn't mind that. You an' me, we was buddies. We bulldogged together, boxed together, hunted together. Drank together."

"Well, to be fair, you did most of the drinking."

Hague laughed. "Yeah! Haha. I forget. Tea drinker. So whatever. Anyway, we were buds. And I never minded a face to face fair fight with a bud. But them others, they tried to stop even that. Started trying to hold me down till you told them to let me go. You know, the whole school laughed at me after that. The whole friggin' school. But not you, man. You were always square with me."

"So that's why they all had to die? For something that happened in high school?"

"They made my life hell! Made it so I couldn't even show my face around Salmon without wonderin' what people were sayin' behind my back."

"Then what about me? How come you decided to kill me?"

"Aw." Hague waved a hand dismissively. "Sorry about that, old buddy. I was out of my head. I guess I wanted to see if I could. I didn't mean any harm."

"Wha—? Shooting me with a thirty-ought-six is 'no harm'?"

"Shut the hell up already! I told you I was sorry."

A shiver ran down Coal's spine. He knew he was standing in the presence of the most insane man he had ever known.

"What about today, Hague? And what about my daughter? She didn't hurt you. Let her go."

"Oh, give me a break, bro. I didn't hurt her. Come on. I'll let the slut go when we're done. And you'd be better off without her anyway. She's gonna screw up your life if you let her stay around, like my so-called mom did mine."

Coal felt his face redden, but he tried for all he was worth not to let his anger show. "She's my daughter. She's not a slut. She's my daughter. If you had kids of your own, maybe you could understand."

Hague stared at him, reddening around his eyes. Suddenly, he belted out a laugh. "Oh, yeah! Like my bitch of a mom and my dad. Threw me to the wolves as soon as I got kicked out of the Corps. Didn't even give me a chance to tell 'em what happened. And then they told everybody I died. Damn. Who'd do that to their own kid? I guess they won't do it again."

"What's that supposed to mean?"

"Well, you don't think I just left 'em there to tell everybody all about me, do you? Hell. Once a traitor, always a traitor."

"You killed them?"

Again, Hague laughed. There was no humor in any of his laughter. It was worse than listening to Snidley Whiplash rave about killing Dudley Doright's "Nell." But at least Whiplash was fiction. "Kill them? Hell, no! My old man's gonna wish I did, though. As for that old hag, she's gonna fry. Ain't that right, Mom?" Coal gave Hague a queer look, then followed his glance to the cabin door. Before he could ask another question, Hague roared, "Ain't that right, Mom?"

Now Coal heard Nonie Freeman break down crying inside the cabin. Hague laughed once more. "Yeah, so as you can see, Mom's gonna go up with the cabin—after you and me are done here."

"What's 'done', Hague? We going up the hill to see who gets their deer first? It's out of season, you know."

"You're real funny, Coal."

"I'm not trying to be funny."

"Coal, we started a fair fight, back in school. Had a good one too. If it hadn't been for all those others steppin' in and gettin' me off my rhythm, that might've turned out different. Now we get to see."

"A fair fight?" Coal echoed, feeling the first sense he had felt of anything near relief in hours. "You want to fight me? Hague, you can't hope to win. Look at you. You're wasting away."

"Haha. Yeah, and look at you, old Mr. King of Pushups. You're too bulky to beat me. This is lean muscle on me. I bet you can't say the same."

"Well, if that's what you want, then let's get to it."

Again, Hague laughed. The eerie, forced sound was really starting to wear on Coal. "You don't really think I want to box you, do you? Judas priest, Coal! We had that fair fight back in school. I'm talkin' about a *real* fight, bucko. A gunfight. Just like old Marshal Dillon. Or Palladin. Or big Cheyenne! That's how you get into the history books for real: a gunfight to the death!"

CHAPTER TWENTY-EIGHT

Coal stared at Hague, breathless. A fight to the death? Hague Freeman wanted a gunfight? Coal had not had to shoot anyone for so long. It felt good. A kind of freedom he had not understood since landing in Vietnam. But if he had to go into a quick draw, like they did in the old TV series, Hague really was no match for him. He was a fool if he believed he was.

"Hague, you don't really want to do this," Coal said. His voice sounded calm, at least to his own ears, and indeed, it was the calmest he had felt in some time.

"No, you're dead wrong, Coal. On the contrary, I've been thinking about this for so long I can't even remember when the dream began."

"Why?"

"I told you. We had our little kid fight back in high school. Everybody was on your side, and they kept trying to stop it. The whole thing messed up the idea of a fair fight. This is different. This is how we finally get to prove who the best man is."

"So we stand here and wait until someone says 'draw.' Is that it?"

Hague started laughing crazily again. "Oh, yeah, you'd like that, wouldn't you? No. This is a lot bigger game than that. This is my turf."

"I don't want to take away all the suspense you're trying to build up, Hague, but what the hell are you talking about?"

"A match! With rifles. You, me, and nothing but the mountains. Winner takes all."

A chill went over Coal as it began to dawn on him just what kind of a fight this was going to be. It was something he had half expected but was hoping fervently against. This really was going to be Hague's "turf." Hague, the best long-shot rifleman Coal had ever known, and an incredible stalker of game besides, had set up a stalking game where the opponent was like a wild game animal. He had yet to hear all the rules, but there was no doubt they would be good.

As Coal stood in dismay, Hague explained how he was going to be handcuffed while Hague got him into his Power Wagon and drove him way up the mountain. At that point, both men would be unarmed, and both rifles would be down near the cabin, some two hundred yards distant from each other, on opposite sides of the meadow. Hague would drive to a place on the mountain that he had measured out exactly, according to him, where a normal man should be able to walk down to the cabin in about twenty minutes. Here, he would remove Coal's handcuffs and leave him standing on a stump, where he could see him perfectly and keep track of him.

Hague would then drive to another place, some four hundred yards away from Coal, but again a place from which it should take a man about twenty minutes to reach the cabin.

Once Hague reached the place where he was to begin, he would lay on his horn as a signal, and both men would head down the mountain on foot as fast as they could—down the mountain and to their own rifles which awaited them. From that point, it was winner take all. Whichever man reached his rifle first, while not the clear winner, definitely had the edge. But once the other man reached his rifle, if he made his escape into the timber, it became a cat and mouse game—exactly like Hague's job in Vietnam. A game at which no one could beat him.

Coal looked over at Katie, and his heart fell. How was he to beat this man? Katie stared at him. Really looked into his eyes, for the first time in almost as far back as he could remember. As he watched her, the tears started flowing down her cheeks.

"Don't worry, Katie. It'll be okay."

Hague laughed. "Yeah, Katie. It'll be okay." He was speaking to both of them, and loud enough for his mother to hear from inside the cabin, when he said, "I know one fat cow that's going to roast today, and one little doe that's going to get its throat slit or get blown into a million pieces if her daddy tries anything funny. I've killed lots of little girls like you in Nam, missy. I won't blink if I have to blast you to eternity too."

Katie broke and started to sob, but then she steeled herself and turned her tear-filled eyes on Hague. Somehow, through her tears and the lump that must have formed in her throat, she managed to say, "I hate you."

Quiet and seemingly as calm as a summer's day, Hague Freeman said, "Yeah, don't we all. Well, Daddy. You ready?"

Coal just nodded.

"All right. Let's go to your truck. I'm sure you brought an arsenal."

Seeming to ignore the killer, Coal turned suddenly back to Katie. "Sweetheart, I hope you know I've always loved you."

Then, unable to bear the thought that she might not reply, Coal turned and followed Hague across the ever-lightening snow.

They reached the truck, and Hague jerked open the door. He started laughing. "Holy crap! Did you think I had the whole Marine Corps up here with me?"

Coal stared at him, full of despite.

Hague cocked his pistol and pointed it at Coal's forehead. "Step back, cowboy."

Coal did so. Hague was insane enough to throw away his entire game and shoot him right now if he got angry.

Hague leaned in and looked over Coal's arsenal. Finally, he stepped back out and turned to Coal. "A Model 12, an ought-six, and a freaking .44-40. You that dumb, to think you'll get that close to me? What was the lever action gonna be for, Coal?"

Coal continued to stare the other man down. "For you."

Hague gave out with a long, hearty laugh. "For me? Okay, is that what you want? It sure isn't what I'm going to use. I'll have my old ought-six. The same one I used to break up those pebbles with at six hundred yards—remember?"

Coal did not reply.

"Sure you do. We both do. Hey, Coal, you never know. You might get lucky today. Lucky enough that I kill you with one head shot." Hague gave his crazy laugh again. "Pick your weapon, big man. And remember—this .45 will blow a hole in you as big as a barn if you try anything."

With his heart pounding, Coal walked to the door of the truck and stared at the weapons leaning against his seat. He wished he had the shotgun in his hands right now. Any of his weapons, actually. He thought of the terrain he had seen on the hillside, of the thick, gnarly trunks of trees, the patches of exposed volcanic rock. There might be a lot of chances for some fast shooting up there. And fast shooting called for a gun like the .44-40. But there could also be some long distance shots. And if there were, a scoped .30-06 would be invaluable.

Reaching far across the seat, he picked up the ought-six, bringing it out with him as he prayed with all his heart that it was still at least close to being zeroed in at one hundred yards, the way he had left it. He turned to Hague, who had his .45 auto centered on Coal's chest.

"All right. Smart move. Now turn away from me and very slowly take all the rounds out of the magazine and the chamber."

Coal did as ordered. Then he turned and held them out to Hague. "You might want them later," said Hague with a smirk. Put 'em in a pocket."

When Coal had done so, Hague said, "All right, now get out the shotgun and empty it. And the rifle." Coal complied, and when he handed the cartridges to Hague, he took them and hurled them as far as he could out into the snow.

"No point givin' you any second options."

Now, he made Coal move away from the truck and leaned inside the cab, plucking the key out of the ignition and shoving the driver's door handle down to lock it. He got out and locked the passenger door with the key, then put it in his pocket, smiling at Coal. "For safe keeping. Come on."

He led them over to the stump of a tree fifty yards to the right of the cabin. "Set it on the stump, Coal." Coal carefully laid the ought-six on top of the stump. "Now, so you know this is all above board, come with me."

Hague started across the meadow, watching Coal out of the corner of his eye. They went to another stump that was a good two hundred yards from the one where Coal had left his rifle. There across its top lay a battered rifle with a newer Redfield scope attached to it. The bolt was open.

"Pick it up and look, if you want," said Hague. Coal made no move. Then Hague laughed, shaking his pants pocket. The muffled rattle of a handful of cartridges was a familiar sound.

"All right then. Let's go get in my truck."

Coal followed Hague around behind the cabin, where the Dodge Power Wagon with the pathetic looking, splotchy green paint job was parked, waiting. There was a scoped rifle in a rack in the back window.

"I thought we were leaving our guns down here," Coal said. "What's that for?"

"Just in case," said Hague with a laugh. Then he growled, "Come around here." Coal went with him to the passenger side. While still holding the pistol centered on Coal's chest, Hague rolled down his window, then took a pair of handcuffs from a back pocket and made Coal put one side on his left hand. "Now get in." Coal slid into the seat, and Hague, with the cocked pistol practically jutting into Coal's throat, said, "Give me your left hand." With the loose handcuff dangling, Coal held out his hand, and Hague took it ungently and snapped the other cuff around the outside door handle. "There, that ought to keep you tame."

He came back around the other side and climbed in, firing up the two hundred-thirty horses. "Let's go for a drive, Coal. It'll be your last one, so enjoy it." Laughing, he wheeled the truck around through the trees and pulled up in front of the house. He stared at Katie Leigh, who was quietly crying, but fiercely staring him down. "Aww. Would you look at that. Such a shame. Such a shame."

Alarm rose inside of Coal. "You're letting her go when this is over, Hague. She didn't do anything to you."

"Haha. Nope, she sure didn't. Oh, I'm letting her go, all right. She'll be gone. Long gone." With that, Hague slammed it into first gear and jerked them back in the seat as the rig lurched forward in the snow. And suddenly Coal knew that no matter what happened today, Hague Freeman planned to take apart that cabin with nitroglycerin, his mother, Katie, and all. No one was to survive to be a witness to what would happen here today. Coal knew that as surely as he knew his own name.

The old logging road was badly neglected. Coal wasn't sure the GMC would have made it. Even the Power Wagon struggled, here and there, sliding back and forth, and two different times stalling. "Sure hope we don't get stuck up here, Coal," said Hague with a laugh. "If the whole game gets ruined, I might have to bash your stupid head in with a rock."

He revved the engine and slowly pulled away from the road edge where they had bogged down in deep snow.

"I have to admit, Coal," said Hague all of a sudden. "This isn't really a fair fight. I already know you can't beat me. You know it too." Coal was silent, and finally Hague said, "Cat got your tongue?"

"I don't have a word to say to you, Hague. I'm ashamed I ever called you a friend."

"You always were a bastard, Coal. You always had to show how much better you were at everything, didn't you? You always had to have the spotlight."

There was no reason for Coal to speak. Then Hague slammed him in the side of the head with his forty-five. "Answer me when I'm talkin'."

"There was never a spotlight," Coal replied, rubbing the side of his head with his right hand as he strained to turn his head far enough to see Hague over his left shoulder. His left hand was starting to go numb, with his wrist jammed tight against the inside of the cuff. Every jolt in the road was agony. He tried to look back and see the cabin, but now he could see nothing past the trees and rocks. "The only spotlight was what you had in your own head. I was just trying to be your friend."

"Oh my hell," Hague growled. "I couldn't even keep a girl with you and Batterton around. I wasn't good enough for anybody. Even my own dad and my witch of a mom liked you better than me. You and Batterton both."

Coal thought he actually heard Hague's teeth grind together. Again, he held his silence, hoping not to provoke his old hunting partner even further.

Needlessly, Hague slammed on the brakes on a downhill grade, jerking Coal forward until he wrenched to a stop. His hand felt like it had almost torn off, and his shoulder felt nearly dislocated. He listened to Hague laugh for a while, and when he finally got over the pain and Hague stopped laughing, he said, "You're not going to prove anything to me or even to yourself if you keep it up, Hague. If you cripple my shoulder and my hand, you might as well just shoot me like you did them."

Hague was quiet for a moment. Coal sat and gritted his teeth. He wondered how bad his hand was and if he would even be able to use it if he beat Hague down the mountainside. "Yeah, okay," he heard Hague saying. "You're right. But that sure felt good to me." He gave another laugh, then drove on.

Forty yards farther, he pulled up. There was a wide spot here, and the road appeared to come to an end. Coal could see a rock circle under the snow, and all of a sudden he recognized this as a place he and Hague used to come to make themselves a fire and fry deer back straps, or sometimes a grouse or a snowshoe hare. He didn't know if it was the same circle of rocks, but it was a good bet.

Hague jockeyed around until they were facing back down the road. Looking downhill, Coal could now see the cabin, through the trees. "Well, old buddy, this is it," said Hague suddenly. "This is where we part ways, at least for fifteen or twenty minutes." Coal was silent. "You remember that last rise we came up, before we started down that incline and I busted your wrist?" Hague asked, then let out a laugh. "Do you?" he asked angrily.

Coal nodded. "I remember."

"All right then. That's more like it. You can see it from right here, in fact. So that's where I'm going to start from. I'm going to pull the truck up there, and then I'm gonna park and get out. When you hear my horn, we both start down the hill. I'm telling you, I've walked from both these places half a dozen times, and it should take about twenty minutes if you walk at a hiking pace. If you're smart, it better be a lot shorter. I sure as hell won't be hikin'.

"But I'm warnin' you, Coal. If I get over there and I look back here and you ain't still standing here—on that big stump right there—then I'm just gonna finish driving the rest of the way down the mountain, get my rifle, and light up that cabin like the Fourth of July. And then I'm gonna light you up too. The choice is yours. If you make the wrong one, just remember—there's a little doe down there that gets its throat slit."

"I heard you the first time," Coal said with gritted teeth.

His anger only made Hague laugh. He got out of his side and came around to Coal's, putting the key in the handcuff that was attached to the door handle and setting him free. Then he stepped back and pulled his pistol out of his waistband again, sticking it in Coal's face. He held out the key. "You can undo the other side yourself."

Coal did so, then got out, throwing the cuffs and the key back inside the cab. Hague wiggled the barrel of his pistol toward a stand of timber ten or twenty feet from the stump where Coal was to stand. "Walk that way. When you hear the truck taking off, you come back over here and stand on this stump. And you'd better damn well still be here when I get to my starting place and look back, Coal. Or the game's over."

"I'll be here."

"I'll just bet you will." Hague laughed. Coal wanted to scream at him to stop laughing. But it would have only made him laugh harder.

He walked away with his back to Hague, his face toward the stand of firs. The hair prickled up on the back of his neck. He thought how easy it would be now for Hague to put a bullet in his back, to end it all. But then he would never have gone through this kind of work if he were going to do it that way.

No, Hague Freeman wanted to thoroughly shame him, to prove once and for all that he was the better man, and then cut him to pieces with lead.

Killing his own mother and Katie was going to be icing on the cake.

CHAPTER TWENTY-NINE

Behind him, Coal heard the rev of the Dodge's motor. The gears grinded, and the pickup crept away back along the route they had just come. Coal's heart seemed to be pounding out of his chest. Looking down the hill, he could not see Katie, because the cabin was quartered away from him. But he was confident that Hague could. He would have made sure his route was in the best position to see down through the trees and view the cabin as much as possible.

Sucking in a deep breath, Coal turned and walked back to the stump, stepping up onto it the way Hague had demanded. He could not afford a slip-up now. He had to do everything the way his enemy had set it up. Taking chances was taking chances on Katie's life.

Standing on the Douglas fir stump, he watched the Dodge angling away from him, and his heart fell. While trying to massage the feeling back into his left wrist and his hand, he turned his head and looked down-slope. Hague had all this planned. How did he even know the other man had really given him an equal distance from the cabin? Sure, he claimed he had. So what. He was a murderer. An assassin. It wasn't like such a man should care about being a liar too.

A surge of adrenalin rushed up through Coal's body, and for a second he thought about bolting. If he took off now, throwing caution to the wind, could he make it down the hill before the truck? The slope was covered in snow. Snow half-buried millions of bushes and tree limbs and rolling rocks—any number of things that could easily trip him up and send him careening down the steep decline. Snow would have soaked into fallen, bark-less logs, making their surface slippery and treacherous—to say nothing of the ice that would have formed on many of them in these sub-freezing temperatures. At best, he might tumble all the way down the hill more than he would run. At worst, he could break a leg—or his neck. And then Katie would be left at Hague's mercy, and Coal could do nothing but watch her die. From what he had seen of Hague's capability as a murderer, looking down at Jennifer Batterton's dead body, he knew already that Hague would make it a point to give Katie the most gruesome death possible, to make Coal pay for trying to take advantage of him.

There was no choice. He had to stay.

The pickup went over a rise, and for a moment it vanished, now some three hundred yards distant. Coal stared that way, anxious for it to reappear. How many yards were left until Hague would park? How many yards until Coal must make the run of his life, in temperatures that were sure to fill his lungs with ice, over terrain that would threaten to break an ankle, a leg, or his neck, at every slippery step?

Where was the pickup? It had not yet reappeared. He expected to see it. Had he mistaken the place where Hague said he was going to park? Was Hague already out, making ready to head down the hill? Or gone even now? Where was the horn honk? Hague had said that was the signal to begin the race of death.

Tears from frustration and from cold filled Coal's eyes, and he blinked them away. He looked down the mountain. He peered through the trees back the way Hague's pickup had gone. Where was he? Where had the madman gone?

Coal's body was filled with adrenalin now, head to foot. The sound of Katie's name startled him, and he realized it had come in a whisper from his own lips. He bunched his leg muscles. Hague was making the run without his own promised signal. He just knew it. He had either forgotten to honk the horn, or he was purposely tricking him and starting before the clock.

Coal felt like he could barely breathe.

And then it came. Loud and clear on the crisp morning air. Ringing up through the trees, seeming to strike against the cold, dead pall of the low-hanging clouds. The long blare of the horn.

Almost forgetting to breathe, Coal leaped off the stump, facing downhill. His first contact with the ground told him how the rest of the descent would go. Slipping and sliding, he went down on top of a fallen limb, striking a buried rock hard on his tailbone. Desperately, ignoring the devastating pain in his tailbone, he clambered up. His eyes went up to where the truck would be. He looked desperately for Hague, but he wasn't there. Anywhere.

Coal turned and moved again. He started to slip but grabbed onto a sapling and caught himself. The move spun him around, now facing uphill. He turned and zeroed in on a fir that was some three feet across, and with abandon he made for it. He slammed against the trunk, bringing his sliding momentum up short. He sucked in a deep breath, then once again turned to look up the hill.

And this time the truck was there.

The Power Wagon had just pulled up onto the rise where Coal had thought he was going to stop. Hague was still moving. Coal's heart leaped. What? But— He had heard the horn!

Confused and panicked, Coal turned to look down through the trees again. Suddenly, he heard the sound of a vehicle's door slamming shut. It rocketed up from down below, ringing against the trees, against the dead gray sky. Coal whirled back to the Power Wagon. Hague was getting out! He would look first to see if Coal was on the stump, following his rules and waiting for him. If Coal wasn't there, he would race the truck down the mountain, and the game was over!

With fear flying through him, Coal whirled to look back uphill. The stump wasn't even in sight anymore! He had to get back there. He had to move as fast as he could, to make Hague see him, to make him know he was not trying to break his rules!

But Hague was out now, and he raised a pair of binoculars, turning to look toward the stump. Coal froze. There was no way back up the hill. Someone else had honked their horn, down below. Suddenly, Hague dropped his binoculars and bolted for the truck. Coal swore.

He turned downhill again as the sound of grinding gears came to him from Hague's direction. The Dodge was moving again!

Coal slipped and slid, went down in the snow. His hands were icicles, even in his gloves. His butt felt numb from hitting hard, frozen objects under the snow. He tried to clear his blurry vision, wet with the tears of panic. Sliding, he grabbed for a tree limb as he went by. It caught him, whirled him around. He went to a knee, the momentum wrenching his arm. Taking a deep breath into already frozen lungs, he got up and pushed on.

Calm yourself, damn it! It was as if he heard the words out loud, but they were only in his head. They were right, though. He had to stay calm. This wild flight of terror was not going to save Katie. Calm!

He looked up to see the Power Wagon sliding on the road above him. The Dodge was almost closer to the cabin than he was now, and moving fast. He heard the motor grind and rev. Was Hague stuck?

He couldn't wait to see. Trying to carefully pick a next goal to reach, he moved forward, slipping, catching himself on a rock. There, a solid tree. Get to that. He reached it. He ignored his frozen feet and hands. Ahead was a stubby outcrop of broken rock. He slipped and slid down to it, catching the uppermost tip of it as he went by, again going to a frozen knee.

He looked across the slope in time to see the Dodge sliding again, but it had already reached a point closer to the cabin than he was now. Hague was going to make it before he did.

He was moving, lurching down the hill, digging the sides of his boots into the slope as he went, slipping on the snowy grass and shrubs. A rock or log rolled under him, and he felt himself going down. There was no stopping. He rolled several times, then pitched headlong and landed in a shallow depression, possibly an elk wallow. He lay there, head spinning. From across the forest, hundreds of yards away, he heard the violent grind of gears, and then Hague's tires spinning.

Coal sat up, shaking his head and grabbing his temple. A stream of warm blood ran down the side of his face.

Down through the timber, he glimpsed another pickup. It took a moment for reality to sink in. It was Todd Mitchell's!

With a surge of hope, Coal whipped his eyes over to the Power Wagon. He heard the echoing ring of the truck door slamming, which must have happened a couple of seconds earlier, judging by the slow movement of sound. By now, Hague was already standing beside it, a rifle at his shoulder.

"Todd!" He screamed down the slope. "Katie!" And then he saw the rifle buck against Hague's shoulder. Two seconds later, he heard the solid report.

The feeling of terror swept over him again. Now he was dead. Hague had a rifle in his hands, and with a rifle in his hands, Hague was a god.

Coal picked out an aspen up ahead, its stark white trunk blending into the snow that glared back at him, even in the dim, gloomy light of day. He leaped toward it, slipping in the snow. The sound of a bullet pinged off a rock close by as he felt himself hit the ground hard. It was followed moments later by the crack of the shot. Coal lay in a depression, and rolling wildly to look across the slope he could not see Hague. His fall had saved his life.

Throwing himself forward, on hands and knees, he made it to the dubious cover of the aspen and leaped and rolled to get behind it, turning to look for Hague. A glance around the tree trunk showed him the gunman racing downhill. He was going to beat him to the meadow.

Coal turned his eyes down toward the meadow and the cabin. His first revelation startled him. There was no Katie on the porch! Had she escaped? Had she gone into timber? Or was she inside the house? He saw movement inside the door, and he screamed. "Get out of the house!"

With renewed urgency, Coal leaped up and took off running.

Once more, he stopped and screamed toward the cabin to get out. Suddenly, he slipped on a loose rock and fell on his back, striking the rock directly on his spine. He lay there wanting to die, with pain bursting in little explosions all throughout his body. At last, clenching his teeth, he rolled and saw Hague with the rifle to his shoulder.

He heard the panic in his own shout. "NO!"

And then the rifle hammered back against Hague's shoulder, and a terrifying explosion ripped through the forest. Coal was thrust sideways. When he sat back up, the cabin was gone, and bits of smoking log were lying about the meadow. One of them lay directly in front of his pickup, a log that would surely have mangled the front of it had it been ten feet closer.

Coal stared at the place where, as far back as his deepest memories, the trapper's cabin had stood. It was gone now. The roof, the walls... the porch where Katie had sat only minutes before. A feeling of horror welled up inside Coal, and he looked back toward Hague Freeman. He had done it. Coal would never see his daughter again. He had never had a chance to hold her in his arms, to tell her eye to eye how much he adored her. Hague had stolen from him his one last chance at redemption.

But he had not taken his will for justice.

Getting up, Coal looked over toward Hague. He, too, was just beginning to recover from the nitro's blast. Coal turned and raced down through the trees. He knew Hague could hit him on the run, but he had no choice. To stay where he was, he was a sitting duck. To move was the only way he had any hope to get to a weapon.

Instead of the shot he expected to come, Coal glanced over to see Hague also driving headlong down through the trees, paralleling him. He was trying to get down to the flat first, where he could then wait for Coal to emerge. Coal pushed himself harder. The ground had started to grow more level, and it was easier to run, to dodge tree limbs and leap over bushes. Hague, although much closer to the meadow, was still on steeper ground. It was the only edge Coal had.

But he couldn't imagine Hague continuing to race him. The ex-Marine was not built for a hard race like this, not anymore. He had let himself go. Surely, at any moment, he would turn his rifle on Coal once more. Coal, running hard and feeling the ice seem to form in his throat and lungs, told himself he would see Hague's movement cease whenever he decided to shoot at him again, and he would drop for cover. Maybe he would have time.

But Hague didn't stop. Instead, his feet swept suddenly out from under him, and he hit the slope hard. Coal lurched to a stop against another aspen, which were much more numerous than the conifers, now that they were this far down the slope. He dared a glance toward Hague and saw him on his knees, looking at his rifle. Then Hague angrily threw the weapon aside and got back up, continuing his headlong flight down the mountain. He was unarmed! Coal's heart leaped with hope. Even while his body ached, he might make it to the meadow. He might reach his rifle, lying there on that stump, waiting for him.

But Hague Freeman reached the meadow first. He reached the meadow, and then he reached his rifle.

CHAPTER THIRTY

With sickness sweeping over him, Coal heard the crackle of the logs of the cabin, settling into the snow and ice on the ground.

He looked beyond his truck, at the stump that seemed so endlessly far away now. Everything was moving in slow motion. He saw Hague fumbling with frozen hands to load his rifle. Coal's was still a hundred yards away. It might as well have been back in D.C.

Coal looked at the GMC, and hope surged through him. He looked toward Hague again, and the other man was coming to his feet. Coal's eyes swept the ground. He saw a lump in the snow, and he dropped to his knees and reached for it. It was a rock!

He dug at the rock, trying to pick it up. But it was frozen against the ground.

"I'm comin', Coal! I got your little angel and I got my mom. I got whoever you brought up here to save your worthless life. Now I'm comin' for you."

Coal fell over onto his back and kicked with all his might at the rock. The icy grip of the snowy ground broke free. Gritting his teeth, Coal raked at the rock. It rolled loose. He tried to grip it. His gloves had become wet, now were frozen in place and useless. He struggled with them, pulling them loose. The first one came off and fell like a dead bird onto the crusted snow.

He heard Hague yell something at him. The frozen fingers of his free hand clawed at the other glove, finally pulled it loose.

With fumbling fingers, he picked up the rock and ran. Something seemed to be dragging at his feet. He could see Hague moving toward him across the meadow, talking to him. At least his lips were moving. But Coal could not hear a sound. There was only an aimless, taunting ringing in his ears.

As he came up to the pickup, he drove the rock through the side window. His glimpse of Hague's face showed a man who seemed to be laughing. He had his prey like a fish in a barrel. He was coming. He was confident. He could not lose.

Something registered in Coal's mind about a useless, empty rifle. He did not know if Hague's words were actually slurred, or if it was his own fevered mind that was bending them into syllables of nonsensical gibberish.

Coal reached under the pickup seat, and his fumbling fingers dug out his father's old .44-40 Colt Peacemaker. He looked up, and Hague was only one hundred feet away. But much too far for the Colt.

His frozen fingers managed to get the Colt to half-cock. Shaking like an aspen leaf in high winds, he worked the loading gate open. Hague was ninety feet away. He was grinning. His rifle was half-raised.

Coal managed to thumb out two shells. He grabbed for the lever action rifle. His vision was blurred. He tried to shove a round through the loading gate, but it fell, struck the floor inside the door, then bounced off and disappeared into the snow.

Coal saw Hague's rifle coming up. He stared at the Winchester's loading port. It seemed so small. He fell onto his knees in the snow and drove the last icy cartridge into the gate. He almost could not feel his fingers. He jacked the lever, throwing the hammer back.

Suddenly, he could hear the laughter of his nemesis ringing against the timber. "I got all your friends and I got your daughter. When I leave here, I'm going after your mom, too. There ain't gonna be one thing left in the valley but sour memories of you, Coal Savage."

As Coal turned and moved, he heard the mighty explosion of the ought-six, and dirt and snow flew from the ground where his foot had been half a second before. He came up over the back of the pickup bed, the Winchester already level.

His sights settled on Hague Freeman's chest as the other man was working the bolt of his rifle, sending an empty casing winging out into the air. He saw the look of surprise flash over Hague's face as his eyes came back up to land on Coal.

And as the crescent butt of the Winchester hugged into his shoulder, Coal squeezed the trigger.

Against the steel of the GMC, in the dead-cold air of the wintry day, and with ice magnifying the sound, the crack of the .44-40 sounded much louder in Coal's ears than it ever had before. He saw Hague Freeman's mouth drop open and the rifle fall out of his hands. He went to his knees in the snow, looking down at his rifle. He so badly wanted to reach for it. Coal could see that by the way he stared. But apparently his arms would not move. He stared and stared, then finally raised his eyes to Coal.

Coal stepped back to the cab and took out the other three cartridges from the Peacemaker. Working with painful slowness against the ice crystals in his fingers, he pushed them all into the Winchester's loading gate, then jacked the lever again and let the empty bounce onto the floor of the pickup.

Coal walked around to the hood of the truck, then beyond it. Hague was still kneeling there, staring. To Coal, the .30-06 was invisible in the snow in front of Hague. But it must be glinting up at the dying man, taunting him.

Coal could not feel his feet as he walked across the meadow. He had one thumb on the hammer of the Winchester, another in front of the trigger. And three .44-40 slugs that were soon going to tear Hague Freeman's skull to pieces.

"Coal!"

The sound made him whip to the side. The face of Todd Mitchell registered on him somehow, through his hate and his ice-cold fury. Somehow, Todd had survived the explosion. But how? Right now, it didn't matter.

"Get away from here, Todd!"

He raised his rifle and pointed it at Hague Freeman's forehead. Hague was like a wounded bear, waiting to be dispatched.

"No, Coal! No. Man, you've got to let it go."

Coal centered the sights. He had never had a sight picture on anything more clear than on the center of Hague's head.

"Turn around, Todd. You don't need to see this."

"Daddy, no!"

Coal's finger had started to creep back on the trigger, but somehow he stopped. He froze. That voice. That voice... His heart seemed to have ceased beating. Now it started again, with a vengeance. He eased his finger away from the trigger and looked around.

Katie Leigh was walking out of the trees, with tears on her face. "Daddy, don't do it."

But her words were wasted. When Coal looked back, Hague had fallen onto his face in the snow.

He turned back to Katie and Todd, who stood some ten feet apart on the edge of the trees. Beyond them, he saw Don and Nonie Freeman, standing in shock. The old man, his face wreathed in ugly bruises, had one arm drawn tightly about his wife. The other appeared to be held up by some kind of makeshift sling.

Katie started running through the snow. Coal had only the presence of mind to let down the hammer of the Winchester before she reached him. With abandon, the girl threw herself hard against his body, openly weeping. "Oh, Daddy. Daddy," she cried over and over again into his coat. "Daddy. I love you too."

There would be years of time for Coal to learn the details of how Todd Mitchell had managed to find him, assumedly with the help of Don Freeman. There would be years to learn how he had saved Nonie and Katie from the fiery explosion that laid a nostalgic old structure to the forest floor.

And there would be years to sit and contemplate the sound that rang like a whip-poor-will's sweet song through Coal's ears, through his heart and soul.

His daughter who had for so long hated him had told him she loved him. In Coal Savage's broken universe, nothing mattered more.

♦ THE END ♦

Look next for: *Savage Law, Book 2: River of Death*

Author's note

I'm not sure if it will come as a surprise to my readers or not to know that *Law of the Lemhi* began its life as a single, all-inclusive book. Unfortunately, what began as a fairly simple plot soon branched into a dozen sub-plots and quite a major story, and when I realized it was by close to one hundred pages the biggest book I have ever written and that publishing it in that form was going to cost a fortune, both to myself and to my readers, I made the decision to publish it in two parts—much like a two-part pilot of a television series.

Thus, the two parts are not only closely intertwined, but it is imperative that both be read to follow the story. Similarly, I have planted seeds of future plots in these two books that will carry on into forthcoming books in the *Savage Law* series.

It is with great relish that I look forward to the ongoing series. I have sworn in the past that I did not care to write any books that carried on from one to the next, but I have become so attached to, and interested in, the *Savage Law* characters as to feel I know them personally and am invested in them emotionally.

I hope you, my readers, feel something similar.

And I hope you enjoy these books with even a spark of the

same joy I had in writing them. See you in the next one: *River of Death.*

As a final note, I would like again to thank all of those who allowed their names to be used within these pages. All are the same names that were used in *Law of the Lemhi, Part One*, with the exception of my friend and good sport, Nancy Pearson.

Remember that none of the things done within these pages by any of these characters who are also real people reflects in any way upon anything they have done in reality and should not be construed in any way as being a factual account of any circumstance in their lives, past or present.

About the Author

Kirby Frank Jonas was born in 1965 in Bozeman, Montana. His earliest memories are of living seven miles outside of town in a wide crack in the mountains known as Bear Canyon. At that time it was a remote and lonely place, but a place where a boy with an imagination could grow and nurture his mind, body and soul.

From Montana, the Jonas family moved almost as far across the country as they could go, to Broad Run, Virginia, a place that, although not as deep in the timbered mountains as Bear Canyon, was every bit as remote—Roland Farm. Once again, young Jonas spent his time mostly alone, or with his older brother, if he was not in school. Jonas learned to hike with his mother, fish with his father, and to dodge an unruly horse.

Jonas moved to Shelley, Idaho, in 1971, and from that time forth, with the exception of a couple of short sojourns elsewhere, he became an Idahoan. Jonas attended all twelve years of school in Shelley, graduating in 1983. In the sixth grade, he penned his first novel, *The Tumbleweed,* and in high school he wrote his second, *The Vigilante*. It was also during this time that he first became acquainted with Salmon, Idaho, staying toward the end of the road at the Golden Boulder Orchard and taking his first steps to manhood.

Jonas has lived in six cities in France, in Mesa, Arizona, and explored the United States extensively. He has fought fires for the

Bureau of Land Management in five western states and carried a gun in three different jobs.

In 1987, Jonas met his wife-to-be, Debbie Chatterton, and in 1989 took her to the altar. Over some rough and rocky roads they have traveled, and across some raging rivers that have at times threatened to draw them under, but they survived, and with four beautiful children to show for it: Cheyenne, Jacob, Clay and Matthew.

Jonas has been employed as a Wells Fargo armed guard, a wildland firefighter, a security guard, and police officer. He is currently employed both as a municipal firefighter for the city of Pocatello, Idaho, and in part-time armed security, guarding federal facilities in Pocatello.

Books by Kirby Jonas

Season of the Vigilante, Book One: The Bloody Season
Season of the Vigilante, Book Two: Season's End
The Dansing Star
Death of an Eagle
Legend of the Tumbleweed
Lady Winchester
The Devil's Blood (combination of the *Season of the Vigilante* novels)
The Secret of Two Hawks
Knight of the Ribbons
Drygulch to Destiny
Samuel's Angel
The Night of My Hanging (And Other Short Stories)

***Savage Law* series**
Law of the Lemhi, part 1
Law of the Lemhi, part 2
River of Death (forthcoming)

***The Badlands* series**
Yaqui Gold (co-author Clint Walker)
Canyon of the Haunted Shadows (forthcoming)

***Legends West* series**
Disciples of the Wind (co-author Jamie Jonas)
Reapers of the Wind (co-author Jamie Jonas)

Lehi's Dream series

Nephi Was My Friend
The Faith of a Man
A Land Called Bountiful
Shores of Promise (forthcoming)

Books on audio tape

The Dansing Star, narrated by James Drury, *"The Virginian"*
Death of an Eagle, narrated by James Drury
Legend of the Tumbleweed, narrated by James Drury
Lady Winchester, narrated by James Drury
Yaqui Gold, narrated by Gene Engene
The Secret of Two Hawks, narrated by Kevin Foley
Knight of the Ribbons, narrated by Rusty Nelson
Drygulch to Destiny, narrated by Kirby Jonas (forthcoming)

Available through the author at www.kirbyjonas.com

To order books, go to www.kirbyjonas.com or write to:

Howling Wolf Publishing
1611 City Creek Road
Pocatello ID 83204

Or send email to: kirby@kirbyjonas.com

Made in the USA
Columbia, SC
26 October 2018